"Yeah, so you've written a book about this [customs harassment]. But you're not going to be able to publish it, are you?"

former US Customs Service senior agent,
in conversation with the author, Durango, Colorado, 1999

"Thanks to Martha Egan for giving us Beverly—
a river running, shop-keeping protaganist who doesn't
look like a Barbie doll—to propel her page-turning story
about a brave new world where privacy does not exist.
Read this book at your own risk.
You may never feel the same about your mail,
your phone, or your life."

ELIZABETH COHEN
author of *The House on Beartown Road*

"If you suspected the government was tapping your phone,
following you around, and otherwise harassing you unjustly,
you could passively ascribe it all to paranoia, or, like Beverly
Parmentier, the protagonist in this exciting novel, you could
fight back. I'd bet that, in a similar situation,
the author, Martha Egan, would do just what Beverly
Parmentier did and that she'd be as successful at it
as she is in the writing of this terrific
and engaging story."

FRED HARRIS
former US Senator (D-OK),
author of *Following the Harvest: A Novel*

"Has Carl Hiaasen switched states and gender or what? Is the best-selling mystery novelist now targeting his noir satires not at Florida but New Mexico, going undercover as a Santa Fe gallery owner named Martha Egan? Egan's *Clearing Customs* wages jihad on the same brand of self-serving cretins that overpopulate Hiaasen's Miami, heavy-handed, power hungry, sloppy politicos and so-called public servants too ready to break the law to enforce it. And anybody who loves Hiaasen will have a ball reading Egan's fast-paced, chili-flavored, and always entertaining mystery."

BOB SHACOCHIS
author of *Easy in the Islands* and *The Next New World*

"In *Clearing Customs,* Martha Egan has written a flaming indictment of government bureaucracy run amok... Humor and compassion abound in this personal odyssey of Beverly Parmentier, an importer of folk art, whose adventures transport her from the American Southwest to Mexico to the French Caribbean and back again. Supported by a tiny coterie of fellow individualists, the River Rats, Ms. Parmentier feistily challenges corrupt government agency officials and their minions...."

JACK LOEFFLER
ethnomusicologist, radio producer, aural historian,
author of *Adventures with Ed: A Portrait of Abbey*

CLEARING CUSTOMS

CLEARING CUSTOMS

A NOVEL

Martha J. Egan

Papalote Press

Santa Fe

Copyright ©2004 Papalote Press

Papalote Press
P.O. Box 32058
Santa Fe NM 87594
www.papalotepress.com

ISBN 0-9755881-0-9 cloth
ISBN 0-9755881-1-7 paper
Library of Congress Control Number 2004107829

FIRST PRINTING
This book is printed on acid-free, archival-quality paper.
Manufactured in the USA.

9   8   7   6   5   4   3   2   1

Fate is unmoved

By one's pitiful hopes.

What changes,

Bowing to fate,

Is what one hopes for.

Lady Murasaki
The Tale of Genji
twelfth century

BOOK ONE

One

January 1988

Beverly Parmentier stepped out of a taxi in front of Puerto Escondido's Hotel Santa Fe, and the brilliant Mexican sunlight hit her like a photoflash. Squinting, and a little wobbly on her legs after hours in airplanes, she fumbled in her purse for sunglasses and the money to pay the driver. He took the bills, deposited her suitcase at the entrance to the hotel, and drove off in a cloud of dust that left her blind and coughing.

Once she could breathe again, she put on the sunglasses and took in her surroundings. Inland, a ridge of dense vegetation held clusters of houses facing a beach that gleamed pearl-white along an azure bay. Above, gulls winged through a cloudless turquoise sky that tented the Mexican coastline to the north, south, and west, and disappeared in the milky haze hanging over the mountains to the east. A brick arch framed the entrance to the colonial-style hotel, and a pretty courtyard of tropical foliage and flowers beckoned.

Grinning like a lottery winner, she set a straw hat atop her mop of curly auburn hair and strode into the patio, her huaraches creaking and the wheels of her suitcase rumbling across squares of river rock like a seaside squall. As if in welcome, a playful, teasing sea breeze lifted her hat brim, ruffled the hem of her gauzy dress, and rattled the fronds of tall palms overhead. She stopped in the courtyard, breathed in the essences of sea and sky and greenery, and restrained herself from screaming for joy.

Suddenly, a raucous, cawing laugh Beverly had known all her life burst forth from a nearby thatch-roofed *palapa,* where tanned beachgoers sat eating, drinking, and enjoying protection from a searing mid-afternoon sun. She knew she was in the right place. Scanning the crowd, she quickly found her Aunt Magdalena, a striking older woman with shoulder-length hennaed hair. Wearing Maria Callas sunglasses, Magdalena presided over a drink-cluttered table with a trio of men half her age. Just then, she slapped a hand of cards on the table and let out a resounding whoop. Heads in the *palapa* turned toward the poker players' table. The other cardplayers put down their cards in disgust. They caught sight of pale, plump Beverly trundling her suitcase across the patio and stared as she approached their table. Magdalena turned, screamed, and jumped out of her chair to enfold her niece in an *abrazo.* The women were oblivious to the stares they drew.

Beverly plopped into an *equipal* chair, draped an arm around her aunt's shoulders, and released a deep sigh. "You can't imagine how I need this, Mag," she said. "Pinch me. I think I'm in heaven."

Just after Christmas, Aunt Magdalena had called from New York.

"Bev! What would you say to a week on the beach in Mexico? I'm going to Puerto Escondido in a couple of weeks. There's a wonderful little resort right on the shore, and I'd love to have you join me."

"Mag, it sounds fabulous, but...I don't have the money and..."

"Silly girl. I'm inviting you. This is on me!"

"Really?"

"Of course. Ticket, room, food—my tab."

"Gosh, Mag, that's tempting. But who'd take care of my business?"

Beverly ran a small, struggling import store in Albuquerque with the help of Lucille, a part-time employee working her way through the University of New Mexico.

"Couldn't your employee manage for a week?"

"Maybe. She'll be on semester break for most of January, but I've never left her alone with the store before."

"Darling, say yes. Things will be fine. You always tell me what a sharp cookie Lucille is, dependable, honest, hard-working . . ."

"Well, I'll talk to her and get back to you in a couple of days, OK?"

Beverly hung up the phone. She was in a daze. *¡México!* A week at the beach! Free! She immediately called her friend Pancha Archibeque, who managed a gallery in Santa Fe, and told her about Magdalena's invitation.

"How could you possible say no to a week at the beach, *mujer?*" Pancha scolded her. "If you don't go, I will. There's hardly any business from now until Valentine's Day, Lucille will do a great job, and if she has any questions, she can call me anytime. You need a vacation. You told me Christmas had been worse than usual."

"It was exhausting. Ten-hour days, seven days a week from Thanksgiving until after New Year's. Lucille had the flu the week before Christmas, and I couldn't find anyone else to help out. Now I'm working on my odious year-end bookkeeping. Ugh. But I'm almost done."

"You need this vacation, Bev. And you've always told me you wanted to spend more time with your aunt. Call Lucille, and if she can do it, you call Magdalena right back and say yes. That's an order."

"*Ayyy, ayyyy,* Pancha."

. . . . .

Puerto Escondido was a visual and sensual feast. The Hotel Santa Fe's cozy whitewashed rooms, decorated with bright-colored furnishings, were set in a compound of thick greenery around a turquoise pool. Except for the chorus of birds that noisily heralded dawn and dusk, the resort was tranquil. Mornings and evenings were cool, but by midday the sun's heat encouraged guests to seek respite in the shade of their rooms, the *palapa,* or hammocks in the leafy patio.

The barren gray chill of the Albuquerque winter Beverly had left behind quickly became a remote memory. In Puerto Escondido, she and Magdalena reveled in Mexico's gentle and colorful January and enjoyed a beach bum's life. They took long strolls along the shore, then leapt over the rolling surf to paddle in the tranquil ocean beyond. They meandered through the shops and the market, or lounged around seaside restaurants nibbling shrimp and avocado cocktails.

Although Beverly's aunt was well over seventy, she had the stamina of a twenty-five-year-old triathlete, thriving and energetic even in the sultry heat of coastal Mexico. One day, however, Beverly came back from an early morning swim to find Magdalena in bed, writhing in pain.

Beverly was alarmed. "Should I get you a doctor?"

Magdalena waved her off. "It's just a stomach thing. *La turista.* It'll pass. Can you get me my pillbox and a glass of water? I'll be fine in a minute. Go on to breakfast without me, OK?"

By the time Beverly returned, Magdalena was sitting in a chair outside their room reading a book and sipping a cup of tea. Although pale, she seemed much better. For the rest of the day, they took it easy.

By the following morning, Magdalena was her old self again and soon engaged in a marathon poker game with the same three men who'd shared her table the day Beverly arrived. Beverly didn't mind having time to herself. For years, she'd lived alone and treasured solitude. While her aunt played poker, she read her favorite trashy mysteries, swam for hours in the ocean, and devoted herself to *il dolce farniente*. Often she went to bed long before Mag was ready to fold her cards for the evening.

Magdalena was easy to be with, and Beverly especially enjoyed their long soulful talks about life, love, and invariably, their family.

"I wish they supported me," Beverly said late one afternoon as they sat beneath slowly twirling ceiling fans in the *palapa*, sipping fresh pineapple daiquiris while watching the sun slide beneath the western horizon in a gouache of *rosa mexicana* and tangerine orange. "I don't mean financially. I simply wish they were proud of me, even a teensy bit. I always get the feeling I'm an embarrassment to them—especially to Mom—because I haven't done the only thing they ever expected of me, to get married and help populate Upper Michigan with more Parmentier offshoots."

"Your family has its limitations," Magdalena said. "They don't understand anything beyond their own small world, and maybe they don't want to. I've always thought your mother was jealous of you and what you've done with your life."

"Mom, jealous of me? You've got to be kidding."

"No, I think you've done things she always wanted to do, but maybe never had the courage to try. She always talked about becoming a pediatrician like her father, but she married my brother right after high school and started having kids. Maybe she was afraid to leave home. You, on the other hand, hopped a train to New Mexico by yourself at seventeen. You put yourself through college, you went into the Peace Corps, and now you've got your own business, all of it with no help from anyone."

"Not true. You've always supported me, Mag. You helped me get through school emotionally and financially, and you gave me seed money for my store."

"Peanuts, kid."

"It wasn't peanuts. It was the difference between my being able to squeak by or lose my shirt, especially that first year. More importantly, all along, your believing in me helped me believe in myself. I'll always be grateful to you." Beverly reached across the table to squeeze Magdalena's hand.

From time to time, one or another of Magdalena's poker pals, especially Al, the tall Texan with acne scars, tried to chat Beverly up in the swimming pool or on the beach.

"He's too interested in me," she told her aunt. "It's fishy. I'm not date-bait. I'm short, fubsy, and forty-two. Like Woody Allen said, I'm not sure I want to belong to a club that would have someone like me as a member. Even I, liberal that I am, might not ask me out."

"Woody stole that line from Groucho Marx. Enjoy the attention, Bev," Magdalena said. "You're not as unattractive as you think, and you're approachable and friendly. It's one reason why you're good at retail."

"Al's more interested in my import store back in Albuquerque, my travels, and my politics than he is in me. And so are his pals. There's something cold and steely about those guys that makes me uncomfortable. I know they've invited us on a deep sea fishing expedition tomorrow, but I'm not going. I hope you don't mind."

"Of course I don't mind," Magdalena replied. "But be nice to them, kid. They're paying for our trip."

And indeed they were. At the end of the week, when it was time to check out of the hotel, Beverly watched in amazement as Magdalena piled twenty, fifty, and hundred dollar bills atop the cashier's counter, a look of smug and impish satisfaction on her tanned face. One of the poker pals cruised past and wordlessly glared at the heap of rumpled bills.

Beverly and Magdalena's farewell lobster and margarita lunch in the Hotel Santa Fe's *palapa* ended with them a little drunk and teary-eyed.

"We've got to get together more often," Mag said.

"This has been my best vacation ever," Beverly said. "I can't thank you enough. Promise you'll visit me in New Mexico soon so I can give you the grand tour."

Magdalena smiled and kissed Beverly's forehead. "You're on."

At the Puerto Escondido airport, they shed more tears when they separated. Magdalena began her journey back to Manhattan, and Beverly boarded a flight to Dallas-Fort Worth on her way home to Albuquerque.

Bright white lights, blank walls, and shiny metallic fixtures in the cavernous customs clearing area at DFW International gave off an antiseptic, arctic glare that reminded Beverly of a hospital operating room when she emerged from the maze of corridors leading from the jetway into the airport. Only two lines at the immigration counters were open, and through her half-closed eyes she soon saw she'd chosen the slower one. With resignation, she shuffled slowly forward with dozens of other tired passengers. Suddenly, lights went on in additional booths, and more immigration officials appeared. Travelers madly changed lanes like freeway drivers, trying to outrun each other in a dash toward the new booths. Beverly was too tired for the chase and stayed put. Eventually, it was her turn to cross the yellow line, step up to the counter, and slip her passport under the Plexiglas window.

The official peered over the top of his glasses and stared hard at her. She wondered if he was trying to determine whether she was as ugly in person as she was in her five-year-old passport photograph. After a week at the beach, she felt like a new person. Maybe her looks had changed, too. The gray in her thatch of reddish hair had been joined by a few beach-blonde streaks, her eyes were a little bloodshot from one margarita too many at lunch and hours in airplanes, and her newly acquired sunburn had tightened her wrinkles and crow's-feet.

The official turned to his computer, typed, then read. And read some more, his eyes following the words that marched across his screen, words Beverly couldn't see. Several minutes went by, but still he read on, typing now and then. She began to fidget. What was taking him so long?

The businessman in line behind her groaned and dropped his attaché case with a slap on the linoleum floor next to his shiny loafers. He folded his arms across his Armani suit and glared at Beverly, as if the delay were her fault. She shrugged him an apology. He scowled and began to shop for a line that was moving faster, but just then, the official scrawled a capital A on Beverly's customs declaration form with a red pen, circled it, and shoved her papers back under the window. "Next!" he called out.

The businessman nearly trampled her as he rushed forward.

Her paperwork and carry-on in hand, she approached the luggage conveyor belt that snaked in and out of the airport's backstage area. As she searched the carousel for her battered suitcase, she saw Magdalena's poker pals and waved at them. They'd been on both of her return flights, the propjet from Puerto Escondido to Mexico City, and the connecting 757 to Dallas. They nodded a silent greeting to her, collected their luggage, and passed quickly through the customs inspection station into the airport.

One by one, the other passengers retrieved their luggage, loaded it onto carts, and wheeled away toward the customs counters. Soon the carousel was empty, and with a thunk, the conveyor belt stopped. Beverly's heart sank. She was luggageless and alone.

Just as she was about to storm the airline's freight office, she heard another thunk, and the conveyor belt began to move again. Like the Red Sea, the rubber flaps parted, and her suitcase, the much-abused and duct-taped veteran of her many trips south of the border, jerked toward her on the shuddering belt. Sighing with relief, she dragged the heavy bag toward the customs line. A uniformed inspector intercepted her, glanced at the red scrawl on her declaration form, and pointed her toward a table at the far end of the room.

Oh, boy, she muttered to herself. Siberia.

At the table, a Latina inspector was giving an elderly Mexican Indian woman a hard time. The *mexicana,* unable to understand the inspector's garbled Spanish, was nearly in tears.

Beverly spoke quietly to the Indian woman. *"Ella solamente quiere ver lo que usted tiene en los paquetes,"* she said. "She just wants to see what's in your packages."

"Step back and stay out of this!" the inspector yelled.

Beverly jumped. "Just trying to be helpful," she said, retreating to the far side of the yellow stripe.

The Indian woman hastily unwrapped several parcels of food. The inspector poked at them with gloved hands. Then, with a scowl and a grunt, she ordered the woman to pack up her things and go on through. When the woman looked at her blankly, the inspector barked at her. *"¡Vaya!"*

She quickly rewrapped her bundles, tossed them into plastic shopping bags, and hustled away on short, thick legs, her braids swaying across the back of her thin sweater. The inspector motioned Beverly forward.

She handed over her documents, hoisted her luggage onto the metal examining table, and went to open her combination locks, but both were already open. "That's odd. I made a point of locking this suitcase back in Puerto Escondido," she muttered aloud.

"What did you say?"

"Just talking to myself."

The inspector grunted. As she rummaged through Beverly's luggage, she fired off questions. "What kind of work do you do?"

"I have a store."

"Where?"

"In Albuquerque."

"What do you sell in your store?"

"Folk art."

"Where were you in Mexico?"

"Puerto Escondido."

"Where else did you go in Mexico?"

"No place else."

"How long were you there?"

"One week."

"How often do you go to Mexico?"

"Maybe once every year or two."

"What did you buy?"

"Gifts for my family."

The inspector let the lid of the suitcase fall and glanced at the declaration form. "Twenty-two T-shirts?"

"Yes, I have fifteen nieces and nephews, five brothers, and a sister."

"That's twenty-one, not twenty-two."

"Right. One of the T-shirts is for me. Is that OK with you?"

"Don't get smart."

"I'm not getting smart. I'm just wondering what this is all about. I have receipts if you want to see them. I don't sell T-shirts in my store, if that's what you're wondering. I don't know why you're giving me the third degree, and I'm worried about missing my connecting flight."

"Do you want me to really give you the third degree?" the inspector said, her voice rising, her face flushed, her hands on her hips. At nearby tables, heads turned toward the inspector and Beverly.

Just then, a male customs official stepped up. "I'll handle this, Pérez," he said smoothly. "I think you're due for a break here."

The woman thrust Beverly's paperwork at the man and stomped off.

Beverly knew her face was flushed, and she could hear her heart pounding. As upset as she was at the inspector for hassling her, she was even more annoyed with herself for losing her temper. Being tired, sweaty, and short-tempered after a long day of traveling was no excuse. From fourteen years of professional dealings with customs, she knew that whether you're right or wrong, you keep your cool with border cops.

The new official, a tall, balding Anglo with hairy arms emerging from his short-sleeved shirt, narrowed his ice-blue eyes and attempted a smile. He reminded Beverly of a snake about to strike. He motioned the two men in line behind her to another table. Bad sign, Beverly thought. But she took a deep breath, forced a smile, and watched the official page through her passport, turning it this way and that to look at the stamps before he handed it back.

"You seem to go to South America often," the inspector said, flashing her a mouthful of large, shiny teeth. "Can I ask you the nature of your trip to Mexico?"

"My Aunt Magdalena and I spent a week on the beach in Puerto Escondido," she said evenly.

"And what kind of business are you in?"

From the way he peered at Beverly, she knew he knew exactly what kind of business she was in. "I import folk art from Latin America. I have a store in Albuquerque."

"Hmmm," the inspector said. "And what did you buy in Mexico?"

"It's all right there on the declaration form, . . . sir."

The man shifted his weight from one foot to the other and smiled. "Well, of course. But what did you buy for your business?"

"Nothing. If I'd bought commercial goods, I'd have prepared

paperwork for an informal entry, sir. The items I bought are personal. The truth is, I rarely buy in Mexico for my business. Things are too expensive, the quality's not that great any more, New Mexicans prefer to buy in Mexico themselves, and the exporting is a hassle. I was in Mexico for a vacation."

"Hmmm," he said. "So what do you handle in your store— clothing, wood carvings, wall hangings, pre-Columbian art—that sort of thing?"

"I don't handle pre-Columbian art."

"No?" The inspector raised one of his furry eyebrows and grinned broadly.

"No. I've had my store for fourteen years, and there have never been any irregularities with my import shipments. Is there something going on here, sir?"

"Why, no," the inspector beamed. "There's nothing going on here. Thank you for your cooperation, Miss Parmentier." He handed her passport and declaration form to her. "Have a nice day."

Later, aboard her flight to Albuquerque, Beverly munched peanuts, sipped a screw-top burgundy, and ruminated on the scene at Dallas-Fort Worth. A veteran of dozens of trips to Central and South America, she hadn't been questioned like that by customs since 1975, when she was returning from a two-week visit to the village in Colombia where she had served as a Peace Corps volunteer in the late sixties. Then, like anybody getting off a plane from Colombia, she'd expected extra scrutiny from border officials, and she'd gotten it—the drop-your-drawers-bend-over-and-say-ah routine. The DFW experience wasn't nearly as hideous or humiliating, but it was unusual. Pestering her about a bunch of souvenir T-shirts? Asking her about pre-Columbian art?

It was almost as if customs had been waiting for her at DFW. It was a scary thought, but within the realm of possibilities.

With computers and airline cooperation, customs could easily track anyone's border crossings, she knew. But why would they track her? If the agency was any good at discerning who was involved in illegal activities and who wasn't, they'd know she wasn't worth a second glance. For one thing, if she were involved in illegal activity, wouldn't she have money?

Beverly thought her threadbare life style and pitiful bank accounts made it obvious she was almost penniless. Moreover, she didn't hang out with shady characters. She'd gotten a few parking tickets in her day, and if tortured, might admit to driving over 25 in a residential zone a time or two, but she'd never been in any real trouble with the law. Customs was probably on some new kick, she decided. No doubt one that meant more hassles for small importers like her.

She leaned back in her seat, gazed out the window, and tried to put the experience at DFW behind her. As the jet chased the sunset westward, cottony clouds just beyond the plane's windows turned a faint rose against the deepening indigo sky. Puerto Escondido's pristine beaches, its swaying palms, grenadine sunsets, and the tropical torpidity of the Mexican January she'd left just hours before suddenly seemed long ago and far away.

The plane soon tipped earthward on its approach to Albuquerque. Beverly pressed her nose against the cold glass and peered through the pastel dusk at the earth below. In her absence, snow had blanketed the plains of eastern New Mexico. The outlines of roads, waterholes, salt lakes, and irrigation-system circles were now only lightly traceable beneath the cold, white flannel that covered them. A wintry chill settled into her bones. She drew an alpaca shawl around her sunburned shoulders.

Two

The following morning, although she awoke feeling achy and jet lagged from the trip, Beverly was eager to get to the store to see what had happened in her absence. She drove her fifteen-year-old Datsun—the station wagon her friends called the Dumpster—from her home in the North Valley to La Ñapa, her store, housed in a century-old adobe on the edge of Old Town.

Like a trained chimp going through her daily paces, she slipped her worn brass key into the locks on the store's rear door, used another key to turn off the burglar alarm, and walked into the old house's kitchen, which doubled as a storeroom.

Even if space aliens had kidnapped and blindfolded her and driven her around the galaxy for hours, her nose would have told her she was back in La Ñapa. The store had a specific odor, an offbeat masala of familiar scents that reminded her of various parts of Latin America: the nutty odor of etched and burned gourds from Peru; the slight mustiness of Kuna Indian molas from Panama; the wet-earth smell of pottery from Guatemala; and the lanolin-rich scents of alpaca and sheep's wool textiles from the Andes.

In the mid-1970s, Beverly had opened La Ñapa with her savings and a $2,000 loan from Magdalena. In the Andes, vendors give their customers an extra little gift, a *ñapa,* as a token of appreciation for their business. Beverly wanted to give her customers that extra something, something personal, she found missing in the modern-day Wal-Mart world of wage-slave-produced goods and surly service. Ever a pipe dreamer, she hoped to build a bridge, however tiny and insignificant, between hardworking Latin American artisan families and her customers. Beverly saw La Ñapa as her personal foreign aid program.

Her on-again-off-again boyfriend, Steve Bronstein, whom she'd met while in the Peace Corps in Colombia, frequently reminded her she was hopelessly mired in outmoded sixties sentiments like doing good in the world.

"You're destined for a life of penury if you don't tailor your business more to fashion trends, advertising, and a heftier markup," he warned her.

Beverly ignored Steve's admonitions to join the "real" business world. It bored her. "I'll happily pump gas or flip burgers for a living before I join the panty-hose-and-heels business world," she told him. "It's true my income as a self-appointed bridge tender will always be modest and precarious, but as long as La Ñapa provides me with enough money to pay bills and keep myself in vino and chocolate, I'm happy."

As Beverly tarried in the storeroom, she heard a knock at the front door. The clock told her she was five minutes late opening for business. To her chagrin, her best customer, Helen Benton, stood waiting patiently on the porch, clutching her alligator purse in front of her mink coat.

"Mrs. Benton! How nice to see you! I'm so sorry to keep you waiting."

"Perhaps I'm a little early. "

"No, it's me. I got home last night from Mexico, and I was moving a little slowly this morning."

"Take your time. I'm in no big hurry today. I'm not meeting my granddaughter Alicia for lunch until noon."

The elderly woman came in, a little unsteady on the vintage alligator heels that matched her purse, and waited patiently as Beverly scurried around the store, turning on the overhead lights in her four showrooms. She helped Mrs. Benton out of her coat and draped it over the back of a blue denim sofa.

Just then, a heavy-set, middle-aged man in a Hawaiian shirt came into the store. He wore aviator sunglasses and a grim, tight-lipped expression. With hulking, slightly stooped shoulders, he looked like an old linebacker. She greeted him cheerfully, but he ignored her. Walking gingerly on what might have been football-injured knees, he approached the pottery display at the entrance to the clothing room and paused over the pots and figures on the shelf.

"Can I help you?" she asked.

But the man acted as if he hadn't heard her. He picked up pots one by one, inspecting each carefully, turning it over in his meaty hands. Doubting he would buy anything, Beverly turned her attention back to Mrs. Benton.

"It's Alicia's birthday today," the elderly lady said. "I'd like to get her something special. Perhaps she could use one of these wool wraps." Mrs. Benton approached a rack of clothing and stroked an emerald-green brushed wool ruana from Colombia.

Although the man had his back toward Beverly and her customer, she sensed he was listening to their conversation.

"Alicia might also like one of these hand-knit coat sweaters," Beverly said. "In fact, when she was in here a few weeks ago, she was rather taken with this brown-and-white one. She thought about putting it on layaway, but decided she couldn't afford it."

"These pre-Columbian?" the man asked in a raspy, high-pitched voice.

"No. They're contemporary pots from the Peruvian jungle. Shipibo Indians' work."

He huffed.

Beverly held out a snowflake-patterned coat sweater for Mrs. Benton to inspect. "I import these sweaters from a women's cooperative in southern Ecuador. It's all handspun wool and natural colors of the sheep, so the sweaters are washable. They're popular with the college kids."

"Which ones are your pre-Columbian?" the man interjected.

"The pots? None of them, sir. I don't handle pre-Columbian material."

"Huh," he muttered in a tone that indicated he didn't believe her.

The man made Beverly uneasy—his florid face, his narrowed eyes, the way he wouldn't face her when he spoke. Everything about him was so unpleasant that she decided to ignore him.

Mrs. Benton fingered the soft, nubby sweater and looked at the price tag, which dangled from a sleeve. "It's a lovely sweater, dear, but it's half the price of the wool wrap. Shouldn't you be trying to sell me the more expensive item? That's what everyone else in this town does when I go shopping."

Beverly laughed. "I want you and your granddaughter to be happy with your gift. That's what's important to me."

"You take such good care of me. I'll take the sweater, if that's what you think Alicia would prefer. And I'll take the lovely green poncho for *moi.*"

"Done. Can I gift wrap the sweater for you?"

"Thank you, dear. That would be lovely."

"So where's your pre-Columbian?" the man asked over his shoulder. Mrs. Benton glared at him, and Beverly thought she was going to tell him to mind his manners. "You keep it in the back?" he added.

"I already told you I don't handle pre-Columbian art."

"Yeah," he grunted again. He clumsily set a fragile Shipibo water jar onto the shelf and walked briskly out of the store.

Mrs. Benton and Beverly rolled their eyes at each other and watched the man hobble down the steps and get into a baby-blue Lincoln Continental parked in front of the store.

"What a rude man!" the elderly woman said once he was out of earshot.

· · · · ·

After Mrs. Benton left, Beverly sat at the sales desk and looked over Lucille's daily reports. She was cheered to see her employee had made good sales in her absence—lots of small things like tapes, books, Tarahumara Indian baskets, and *milagros,* little silver charms. She had also sold some clothing and an $800 santo, a wooden figure of St. Joseph, although she had written "San Judás" on the receipt. The sales added up to more than enough to pay Lucille's salary and the coming month's rent. Brava, Lucille! she thought.

She turned to the pile of mail that had accumulated. The corner of a blue airmail envelope caught her eye, and she tugged it out of the middle of the stack. Although the letter bore U.S. stamps and a Miami postmark, a glance at the return address confirmed her guess. The letter was from Peru, from one of her main exporters, Delia Quispe. Beverly hummed a little tune. It was a letter she'd been waiting for. But one end was slit open. The envelope hadn't been crunched in a mail-sorting machine; it had been deliberately opened with a letter opener or knife. "This is odd," she said aloud. Lucille never opened mail addressed to Beverly. And other first-class letters as well as junk mail showed signs of tampering. Well, she thought, Lucille would have an explanation.

She hoped Delia's letter contained information about a shipment bound for an exhibit at Santa Fe's Museum of Popular Art. The museum had invited one of Beverly's suppliers, Dionisio Toma, a Peruvian *retablo* maker, to discuss his work and demonstrate his craft, and they were paying for his trip from Lima. Dionisio had been working for a year to prepare special work for the exhibit. The opening date was only a month away, and Beverly was getting nervous.

The *retablero's* trip to the United States was the first visit she'd been able to arrange for one of the folk artists who produced things for the store. If everything went well, she hoped to be able to arrange for more of them to come to the United States and meet her customers.

Dear Beverly,

I've had more trouble than usual getting your shipment out of Peru. Your government is putting a lot of pressure on ours because of drugs, and our customs agents are giving extra scrutiny to all shipments leaving the country. They demanded bribes to let your crates pass inspection, but with the help of a cousin who works at the airport, I was able to get the shipment cleared with minimal "administration fees."

Too, I was able to repack the crates following the inspection. As usual, the inspectors made a mess of our careful packing order. Should any of the retablos get damaged in transit, however, I included a packet of Dionisio's powdered paints to repair broken items.

Beverly read more quickly now, scanning the letter for specifics on the shipment date. When she reached the line where Delia said the shipment was about to leave Peru, she picked up the blue envelope lying on the desk and saw its postmark was only four days old. Delia must have given the letter to a traveler to post in the United States for her. A wise decision: the Peruvian postal system was hopeless.

I'm including a copy of the airbill, an invoice for the goods, and the form A.

But no documents accompanied the letter. Beverly was dismayed. It was unlike Delia to forget to include these all-important papers. She had always been thorough and reliable. Perhaps Lucille dropped the rest of the envelope's contents somewhere in the store or had already filed them.

She dialed Lucille's number and had the luck to find her at

home. "Thank you for doing such a great job while I was away," Beverly said. "And you get gold stars for selling the San José. I never thought we'd sell that ugly thing."

Lucille giggled. "The lady thought it was the prettiest 'santos' she'd ever seen. She was sure it was a Saint Jude, not a Joseph. The customer is always right, so you'll see I wrote 'San Judás' on the ticket."

"Great job. Say, Delia's letter came opened, and there wasn't any paperwork for the shipment, just her letter."

"Oh, no. The letter came open, and so did the rest of the mail. It was really weird. I promise I didn't open the letter. Honest. I never open your mail."

"I know you don't. The missing papers are a real problem. Without the airway bill or its number, I won't be able to keep track of the shipment. It comes to Albuquerque from Lima, via the Miami and Dallas airports. Cargo sometimes disappears if no one pesters the airlines about it. Before you worked here, a sweater shipment to La Ñapa ended up in Tierra del Fuego. When the crates finally arrived in Albuquerque, they were practically empty. The longer a shipment's in transit, the more likely it is to be lost or pilfered."

"Oh, I'm sorry, Bev. At least the shipment's insured, isn't it?"

"Yeah, but insurance is next to useless. I once filed a claim against Eastern Airlines when one of their forklifts ran over a large box of clothing I'd specially ordered from a women's group in Ecuador. The forklift ironed grease spots and indelible tire marks into dozens of beautifully hand-embroidered shirts and dresses. White ones, no less. I'd insured the shipment for the full value of the clothes, but the bastards at Eastern laughed me off."

"They did? They can do that?"

"I took them to small claims court, but it was just me, a female nobody, up against three attorneys from El Paso. The good ol' boy judge and the guys from El Paso were obviously pals, and I lost."

"Didn't you have an attorney?"

"Steve was going to represent me, but at the last minute, he had to go out of town."

"Steve's not very reliable."

"No, he's not. My only consolation is that soon afterward, Eastern was out of business, and years later, I'm still solvent—sort of, anyway. There's a little justice in the world, but not much."

"Can you get copies of the paperwork from Peru?"

"I hope so. The problem is it's expensive to call South America, and it can take days to get through to Delia. In the meantime, the cargo will be rattling around in the pipeline with nobody tracking it."

Beverly's stomach churned at the thought the retablo shipment that Dionisio had spent a year preparing, and in which she had invested the last of her cash, might end up in darkest Argentina. She wanted to wring someone's neck, but whose? After she hung up, she immediately tried to call Peru, with no luck. For several frustrating days and nights, she dialed and redialed. Finally, she reached Delia and told her about the missing paperwork.

"I'm so sorry, Beverly," Delia said. "The documents were all there when I gave the letter to a friend traveling to Miami. He's totally trustworthy. *Qué curioso.* I'll fax you copies immediately."

Within minutes, Beverly had the necessary papers in hand and began tracking her shipment, biting her nails as the shipment spent five days moving through various ports before it landed in Albuquerque.

At long last, American Airfreight called to say her shipment had arrived and customs had cleared it. Beverly immediately drove to the airport. She approached the air freight office at Albuquerque International Airport, her faxed paperwork in hand, excited as a kid entering a toy store with a fistful of dollars. After a year's wait and more than the usual hassles, she was about to see Dionisio's handiwork. Delia had sent some old jewelry, majolica pottery, baskets, and other odds and ends as well. This was going to be like Christmas.

She handed her sheaf of papers to the freight clerk. "I'm here to pick up La Ñapa's shipment," she said.

The clerk flushed slightly. He turned away and rustled through a pile of papers in a wire basket. His eyes downcast, he passed a pile of documents across the counter to her. "That's $652.94. Sign here," he said, pointing to the bottom of the airfreight bill. "Back your car into the loading dock, and I'll get your crates for you."

"I'd like to see the shipment before I sign anything, if that's OK with you," she said.

The clerk hesitated. "Well, uh, I guess so."

He pried off the top of one of the three large plywood crates that were draped in yards of blue-and-white U.S. customs tape, and Beverly's good mood dissolved like sugar in hot water. The interior, which would normally have been a neat puzzle of tightly packed cardboard boxes, looked as though it had been ravaged by a rabid, burrowing badger. A number of Dionisio's gaily painted *retablo* boxes lay in a jumble of crumpled newspapers and ripped cardboard, their doors flung open on their fragile leather hinges to reveal extensive interior damage. Tiny human and animal figures were strewn about in a disaster scene of broken limbs and decapitated bodies. Even the figures that remained whole were loose from their moorings and scattered.

Beverly could barely speak. "What the hell happened?"

The freight clerk shrugged. "I guess it wasn't packed properly."

"Bullshit! This crate was packed beautifully and professionally in Peru by people I've worked with for over a decade."

"Well, you know, they're inspecting all outgoing shipments down there, looking for drugs. That's probably when the damage occurred. Maybe the inspectors didn't repack the crate, just nailed the top back on, and the stuff shook loose in transit."

Beverly's voice quaked with rage. "My expediter is totally

trustworthy, and she told me she repacked the shipment after the Peruvian customs agents went through it."

When she made eye contact with the freight agent, he looked away, his eyes scouring the warehouse walls as if looking for an escape hatch. Something about this stinks, she thought, and it isn't simply the reek of jet fuel from the tarmac. "Which customs guy inspected the shipment?"

The agent scuffled his steel-toed boots on the cement floor. "Things just aren't the same around here without Larry and Gómez," he mumbled.

Beverly nodded in agreement. The two customs agents with whom she'd had an amiable relationship for years had died within months of each other the previous year. "Was it one of those new guys? DiMarco maybe?"

The agent nodded. "Yeah. That guy throws his weight around, like he's Eliot Ness or something. The new kid from Rio Bravo Brokerage was with him. Actually, he was the one who drilled your little painted boxes."

"Drilled?" Beverly yelped, her voice echoing through the vaulted warehouse. "My broker drilled my stuff?"

"Hey, don't blame me, lady!" the agent protested. "I couldn't do nothing about it!"

She carefully lifted an eight-by-ten-inch *retablo* from its nest of crumpled paper and cardboard and saw it had been penetrated by a drill bit. Her heart sank. Wiping her eyes with the hem of her poncho, she picked up several more retablos. Even a two-by-three-inch one was riddled with boreholes.

She shook a little box in the agent's face. "What in hell did they think they were going to find in this teeny thing? They didn't even bother unwrapping it before they drilled it!"

The man sighed deeply. "I guess they were looking for drugs. Those guys are crazy, if you ask me. You couldn't get no drugs in that thin plywood the boxes are made out of. Drilling your merchandise is just plain stupid, and it's destruction of private property. That's my two cents' worth. Customs has this new program that offers big cash rewards to brokers and freight agents if they turn in an importer for shipping drugs, and some people are going nuts."

Her hands shaking, Beverly set the little *retablo* back down in the crate. Depending on how extensive the damage was, the exhibit at the museum might now be impossible. Dionisio was going to be heartsick to see his beautiful work reduced to rubble. And her hopes to make a modest profit on the special work after the exhibit was over were dashed. Although she felt a volcanic eruption coming on, she did her best to regain calm. She drew in a deep breath, gathered her scattered wits, and spoke softly and calmly to the freight agent. "I'll be back this afternoon with a camera. Somebody is going to pay for this."

"Well, not us," the agent said. "They told me to tell you the drilling happened in Peru. I really shouldn't have told you they did it. Me and my big mouth," he groaned.

"I apologize for yelling at you. I know this isn't your fault." Beverly patted the agent's hand. "You did the right thing telling me what really happened, and I appreciate it. I'll do my best to protect you. But believe me, I'm going to raise holy hell about this."

She walked slowly toward her car. Then, changing her mind and pace, she strode to the old airport building nearby, where Rio Bravo Brokerage and U.S. customs were both housed. Although her engines were smoking in low gear and she was in danger of losing her brakes, she did her best to keep a grip.

She sucked in a deep breath and walked into the brokerage office.

"I'd like to see the manager, please," she said to a balding man in his mid-twenties, who was shuffling papers at a nearby desk.

"Your name?" he asked.

"Beverly Parmentier from La Ñapa."

The clerk's eyes widened, and he tripped over a chair leg as he went to fetch the manager. His nervousness led Beverly to peg him as a possible culprit.

A young woman soon appeared, introduced herself as Alma Briones, and shook Beverly's hand.

"Can we talk in your office?" Beverly asked.

"Certainly." Ms. Briones pulled out a chair for Beverly and sat down behind a large neat desk, folding her jeweled fingers together on it. "What can I do for you?"

"A freight agent at American, who shall remain nameless, said Rio Bravo's broker drilled items in my Peruvian shipment. My own broker drilled my stuff! Very valuable, specially crafted things going to a museum. This is beyond belief!"

The manager frowned. "I'm sure the agent was mistaken. It had to have been the customs inspector."

"No, the agent clearly saw your employee initiate the drilling. I can't tell you how outraged and enraged I am about this."

In striving to control her temper, Beverly felt as if she were holding back Niagara Falls with a piece of cardboard. "I have been an exemplary customer of this company for fourteen years, as the former manager can tell you. This shipment contains work specially prepared for an exhibit at the Popular Art Museum in Santa Fe, and a good portion of it appears to have been deliberately damaged by your employee."

"I have no idea why he would have done such a thing."

"I hear customs is now rewarding people who find drugs in shipments. Maybe he was hoping to strike it rich."

"Let me see who cleared your shipment." Alma Briones left the room. She returned in a few minutes with a handful of documents. The bald, chubby clerk followed her into the office, wiping his palms on the sides of his khakis. He slumped into a chair next to Beverly and sat jiggling his legs.

She turned toward him and stretched out her hand. "I'm Beverly Parmentier from La Ñapa, and you're. . .?"

"Delbert Solecki," he mumbled, giving her a limp, dead-fish handshake while avoiding her eyes.

She took out a notebook. "How do you spell your name, Mr. Solecki? I want to make sure I get it right."

Solecki mumbled his name to her. "I didn't drill your stuff," he stammered. "Well, I did some, but it wasn't my idea. It was customs."

"Whose drill was it?" Beverly asked.

"Well, it was ours," Solecki admitted.

Alma Briones gasped and fell back in her chair. "I didn't even know we owned a drill."

"I—we—bought it last week," Solecki said. "You know, sometimes these shipments from Bolibya or wherever have drugs in them. There was a packet of colored powders right on top in one of the crates. It looked suspicious, so we decided to drill some of the little boxes."

"The powders are special paints, and now I need them to repair the damage you did," Beverly said tersely.

"Well, uh, customs has them. They're running tests to see if they're drugs."

Beverly closed her eyes for a moment, then turned to the manager. "I'll never see those paints again. I expect Rio Bravo to pay for the repairs to the damaged work, and I think compensation for the loss in value due to the vandalism by your employee would be in order."

Solecki squirmed in his chair.

Ms. Briones frowned. "I'll have to discuss the matter with my supervisor in El Paso."

On her way back to the store to fetch her camera, Beverly felt compelled to vent her anger. Her first instinct was to stop her car in the middle of Lomas Boulevard and scream at the blameless blue skies overhead, but she was afraid that could get her a padded cell. Instead, she drove to her friend Steve's law office. Sometimes he was next to useless when she needed a sympathetic ear, but sometimes he had valuable insights.

As he listened to her tale, Steve leaned his tall, lanky torso back in his creaky office chair and made a little church and steeple with his long, narrow fingers. Like a preacher looking down at the congregation from his pulpit, he peered over the tops of his bifocals at Beverly. "Don't go overboard on this, Bev. Can't you file an insurance claim for the damages? Or simply write it off? Raise the prices to cover the losses? Get the guy in Peru to make you more stuff?"

"You don't understand, Steve. This isn't just *stuff*. It's special work Dionisio has been preparing for a year now. The exhibit at the Popular Art Museum is the first show he's ever had outside Peru, and it opens in a few weeks. It can take months to make one of those boxes. There isn't time for him to make more. And I had collectors lined up to buy his work after the show."

"Can you fix the *retablos?*"

"Well, I can try to glue them back together, but they won't be the same, and they can't sell for as much as ones in pristine condition. Maybe Dionisio will be able to work on them. He gets here a couple of days before the exhibit opens. But he's going to be devastated when he sees what those cretins did to his work. Can you believe the fucking nerve of those guys? My own broker—a guy I pay to clear my goods—dives into my shipment with a drill, hoping to find himself a big cash reward."

"It's the Holy War on Drugs, *niña*. I'm telling you. It's a Trojan horse devouring the Bill of Rights as if it were new mown hay."

"Well, I'm going to the CEO of Rio Bravo Brokerage with this, I'm going to the commissioner of customs, and I'm going to Congressman Ovni."

Steve shook his head in dismay. "What's any of that going to get you? Maybe it'll help you blow off a little steam. You'd better chill out before you have a heart attack. And when you plan your reprisals, remember you have to keep a civil relationship with customs if you want to continue importing, and that Rio Bravo is the only customs broker in town."

"I've never had a problem with Rio Bravo before, and I had a perfectly decent, mutually respectful relationship with customs until they brought in these storm troopers."

"*Buena suerte, niña.* You'll need a lot of luck to get anywhere with them."

Steve was right. Her fax to the CEO of Rio Bravo Brokerage, a large corporation with offices in every port in the Southwest, earned Beverly a reply from a flunky in customer service. He was sure the unnamed airline employee was mistaken when he said one of Rio Bravo's Albuquerque employees had drilled her *retablos*. It had to have been the customs agent. Rio Bravo Brokerage valued La Ñapa as a longtime customer, but nonetheless they could not be held responsible for damages to her shipment.

A lawyer in customs headquarters in Washington replied to Beverly's letter to Customs Commissioner Gustav von Gier. The response was smug and blunt. The attorney cited a number of statutes that permitted customs to search all goods entering the United States from abroad and virtually dared her to sue the federal government for damages.

The response from Congressman Ovni, a conservative Republican, was a huge surprise:

I am appalled that Albuquerque customs has engaged in such unnecessary destruction of your private property. Please be assured that I will

bring the matter to the customs commissioner's
attention.

   I fully understand the cultural value and unique
nature of your damaged goods and hope the exhibit
at the Popular Art Museum will nonetheless be able
to go forth. Please extend my deepest apologies
to Dionisio Toma for the harm done to his work.
I hope his stay in New Mexico will be a pleasant
one, in spite of this unfortunate incident.

Ovni's letter made Beverly feel a bit better, but it wasn't going to
result in what she wanted: a heartfelt apology from customs, fair
compensation for her losses, and crucifixion of the guilty parties.

Three

Dave Carney, a twenty-two-year veteran of the U.S. Customs Service, was a patient man. But his boss, the Albuquerque Office of Enforcement's special agent in charge, Ray Zoffke, had already kept him waiting for more than a half hour past his seven a.m. appointment, and Dave was annoyed. To pass the time, he sipped cup after cup of bitter, office-brewed coffee and made small talk with Melissa Montoya, Zoffke's executive secretary. When they ran out of comfortable topics, Dave adjourned to the window of the fourth-floor Federal Office Building in downtown Albuquerque to watch the sun steadily rise above the rim of the Sandía Mountains to the east of the city. A high-altitude wind swept dunes of snow from the ten-thousand-foot peaks onto a celestial canvas that evolved from white to pale blue to deep turquoise as the sun slowly warmed the winter sky. And still Dave waited.

Suddenly Melissa's intercom came to life. "Carney still there?" a high voice said.

"Yes, sir," she replied.

"OK, send him in."

Melissa led Dave into Zoffke's office. The official didn't look up from the pile of paper atop his desk as Dave folded his narrow five-foot eleven-inch frame into the only available seat in the room, an ancient GSA-issue straight-backed wooden chair. The uncomfortable chair was a typical Zoffke ploy. Both men knew Dave had requested the meeting to discuss his long-promised promotion, but Dave figured his boss didn't want him to be too comfortable. Zoffke had probably searched out the damn thing in the basement.

After enduring a few moments of uncomfortable silence, Dave spoke. "Thanks for taking the time to meet with me."

Zoffke, a paunchy, red-faced slab of aged beef, looked up and stared at his underling with little pig eyes, drumming his fingers on his desk.

Dave was damned if he was going to let Zoffke intimidate him. He yawned into his fist, casually crossed one knee over the other, and smiled.

Clasping his hands behind his head, Zoffke leaned back in his plush ergonomic chair, swung his cowboy boots one at a time up onto his paper-strewn desk, and launched into a monologue about his career in customs and what an outstanding, important guy he was.

Dave had been forewarned he would do this. According to the guys in the Office of Enforcement who had served under Zoffke longer than Dave, the SAC always talked about himself at length when a subordinate tried to discuss a promotion.

Dave recrossed his legs, held his hands in his lap, and feigned rapt attention. While his *jefe* rambled on, he discreetly checked out Zoffke's décor. The office was filled with numerous testimonials to the boss's illustrious past—trophies commemorating his career as an all-conference tackle at the University of Alabama, photographs from his Special Forces days in Vietnam (and probably Cambodia and Laos as well), his framed Silver Star won in the Tet Offensive, certificates from training programs attesting to his prowess in various types of weaponry and law enforcement techniques, merit awards from the agency. Reinhardt (Ray) Zoffke wanted to remind visitors, especially flunkies like Dave, that the boss was a man of many accomplishments.

A large, somewhat-faded photograph on the wall behind Zoffke's desk caught Dave's eye. In it, a diminutive middle-aged woman—a Mamie Eisenhower look-alike—hugged Zoffke in front of a cargo plane. Dave figured the photo commemorated Zoffke's hero's return from Southeast Asia. The boss was a lot thinner in the photo, and he had a full head of hair.

Zoffke saw Dave looking at the photograph. "That's my mother," he said in a muted voice. "She's the most wonderful mother a boy could have. She's in a rest home in Florida with round-the-clock nursing care. It's astonishingly expensive, but that's the least I owe her. She protected me from Russian soldiers when they invaded Berlin."

Dave was surprised by the boss's uncharacteristic candor. Zoffke's fidelity to his mother made him a slightly more sympathetic character. But nobody in OE/Albuquerque liked him, including Dave. With his weird, high-pitched choirboy voice, his hair-trigger temper, and his reputation as an untrustworthy hardass who never let anyone forget he was boss, he wasn't a regular guy. While Zoffke saw himself as a key player in the El Paso region, his underlings considered him a paper pusher, although he had been with the agency twenty-four years and had moved steadily up the food chain.

"Things are about to change around here," Zoffke said with a grin.

Dave sat up and paid attention.

"Washington has a new show," Zoffke explained, "the Cultural Patrimony Initiative. The administration is intent on helping certain Latin countries stop people from trafficking in their national treasures, such as pre-Columbian art. Commissioner von Gier believes that international traffic in stolen art is nearly as lucrative as the drug trade."

Ha, Dave thought, that's a good one. Like anyone with street-level knowledge of the drug business, he saw the stolen art "threat" as a political ploy. Yet, he quickly realized, the initiative could serve a number of purposes. With this new mandate, together with the considerable powers Congress had already granted customs under the war on drugs, the agency could beef up its presence in seaports, airports, and cities well within U.S. borders. And overseas, too. Customs already had offices in more than two dozen countries. Some of the new activities had caused a stir, such as when the Office of Enforcement's agents began to open U.S.-originated as well as foreign-originated mail, packages, cargo, and travelers' luggage without search warrants. A few people complained, but not enough to make a difference. Most people didn't know their property had been searched, and customs was not required to inform them.

"It's about time the agency flexed a little of its considerable muscle," Zoffke said. "After all, we're the U.S. Treasury's second most important source of revenue after the IRS, and the nation's fourth largest law enforcement agency. You know, Dave, this Cultural Patrimony Initiative could be manna from heaven for those of us who are team players."

"I'm on your team, Ray. You can count on me."

It was only a half-lie. Dave was a team player, within reason. But he feared what this effort might mean. The Cultural Patrimony Initiative was one more self-serving, politically motivated push, one that everyone would forget about in a year or two. He and Zoffke had both seen dozens of such initiatives come and go over the years. But they'd also seen the career paths of people who didn't play the game end in blind alleys. That was probably what Zoffke was insinuating—play ball with me, or kiss your promotion goodbye.

He knew Zoffke needed him. He was more street savvy than anyone else in OE/Albuquerque, certainly way more than Zoffke. Scuttlebutt indicated Washington had recently intensified pressure on the special agent in charge. For several years, he'd run Albuquerque's twenty-five-person Office of Enforcement. Yet in spite of a hefty budget and abundant manpower, as well as the agency's multimillion-dollar investment in air surveillance equipment for the Southwest region, customs hadn't made a significant drug bust in New Mexico or at the El Paso border in more than two years. In the meantime, the DEA, FBI, Border Patrol, and even local sheriffs were continually uncovering drug shipments throughout New Mexico and West Texas.

"We're going to nail some of these cultural patrimony smugglers," Zoffke said, grinning like a coyote with a mouse in its teeth. "The search warrant I've been waiting for just came across my desk.

"What's up, Ray?"

"The attorney general is giving us authorization to raid a Santa Fe gallery that deals in cultural patrimony items smuggled out of Mexico and Central America. Unfortunately, the gallery's owner, Galo Rivas Griswold, a notorious commie pinko, is out of the country, at home in El Salvador. But we'll still be able to nab the store manager, Pancha Archibeque, who has signed for a shipment of artifacts Rivas sent her from Central America. The customs detail in Central America contacted us with information that Rivas, a black-sheep member of the Salvadoran oligarchy, is heavily involved in pre-Columbian art. I have the impression the administration's Salvadoran friends are anxious to nail Rivas, probably for his traitorous left-wing politics, but I didn't press our colleagues for details. A lot of this has to remain hush-hush."

"Right, Ray."

"I approached Bert—the local U.S. attorney, Bert Schwentzle—with a request to search Rivas's Santa Fe gallery, apartment, storage locker, and Pancha Archibeque's apartment. But Jesus H. Christ! He insisted he needed physical evidence before he would issue a warrant. These lawyers, I tell you. What a bunch of assholes!"

"I'll say," Dave nodded in agreement.

"Providentially, an informant in the local customs broker's office called us just last week about a shipment of stone artifacts from Guatemala addressed to the gallery. The broker-informant program is working better than anyone expected, although the payoffs are shooting holes in our budget."

"I'll bet," Dave said.

"The artifact shipment looked like a box of rocks to me, but I was able to get a curator at the Art Museum to agree the artifacts were pre-Columbian and Mayan. Once I had that, Schwentzle was only too happy to approve the search warrant."

Dave surreptitiously looked at his watch. Time was flying by. He was about to break into Zoffke's patter to bring up the subject of his promotion when a blinking red light on the intercom caught Zoffke's eye, and he pressed the button.

It was his secretary. "You have a call on line two from Congressman Ovni's special assistant, Dalton McGowen."

Zoffke swept his boots off his desk, tucked his shirt back inside his belt, and sat up straight before punching line two. "What can I do for you?"

McGowen spoke so loudly, Dave could hear him halfway across the room. "I'll get right to the point, Mr. Zoffke. We've received a complaint from a constituent indicating your guys at the airport drilled holes in a shipment of her stuff from Peru, special things she was bringing in for an exhibit at the Popular Art Museum in Santa Fe. The congressman has taken a personal interest in this and asked me to contact you. We faxed you about it this morning."

Zoffke, looking a little gray, quickly flipped through a pile of papers on his desk to a sheet of fax paper that Dave saw bore a congressional seal. "Sorry, sir. I don't know anything about this alleged incident. I guess your fax didn't come through."

"We'll fax the materials again," McGowen said. "Her letter is quite hard hitting. She calls customs officials 'thugs' who 'witlessly destroyed' her Peruvian imports."

Dave watched Zoffke's face redden. The boss was no doubt furious that an importer had the *cojones* to embarrass the agency with a complaint to Congressman Ovni, a key member of the House Ways and Means Subcommittee on Trade, the committee charged with customs oversight.

McGowen continued. "I've done a little checking around, and this woman is pretty well known in the community. People say she's on the level, and she has a nice store. My wife and daughters shop there, in fact. Why would you drill her folk art? She says all the items were small enough to be X-rayed."

Ray Zoffke cogitated for a few seconds. Then, as if a lightbulb had gone on in his head, he brightened. "Is this complainant Beverly Parmentier?"

"As a matter of fact, it is."

"Well, I can't go into details at this time, Mr. McGowen. But we have reason to believe this importer is heavily involved in pre-Columbian art smuggling and possibly drugs as well. If we drilled her shipment, believe me, we had probable cause. We've been keeping an eye on these small importers. A lot of them are engaged in illegal activities."

"Really? Well, if you say so."

"I'm sure you understand that we can't allow this intel to be disseminated. I'd appreciate your discretion."

"Hmmm, well, yes, of course. I'll explain the circumstances to the congressman, and I guess we'll drop it. Thank you for your assistance."

"Anytime, sir, anytime."

Zoffke hung up the phone and looked at Dave with a nasty smirk. "I'll teach that bitch to make trouble for us. Come to think of it, maybe we can get a search warrant to raid her store, too. The fact is, my investigation of Rivas's gallery and his manager, Archibeque, shows numerous phone calls between the two businesses. Parmentier sells jewelry and folk art to Rivas's gallery, and she and Archibeque are pals. My bet says they're in this together.

"Schwentzle will demand something 'evidentiary' before giving us search warrants to raid Parmentier's place," Zoffke said, his fingers rapping the pile of mail in front of him. "I'll come up with the probable cause. By the way, our Cultural Patrimony Task

Force, code-named Operation Pillage, is meeting tonight at seven in the office over the tire store. Be there. I'm sure we can easily dig up something on Parmentier. You, Dave, are going to be my point man on this."

Dave stifled a groan. This was the first he'd heard about any Operation Pillage, and he doubted it was going to be a fun assignment.

Zoffke picked up the phone. "I'm going to call Eistopf in Washington to tell him the good news about the search warrant on Rivas and about my idea to raid Parmentier's gallery, too. I'll put the call on speakerphone so you can listen in."

Dave crossed one knee over the other again and resettled his bony bottom in the chair.

A secretary in Washington answered Zoffke's call, and soon his boss, Rupert Eistopf came on the line. Zoffke outlined his plan.

"Bravo, Ray," Eistopf said. "I like your idea of raiding that Albuquerque gallery at the same time you do Santa Fe. Why is that woman's name familiar?"

"She complained to the commissioner and Congressman Ovni about customs drilling her imported art. Your office sent me a fax about it this morning."

"Ah, yes, the pushy bitch who demanded the agency pay for damages to her shipment. Get her. She's caused us a lot of trouble. I hate dealing with congressional inquiries."

"I'm working on getting the search warrant now, sir."

"Good work. Your timing couldn't be better. As a matter of fact, on March 15 San Francisco is going to stage a major raid on a textile dealer who stole some ceremonial cloths from a village in highland Bolivia. The Bolivian president's cousin and some of the villagers have just arrived in California to help us publicize this thing. They're at Disneyland now, sightseeing, but on the weekend, they'll join the team that's set to nail the textile dealer at the Ethnographic Art show in Marin. A second team will toss his house while his kids are home alone. If you can be ready in the next few days with your raids on Rivas and Parmentier, that will mean a one-two-three punch for us and an improved chance of getting some national media attention. We need to publicize the Cultural Patrimony Initiative. Nat Pat is one of the agency's top priorities for this fiscal year."

"I'm trying to do my part, sir," Zoffke replied. "I'm sure we can get something on Parmentier."

Zoffke hung up the phone just as a knock came at his office door. "Come in," he called out gruffly. A frizzy-haired young man wearing tight-fitting jeans and a black leather jacket over a T-shirt sauntered in.

"Ah, Mr. Hardin," Zoffke said. "Operation Pillage's very own electronics wizard. How is the world treating you today?"

The young man shrugged noncommittally. He barely acknowledged Dave's presence as he tipped his head to one side and eyed Zoffke obliquely. "I could be better," he said in a soft voice.

Zoffke smiled—a little nervously, Dave thought.

"I have something I'd like you to do for me. Maybe we could meet later to work out the details, maybe after the task force meeting."

The young man grinned. "Sure, Ray. Anytime." He left the room, closing the door carefully behind him.

Zoffke turned to Dave. "Sure glad you stopped by. I hope you don't mind our putting off whatever it was you wanted to talk to me about. As you can see, I'm up to my ass in alligators with all the preparations for these raids. In the meantime, I'm looking to you for leadership in procuring evidence for a search warrant on Parmentier. You're one of Operation Pillage's most important assets, I hope you know. I need someone with your experience and reliability to get this show on the road. See you at the meeting tonight, OK?"

Dave knew he was being dismissed. "Sure, Ray," he said, containing his anger. He got up from the chair, restrained himself from the impulse to hit Zoffke over the head with it, and walked out.

Four

One morning shortly after the Peru shipment arrived, Beverly was in her office at the rear of the store, organizing end-of-the-month paperwork for her bookkeeper, when she heard Lucille greet a couple of men in the clothing section.

"I'm looking for a Mother's Day present," one said in a heavy Spanish accent. "What do you have from El Salvador?"

Alarm bells went off. Since Beverly's return from Mexico, a number of strange visitors had come into her store, asking odd questions, especially about pre-Columbian artifacts. This sounded like more of the same. Mother's Day was months away.

She put down her paperwork, strode into the clothing room, and greeted the men cordially. "Can I help you?"

"They're looking for a Mother's Day present, Beverly," Lucille said in her soft, breathy voice, nervously nibbling at a couple of her green and purple fingernails inserted into a corner of her orange-lipsticked mouth. "Something from El Salvador, maybe. Do we have anything from there?"

"What did you gentlemen have in mind?" she asked.

The taller man glanced at the Latino "Well, maybe a shawl."

Beverly watched him nervously rock back and forth on the heels of his spit-polished Florsheims, his hands shoved into the pockets of his dirt-brown suit. His cloudy khaki-colored eyes reminded her of a neglected swimming pool. "Cops," a tiny billboard in her head flashed, and she went on alert. Unless she was being paranoid, these men were fishing for something, and it wasn't a Mother's Day present. "Why El Salvador?" she asked Brown Suit. "I didn't know they made any special shawls there."

"Well, uh, I thought maybe my mother would like something from there because, uh, I was down there last month," he replied.

"Oh, really? Why didn't you buy her one then?"

"Well, you see, he was very busy in my country," the Latino interjected. "And there was no time for to buy the shawl for his mother. And now he feel a little bad for his mother. So now he come to buy the shawl from you."

The man, pleased with himself, smiled broadly at Lucille and Beverly, then reached into the rack to feel the texture of an alpaca shawl with his perfectly manicured fingers. Beverly noted his wide, muscular shoulders that tapered like an inverted pyramid to tiny feet, which were encased in see-through black nylon socks and highly polished loafers.

The Latino turned to Lucille "So what is the fiber content of this shawl?"

"Fiber content?" she giggled. "You're not going to eat it, are you? I don't think it would be good for you—or his mother."

The Latino looked puzzled. Brown Suit was trying hard not to crack a smile, and so was Beverly. Fiber content? She thought. These aren't garden-variety cops. They're from customs. "It's supposed to be alpaca," she said. "But I think it's mostly llama with some acrylic thrown in for stability. Maybe you gentlemen could tell me?"

Brown Suit stepped up to the rack and rubbed a corner of the shawl between his fingers. "Yeah, maybe some acrylic," he said. Then he searched the shawl until he found a label. "Bolivia, huh. So you import a lot from Bolivia?"

"Just folk art, no clothing. I bought these things from another importer."

"Say," he said to the Latino, "maybe I could get her a necklace or something. What do you think, José?"

"Certainly," José replied, again flashing a white-toothed grin at Lucille, his eyes resting on the front of her plaid dress with its tiny red bows and rows of white lace. "Perhaps the young lady could show us jewelry."

He gripped Lucille's elbow and steered her toward the front of the store. She silently called to Beverly for rescue, but her attention was focused on Brown Suit, who was still systematically going through other garments in the clothing rack, inspecting labels.

He stopped when he noticed her watching him. "So you have things from lots of places, don't you," he said. "Do a lot of importing from Bolivia?"

"You already asked me that. What's the big deal about Bolivia?"

Brown Suit flashed a phony, open-mouthed smile, revealing mismatched teeth yellow with nicotine. He ignored her question and strode to the front of the store, where Lucille stood chewing on a mouthful of fingernails, pinned like a butterfly between José and the wood-and-glass floor case that displayed several shelves of jewelry.

Beverly followed Brown Suit, her hands tightened into fists in an attempt to keep them from trembling.

"So maybe you have something Mayan," José said to Lucille. "His wife like Mayan things."

"I thought you were looking for something for his mother," she said, deftly sliding around the floor case to put it between José and herself.

"Oh, we are looking for something for the both of them. Is not the true, Peter?"

"Uh, yeah, right, José. Of course." He approached the jewelry case. "And they both like Mayan things. What do you have?"

"Mayan?" Lucille asked. "You mean, like the Indians?"

"Yes, the Indians," José said. "You know, nice old stuff. Maybe a jade pendant. Something really old, really special. For the Mother's Day, you know."

"Where did you say you were from?" Beverly asked José in a soft, friendly voice she hoped was tremolo free.

"I am from El Salvador," he said with pride. "And my partner here . . . uh, my friend, I mean, he from Chicago. Right, Peter?"

"Yeah," Brown Suit grunted as he systematically inspected the display of earrings, pins, and crosses.

"Oh, really?" Beverly said. "What kind of work do you do?"

The men looked at each other. "I'm a child psychologist," Brown Suit said. "And, uh, so's my partner. But he's just here for a little while. For training."

"Yes, for training," José said brightly. "Then I go back to my country. I have a clinic for treatment of the childrens which have psychological problems. With the war in my country, you know, is many childrens with the psychological problems."

"Oh," Lucille sighed heavily. "That's so sad."

"Yes, is the true," José said. "But let us not talk of sad things, *mi amor.*" He placed his soft, hairless hand over her hand, which clasped the jewelry case keys. "Show us some pretty jades."

Lucille slid her hand out from under his. "We don't have much old jewelry. And I don't think we have any—what was it you wanted?—Aztec stuff? But we have lots of pretty things. Here, maybe you'd like this." She opened the case and handed him a silver pin with a large smooth green cabochon in its center.

He quickly examined the pin. "Oh, perfect! Yes, is very pretty. Is the color of your eyes, no, *amorcita?* Such a lovely jade!" José flashed his partner a wide grin.

"Hey, that looks good," Brown Suit said brightly, looking over the Latino's shoulder at the pin. "We'll take that. Right, José?"

"Well, uh, sure. We take that. And the alpaca shawl too. We take the both."

"We do?"

"Sure, *compadre.* Don't you remember? We need something for you mother and for you wife. So we take the both, OK? Give to the lady you credit card."

"Sure, sure," Brown Suit said. Reaching into his back pocket for his wallet, he pulled out a green plastic card and handed it to Beverly.

She looked at the name on the card, Peter P. Geiss, and handed it back. "I'm sorry. We don't take American Express. Visa or Master Card is fine. Or a local check." She was doing her best to act normally, but worried the men would notice she was shaking and her voice was quivery.

"You don't take American Express?" Brown Suit said. Then he turned to his partner. "I don't have enough cash," he said quietly.

"So give the lady you Visa card," José said.

"Really?"

"Yeah, really. It don't make a difference."

Brown Suit shrugged, then handed Lucille a Visa card.

While Beverly wrapped the shawl and put the pin in a jewelry box, Lucille processed the credit card. When the machine kicked out the receipt, she handed it to Brown Suit and watched as he signed the tiny paper chit with a large flourish.

José leaned across the desk until his face was just inches from Lucille's. "What you are doing for dinner tonight, my love?" he crooned in a velvety voice. "I could take you out for some drinks, a big yoosie esteak, maybe some dancing. I could tell you all about the childrens in my clinic and my country. Is not all war and poor, you know. For example, we have very, very beautiful bichess."

Brown Suit corrected him. "Beeeeches, José. 'Bitches' are something else." He smiled at Beverly.

José repeated his offer to Lucille. "A free esteak, *mi amor!* What time I pick you up? Where you live?"

She didn't look up from wrapping the purchases. "I'm sorry," she said tersely, "I don't eat animals."

Brown Suit guffawed. "She don't eat animals! Hear that, lover boy? She don't eat animals!"

A flush of color rose up José's thick neck into his face as he glared at his partner.

"She's a vegetarian," Beverly explained.

"That means she only eats fruit and nuts, José. She gonna eat you only if you're a fruit or a nut." The tall man roared at his own joke.

José grabbed the bag from the counter and brusquely left the store. His partner, still chuckling to himself, followed.

Lucille called out cheerfully to the retreating figures. "Actually I have a kinematics test tomorrow—but thanks anyway."

The two men walked quickly down the sidewalk and headed toward the corner.

Once they were out of sight, Beverly growled. "Bastards! You don't have to be nice to them, Lucille. They're cops. Here, give me the Visa slip. What was his last name?"

"It's Luger. Paul P. Luger. Hey, I thought his name was Peter."

"His American Express card said Peter P. Geiss. You'd think these guys would be a little better at this. Let's check something out. Give me the phone book."

Beverly thumbed through the white pages. No Peter Geiss in Albuquerque, but there was a P. P. Luger on Montgomery Boulevard. Then she flipped to the business pages and called a friend who taught child psychology at the university. Neither of the gringo's names rang a bell with him, nor did he know anything about a local training program for Central American or any other foreign clinicians. A call to the New Mexico Association of Child Psychologists in Santa Fe produced the same answers.

"So now you're going to call and see if they're cops?" Lucille asked.

"No. That's just my guess. What's going on here? At least they bought something."

"Yeah, $243.57. They didn't even ask how much the pin was," Lucille said.

"What a bright pair of guys. Don't even know the difference between jade and turquoise."

"I didn't know that was turquoise," Lucille said. "It wasn't blue."

"It's old turquoise, from Cerrillos. Some of the turquoise from that mine was green to begin with, and most turquoise turns green with age and use. Jade, my ass. And gee, Lucille, you missed your chance for a hot date and a free steak."

"That guy gave me the willies. I wouldn't have gone out with him even if it was for fruit and nuts. Why did the other one think eating fruit and nuts was so funny?"

"Oh, never mind. Listen, if you ever get any other people like that in here asking dumb questions and acting weird, pay attention to what they look like, how tall, color of eyes, hair, what they're wearing and write something in the log book about it after they leave. Oh, and if you can get a license number and make of their car, write that down, too, OK?"

Something strange was going on, but she didn't know what, and she didn't want to frighten Lucille unduly. This wasn't her problem; it was Beverly's. She looked at the clock on the sales desk. "Hey, it's after five. Let's close up this joint. I'll take care of the daily report in the morning. Need a ride home?"

"No, I have my bike, thanks." Lucille put on a pair of royal-blue spandex biking shorts under her plaid dress and exchanged her flats for running shoes. She swung a lime-green backpack over her shoulders and headed for the back of the store, the bike shorts swishing audibly as she walked.

"Good luck on your test tomorrow," Beverly called out as she took the cash box out of the drawer.

"Thanks. But I don't have a test. And I took kinematics last semester." Lucille called back as she went out of the store, the screen door banging shut behind her.

Beverly had to laugh. Lucille often came across as a ditz, but she was no dummy. She was a dean's list student, in fact, a micro-biology major and a dance minor, taking eighteen hours a semester and working fifteen hours or more a week at La Ñapa.

As she went about closing up the store for the evening, Beverly tried to look on the bright side of things. Whatever the cops had been after, she was a couple hundred dollars richer for their visit.

Five

Beverly left through the back door. Ten minutes later, she parked in the driveway of her nine-hundred-square-foot adobe house and walked across the street to her neighbor's house. Ricky Sandoval, a thin teenager wearing a black shirt and pants and a black rubber Batman hood with peaked ears, sat waiting for her on the porch in his wheelchair.

Ricky was one of the constant companions in Beverly's sometimes solitary life. Since he had come to live with Doña Lupe, his foster mother, Beverly had gotten into the habit of spending time with him after work, chatting with him on the porch. Their conversations were somewhat one-sided. He couldn't really talk, but there was no mistaking the intelligence in his bright brown eyes, and over the several years of their friendship, she and the boy had developed their own esoteric way of communicating with one another. Their porch visits might have been the highlight of Ricky's day. They certainly were a highlight of Beverly's. He was a good listener. And not just because he couldn't speak. If she had an important decision to make, she often discussed it with him first. Before she could explain something to him in terms a kid could understand, she had to think through the issue and organize her thoughts.

She wished she had the money to buy Ricky a talking computer, so he could express himself better. It had to be frustrating for him to have his thoughts, words, and desires locked up inside a body that didn't work. And she'd love to buy him a motorized wheelchair. Then he could be more independent of Doña Lupe and his aide at school. But neither a talking computer nor a motorized wheelchair was a priority for the only parents he had ever known, the state of New Mexico. His mother had abandoned him in a truck stop restroom shortly after his birth.

Doña Lupe took wonderful care of the boy. She showered him with toys and clothes that surely cost her more than the state paid her for his keep. But Beverly worried about Ricky's situation. How much longer could Doña Lupe continue caring for him? He was a lot of dead weight to lift, and she was over sixty. At fourteen, maybe he should be with other kids his own age, maybe in a group home.

As Beverly approached the porch, a bouncy little reddish-black dog hurled itself at her knees, nearly knocking her over. This was part of the daily routine. Beverly grabbed the porch railing to keep her balance. "Help, Batman! Pooh—I mean Robin—is attacking me!"

A garbled laugh came from inside the boy's Batman mask as the dog yipped and barked, bounding up and down like a yo-yo against Beverly's legs. When Pooh was through greeting her, the little dog lept into the wheelchair and settled herself in her master's lap. He stroked her coat with a bony, gnarled hand.

Beverly dragged a lawn chair close to Ricky and sat down. She ruffled the dog's ears and patted Ricky's hand. "I hope your day was better than mine, Batman. Let me give you all the gory details."

"Unnnhhh!" a small voice responded from inside the rubber mask.

Holding his hand, she gave Ricky the lowdown on the men who had visited her store. Inside his mask and Batman persona, he listened intently.

"I'm pretty sure they were cops."

"Unnnh?" the boy asked. "Cccccppps?"

"I know, it doesn't make sense to me either. I'll guess I'll find out soon enough what this is all about. In the meantime, I'd better tell Steve about it. But before I do that, would you like to go for a stroll and see if the chickens left us any eggs today?"

"Yeeeeennnhh!" he said.

Pooh jumped down from the wheelchair, and strutting proudly like a four-legged majorette, she led the way across the street to Beverly's chicken coop.

Six

Although it was nearly six o'clock when Beverly telephoned Steve, she found him at his office. "No rest for the wicked, huh?" she said.

"It's a wicked, wicked world out there," he said, "and we denizens of the law have to work hard to be more wicked than our opponents. I'm preparing a brief. A woman on the police force is going after her boss for sexual harassment. He refused to promote her unless she put out for him."

"I'd love to hear about it. And I need to tell you about my day, too. A real bummer. Could I interest you in dinner?"

"Let me guess. Soy burgers?"

"Actually, I was going to offer you the braised lamb shanks I made yesterday, with nice crusty sourdough bread, an endive salad, and a pleasant little burgundy. But if you're going to be a food snob, how about a *sanduiche de buerre de cacahuètes avec de gelée?*"

"Wow. I'm drooling all over my keyboard. But I'd hate to put you to the trouble of making me a peanut butter and jelly sandwich. Allow me to do you a big favor. Just heat up that leftover lamb. I'll be there in a half-hour."

Beverly's twenty-year relationship with Steve was ever a puzzle to her. He was as familiar to her as her right hand, but she wouldn't say she'd be lost without him. And the "love" part of their relationship? They engaged in a bit of ardent lust now and then and basically got along most of the time. Hmmm, was that love?

Steve soon rang the doorbell. Beverly opened the door, and he pecked her on the cheek on his way in. "I'm ravenous!"

"I'm fine. Thanks for asking," she said, closing the door behind him. "I'm forewarning you that I'm a little edgy tonight. A couple of cops came to the store today, and I think they were from customs."

"Huh. Let's have a glass of wine, and you can tell me all about it. Funniest thing, I had to deal with cops today, too. I deposed several, in fact, deftly nudging them into giving me the testimony I needed to nail the captain who's been hassling my client. I bet the city will want to settle now. Ah, yes, another for my win column. I can already scent the sweet smell of success. Let us celebrate, wench!"

Beverly fetched a bottle of wine.

He inspected the bottle she set on the table. "Don't you have anything better than Mondavi?"

She sighed. "I suppose we could drink that lovely petit Rothschild you brought."

Steve wagged his finger at her. "Tut, tut." He poured two glasses of wine, handed her one, took a sip from his own glass, and smacked his lips. "Ah, yes, October was a good month. So, what's this about INS cops in your store?"

"Customs."

"Hmmm. I told you to be careful about raising the ire of those lads."

"I was careful. I didn't bust down the door to the customs office at the airport and ream out the bastards like I wanted to. And I was careful with the broker, although I did write to their CEO in Dallas, as well as the customs commissioner and Congressman Ovni. But I got nowhere with anybody."

"Exactly my point. What good did it do you to write those letters?"

"Oh, silly me. I should have let customs and my broker bust up my stuff and not said a word. Maybe you think I should give them sledgehammers and invite them to finish the job."

Steve shook his head. "Oh, Bev, really. Is dinner ready? I'm famished."

They ate mostly in silence. As usual, Steve wolfed down his meal like a starving peasant. Beverly picked at her food, dismayed he didn't seem to care about her damaged shipment or the cops' visit to her store. In fact, she regretted inviting him.

Toward the end of the meal, however, he grew more attentive. He leaned over and stroked her cheek with the back of his hand. "That was an absolutely superb repast, Bev. Thank you. I needed a hearty meal. Now tell me about the strange visitors to the store. I know you don't think I care, but I do."

She cleared the table while he built a fire in the kiva fireplace in the living room. They sat next to each other on Beverly's homemade sofa sipping wine. She told him about the day's mysterious visitors and the recent visits from other coplike men.

"They all ask me about pre-Columbian art," she said.

"Are you buying from any suspicious characters, or do you have anything in the store that's iffy?"

"You know the answer to both questions is a resounding no," she said heatedly. "And I've never handled pre-Columbian art. So what's going on?"

"Just stay cool. Sooner or later they'll give it up and leave you alone. You have nothing to worry about. Say, what's for dessert?"

"Well, there's that death by chocolate cake you brought me from the Double Rainbow. Or was it a pair of crème brulées?"

Steve sighed. He put his arms around her, nuzzled her neck, and whispered in her ear. "Perhaps I'll take you out for dinner this weekend. A big splurge. Burger King, maybe. Don't you have anything sweet in the house, Bev, honest?" His breath was warm on her neck, his hands moving upward under her *huipil.*

She wrapped her arms around him and drew him closer.

Steve laid his head on her shoulder. "I'm desperate," he simpered. "My sweet tooth is killing me. Aren't you at all sympathetic?"

"OK, well, as a matter of fact, I do happen to have a couple of truffles around here somewhere, dark chocolate with a mint chocolate filling."

"Oh, my God! My favorite!" He sat up and kissed her noisily. "They're gonna cost you, though.'"

"Oh, really? How much?"

She leered, took his hand, and led him into her bedroom.

Sometime later, Steve rolled over in bed and kissed Beverly's bare shoulder. "Are you awake?"

She pulled a sheet up over her head. "No."

"Bev?" Steve asked in a plaintive voice, pulling down the sheet to stroke her cheek and kiss the nape of her neck.

"Oh, all right," she said. "The truffles are in the refrigerator, second shelf from the top on the right, in a little white box next to the yogurt. There are three of them. You can have two, but if you take the third one, I will saw you into little pieces with a rusty grapefruit spoon."

Steve threw off the sheets and danced naked into the kitchen.

For hours after Steve slipped out of the house to drive home, Beverly lay awake in the bunched bedcovers, listening as dry branches scraped against the window screen. In her back yard the wind rattled through the last leaves hanging on her black walnut tree. Steve's slightly sweaty, earthy smell still enveloped her, the sheets and pillowcases, and her whole body glowed from their lovemaking. But she couldn't sleep. She flipped and flopped about in the rumpled bedclothes, ruminating on her feelings about Steve. Like chewing on old gum, trying to decide whether their two-decade-long relationship was good for either of them was a pointless and unsatisfying exercise, but one she indulged in after nearly every interlude with him. At times she thought she loved him. He was smart and funny, his politics mostly meshed with hers, and they shared a lot of interests—art movies, classical

music, bluegrass, Thai food. He liked her cooking. He was a better roll in the hay than most guys. They made each other laugh.

But she knew she wasn't the glamorous babe he'd like to hang
on his arm to impress himself and his friends. And in truth, a
number of things about him were neither lovely nor admirable.
For one, his relentless self-centeredness annoyed her. For another,
he seemed not to take her seriously. To him, she was an unre-
constructed hippy.

She didn't expect perfection. She was far from perfect herself.
She longed for a partner, an equal partner, a life partner. At times,
it seemed like what she had in Steve was not much more than a
rent-a-guy.

Seven

For more than a week, Beverly and Lucille put off dealing with the Peruvian shipment. It was too demoralizing. Like oversized toy blocks, the three crates, each a cubic meter, filled La Ñapa's storeroom. The rough-sawn mahogany corners snagged their clothing every time they walked past, as if trying to grab their attention.

Lucille and Beverly finally tackled the grimy task. Dressed in T-shirts and jeans, they unpacked the crates between customers. Mounds of crumpled paper and cardboard at their feet, they carefully sorted through the mess of packing materials in the first crate, looking for broken pieces of Dionisio's retablos. Beverly was heartsick at the destruction. Lucille was more upbeat. Sometimes her unrestrained cheerfulness drove Beverly nuts, but she had to admit it was refreshing to be around someone who was unfazed by adversity. Or reality, for that matter.

"We sure have lots of little things to glue back together," Lucille chirped, shaking her bouncy blond curls from side to side. "Gee, this reminds me of kindergarten."

"It's sinister, though," Beverly said. "All these decapitated bodies, legs, arms, and torsos. It looks as if somebody set off a miniature bomb inside this crate. Fortunately, the drilling duo seems to have run out of boyish enthusiasm for the task. Look, they didn't even open the second and third crates. They just bored dozens of holes in them."

Lucille ran her crossing-guard-orange-tipped fingers over the holes in the crates' plywood sides. "It looks like a hallucinating woodpecker attacked these boxes."

"It was more likely a hallucinating peckerwood. Same difference."

For the most part, the merchandise in the second and third crates was intact, with only a few things damaged. The shipment wasn't a complete loss. Beverly thought maybe she could breathe again.

As per the invoice, the second crate contained a small cache of old but not ancient Andean Indian jewelry and artifacts that had escaped the ravages of the broker's drill bit.

"Oooooh, play time!" Lucille squealed when Beverly opened the small carton Delia had labeled *cositas,* little things. The women rummaged through the box of treasures, carefully un- wrapping each trade-bead necklace, earring, tiny silver votive plaque, soapstone amulet, and one-of-a-kind trinket. Like girls on the loose in their grandmother's attic, they draped each other with necklaces and tried on earrings, standing back to see which things they liked best. There were a half-dozen *rosario* necklaces, loops of eighteenth-century multicolored Venetian glass beads in- terspersed with silver *milagros* and coins, each with an antique sil- ver cross at the end.

"These are gorgeous," Beverly said. "But now I've got more than I need."

"I'll take one," Lucille offered.

Freight and landing costs on the shipment had drained the store's bank account to a perilously low level. Beverly decided to wholesale some of the jewelry. Pancha came to mind, and she called her at Galería Galo in Santa Fe. They hadn't spoken since Beverly's return from the trip to Mexico with Magdalena.

"Panchiiiiiiiiita, I'm back!"

"How was Mexico, Bev?"

"Absolutely terrific. Puerto Escondido is gorgeous, the weath- er was perfect, and I had a great time with Magdalena. We ate ice cream and papaya for dinner and tacos for breakfast, we talked until all hours about everything under the sun, we slept late, we vegged out by the pool, and it's all your fault."

"My fault?"

"Yup. You're the one who talked me into going. I hope you get to meet Magdalena sometime. She's dynamite. Except for one day when the *turista* laid her low, she was up until all hours every night playing poker with these three guys who couldn't stop drooling all over her and following us around everywhere. She's twice as old as any of them. It was a riot."

"Were any of them cute?"

"They were OK looking, but none of them made my heart go pitter patter. They were kind of annoying, in fact, continually asking me about the store and the import biz. Mag got along fine with them, though, and cleaned their clocks at poker."

"I was hoping you'd meet some buff, bronzed macho man on this trip."

"So was I."

"Seriously, you need to hustle yourself up a new sweetie. Steve is never going to make an honest woman out of you."

"After twenty years, of course I know he's not. And even if he wanted to marry me, I wouldn't marry him. He has some good qualities, he can be fun. Frankly, Steve's like a can of Campbell's celery soup. Not all that tasty, but he's on the pantry shelf, I know how to open the can, I know what I'm getting. And some days, that's better than nothing."

"Ayyyy, Bev."

"I know. It's a sorry state of affairs. Enough about me. How are you feeling? Are you still having morning sickness?"

"No. I think I'm over that. But now I'm getting fat. Tom calls me his *cochinita.*"

"You are not a pig, Pancha. You're pregnant. You're supposed to put on some weight. Hey, what's the matter with your phone? Did you hear that funny noise?"

"Yeah. I thought it was from your end, call waiting or something."

"No, I hate call-us-interruptus. Maybe it was Lucille trying to make a call. My Peru shipment finally came in. What a nightmare that was."

Beverly heard several clicks and a whirring sound. "Ay this phone. Maybe it's my cord. It looks like spaghetti. Anyway, I have some beautiful trade-bead *rosario* necklaces I think you'd like, some silver-and-glass earrings, and a terrific assortment of the soapstone *chacra* amulets your boss always goes nuts over. Are you interested?"

"Truth is, I'm a little low on inventory now, and our cash situation is pretty healthy. I'd love to see what you have. Can you come up to Santa Fe?"

"Sure. In the morning, say, ten?"

"*Fantástico.* This time of the year, we're not usually busy before noon."

"I can't wait to show you the tan I got in Mexico before it fades completely. I am definitely dark white, or at least I was a month ago."

"Oops, got a customer. Gotta go. See you *mañana,* OK?"

"OK. *¡Hasta la bye-bye!*"

"Ay, Beverly, *tu español. ¡Qué desastre!* 'Bye, *chula.*"

The bells of St. Francis Cathedral were striking nine forty-five when Beverly walked into Sena Plaza, a quadrangle of historic adobe buildings across from the church in downtown Santa Fe. A basket of Peruvian jewelry swung from her forearm. A few minutes early for her appointment, she sat down on the edge of the time-worn stone fountain in the center of the courtyard to savor the balmy late March morning.

For the moment, the garden was hers to enjoy by herself, no tourists in sight. She inhaled a deep breath of the damp, musty aroma of newly turned soil in the flowerbeds beneath spreading cottonwoods. Finches flitted from tree to tree, trilling happy songs. The sun, filtered through the trees' canopy of shiny new leaves, dappled the worn brick walkways with fractured light and warmed her face and hands. Wisteria vines and lilac branches weighted with fat green buds bent in graceful arcs toward the loamy earth. Spears of daffodil and iris shoots poked through the bare soil, point ng toward the cloudless turquoise sky. Tiny purple and yellow crocus fluttered in a light breeze.

The enthusiasm of the emerging plant life and the giddy chirping of the birds energized Beverly. She crossed the plaza, trotted up a brick stoop, and pulled on the handle of Galería Galo's screen door. The door was latched, but she could hear voices inside. Shading her eyes against the bright sunlight and pressing her nose to the screen, she peered in. Pancha, looking pale and frightened, stood in a swirl of huge men in dark jackets. Beverly rapped furiously on the door and pulled at it as her heart banged against her rib cage.

A tall black man in glasses opened the glass-paned door, but didn't unlatch the screen. Beverly recognized the U.S. customs emblem on his navy blue jacket. The contents of her stomach threatened a revolt.

"Ma'am, the store is closed," the man said abruptly.

"It's my friend, Pancha. Is she OK?"

"If you mean Mrs. Archibeque, the manager, yes, she's fine. But I must ask you to leave."

"Leave? I have an appointment with her. What's going on here?"

From inside the store an angry male voice squawked. "Tell her to go away and shut the damn door, Washington."

The man turned to the store's interior. "Sir, my name is Chardon, if you don't mind, and I am telling the lady to leave."

"I'm not going anywhere until you let me talk to Pancha!" Beverly yelled, rapping her knuckles furiously on the screen door. "She's my friend. And she's pregnant!"

"I assure you Mrs. Archibeque is fine. Now, please leave the premises."

"Call a lawyer, Pancha," Beverly shouted as the agent closed the door in her face.

Beverly ran to a nearby restaurant and telephoned Lynne Deutsch, a Santa Fe attorney who was a friend of Galo Rivas, the store's owner. A secretary answered. "Pancha just called. Lynne is on her way. Don't panic."

Beverly's next call was to Tom, Pancha's husband. Her third call was to a reporter friend who worked in the *Albuquerque Sentinel's* Santa Fe office. Then she telephoned a dozen of Pancha's friends and relatives and an Albuquerque television station. Within minutes, the lawyer, Tom Archibeque, a *Sentinel* reporter-and-photographer team, and a number of Pancha's friends arrived at Sena Plaza. The customs official, Chardon, let the attorney into the gallery but refused entry to all others. The crowd gathered in the courtyard in front of Galería Galo, talking angrily.

"This is outrageous!" said Tom. "Who the hell do those bastards think they are, forbidding me to be with my wife?"

Beverly took his arm. "She's OK. They're not going to hurt her."

A Santa Fe based crew from the television station soon appeared. As friends and curiosity seekers stood by, a pert blonde TV reporter Beverly recognized as a La Ñapa customer interviewed a customs agent who had emerged from the gallery when the television crew began filming in the courtyard. A chill ran down Beverly's spine. The agent was the rude guy who had come into La Ñapa the previous month during Helen Benton's visit, asking about pre-Columbian art. Then he had worn sunglasses and a Hawaiian shirt; now he was dressed in a customs uniform. This customs official had been snooping around her store. Would they raid La Ñapa next? Her home?

The agent identified himself to the reporter as Special Agent in

Charge Ray Zoffke. His face flushed, his fingers holding a soggy, unlit cigar against his chest, Zoffke turned toward the camera. "This raid should serve as a warning to importers that the United States Customs Service is serious about Public Law 97-446, the legislation that forbids the smuggling of national patrimony items into the United States from impoverished third world countries."

"What sort of smuggled items did you find in this gallery?" the reporter asked.

"We uncovered important national treasures from Guatemala, about a quarter of a million dollars worth of pre-Columbian," Zoffke replied.

"Pre-Columbian what?" the reporter asked.

"Uh, statues, jewelry, pottery, things like that. If you'll excuse me." He pushed the microphone away from his face and walked back into the gallery.

Next, the news reporter interviewed Lynne Deutsch.

"Customs trashed a beautiful gallery," the attorney said. "Their allegation that this reputable business handles stolen national patrimony items is absurd and unsubstantiated. What happened here today was a major violation of the gallery owner's and manager's civil rights. It was an especially serious assault on the Fourth Amendment, the right of the people to be secure in their persons, homes, and businesses against unreasonable search and seizure."

When the reporter finished with Lynne, she asked Beverly to comment on the raid.

"This is crazy," she said. "What country are we in? Iran? Iraq? China? Russia? Customs claims to have seized nearly a quarter million dollars in illegal pre-Columbian art here. And that quite frankly, is nonsense. Galería Galo handles mostly folk toys, vintage silver jewelry, and religious folk art. Do these guys think Catholic santos are pre-Columbian art?"

. . . . .

That evening, Beverly called Pancha at home. "Are you OK, *chula?*"

"I'm OK. Thanks for calling. And thank you for your support this morning. God, what a nightmare." Pancha's voice echoed, and the phone made strange sounds. "Are you there, Bev?"

"Yes, but I think somebody else is, too."

"Maybe we better not talk now."

"Pancha, it's not as if you're Manuel Noriega and I'm George Herbert Walker Bush and we're discussing how to get you your CIA payments. Hello, Nazi creeps. Are you enjoying our . . ."

A dial tone drilled Beverly's ear. With a burst of anger, she punched Pancha's number again and got a busy signal. For an hour she tried repeatedly to call her back, to no avail. The next morning her call finally went through.

"What happened?" they asked each other, their voices rebounding through the wires as if they were speaking with tin buckets over their heads.

"Was the disconnect on your end?" Beverly asked.

"No. Was it on yours?"

"No. In case we get cut off again, I just want you to know that I'm behind you one thousand percent. Hey, do you hear those clicks? Yo, Nazis, don't you have anything better to . . ."

The line went dead again.

Eight

At customs headquarters in Washington, Ray Zoffke's boss, Rupert Eistopf, stood at his office window looking onto the Ellipse, where a group of Japanese tourists wearing identical bright red caps swarmed around the base of the Washington Monument. From a distance, the tour group appeared to be a colony of red-hatted ants on the move. Eistopf sat down heavily in his chair and using his pen snapped a two-four beat on a piece of paper atop his desk blotter. Then he picked up the phone and called Zoffke.

"Did you receive the newspaper reports and the TV footage on our raid, sir?" Zoffke asked.

"Yes, but it's not what I'd hoped for. Frankly, I'm disappointed in you, Ray. I thought you were going to get a search warrant for Beverly Parmentier's place. We were hoping simultaneous raids in Albuquerque, Santa Fe, and San Francisco would get us national press coverage on the cultural patrimony thing."

"I'm sorry, sir. The AG wouldn't give us the go on Parmentier. Said we didn't have enough probable cause for a search warrant. But we got great publicity on the Galería Galo raid."

"Not exactly. I heard that Parmentier, of all people, showed up during the raid for an appointment with the gallery manager. Your guys should have known about that from your wiretaps. Then she brought in a crowd of protestors and the press, and I'm told customs looked terrible on the evening news. You call that great publicity?"

"But sir, we nabbed significant national treasures from Guate-mala in the raid."

"*El Salvador,* you numbnuts! You were supposed to say you'd nabbed numerous grave-robbed Mayan artifacts from the Cara Sucia region of El Salvador. Moreover, the gallery's lawyer walked all over you in the papers, claiming all you found in the raid were a few worthless necklaces made of stone beads and a couple of reproduction pots that might have looked pre-Columbian to an untrained eye."

Eistopf tapped his pen on the paper that lay in front of him, a cable from the embassy in Guatemala. "And now, because you can't tell the difference between El Salvador and Guatemala, Ray, I've got to deal with the goddamn Guatemalan Ministry of Culture!"

"How so?" Zoffke asked, his voice small.

"The Guats got wind of your seizure of artifacts you identified as Guatemalan national treasures, and now they're pressuring the embassy to return them. I just got a cable on this from our cultural affairs officer in Guatemala City. A group of Guatemalan honchos is ready to fly to Albuquerque to take possession of the artifacts. They expect the embassy to pick up the tab for the trip. And to pay for a side trip to Disneyland while they're in the U.S."

"Disneyland? These Latins expect us to pay their way to Disneyland?"

"Fuck Disneyland, Ray. What are we supposed to tell them about their valuable artifacts?"

Without waiting for Zoffke's answer, the senior customs official slammed the phone down on the receiver and whapped his ballpoint on the cable so hard the pen bent. He tossed it across the room into a wastebasket. Grabbing another pen from the large brass shell casing that served as his pen holder, he composed a cable to the CAO in Guatemala. "Stall them. Tell them the Office of Enforcement in Albuquerque has not yet concluded its inventory of the seized objects, and they haven't positively identified the artifacts' countries of origin."

When he finished writing the cable, Eistopf stood up from his chair, jammed his hands into the pockets of his navy-blue pants, and turned to stare out his window at the Washington Monument. "I've never understood why every Latin American visiting the agency wants a side trip to Disneyland—at agency expense, of course. Disneyland. This whole thing's a fucking Disneyland!" he grumbled aloud.

Two days later, Eistopf took a call from Bert Schwentzle, the usually friendly U.S. attorney in Albuquerque, who was a law school classmate.

"What kind of a shop are you running, Eis?" Schwentzle asked. "Your guy, Zoffke, was in here a couple of weeks ago. He tried to tell me a New Mexican turquoise pin his men had bought in a local import store was museum-quality Mayan jade the owner had smuggled into the country. And he wanted—no, he demanded—search warrants to raid the owner's home and business. It was amusing."

Eistopf managed not to groan. No, he thought to himself. It's not funny. It's a fucking disaster. He did his best to brush Schwentzle off in a casual, good ol' boy sort of way. "Yeah, that Zoffke, he's so far out in front of things and moving so fast, he's gonna run himself over one of these days," he chuckled. "I'll get back to you when we've got something more substantive. Don't hold this against me. The cultural patrimony thing is big, and some of our guys aren't quite yet up to speed."

For days, Zoffke's latest faux pas weighed heavily on Eistopf. He often found himself thinking about it. If the cultural patrimony initiative were going to have any chance of succeeding—and it had to succeed; it was his baby—a few things would have to change. For starters, his goddamn agents didn't know jack shit. They couldn't tell the difference between a bunch of rocks and valuable pre-Colombian artifacts worthy of the national patrimony designation.

The way Eistopf saw things, the agency couldn't afford to look like ignorant assholes. They were already getting too much negative ink in the papers. There was talk on the Hill about hearings.

Commissioner von Geier said he wasn't worried. He claimed the Ways and Means Subcommittee on Trade, charged with customs' oversight, was in his pocket.

But Eistopf thought there was a problem. He'd been with the agency a long time, and like a lot of other old-timers, he didn't like von Geier's way of doing things—nor Zoffke's. He considered them too heavy-handed, too power hungry, too sloppy, and too ready to break the law to enforce it. To his way of thinking, they were borderline thugs, causing a major morale problem in the ranks. And they were pissing off the wrong people—like congressmen and the airline industry. So what could he do about it? *Nada.* But he thought he could do something about the problems in his own shop.

Training, that's the ticket, he decided, hammering his hand down on his desk as if making a point with a rapt audience of underlings. Everybody had to be brought on board about the patrimony issue. And, for chrissakes, the troops had to know how to identify artifacts. Not only did they need to be able to tell the difference between turquoise and jade, they had to be able to recognize even more arcane stuff like Caroma textiles from Bolivia and Salvadoran Cara Sucia pots—items the Cultural Patrimony board had recently listed for protections under the 1983 law.

"That fucking Philistine Zoffke could obviously do with a few lessons on art," Eistopf muttered to himself. The agency was already training new agents at the All Agency Training Academy at Kirtland Air Force Base in Albuquerque. It wouldn't be hard to add a few more components to the program.

Eistopf smiled. A beefed-up training program at AATA would also give him more opportunities to interact with Lita Liebling, the agency's liaison officer with the contractor running the program, Schlacthof International. An attractive woman. A very attractive woman. Maybe he'd call Lita back to Washington for consultations.

Eistopf picked up the phone and called ATTA.

Níne

One fine spring morning shortly after Dave Carney's failed meeting with Zoffke about his promotion, and Zoffke's failed effort to obtain a warrant on Beverly Parmentier, Dave found himself kneeling on a little square of Astroturf in front of La Ñapa, yanking weeds out of the flower bed. Customs undercover agent extraordinaire, twenty-two-year-veteran of special ops and derring-do in the war on drugs, Dave was now a weed puller in the war on importers. *"¡Coño!"* He grumbled.

When Zoffke assigned him to get a job as a gardener at Parmentier's store so he could get the goods on her and engineer the raid his boss hungered for, Dave had been offended. Jesus! Snooping on a two-bit importer like Parmentier was way beneath his talents and experience. A waste of valuable manpower.

He'd considered telling Zoffke to shove it, but then thought better of the idea. Buck up, Dave, he told himself. And make the best of the situation. Maybe you'll have to do a little ass kissing with Zoffke before he'll sign off on your promo. Look on the bright side of things, dude. The job's not going to get you killed, and it's not forever. If Parmentier's involved in pre-Columbian smuggling or other illegalities, you'll figure that out quickly and be on to a more challenging assignment. You've had worse jobs. You grew up on a pig farm in Iowa, for chrissakes. You've had waaaay worse jobs.

The day was balmy and beautiful, and the weed pulling mindless enough to let Dave's thoughts wander.

For this undercover job as a gardener, Zoffke insisted Dave ride a bike.

"What? A bike?" Dave said.

"Don't question my judgment," Zoffke said tersely. "You'll

only be making $4.25 an hour minimum wage at Parmentier's. You shouldn't be able to afford a vehicle."

Dave opened his mouth to tell Zoffke to fuck himself, then closed it before he said anything stupid. Chill, dude, he told himself. Maybe the bike's not such a bad idea after all. It'll help me get back in shape.

Dave had just returned from a two-year assignment in Peru, where he'd worked a dangerous undercover assignment with the DEA as oilfield trash in Tingo María. Life in the jungle had been damn hard on his forty-eight-year-old body. Too much sitting around smoky bars and acetone fume-laden paste labs. Too many bouts with jungle fevers, dysentery, and worms. Too little decent food, too much cheap booze. The coke-snorting he had sometimes been unable to avoid as part of his undercover role—he wouldn't miss that. Coke made him squirrelly.

After almost two decades in and out of Latin America, Dave was quickly at home in New Mexico. Truth was, he wasn't comfortable in white-bread, English-only America anymore. New Mexico had many of the best aspects of both worlds—Latino and gringo. People often spoke English mixed with Mexican Spanish or the odd, archaic brand of *castellano* that had survived in the northern mountains of the state.

New Mexicans were usually pretty hospitable. Nobody tried to pick his pocket or beg his watch, boots, jeans, or a few *soles* off him every time he turned around like they did in Peru. Guys he'd barely met would buy him a beer in a sports bar, especially if he mentioned he was in law enforcement. Neighbors were neighborly. Stores would take a check from him, sometimes without an ID.

In New Mexico, Dave didn't have to deal with crazed *sinches* or coke dealers or *militares* with long knives and short tempers coming at him in the filthy hovels that passed for bars or whore-houses in South America. He didn't have to carry a gun in New

Mexico. At first, it felt strange to be sleeping without a Glock under his pillow or a mosquito net overhead, but he was soon pretty well adjusted to life in Gringolandia. Some of the horrors of Tingo María were still with him, however, like the weird skin fungus on his forearms that mystified his dermatologist and wouldn't go away. Then there were periodic bouts of diarrhea that seemed to indicate he still had amoebas in his system. Worse yet were the nighttime ghosts that invaded his dreams, oilfield co-workers he'd had to betray as part of his job.

Paulette, his wife, told him he was jumpy. "Honey, what's with you? You wake up yelling. The least little thing sets off your temper. The girls don't know what to make of you."

"They treat me like some kind of exotic houseguest. They don't talk to me, and they giggle behind my back. They weren't like that before."

"Oh, honey," Paulette said. "They're teenagers now. April's thirteen and June's fifteen. They're not used to having a man around. It kind of upsets them when you wander around the house in your shorts."

"It's my house, goddamn it!"

"Honey, it's their house, too. Give them time. It'll take awhile to rebuild family ties."

"Getting a place with a second bathroom would sure help. Damn, you women spend a lot of time in the john."

"I'm sorry, honey. After your two years in the jungle, I thought you'd be happy to have a bathroom at all."

Paulette had a point. "OK, OK. I'm a little short-tempered, and this new assignment isn't quite what I expected. Be patient with me."

"Are you happy to be home with us?"

"Of course I am," he'd said, kissing her. "You're right. It's going to take a little time to get back in the swing of family life."

. . . . .

Indeed, Dave was very happy to be back in the good ol' USA. Every day of the couple of months since his return from Peru, he blessed the wonders of daily life in America, the things most Americans never notice. Like safe water, hot or cold, right out of the tap. And one of man's greatest inventions ever, the hot shower. He'd had enough of river bathing to last several lifetimes. No more worrying about catching some horrible disease or getting zapped by a caiman or a snake. Laundry? Give it to the wife to throw into the washing machine. To get clean clothes in Tingo María, he'd had to tussle with the toothless old washerwoman in his *pensión,* a semiretired whore who'd steal his jockey shorts if he didn't count them out to her. Sometimes it had taken a week to get his clothes back from that *puta.* Invariably, his shirts came back with the buttons smashed because she'd whacked them on a river rock trying to beat out the dirt and sweat.

The sun was warm on his back, and he whistled as he weeded the flower beds along the brick walkway that lead up to the store's entrance. Bars of a *ranchera* tune he'd been trying to shake for days buzzed madly around inside his head like the slow, fat flies that hurled themselves against farmhouse windowpanes in spring. Oompah, oompah, oompah, *mi corazón* this, *mi corazón* that. Over and over again. Strains of the ballad escaped the confines of his head, coming out of his mouth at the damnedest times.

As the jouncy accordion music played on inside his head, he attacked a cluster of elm seedlings, grabbing a fistful and pulling. The tiny leaves slipped easily off their stems into his hand, but the stalks left miniature rope burns on the insides of his fingers. "Damn," he said, shaking his hand in pain.

A melodic female laugh interrupted the *ranchera* band's noisy gig, and he looked up. Beverly Parmentier, his new employer, stood on the porch of her store, coffee cup in hand.

"Those elms seedlings are murder, aren't they?" she said. "You might try watering the ground first. They come up easier then, roots and all. You have to get the whole root, or they'll come right back. I have a weeding tool around here somewhere, if you'd like to use it."

Dave wanted to tell her to come on down and do the weeding herself if she knew so damn much about it. Instead, he flashed her a big-toothed monkey grin and said nothing. Normally, he was put off by tubby women like Beverly. But she was sort of attractive, in a voluptuous way. She had some nice features. A longish, Mediterranean face and thick, dark, copper-colored hair down to her shoulders. *Verde claro* eyes—a clear, light-refracting green. Smooth, rosy skin. Too bad she hid herself in those garish, shapeless Guatemalan *huipiles*. The Operation Pillage task force wag, Joe Scarafaggio, called her the elephant under the circus tent.

"Care for some coffee, Mr. Carney?" Beverly's voice interrupted Dave's reverie.

"Yeah, sure," he said, getting slowly to his feet and brushing dirt off his jeans. As he walked up the porch steps into the store, the phone rang.

"It's for you," Lucille called to Beverly.

"The coffee's in the kitchen. Help yourself," Beverly said to Dave. "But I had better warn you. It's *café,* not coffee."

"Hi, Estéban!" Dave heard her say. Estéban? He dropped to one knee to tie a shoelace that was already tied and listened. A supplier? Another retailer? A contact?

"Thanks for calling back. I'd like to come talk to you. Yeah, they've been coming around every day since the raid on Pancha's. Usually in pairs, like nuns or Mormons. No, they don't look like nuns. They look like Mormons or Marines or maybe Martians. I thought you might have some ideas, and I'd rather talk it over in person, OK?"

Dave stood at a clothing rack, listening to Beverly's conversation as he feigned interest in some embroidered shirts. She switched to Spanish.

"Tengo que ir al banco antes de las tres. ¿Puedo pasar por tu oficina? ¿Tienes tiempo?"

She had to get to the bank before three, and she wanted to see Estéban in his office after that. It had to be somebody nearby. Ah, she was talking to Steve—*Estéban*—Bronstein.

Whistling his *ranchera* tune, Dave strode through louvered doors into the kitchen, where he poured himself a cup of steaming black brew from an Italian espresso pot sitting on a hot plate. The thick aroma of Beverly's *café* tickled his nose hairs to attention.

During his two-year assignment in the Peruvian jungle, he had lived on *café*. He hated American coffee now. It tasted sour and burnt, and it gave him the jitters the way a rich *tinto* never did. He found the sugar bowl and dumped several spoonfuls of sugar into the cup, then poured half the contents down his throat. Ahh, he thought, as he banged the cup down on the counter; that, *señores míos,* is *café*.

Beverly had caused the agency a lot of grief by writing letters to her congressman and the customs commissioner. Her calling in the press and Pancha Archibeque's friends during the raid on Galería Galo further infuriated Zoffke and Washington, and they were determined to pay her back. Maybe she was into some kind of funny business. But Dave didn't think so, and his instincts about people were almost always right. He was certain of one thing. She knew how to treat a coffee bean.

Beverly walked into the kitchen. "So, Mr. Carney, how's it going?"

"Fine," he said, taking a final sip from his cup. "Whew! This is pretty potent stuff. What's in there? Motor oil?"

She laughed. "Naaaaw. That's real coffee. This is how it's supposed to taste."

He sputtered and shook his head. "Your coffee, ma'am, would

put hair on Mrs. Olson's chest. That's not Folger's, is it?" He smiled at his private joke. He knew it was Guatemalan *altura* and that one of Beverly's importer friends had given her a bag of it a few days before. Truth was, he probably could have identified the type of coffee by its taste alone, being something of a connoisseur.

"It's Guatemalan," Beverly said. Then she changed the subject. "Say, what about putting some rose bushes in front of the store? It's so bare out there. We really need some color by that wall."

"Well, uh, Miss Parmentier . . ."

"Beverly."

"I don't know. It might be too sunny for roses out there, facing south and all. And then there's always the problem of people stealing stuff. The rose bushes would be right on the street."

"What faith you have in your fellow citizens," she laughed. "Well, if not roses, then what would you suggest?" She crossed her arms over the bright floral embroidery of her *huipil* and tilted her head, awaiting his response.

Dave was stumped. As a Midwestern farm boy, he knew a lot about alfalfa and corn. And as a twenty-two-year veteran of the U.S. Customs Service, he knew a lot about coca and marijuana. But he knew nothing about flowers, except for opium poppies, of course. "Well, I'm going to have to think about it. We don't want to plant the wrong thing there," he said.

"Right," she said, squinting at him with her jade-green eyes.

"Hey, I have a dentist appointment at three, and it's 2:20 now. I'd better get going. I'll be back Thursday, OK?"

"Sure. Can I give you a lift somewhere? I'm on my way downtown."

"No, no. I've got my bike, and the dentist's office is pretty close. But thanks for the offer."

As Dave worked the combination lock on his bicycle, he knew Beverly was watching him from the doorway. When the lock snapped open, he looped the chain around his neck rather than put it in the small pouch behind his bicycle seat. With her standing not ten feet away, he was worried she'd see the mobile phone inside the pouch. He didn't think minimum-wage gardeners usually carried mobile phones. "I'll have some suggestions for flowers on Thursday," he said cheerfully.

With a wave of his hand, he rode down the driveway. He needed help *muy pronto* about the flowers. And even faster, he needed to let the Operation Pillage office know Beverly was meeting with a lawyer. Her phone conversation with Bronstein would be on the tapes, but he couldn't be certain the ATTA trainees were actively monitoring her phones.

Ten

Looking out the window that faced Lomas Boulevard, Beverly watched her new gardener ride his bike down the driveway and head toward Old Town. He struck her as a little quirky, but she couldn't be too picky. Good, cheap, reliable gardeners were hard to find. The day after she groused to Pancha on the phone about the terrible state of the store's landscaping, Dave rode up on his bike and offered his services. It had been like magic.

She turned away from the window and picked up one of the dolls she'd been tagging, a sweet-faced Bolivian *chola* with a felt bowler, braided hair, and short, wide skirts. On her back, a tiny baby peered up from the edge of her mother's *lliclia,* her carrying cloth. Beverly inspected the doll's fine detailing: the soft alpaca hair, the stitching on the layered skirts, the tiny knit *chullo* on the baby's head. The doll was beautifully made, and it felt good to hold her.

"What do you think of our new gardener?" she asked Lucille as she wound a price tag around the doll's arm.

She looked up. "Dave? He walks funny, like he's *en pointe* all the time, and he's a little goofy. I guess he's OK looking, in a kind of goony, string-bean way. Not bad for an old guy."

"Old? What do you think I am?"

"You're not that old. He has gray hair, and I think his glasses are bifocals."

"So?"

"Well, let me put it this way. He's better looking than Steve, but then, most men are."

"Steve!" Beverly jumped up. She'd forgotten about going to the bank and then to his office. "I've got to run."

As she drove toward the building-block towers of downtown

Albuquerque, she noted that the flower beds in the medians along Lomas Boulevard were filled with snapdragons, pansies, petunias, dianthus. In another month or so, when the late spring heat had zapped them, the city usually planted marigolds and zinnias, which, if well watered, could tolerate Albuquerque's blast-furnace summers. "Maybe I should tell Dave to plant whatever the city is planting," she thought. "For a gardener, he doesn't know much about flowers. Roses love full sun."

At Fifth Street, she maneuvered into the drive-up bank's commercial lane and deposited her bank bag in the drawer. As she listened to the whoosh and clunk of her store's modest earnings being whisked by vacuum tube into the bank's inner sanctum, she noticed an old, battered, white Dodge van with darkened windows easing into the lane alongside her. The driver—late twenties, kinky blond hair in a military haircut, aviator glasses— was writing something down on a clipboard. Nice looking, but not her type.

The young man glanced up from his clipboard and glared. His tight, squarish jaw was slashed by a hard mouth, and there was no humor in his squinty eyes. She turned away.

Another whoosh and clunk announced her bank bag's return.

A few blocks east on Lomas, she drove into Attorneys' Acres, the old neighborhood adjoining downtown Albuquerque where lawyers had gentrified simple prewar bungalows into too-cute office buildings. She parked behind Steve's mint-green clapboard with pink gingerbread trim and locked the Dumpster. Her friends always laughed when they saw her lock her car. "What do you think somebody's going to steal, Beverly, your pizza crusts?" one of them once asked.

When she walked into Steve's office, he was on the phone. He motioned her toward a chair in front of his desk, which was piled high with columns of paper. The floor, too, was littered with heaps of files and notebooks, law books, coffee cups, and candy wrappers. As Beverly waited, she considered the likelihood that had she married the man, they would have had neatnik children for sure—two negatives making a positive. Fortunately, that hadn't happened. When they were volunteers in Colombia, Steve's mother had come to visit. Obviously, she feared her only son was getting too serious about a *shiksa*. Beverly's encounter with Mabel Bronstein in the posh Hotel Tequendama's restaurant in Bogotá had been a nightmare. After nearly two years of a populist diet of hominy-cake *arepas,* boiled potatoes, eggs, and thin soups, Beverly's stomach rejected the rich dinner—filet mignon in a mushroom and wine sauce, potatoes Anna, Chilean cabernet, and chocolate mousse. She had not only thrown up, she had thrown up on her prospective mother-in-law. Steve claimed she had purposely barfed on his mother. "If only!" Beverly had replied. They had a huge fight and didn't speak for several years.

Steve finished his telephone conversation and swiveled his desk chair around to face Beverly. "So what's up?" he asked, tapping the tips of his hairy fingers together.

"I'm a little stressed out. I told you something's going on and it is. Weirdoes come into my store on a daily basis. The phones make funny noises, and if I say anything negative about customs, the call gets cut off. My mail and packages come ripped open. And ever since the raid on Pancha's, I've lived in terror that cops are going to come to my door, wave a piece of paper in my face, march in, and bust up my store or my home. Zoffke, the guy who headed the search-and-destroy mission at Galo's, was in my store a month before the raid, insisting we had pre-Columbian things. When I told him I never handle the stuff, he became belligerent."

"How do you know it was Zoffke?"

"I recognized him when he was interviewed on TV during the raid on Pancha's."

"They're not going to bust you, Beverly."

"They did it to Pancha. They trashed her house, Galo's store, his storage locker, his apartment."

"Yeah, but she signed for boxes Galo sent her from Central America. And maybe there's something there you don't know about."

"How is she supposed to know what's in the boxes? And even if she did know—which she didn't—did that give those cretins any right to wave guns in her face, and terrify her so much she almost lost her baby?"

"No, of course not. But I think you're exaggerating. I don't think they waved guns at her. They may have *had* guns."

"Pancha says they had *big* guns. And they had on these navy-blue nylon jackets and caps with 'U.S. Customs' emblazoned on them, like they're some jaunty baseball team out for a bit of mid-morning male bonding."

"Take it easy. What can I do for you? I have to get over to the courthouse before it closes."

"I'm upset about the creeps coming into the store. They ask me a lot of stupid questions, and they're taking up an awful lot of my time and Lucille's."

"Hey, that's retail for you, stupid people asking stupid questions. Every night, my grandfather came home from his dry goods store and regaled us with stories of human idiocy. How do these people differ from your usual customers?"

"First of all, they're almost all white guys between maybe twenty-two and thirty. Buzz haircuts, military tattoos, shiny shoes, pressed pants, and aviator glasses. They drive muscle cars and park around the block when there are parking spots in front of the store or out back in our parking lot. They want to know how I 'smuggle' my stuff across the border. How I 'steal' old things out of churches. Stuff like that. They're hostile, they're nasty, and they smirk. Like they know the punch line, and I don't even know the joke. There's an edge to these guys that my regular customers—even the rare unpleasant ones—never have. And nearly every day some asshole comes in and asks me about pre-Columbian art."

"Quit talking to them."

"I try. But sometimes it's impossible to tell the real customers from the snoops. Talking to people and educating them about what we handle is how we make our sales. Latin American folk art is not groceries."

"You've been under a lot of pressure. Customs may indeed be snooping around because of your relationship with Galería Galo. But you have nothing to worry about. You weren't part of whatever Galo was up to. But your calling in the press when customs was raiding the gallery and leading the hiss parade in Sena Plaza was highly intemperate of you."

"So? If that was a legitimate raid, why should it be hidden from the public? I was expressing my First Amendment rights, and so were the rest of Pancha's friends."

Steve frowned, shook his head, and patted his fingertips together. "Be patient. Let them come around. They've got nothing on you."

"But you recently told me the U.S. attorney—Pizzle or Schwizzle or whatever his name is—is capable of indicting a ham sandwich."

"It's Schwentzle, and I'm sure I said cheese sandwich. Look, they can come into your store, and they can follow you around town. It's perfectly legal. After a couple of months, they'll give it up and leave you alone. Believe me, the federal government has a lot better things to do than watch you tag Christmas ornaments. Why would they harass you for no reason? Moreover, it's way too expensive for them."

"I never had any problems with customs until the nice old guys at the airport were replaced with the new, gung-ho facists from the Attila the Hun School of Cargo Inspection. I sometimes wonder if customs doesn't have it in for small importers. Women in particular."

"Oh, Bev. Spare me the feminist crap."

"Hey, when Reagan came into office, not only did customs start breaking small importers' goods intentionally, but they'd fine us for breaking rules that had changed after our shipments left the country of origin. And if we complained about the fine, they'd threaten to confiscate the entire shipment. It was almost as if a directive had come out from Washington to hassle small importers right out of business, and the women always get hassled far more than the men. I know you don't think I should have written Congressman Ovni about my Peru shipment, but isn't this a free country?"

"These are not the best of times for people who think the Bill of Rights ought to protect people from their government," Steve said. "Maybe it would help if you started dressing like an American."

"What do my clothes have to do with this?"

"It's not the sixties any more, dear. It's nearly the end of the twentieth century. You're supposed to dress for success."

Beverly felt her mercury rising. "Frankly, dear, this *huipil* is worth more than that Jacques Penné lawyer uniform you're wearing, and next year it will be worth more, not less. You really ought to give that tie to Goodwill. It's disgusting." She leaned across the desk to take a closer look at his tie. "Are those yellow blobs mustard spots?"

Steve grimaced. "Mother gave me this tie. It's a Sulka, in case you're interested. And the yellow patterning is butterflies." He sighed. "Truce, Beverly. Let's not fight."

She flashed Steve the peace sign and smiled, hoping he couldn't see that she was near tears. "Can't I do anything to get this harassment stopped?"

"Well, if you had money and influence, there would be a number of things you could do. But you don't. So I suggest two things. One, develop a sense of humor about this. I know it's not funny, but make jokes about it when you can. And two, you don't have to tell them the truth. When they ask you stupid questions, give them stupid answers. Look, it's going to pass." He reached across the desk, held her hand, and gave it a squeeze. "I have to get over to court, *niña*. You take care of yourself, promise? I'll see you soon."

"Dionisio arrives tomorrow, and the opening at the museum is Friday night. You're coming, aren't you? I have a ticket for you."

"Uh, I can't. A friend has tickets for the symphony."

The news hit Beverly between the eyes like a line drive. "You know how important Dionisio's exhibit is to me. I've been talking about it for more than a year. I assumed you'd attend the opening with me."

"Sorry, Bev. It totally slipped my mind."

Beverly was more hurt than angry. She left his office quickly, before he or his secretary could see her tears. Through her bleary eyes, she found her car and inserted the key into the lock, only to discover the car was already unlocked. She cautiously opened the door and inspected the Dumpster. Everything seemed to be in place, all trash present and accounted for. Even the mass mailing from the Republican National Committee that had come in the morning mail, right? No. The red, white, and blue envelope she'd left unopened on the front passenger seat was no longer there. In a panic, she thrashed like an antic mole through the papers under the front seat and in the back of her car. The envelope was gone.

"Looking for something?" Steve said behind her.

Startled, she banged her head on the door frame.

"And if you were, how would you ever find it?"

She rubbed the top of her head. "It's gone! My letter from the Republican National Committee. It's not here!"

He put a hand on her shoulder and peered into her eyes. "Are you OK? A letter from the *Republicans?*"

She forced a little laugh. "Oh, never mind. I'm practicing having a sense of humor, just like you suggested."

Steve stood by the Dumpster as she fastened her seat belt and started the engine.

"I'm OK. Really. Thanks," she said to him.

The Dumpster bounded through the potholes in the parking lot behind Steve's office like a lame kangaroo, the struts squeaking in protest. The bouncing jarred fat tears from her eyes, and they dropped onto the front of her *huipil*. Although she was distressed, something caught her attention. A battered white van, like the one that had drawn alongside her at the drive-up bank, idled in the alley beside Steve's office. She wiped her eyes and recognized the driver, the guy who'd been at the bank. Eyeing her obliquely, he ripped the wrapper off a candy bar with his teeth and spat the paper out the window. Was it a coincidence that he was at Steve's office? Beverly didn't think so. She briefly considered ramming the Dumpster into the bastard. Instead, however, practicing Steve's advice to use her sense of humor, she honked her horn, and when the van driver looked her way, she flashed him a phony grin and waved energetically. The driver scowled, and sped out of the parking lot, his tires spurting gravel.

Beverly drove back to her store, gritting her teeth, tears running down her cheeks. Steve and the guy who had followed her from the bank had both raised her temper to dangerous levels. She dug her nails into the steering wheel and said a lot of bad words.

Eleven

The following day, Beverly drove to the airport to pick up Dionisio. It was easy to spot him in the stream of passengers coming off the plane from Dallas. A short, stocky Indian in his late thirties, he wore a fuchsia, red, and lime green alpaca poncho and an ear-to-ear smile on his round brown face. He quickly found Beverly in the crowd.

After they picked up his luggage, two boxes sewn into white plastic feed sacks, they drove to the store. Along the way, they chatted about family and friends in Peru while, wide-eyed, Dionisio took in the city.

Beverly felt she had to warn him before they reached La Ñapa. "There was some damage to the shipment," she said.

"Oh," he said. "I'm sure it's nothing too bad."

When he walked into La Ñapa's storeroom and saw his busted retablos in the open crates, however, it was as if he were coming upon his murdered children. His eyes widened in shock, and anger tinted his face a deep red-purple. With shaking hands, he picked up one of the small gaily-painted boxes and ran his fingers over the numerous bores in its wooden sides. After a long pause, he spoke in a soft, lilting Spanish. "I didn't think they did things like this in the United States."

"I didn't either," Beverly said.

Like a blind man reading Braille, Dionisio slowly fingered the box and the broken figures inside it. "In my country, we're not surprised when police do things like this, especially to us Indian people. We don't have the freedom and civil rights you are supposed to have here in the United States. But maybe your police are no better than ours after all. This is an abuse, *un gran abuso.*"

Beverly's voice caught on the lump in her throat. "I'm so, so sorry, Dionisio."

The maestro shook his head. "It's not your fault." He picked up a *retablo* Lucille and Beverly had worked on and examined the figures inside carefully. Then he smiled. "You did a good job of gluing the *figuritas* back together again. Maybe I should hire you."

"We did the best we could, but it takes time to repair them well, and we've only been able to put a few back together in between waiting on customers. We have four days before your exhibit opens. I had planned to take you around to see some of the local sights, but we have work to do."

"Así es. First we fill in these terrible holes and glue the pieces. Then we do a little painting. Do you have the powdered paints I sent?"

"Oh, Dionisio, customs confiscated them. I guess they thought the paints might be *cocaína.*"

"Cocaína? My paints? That's ridiculous!"

For the next few days, Lucille, Dionisio, and Beverly repaired the *retablos.* Beverly bought paints that approximated those the artist used. Though they weren't quite the same, with some magic, he was able to blend them with the original colors. Working all day and late into the nights, they concentrated on repairing the large, multistoried *retablos* Dionisio had specially prepared for the exhibit. By Wednesday afternoon, they had the most important ones back together. Dionisio wasn't satisfied, but Beverly assured him they'd look intact and fabulous to people who hadn't seen them prior to the damage.

To her eye, even the repaired ones were magnificent, the best work he'd ever done. Some depicted traditional Andean highland scenes of festivals, curing ceremonies, and important events in Peruvian history from an indigenous point of view. Others narrated contemporary events, some quite dramatically, like one that showed murderous assaults on highland farmers by both the Peruvian military and Shining Path guerrillas in the early 1980s. Another portrayed the army's massacre of journalists near Dionisio's village. These large, spectacular political retablos were gaining fame for him. He was not only receiving prizes, but also death threats from both extremes of the Peruvian political spectrum.

On Friday evening, the reception for Dionisio at the Popular Art Museum in Santa Fe was well attended and lively. Museum patrons wore bright-colored clothing from south of the border: the women in gaily embroidered blouses or dresses set off with ropes of glass trade beads or Navajo squash blossom necklaces, and many of the men in *guayabera* shirts, silver bracelets, and bolo ties. A crowd clustered around Dionisio, who stood in front of his *retablos,* wearing his poncho and a knit *chullo* cap typical of his highland village. People peppered him with question after question about his work. A number of well-wishers spoke Spanish, but Beverly stood at Dionisio's side, ready to interpret.

Soon, the crowd parted for a portly man in a navy pinstripe suit, who greeted people loudly and cheerfully as he made his way toward Beverly and Dionisio at the head of the reception line. Beverly recognized him—Congressman Bradford Ovni. He grabbed Dionisio's hand and gave it a vigorous shake. *"Benvenidas!"* he said in a hearty Southwestern drawl.

Beverly whispered in Dionisio's ear: *"El señor es nuestro representante en el Congreso en Washington."*

The artist took off his *chullo* and tipped his head graciously to the congressman. *"Me es un gran honor conocerle a usted. Gracias por haber venido."*

Ovni turned toward Beverly with a blank look.

"He says, 'It's a great honor to meet you, and thank you for coming.'"

Ovni's florid face creased into a practiced grin. *"Gracias, gracias,* Mr. Toma. Say, we're all mighty sorry about the mix-up at the airport with your stuff. Looks like you were able to put things back together again, though."

Beverly translated for Dionisio, whose face clouded at the mention of the damage to his work. Then she spoke to the congressman. "Thank you, Congressman Ovni, for your kind letter and for taking personal interest in customs' deliberate damage to Mr. Toma's work."

The congressman turned on his grin machine again and extended a hand toward Beverly. "Congressman Bradford Ovni, and you are . . . ?"

"Beverly Parmentier, sir. I'm the importer whose shipment customs damaged."

The congressman frowned, dropped her hand, spun on his heel, and disappeared into the crowd.

Dionisio and Beverly stood in open-mouthed astonishment at the congressman's rudeness, as did people standing nearby. In Spanish she whispered to Dionisio. "I guess he knows that if he were running in an election against a pit viper, I'd vote for the snake."

Over the weekend, Dionisio gave hands-on workshops at the museum. Beverly made the hour-long drive from Albuquerque to pick him up at his Santa Fe hotel, drove him to the museum, and interpreted for him as he showed schoolchildren how to make *retablos.* Under his patient tutelage, the children learned how to transform a mashed potato, glue, flour, and plaster mixture into lively, action-packed figurines that they then painted and set into decorated wooden boxes. The children's *retablos* delighted him, the museum staff, the kids' teachers and parents, and Beverly. The workshops were a huge success, and there was talk of his giving more of them in the future.

By Monday, when Beverly put Dionisio on a plane for Miami,

where he would visit relatives on his way home to Peru, she was mentally and physically exhausted. She wanted to flop on the couch at home for a week and do nothing but sleep, eat chocolates, and read cookware catalogues. But duty beckoned. She was behind on work at the store and needed to finish repairing the other *retablos* so she could put them out for sale. On her way back from the airport, she bought herself a Lindt bar to get her through the week. It disappeared before she got to La Ñapa.

Twelve

On a hot, sultry morning in mid-May, two months after the raid on Galería Galo, Pancha drove from Santa Fe to downtown Albuquerque for yet another interrogation with the U.S. Customs Service—her fourth. Although she was by then into her sixth month of pregnancy, she felt like she had the worst case of morning sickness ever. But it wasn't morning sickness that made her nauseous; it was nerves. She dreaded dealing with those men. Each interrogation session was worse than the previous one.

She met her attorney, Lynne Deutsch, in the customs office, and Melissa, the secretary, showed them into the usual hot, stuffy meeting room. As always, she seated the women in old wooden chairs with straight backs across a table from the two customs officials, who sat in comfortable looking armchairs. Zoffke, the man in charge, looked steamed up about something, but he always did. His eyes were like two slits in a tomato about to burst its skin. The second agent, Herman Naranjo, had a much kinder face. He always tried to look and act tough, but Pancha could tell he was basically *simpático,* and almost as unhappy as she was about being there.

Zoffke started the session with his long-winded narrative about Pancha's alleged crimes. While Zoffke ranted on, Naranjo squirmed in his chair, and his eyes moved restlessly from Pancha's face to her big belly, then wandered around the bare, windowless room as he clasped and unclasped his hands atop the table in front of him. Lynne sat quietly. Now and then she would jot down something on a legal pad.

For a while, Pancha listened to Zoffke relate his preposterous tales, then she simply had to say something. "Sir," she said as politely as she could. "You've got it all wrong. When Galo visits El Salvador or Guatemala, he mails me folk art—dolls, ornaments, textiles, inexpensive jewelry—things like that. The stone beads in the box mentioned in the search warrant couldn't have been pre-Columbian. They were machine drilled—not pump drilled."

"Quit trying to sidetrack us, Archibeque," Zoffke said. "Your boss is up to his ears in this artifact smuggling business, and you're a key player. You come clean with us, or it will go badly for you. We'll take that baby away from you and send you to the nastiest federal prison in the country for a long, long time."

"Mr. Zoffke," Lynne interjected. "Don't be ridiculous. My client has been totally cooperative with you. There's no need to threaten her."

"Uh, really, Ray," Naranjo said frowning. He turned to Pancha and spoke softly. "Just tell us how Galo gets the artifacts across the border, and we'll do what we can for you with the U.S. attorney." He folded his hands together and smiled at her.

Pancha had seen enough episodes of *Hill Street Blues* to know that Naranjo and Zoffke were doing a good-cop, bad-cop routine. But that didn't make things any less frightening. She couldn't quite look them in the eye and instead, she looked down at her big belly, where her hands lay curled in fists in the lap of her dress so no one could see they were shaking.

"I've already told you what I know," she said. "To the best of my knowledge, Galo Rivas inherited most of his collection of pre-Columbian art from his mother, who died a couple of years ago. The artifacts came from their coffee *finca* in El Salvador. Galo only has a few artifacts here in the states, the cracked pot you found on top of my desk at the gallery and several tripod bowls you told me you found in his apartment in Santa Fe. I think I remember seeing them on the fireplace mantle when he invited my husband and me over at Christmas. We don't have pre-Columbian art in the gallery, except for some reproduction pots."

"Aren't you forgetting about that gold and jade jewelry?" Zoffke said.

"I already told you about that, too. Galo said it was his mother's."

"So how did he get it across the border?" Naranjo asked.

"In his suitcase, I guess. He had it with him one time when he flew up from El Salvador. I've never been out of the country, except for Juárez. Doesn't customs look at people's luggage when they come across the border?"

"Don't be a smart aleck," Zoffke said sharply.

"I . . . I wasn't trying to be smart," Pancha stammered. "I mean, if there was something wrong with his bringing the jewelry into the country, wouldn't customs have told him that in the airport?"

Naranjo's eyes met Zoffke's. Zoffke cleared his throat and chewed on his unlit cigar. "Let's go on to the animal pots."

"Do you mean the Colima effigy figures?"

Zoffke waved his big hands in the air. "Whatever."

"Galo bought those in Santa Fe. I was totally against his buying them. I don't think we ought to be handling things like that in the gallery, and anyway, I'm pretty sure they're fakes. Moreover, I don't like to do business with the people he bought them from. They're not reputable."

"Who's that?" Naranjo asked, leaning across the table.

"The Lechuga brothers, Ronnie and Elías," Pancha answered.

Zoffke looked up with a start and took his unlit cigar out of his mouth. He adjusted his weight in his chair, and narrowed his eyes at Pancha. "So are you having an affair with Rivas? Is that his baby you're carrying?"

Naranjo's head jerked up. "Ray? Aren't we losing the train of thought here? Let's hear from Mrs. Archibeque about these guys she just mentioned."

Zoffke glared at his colleague. "I shouldn't have to remind you who's running this show, should I?" He turned to Pancha. "So what kind of drugs do you and your boss do together?"

Lynne put down her pen and broke in. "Mr. Zoffke, this line of questioning is unfair to my client."

"Are you trying to tell me my business?"

"Of course not. But I fail to see how this sort of question is relevant to the issues at hand, namely, the alleged involvement of my client with alleged pre-Columbian art smuggling."

Pancha exhaled a breath she had been holding during the interchange between Lynne and Zoffke. She was relieved the attorney had intervened. Sometimes she thought Lynne let him badger her.

"Where does Parmentier keep her pre-Columbian?" Zoffke asked Pancha.

"Beverly? I don't think she has any."

"Oh, come on! Why are you covering up for her? Does she have something on you?"

Pancha shook her head in disbelief. "She's my friend. I've known her for more than fifteen years, and I've never known her to be involved in anything even remotely illegal. She is one of the most honest people I know. She panics if her library books are a day overdue."

Naranjo interjected. "Mrs. Archibeque, we know you do a lot of business with Ms. Parmentier, and she travels to Central and South America frequently. It will go easier on you if you tell us about her smuggling activities."

Pancha felt her face redden. "Beverly's not involved in any smuggling. I don't know where you get that idea. She makes one, maybe two buying trips a year. Is that a lot of trips? And as I have said many times before, I've never known her to come back with anything illegal or pre-Columbian."

Pancha could barely breathe. She saw sparks behind her eyes and she thought she was going to pass out. "Sir, could you turn on the air conditioning or open a door? I'm feeling kind of faint," she said, hanging on to the sides of her chair to keep from toppling over.

Lynne put her hand on Pancha's shoulder. "Yes, it's very stuffy in here, gentlemen. I'll bet it's over ninety degrees. Please open the door or turn on the air conditioning. I'm concerned about my client's health and that of the baby she's carrying."

Naranjo stood up and began to walk toward a switch on the wall, but Zoffke flung out a hand and stopped him. "We'll be through here in a minute, as soon as Mrs. Archibeque comes clean about her boss and Parmentier. If she thinks it's hot in here, wait until she gets to the women's federal prison in Arizona. You'd better start cooperating. I'm getting pretty fed up with your dodges!"

Pancha looked Zoffke straight in the eye. "I'm telling you the truth."

When the interrogation session was over, Pancha held back her tears of anger and frustration until Lynne and she had parted company and she was in her car, heading for Santa Fe. Once she was out of sight of the Federal Office Building, the tears spilled down her cheeks like runoff from a summer cloudburst. She could barely see the road. It was as if she were driving in a torrential downpour without windshield wipers. She pulled a wad of Kleenex out of her purse and dabbed at her nose and eyes as she drove one-handed toward the freeway.

The two hours of interrogation had exhausted her physically and emotionally. The heat and the lack of air. The tension, the innuendoes, the accusations, the never-ending questions. And more than anything, going over territory they had covered in previous sessions again and again.

Pancha thought back to a conversation she'd had with her husband the night following the raid. "I don't get it, Tom. Why did customs raid us? Maybe I'm wrong, but I don't think Galo is the big-time artifact smuggler customs seems to think he is. God knows, I've made mistakes about people, but I don't think I'm wrong about him."

"Unless there's something major about him we don't know, it doesn't make sense," Tom said. "Galo's a dilettante, not a crook. A nice guy, not rich, but with enough family money so that he doesn't have to hold down a regular job like the rest of us."

"Beverly says he probably owns the Santa Fe gallery so he can leave quickly for the states on his business visa if civil war breaks out again in El Salvador."

Beverly. Why was customs continually quizzing her about Beverly? She was the last importer Pancha knew who'd be involved in smuggling pre-Columbian art or drugs. But Zoffke and Naranjo both kept hammering her about her friend. They wanted to know if Galo had sent her packages from Central America. Did he bring her stuff when he came up from Central America? Where was her secret storage locker? Who did she sell drugs to? Where had she hidden her pre-Columbian art collection? On and on it went, Zoffke glaring at Pancha, visually undressing her, treating her like she was some kind of cheap whore who wasn't making him happy fast enough, as he hurled questions and accusations at her in his tight, pipsqueaky voice.

Naranjo countered his boss's aggressive, angry tone with a soft-spoken reasonableness, making like he believed her, pleading with her to help them and herself by simply explaining how Beverly and Galo smuggled artifacts across the border. Although at times she sensed Naranjo was upset by his boss's abusive treatment of her, he never challenged Zoffke's authority or his management of the interrogation. Instead, like a wary street dog, he kept out of his boss's way.

Why didn't they ask me questions about the Lechugas rather than Beverly? Pancha wondered. They're sleazeballs. Everyone in

New Mexico knows they're up to their eyeballs in drugs, and probably pre-Columbian stuff as well.

As she made her way through the stoplights on Lomas heading toward Interstate 25 and Santa Fe, she briefly considered turning around and heading to Beverly's store, which was only a couple of minutes away. She wanted to tell her friend that customs had been asking about her, but they'd made her swear not to divulge the contents of the interviews to anyone. Moreover, Lynne told her not to see Beverly and to go straight back to Santa Fe—no stops.

"Customs might be keeping tabs on you," the lawyer warned.

Pancha drove onto the interstate and wove her way through the jumble of traffic heading north. As she shifted in her car seat, seeking a more comfortable position, her taut belly bumped against the steering wheel. The baby squirmed, as if in protest. She patted her swollen stomach and smiled. *¡Paciencia, m'ijo!* Only three more months.

Later, as her Volvo glided into the deep draw near Santo Domingo Pueblo, a white van ahead of her slowed down suddenly. As she drove alongside to pass him, the driver, a blond man with short frizzy hair, turned and sneered at her. With his teeth, he tore the wrapping paper off a candy bar in his fist, spat the wrapper out the window, and shoved the candy into his mouth in a way Pancha found obscene. Chills ran down her spine. She punched the accelerator of her geriatric Volvo, and the car responded with a steady—if sluggish—increase in power.

A few minutes later, when she began the steep ascent to the Santa Fe plain at La Bajada, she glanced into her rearview mirror and was relieved to see the van had fallen behind.

By the time the Volvo had chugged its way to the top of the mesa, she'd forgotten about the man in the white van. She was now surrounded by a grand panorama, a dramatic display of mountains, tipped planes, shafts of light, and horizons that never bored her, as many times as she'd driven between Santa Fe and Albuquerque. To the northwest, a thin, gray gauze of rain veiled a gash at the foot of the Jémez Mountains, the Rio Grande gorge. And to the southeast, a faint rainbow had formed across a small cloud that was releasing a fine mist over the Ortiz range. The rainbow was right over the old Pegasus Company's gold mine. Pancha smiled. Wouldn't it be nice if there were something to the old tale of a pot of gold at the end of a rainbow? Tom and she could certainly use the *feria*. With the closing of Galería Galo and a cutback in Tom's hours at the furniture shop, their income had taken a nosedive, just as they were expecting their first child. She never let her husband know how much she worried about money. As much as she hated her new job at a downtown schlock emporium and her *pinche* boss, she'd resolved to work as long as she could before the baby's birth. Tom never said much about money, but she knew he was worried, too. He'd begun to work weekends in Albuquerque for a friend who had a construction company.

Suddenly, she heard a loud roar, and the white van appeared alongside her. She gripped the steering wheel tightly and stared straight ahead. For what seemed like dozens of minutes, the van paced her car. Finally, it sped forward and disappeared around the bend in the road where the descent into Santa Fe began.

Pancha let out the long breath she hadn't realized she'd been holding. As if in protest, the baby kicked, sending a sharp pain through her lower ribs.

Nearing the St. Francis Drive exit, she saw that the highway surface was wet from a recent shower. Over the green gumdrop mountains east of the city, dark, fast-moving clouds were dropping curtains of rain on the forests. She rolled down her window to let the car fill with the earthy scent of ozone and the clean, cool fragrance of wet sage and *piñón*, the smells that meant Santa Fe and home to her.

Thirteen

Rays of bright sunshine, filtered through the leaves on the quince bush outside Beverly's bedroom window, played across her eyelids until she opened them. As she struggled to dispel the fog of sleepiness and focus her eyes, the telephone on her bedside table rang. It was Aunt Magdalena, calling from New York.

"I hope I'm not calling too early. I wanted to wish you a happy birthday."

"Oh, that's right. It's my birthday. Thank you for remembering. How are you? Gosh, it's been months."

"Oh, I'm a little under the weather, but maybe it's all this darn rain we've been having. I think the island of Manhattan is about to float into the ocean. Makes me long for Puerto Escondido and all that brilliant sunshine."

Magdalena and Beverly reminisced about their trip and laughed about her poker earnings.

"As a matter of fact, one of my poker pals showed up here last week," Magdalena said. "Your friend Al, the tall Texan with the bad skin. He invited me out for a drink."

"Did he want to play some more poker? Try to win back his losses?"

"No. He beat around the bush a lot, but basically, I think he wanted to talk about you and your importing."

Beverly sat up in bed and took a deep breath.

"The whole thing was pretty strange. He was cagey, but he implied you were mixed up in something having to do with pre-Columbian art. I said not on your life. Maybe I shouldn't be telling you this. I didn't call to ruin your day, especially not your birthday."

"It's OK. I need to know what's going on. I promise you I'm not mixed up in any funny business."

"It was so strange to hear from that guy. You know, I never gave any of them my address or my unlisted phone number. How did he find me?"

"I'm so sorry they've bothered you, too."

"What's up? Has somebody been hassling my favorite niece?"

"Oh, Mag, it has been bizarre beyond belief since you and I parted company in Puerto Escondido," Beverly said.

"Tell me what's been going on, Bev."

Beverly related her story, starting with clearing customs in Dallas.

"Whew, that's astonishing. I'm so sorry," Magdalena said. "Nobody should be subjected to that sort of treatment by a government agency, especially you, of all people. Have you consulted a good lawyer?"

"Well, you know, Steve's an attorney, and he's been helping me."

"Get a smart, experienced civil rights lawyer."

"I don't have the money, and I make too much to qualify for a Legal Services lawyer. Steve's fine. He says I have nothing to worry about. Customs is simply on some kind of tear, and it'll blow over soon enough."

"Maybe so, but I still think you need an expert advising you. Let me pay for one."

"That's really sweet of you, but I can't let you do that. It's fine, really."

They argued for several more minutes.

"You're too proud!" Magdalena protested. "Even from the time you were a little thing, you were feisty. You'd never let anybody help you do anything. I remember how you were always toddling around with your shoestrings tied in knots because you wouldn't let anyone show you how to tie your shoes properly."

"I still don't know how to tie my shoes. Everybody laughs when they see me knotting my shoelaces."

"I wish you'd let me pay for a top notch attorney, but I respect your wishes. Just promise me you'll be careful. Feds are nobody to mess around with. They're omnipotent, and there's little or no oversight. But forget all that. Have a wonderful birthday, sweetie."

"Thank you, Mag. I wish you were here, and we could go have a margarita together."

After Beverly hung up, she stared out the window at the bright green quince leaves moving gently in the early morning breeze. The Texan's visit to her aunt was disturbing news. Did that mean the poker players in Puerto Escondido had been customs agents? Goddamn it! Three guys on an all-expenses-paid jaunt to a posh Mexican resort, deep sea fishing excursion and all, courtesy of a lot of hard-working, struggling taxpayers like Beverly. The only consoling thought was that Magdalena had cleaned their clocks at poker, and with any kind of luck, the money had been their own, not the taxpayers'.

When Beverly opened the door to the store, a cascade of bright-colored balloons and a chorus of "Happy Birthday" sung off-key by a crowd of well-wishers greeted her.

"OK, I'm surprised. I didn't think anyone knew it was my birthday, except, of course, for the Birthday Bobs, three friends named Bob whose birthday is also May 18. We've been celebrating together for eons."

Just then, Pancha walked in with her friend Leona, who worked around the corner from La Ñapa at a counseling center. Beverly squealed and threw her arms around her friend. "I'm so happy to see you! It's been too long. You looked like you swallowed a basketball."

Pancha grinned and rubbed her belly. "Three more months to go."

Beverly and Pancha had talked on the telephone, but they

hadn't seen each other since the day of the raid, a distressing sub-ject neither was going to bring up on this happy occasion.

Even Steve was part of the crowd. He kissed Beverly on the cheek. "Happy Birthday, *niña*. Can't stay long. Got a tennis date with a guy in the federal prosecutor's office. I'll take you out to dinner sometime soon."

"Sure, Steve," she said. She couldn't help notice he didn't have a birthday present for her.

A couple of customers came into the store, and Beverly invit-ed them to join the festivities. She opened silly presents and blew out candles on one of the chocolate zucchini muffins Lucille had baked for the occasion.

As the party was winding down, one of the Birthday Bobs— Bob Newton, a city planner in the mayor's office—stuck his head in the door, and they wished each other a happy birthday. "I can't stay," he said. "I'm late for a meeting, but I wanted to know if we're on for dinner tonight."

"Of course. Same time, same station. Can you and Karen pick me up? If we go in your car, you can be the designated driver, since you don't drink, and I can be the designated drunk, since I do."

Bob laughed. "Sure. See you at seven."

"You'll be sorry," Steve warned him. "An inebriated Beverly Parmentier is an experience that ought to be missed."

When Beverly got into Bob and Karen Newton's car that night, she noticed a white Chevrolet Corsica with government plates parked catty-corner from her house. Asleep behind the wheel was the young man with frizzy blond hair she'd seen in the van at Steve's office. She smiled to herself. Maybe the birthday party with the Bobs would be a private occasion.

They drove to Delgado's, the South Valley steak and enchilada restaurant where the Bobs and Beverly had celebrated their birthday for more than a dozen years. The other Bobs—Bob Aguirre, a social worker, and Bob Stanley, a travel agent—and their wives, Sylvia and Conchita, were seated in the restaurant's brightly lit dining room, sipping drinks, when the Newtons and Beverly walked in.

Beverly was well into her second margarita and halfway through her *enchiladas suizas* dinner when she glanced into a far corner of the dining room and saw a couple of familiar faces. She recognized Galo's sleazy Santa Fe friend, Ronnie Lechuga, who looked drunk, as did the man he had his arm around, Ray Zoffke. Whoa! She thought. This is interesting. The customs official was wearing the same ugly brown and yellow Hawaiian shirt and sunglasses he'd worn the day he'd come into her store. Zoffke, Lechuga, and two Mexican-looking men sat at a table littered with plates of steak, glasses, and a couple of bottles of José Cuervo. Although the Mexicans were laughing, joking, and slapping Zoffke on the back, they looked a lot more sober than Lechuga and Zoffke.

Beverly put down her forkful of beans and reached into her purse for her camera. "Hey, everybody," she said, pushing her chair back and wobbling to her feet. "Photo op time!"

The Bobs and their wives mugged for the camera, and Beverly clicked off a couple of shots. Then she moved around the table and took a few more shots, aiming over her friends' heads at Zoffke and his table.

When the third flash went off in Zoffke's direction, she watched through her lens as he looked into the camera and froze. He hastily hid his face with his hand and said something to Ronnie Lechuga, who sat up, put his hand over his face, too, and spoke to the Mexicans. One, a scarred, mean-looking man with a droopy Pancho Villa mustache, frowned, ripped a couple of bills out of his wallet, and tossed them onto the table. Then they got up and left through a rear door.

As Beverly sat back down, Bob Aguirre whispered in her ear. "You shouldn't have taken pictures of those guys."

"Oops. Caught in the act. Who are they?"

"Nobody you'd want to know or ever mess with. Did you notice the Mexicans' belts when they left?"

"No. I did notice their cowboy boots, though. Silver-tipped white ostrich with lifts. Cute."

"They were both wearing belts with rattlesnakes tooled on them."

"I guess I'm supposed to know what that means, but I don't."

"Well, they're important businessmen here in the valley, associated with important businessmen in Ciudad Juárez, if you get my drift. A lot of my more screwed-up welfare clients have done business with them, as well as some of Albuquerque's well-heeled party types, I'm sure. I'd be real careful with that film if I were you. Guys like them don't like to have their pictures taken."

She was careful with the film. The next day, she gave the roll to Lucille to get developed at a one-hour place and had her wait until the pictures were ready.

Given Bob's suggestion that Zoffke's dinner companions were involved in drugs, she was sorry she'd taken the pictures. But she wasn't about to throw them away. They might come in handy.

One by one, she called the Birthday Bobs on the store's phone, which buzzed, clicked, echoed, and otherwise indicated the line was tapped. "I'm sorry to tell you, but I screwed up the birthday party pictures," she told each. "I don't know what I did wrong, but the roll came out blank. I'm sooooo sorry."

Bob Newton and Bob Stanley were disappointed. "I'm relieved," Bob Aguirre told her.

In reality, the photos of Zoffke and his pals came out perfectly clear. Beverly hid the originals and negatives in her chicken coop and put the duplicate prints in a pink envelope.

. . . . .

To Beverly's surprise, Steve called on the weekend and invited her to dinner at the Café Oceania, a seafood restaurant, to celebrate her birthday. The restaurant was noisy and hopping. Dishes clanged, waiters called out orders, and diners carried on loudly in the high-ceilinged, wooden-floored restaurant. Conversation was difficult with the din. They half-shouted their orders of mixed greens salad, Cajun shrimp, and a pitcher of beer to a waiter.

"How was your birthday with the Bobs?" Steve asked.

"Great. We had a wonderful time. But I did something I shouldn't have."

Steve groaned. "Confess."

She told him about taking the photos of Zoffke and his friends.

He was aghast. "Were you out of your mind? It was probably an undercover operation, and you might have screwed things up for the customs guy. You could get prosecuted for interference."

She shrank in her seat. "Can I ask you a favor?"

He didn't reply.

She handed him a pink envelope. "Here. Would you safeguard this for me?"

"Let me guess. It's the pictures. Jesus, Beverly."

"It could be my will. You don't have to know what's in the envelope."

He shook his head and pocketed the envelope without looking at its contents. "The things I do for you."

At a nearby table, a young man in sunglasses with frizzy, recently dyed black hair peeking out from under a baseball cap sat eating by himself. He seemed intent on his catfish sandwich and beer, but he also paid attention to the couple at the next table and saw the man put a pink envelope in his pocket.

Fourteen

When the weekly Operation Pillage task force meeting was over, Dave quickly trotted down the tire store stairs before Joe Scarafaggio, his least favorite colleague, could buttonhole him. Like a skunk after garbage, Scarafaggio was always rooting around for scuttlebutt and pestering him. Plus his crass Brooklynese drove Dave around the bend.

Scary popped up just as Dave was getting on his bike. Telling Scary he had choir practice at his church, he raced off.

Truth was, Dave never went to church, and, being tone deaf, he wasn't a likely candidate for a church choir. He was on his way to see Clive Jackson, a retired customs inspector he'd worked with in Newark when he first joined the Customs Service. Clive had finished out his career as a cargo inspector at the Albuquerque airport and lived in the South Valley. Dave hoped his old mentor could help him gain some perspective on the troubling assignment at La Ñapa.

The gray-haired retiree was tending his roses when Dave rode up. "Let's go see if that ol' gal of mine will let me have my daily ration of rum," Clive said. "You're the perfect excuse for my running the cocktail-hour flag up the pole."

They sat in the Jacksons' living room nursing rum and tonics.

"I thought Operation Pillage was going to be a plum assignment for my finale on the federal payroll," Dave said. "Boy, was I wrong. It's a harebrained operation that involves unauthorized wiretapping, taping attorney-client conversations, unlawful entry, interference with the mails, theft, and vandalism."

"Let me guess who's in charge—Ray Zoffke, right?"

"Yep."

Clive shook his head in disgust. "That cracker asshole."

"Zoffke has created a conspiracy theory out of thin air—a New Mexico-based pre-Columbian art smuggling ring—and now he's pouring agency manpower and money into proving its existence."

"Who else is on the task force?"

"Joe Scarafaggio and a delegation of AATA trainees."

Clive exhaled noisily. "The stupid leading the more stupid."

"If there's anything funny going on in Santa Fe, the Lechuga brothers—rather than the Salvadoran guy—are likely to be involved."

"Who are the Lechuga brothers?"

"Ronnie and Elías, a couple of low-life importers in Santa Fe who have more money than their lame excuse of a business can possibly produce. They live in pricey eastside condos, drive Jaguars, wear Rolexes, and fly to Guadalajara a lot."

"Have you suggested to Zoffke that he look in that corner?"

"Yep, I did, in a task force meeting before the raid on Galería Galo, but Zoffke shot me down fast."

Clive raised his eyebrows and contemplated his nearly empty drink. "I have never liked or trusted that man. He's a big, mean, powerful, bigoted son of a bitch. Knowing how he feels about black folk, I stayed out of his way. And you'd be wise to do the same."

"I'd like to, but he's the gatekeeper to my pre-retirement promotion."

"Where's Herman Naranjo in all of this? He's a pretty decent sort and fairly senior."

"Agent Orange? On the sidelines, mostly, although he's run the interrogations of Pancha Archibeque with Zoffke. From what I hear, he's uncomfortable with the way Zoffke has been hammering on the woman. But you know Orange. He's not likely to cross his *jefe.*"

"Herman's never been a real courageous guy."

"A lot of people in the agency, especially the women, don't like the way Zoffke is treating Archibeque. She's never been in trouble of any kind, she's cooperating completely with the investigation, and she's six months pregnant. So she signed for the packages that Rivas sent from El Salvador and Guatemala—big deal. She works for the guy; that's her job. How was she supposed to know what was in the shipments? And were the contents valuable enough to classify as national patrimony? Zoffke got a museum curator to identify a strand of stone beads as pre-Columbian Mayan. That's what the search warrant was based on. What a joke! The curator is a specialist in minimalist painting. Any archaeologist will tell you stone artifacts are difficult to date or classify."

Clive shook his head. "A bunch of worthless rocks and Big Ray thinks he's onto a pre-Columbian artifact smuggling ring equivalent to the French Connection. Well, it probably has a lot to do with his need to show Washington something after his four-year leadership of a twenty-five-man office in Albuquerque with not a single narcotics bust to his credit. Do you think the importer you're watching is involved in any illegal activities?"

"Beverly? I don't think so. She's been in the business a long time. The bean counter following her bank accounts and reading her bookkeeper's financial statements—courtesy of the U.S. mails—says there doesn't seem to be any funny stuff in her books. She doesn't pay with cash, and she doesn't buy or sell pre-Columbian artifacts. I contacted one of the cultural patrimony guys in Washington who's investigating artifact dealers on the coasts, and he says nobody in the trade has heard of her. She doesn't have any money—sure as hell not the kind of money you'd have if you were dealing Panamanian Coclé gold or Mayan jades."

They sipped their drinks in silence for a moment.

"I don't know about this 'new' agency, Dave. Guys like von

Geier and Zoffke don't seem to have any appreciation for the old-fashioned street smarts you and I have. When I hear stories like this, it makes me mighty glad that I'm not there any more."

"So what do I do?"

"Zoffke is a lunatic and a discredit to the agency. But you have to look out for Number One and your family. You don't have long until retirement, do you?"

"Twenty-two months."

"I'm sorry to say this, Dave, but if I were in your shoes, I'd do whatever Zoffke told me to do. I'd ride my bike, dig weeds, learn everything there is to know about flowers, and watch Beverly like a buzzard. I'd write reams of reports detailing her every move. And in twenty-two months, you're home free."

"I was afraid that's what you'd tell me to do." Dave's shoulders slumped.

Fifteen

The week after her birthday, Beverly sat in her office, her head in her hands, and listened as Lucille told yet one more GI Joe that the $1 pottery whistles from Peru weren't priceless pre-Columbian artifacts. Damn, this is tiresome, she thought. Will these *pendejos* ever leave me alone?

The phone rang and she picked it up. A husky male voice whispered into her ear. "Do you know what time it is, little girl?"

She recognized the voice. It was Abe Yeates, calling from Steamboat Springs, Colorado. "Yes, I do," she said.

The voice continued, creepy and slow. "Well then, little girl, what time is it?"

"It's river time. Abe, you pervert, I love you! You don't know how much I need a river trip."

"Andrea and I always enjoy your letters. But when you wrote us about customs harassing you, we were pretty shocked. There must be some way to get those idiots to leave you alone."

"I'm out of ideas. Maybe running away from home for a week will help."

"Well, there's nothing like a trip on the Yampa to clear your head."

"Oooh, I can't wait. Who's on the trip this year?"

"So far it's the usual suspects—Andrea and me and Flash and Darryl Goodyear, who's bringing his wife, Lavonne. Priscilla Dobbins, a doctor on the Ute Reservation who was Andrea's college roommate, is coming. So far that's the cast. We thought Doc could ride in your raft. You'll like her. She's a maniac."

"Coming from you, that's a high accolade. When do we go?"

"First weekend in June."

"Perfect. How'd you rate that?"

"By living a clean and virtuous life, dear."

"Ha! That'll be the day."

Beverly and Abe, one of her Peace Corps/Colombia colleagues, discussed details for the trip. She could barely contain her excitement. A river trip was the perfect answer for what had been ailing her, the incessant invasions of her privacy by customs creeps. When she hung up, she felt frisky as a puppy after a bath. She strode into the front room and greeted Lucille's customer, a hulking guy in camouflage pants, black lace-up boots, and a T-shirt stretched like spandex across his muscled chest. "I'll bet you're a pre-Columbian art collector," she said, beaming at the man.

Lucille's jaw dropped.

"Well, I, uh," he stuttered, "as a matter of fact I am."

"I have just the thing for you."

She picked up a chipped, black pottery candelabra from Oaxaca off the sale shelf, where it had languished for months.

"This might be just the thing you're looking for. It's Coyótepec, I'm quite sure. Or some site close to there, Atzompa maybe? What do you think?" She handed the candelabra carefully, curatorially to the young man.

"Well, uh, I don't know," he stammered, juggling the candlestick as if it were a live grenade.

"I mean, it could also be Acatlán, classic period."

"Uh, I'll take it!" He gingerly handed the candelabra off to Lucille and drew an American Express card out of his wallet.

"We don't take American Express," Lucille and Beverly said in unison.

The young man shrugged, put the card back in his wallet, and paid cash for the $30 piece of contemporary tourist pottery. Then, grabbing the package eagerly, he hurried down the steps.

As soon as he was out of earshot, Lucille and Beverly doubled over, hooting and howling with laughter.

"Chalk up one for our side!" Beverly yelled, slapping Lucille's upraised palm with her own.

BOOK TWO

One

June 1988

On the banks of the Yampa River in northwestern Colorado, Frank Tollwut took a final drag on his cigarette and winged it into an adjacent sagebrush. A young park ranger, standing close by with his clipboard clasped to his chest, frowned but held back from saying anything. His superiors had told him to be helpful to Tollwut and his men. And anyway, since May had been damp and rainier than usual, he doubted the bush would catch fire.

"Are you sure you wouldn't like to get on the river, sir?" he said. "The other party should have been here two hours ago. You're more than welcome to go ahead of them."

Frank's attempt at a friendly smile barely teased the corners of his thick push-broom mustache. "Thanks, but we're in no hurry."

The six other members of his party of river rafters—muscular, crew-cut, clean shaven, and dressed like him in identical neon-green nylon wind pants and jackets with matching Nike bill caps—grumbled among themselves. They had been waiting on the riverbank for nearly three hours. One cleaned his fingernails with a penknife. Two took turns throwing a Bowie knife at a nearby log. A blocky, dark-skinned man with gray at his temples stood off by himself, gazing into the distance, his hands clasped behind his back like a general reviewing far-off troops.

The other two sat on their heels under a cottonwood chatting about baseball, their families, previous river trips, fishing. The party's river-running gear—three inflatable rafts, matching blue rubber river bags, coolers, ammo cans, and other baggage—lay neatly piled on the bank, but on Frank's orders, no one made a move to pump up the rafts.

Mickey, a Special Forces veteran with thigh-sized arms, squinted uphill at the dirt road that approached the river from the southeast. "Dust plumes, sir. Maybe it's them."

Soon two pickups with boat trailers and a large van came into view. In a cloud of dust, the vehicles slowed and turned into the road leading to the Deer Lodge boat ramp.

Frank stroked his moustache and smiled.

Two

Under the watchful eyes of a young park ranger, the newly arrived river runners unloaded gear from their pickup trucks and a Yeates Plumbing Company van. The ranger guessed that the black-bearded sequoia of a man was Abe Yeates, the trip leader, and watched as he skillfully slipped two aluminum dories off trailers into the mighty, muddy river with the help of a slight, sinewy, tanned man in thick glasses who reminded the ranger of a river willow. Another man, blond, blue-eyed, with a wispy beard and moustache, did little to help, watching the others work as he sucked on a beer.

Four women, aided by a sturdy, dark-haired fourth man, whom they called Darryl, unloaded two folded-up rubber rafts from the pickups and carried them to the riverbank, where they unfolded them. Using a compressor that worked off one of the pickup engines, they inflated the rafts and slid them down the embankment into the river. They loaded them with coolers, waterproof gear bags and ammo cans, a fire pan and grill, bags of charcoal, a shovel, a pump, and the army surplus rocket boxes that would serve as the ash can and the portable toilet. Once the gear had been settled into a balanced heap on each raft's stern and tethered firmly to the D-rings set into the rubber pontoons, the women covered the jumble with a cargo net and tied that down, too. Next, the party loaded the remaining gear into the dories. The group, with the exception of the beer-guzzler, worked steadily and well, the ranger noted. He was impressed with the care they put into their preparations. When they seemed ready to go, the big bearded guy approached the ranger and handed him a slip of paper, the requisite river permit.

"You're Abe Yeates?" the ranger asked.

"Yup, I is he," Abe answered jovially.

"I've heard about you," the ranger said. "The River Rats, right?"

"Correcto," Abe said. "But don't hold it against us."

The ranger stuttered. "I mean, I've heard you guys are quite knowledgeable."

"About some things," Abe laughed.

Beverly and her seven fellow river runners' departure from the rendezvous point in Vernal, Utah, had been delayed by Jack, an acquaintance of Abe's who'd begged to join the trip at the last minute. To everyone's annoyance, he'd arrived an hour late and hung over, if not still drunk. Then they'd made the obligatory stops along the way to load up on Colorado beer, a higher-octane brew than Utah's 3.2 variety, and enough junk food to see them through their week-long river trip. They reached the Deer Lodge put-in site two hours behind schedule.

Doc, a tall, striking blonde who was Beverly's rafting partner, tipped her head toward the men in identical gear who were clustered around the red Mazda pickup that had been behind them on the road to the ramp. "So how come the parkie wants us to put in ahead of those guys?" she asked Abe.

"Beats me," he said. "When he told me we were to go first, I sure didn't argue with him. This way we get first choice of campsites."

As if Doc had summoned them, the men in neon green came over and stood awkwardly on the riverbank. "Morning, gentlemen," she said, brushing a strand of her corn silk hair back from her face and flashing them a brilliant smile.

"Morning, ma'am," the men replied in cheerful unison. They watched as Abe and the ranger, chewing on a pencil, went over each boat, checking the required safety gear.

As soon as the park ranger gave Abe the OK, Flash, the skinny man wearing milk-bottle glasses, jumped onto the pontoon of his bright yellow raft. "I'm outta here!" He announced as he settled into the tractor-seat rowing perch and grabbed his oars.

Jack, his passenger, unwound the stern line from a piling, scampered down the embankment, and hopped onto the raft as it drifted away from shore.

Beverly, sitting on her rowing perch, pulled on a pair of leather garden gloves. Doc skittered down the embankment and gracefully sat down on the bow's transverse pontoon. Crossing her long legs, she smiled up at the ranger. He turned crimson and tossed the bowline down to her. She caught it expertly, and the women were on their way.

The foamy brown current tugged at the raft as Beverly stroked away from shore. Doc gave the men on the riverbank a wristless Miss America wave and flashed them the winner's toothy smile. They all waved back.

Beverly laughed. "You beauty queens never give it up."

"Why should I? It's so much fun. Men are such dopes. I love 'em, but they're not bright."

With a few deep strokes, Beverly maneuvered the raft into the strongest part of the Yampa's current. The river was high and fast and turbid with cold, muddy snowmelt from the western slope of the Rockies. In the shallows on both sides of the river, tree branches wagged as the current tugged at them, trying to free them for the ride downstream.

"Damn, this is going to be great," Doc said. "A whole week of no beepers, no phones, no responsibilities. This calls for a beer." "You can get me one, too," Beverly said. "It's after 9 a.m., isn't it?"

Doc took a couple of cans out of a cooler and handed Beverly one. "OK, who's who in this movie? Nobody introduced me to anyone."

"Boatman machismo—get used to it. They never introduce

anyone. Up there in the dory with the Perrier umbrella, we have the Yeateses. You know Andrea, and Abe was a Peace Corps volunteer with me in Colombia."

"Andrea and I were roomies at Stanford, but I'd never met her husband before. Who are the goony guys in the yellow raft?"

"The beanpole with the thick glasses is Flash. After twelve years of river trips, I still don't know his real name. He's one of those odd-duck river runners who's barely ambulatory on dry land. But on the water, as you will see, he's a paragon of grace. Jack is new this trip."

"I love his Windex-blue eyes. Who are the straight-looking people in the other dory?"

"That's Darryl and Lavonne Goodyear. They're Mormons. Darryl, Flash, and Abe all grew up together and began running rivers when they were in their early teens. According to Abe and Flash, Darryl's a mere shell of his former self now that he doesn't drink, smoke, or eat mushrooms anymore. They're annoyed Lavonne has come along on a river trip, and it's all your fault."

"My fault?"

"Abe claims that Lavonne's here to protect her husband from such a dangerous gentile as yourself."

"Huh. I know I'm dangerous, but I've never thought of myself as a gentile."

"If you're not a Mormon, you're a gentile, Doc, even if you're Jewish."

Soon the sound of water washing up against rock canyon walls reached their ears. Abe and Andrea, now in the lead, hastily furled their Perrier umbrella. Abe angled his high-prowed dory toward the right bank and nosed his bow into the tongue of the flow, where the boat loped up and down on the series of waves like a Great Dane. The current swiftly carried the dory between massive boulders, around a corner and out of sight. Darryl coolly repeated Abe's run. Beverly was next.

"Don't worry, Doc. I abhor cold water in all forms except as ice cubes in my Scotch. I promise I will not dump us. But hang on!"

She pivoted the craft into the deepest, swiftest part of the current, where tall waves rolled over large boulders just beneath the surface of the water. The raft rocked up and down and left and right all at once. The women screamed as huge slaps of icy water drenched them.

With one hand, Doc clutched the chicken line that encircled the raft, and waved the other high in the air over her head, as if she were riding a bronco. "Yeeeeaawhooooo!" she yelled over the roar of the waves.

When Beverly's eyes cleared, she saw the current was rapidly drawing the raft toward a sharp, pointed boulder on the left. She pulled back hard on the oars and dug deep into the swirling, roiling river to maneuver the raft toward the right side of the current. The raft's blunt nose slid sideways past the rock, clearing it by a foot. Then she pivoted the raft so the bow pointed downstream. The rapids' strong current led the craft up and down the waves' peaks and valleys, past rocky hazards into calmer waters.

The spray from the rapids was cool on Beverly's face and arms, and the early afternoon sun warm as it licked the droplets from her skin. She reached down into the crevice between an ammo can and the pontoon, where she'd stashed her unfinished can of Moosehead, tipped her head back, and took a long draught.

"Just like in the beer ads," Doc said, taking a sip of her beer, too. "Except that the women in those ads are never doing anything more exciting than falling out of their swimming suits. They are definitely not rowing fourteen-foot rafts in whitewater rapids."

Turning to look back upstream, they watched Flash maneuver through the roller-coaster rapids. When his raft cleared the last boulder, he and Jack let out war whoops that reverberated off the canyon walls.

For the next hour, the boats coursed a series of riffles and slow stretches of the river. Mid-afternoon, as Beverly and Doc's raft rounded a bend, they saw Abe and Darryl beach their dories on the river's right bank.

Beverly hauled hard on her oars to cross the current, then eased the raft into the shallows and beached it on the sand upstream of the dories. Doc swung her legs over the side of a pontoon and stood, the bowline in hand. "What, no bellhops?" she said.

Within minutes, all four boats were beached and tethered to trees. The rafters flopped down on the sandy shore. "Tough run," Beverly said to Abe, who lay next to her.

"Killer," he said from underneath the shade of his arms.

"Killer," Andrea repeated from her prone position on the other side of Abe. She took a fat joint from Flash, sucked on it, then passed it on to her husband. Abe inhaled noisily and held the joint out for Beverly.

"Pass," she said, handing the joint to Jack.

"What's the matter?" he asked.

"Nothing. That stuff gives me the munchies and a headache."

For the next couple of hours, everyone puttered about the campsite. Doc set up the portable toilet, while Lavonne, Andrea, and Beverly gathered firewood along the beach. Jack watched everyone work as he stood around knocking back bourbon-and-sevens. The cooks—Abe, Flash, and Darryl—put together the dinner—chicken breasts stuffed with crab in a white-wine béchamel served with asparagus over just-baked sourdough biscuits and a field-greens salad.

The women gathered around the campfire to sip drinks, nibble smoked oysters, and watch the men work.

"Isn't this interesting?" Andrea said. "Here we have men, cooking like world-class chefs, in Dutch ovens over flighty driftwood fires, cooks so fussy they won't let us women chop onions or wash out their precious pots. Are these really the same guys who, in our gadget-clogged kitchens at home, can barely make toast?"

"Yeah," Lavonne said, taking a sip of Diet Seven-Up. "If we could bottle the secret to this magical transformation, we'd be billionaires and heroines to women the world over."

After dinner, the group sat around a campfire sinking their forks into an Amaretto-flavored cake. Jack, by now quite drunk, announced he had a special treat. Wavering on unsteady legs, he pulled a small Ziploc bag of white powder out of his jacket pocket and dangled it in front of Beverly's nose.

"I'll bet you know what this candy can do, little girl," he said, slurring his words.

Everybody stopped eating and watched.

"No thanks, Jack."

"Aww, c'mon," he said. "You've probably seen more of this stuff than everybody here combined. Show us how it's done."

"My mother told me never to take candy from a stranger," she said, staring hard into his bleary blue eyes.

"I ain't no stranger. Abe here and Flash have known me for a long time."

"I'm not interested, Jack. It's not my bag, so to speak."

"I'll bet," he said with some annoyance. "Here, Doc, have a toot."

She shook her head. Jack offered the bag to everyone around the campfire, but nobody was interested. Muttering to himself, he stumbled off into the darkness.

Once Jack was out of earshot, Beverly groaned. "That was weird."

"He's an OK guy," Abe said. "But I didn't know he was into that stuff."

"That was an impressive quantity of coke," Doc said. "Several thousand dollars worth, I'd guess. Assuming it was coke."

"Well, I don't think it was baking soda," Beverly said. "And why me? What did he mean, I must have seen a lot of it?"

"Don't get all paranoid," Abe said. "He's really loaded."

"You haven't been through what I've been through," she shot back. "You have no idea what a toll the last couple of months have taken on me."

Annoyed and hurt, she walked off into the dark to her campsite, where she sat down outside her tent, leaning against a flat rock, and tried to lose her anger in stargazing. The night sky was cloudless and deep, with countless sparkling, winking gems—emeralds, rubies, tourmalines, sapphires, amethysts—scattered across a black velvet backdrop. Several pinpoint-sized satellites blinked across the heavens, and from time to time, a shooting star blazed through the jewel-studded sky. To the west, a glow above the canyon rim foretold a rising moon. The night grew chilly, and a breeze ruffled the tent flaps. She zipped up her jacket and shoved her hands into the pockets.

Andrea's voice suddenly broke through the quiet. "Care if we join you?" Abe was with her.

"I don't mind. Pull up a rock."

"I'm sorry if I upset you, babe." Abe said. He dropped to the ground next to her and kissed her cheek. "Hey, what's this?" He swiped a finger across her tear-stained face.

"It's not you," she said, sniffling into a Kleenex. "It's all the incredible weirdness I've been living with these past months. I truly don't know how to handle it."

"I know you've been having a rough time," Abe said. "But, hey, this is the river. We're a million miles away from all that. Jack's a Bozo."

"Maybe he wanted to impress us with the coke," Andrea said. "You know, the new guy on the block strutting his stuff."

"I suppose," Beverly sniffled. "OK, I'll try to be normal."

"Don't overdo it, please," Abe said. "Normal is not a desirable quality in a River Rat, you know."

Three

The morning sun rose above the canyon wall and quickly burned off a frost that had lightly dusted the tents, grass, trees, and driftwood logs on the beach. As the River Rats set forth on the Yampa, a pair of red-tailed hawks circled slowly overhead in the cloudless sky, and ravens called to each other from clumps of leafy cottonwoods that lined the shore. The river, moving steadily and smoothly, ferried the rafts and dories downstream through sandstone canyons whose high castle walls changed colors at every bend in the river.

Doc took over rowing for a while. With a few pointers from Beverly, she was soon maneuvering the boat well, although she gave the oars back to the captain when they approached the occasional rapids.

In the early afternoon, the rafters beached on a sandbar for lunch. Beverly searched out some shade and lay down to read while eating a sandwich.

Flash sat down at her feet. "How would you feel about being my passenger and letting Jack take your boat for a bit?"

She put down her book. "I guess so, if Doc doesn't mind."

Flash grinned, and the sun glinted off his thick, opaque glasses. "She doesn't mind. I already asked her. I wanted to spend some time with you. You know, catch up on all the year's doings." A grin crossed the boatman's weathered brown face, creasing the corners of his large brown eyes. He studied her. Then suddenly, he patted her leg and jumped to his feet. "I want to try an experiment."

The boats shoved off, but Flash made no moves toward his raft. When the others disappeared around a bend in the river, he whipped off his glasses and tossed them onto his life jacket, spread out on the sand. Then he pulled off his T-shirt and shorts and ran bare-assed into the river, splashing and whooping and jumping up and down. "Come on in. The water's fine," he called.

Beverly shivered. She hated cold water, and besides, she wasn't wearing a swim suit. Yet the hot midday sun on the sandbar was searing her skin, and sweat was streaming from her pores, soaking her clothes. A cool dip might be refreshing, she thought. She picked up Flash's glasses, looked through the blur of his thick lenses, and realized he was nearly blind. Maybe he wouldn't notice she was built like a Buick.

She approached the water with trepidation. Flash bounced up and down, quacking like a duck taking a bath, whacking the water with his long, skinny arms. He reached out for her hand as she timidly tipped her toes into the icy river and tugged her into the water. They both lost their footing and went under. Beverly popped up immediately, gasping from the shock of the cold water, and grabbed Flash's shoulder to right herself in the slippery mud and the swift current. Before she could regain her footing, he raised her water-heavy T-shirt up over her head and flipped it onto the shore, where it landed with a soggy slap. Then, reaching around her back, he expertly unhooked her bra and tossed it onto the shore. Again she lost her balance in the current and toppled over backward with a big splash. Flash whisked off her shorts and panties in one swift motion and pitched them onto the beach.

They played in the water like crazed Labradors, diving, yelling, and splashing, the noise reverberating off canyon walls. Overhead, ravens cawed in disapproval. The sun made mini rainbows in the spray they kicked up. But soon their bones ached with cold. Hanging onto each other, they dragged themselves out of the river and collapsed on the hot sand.

As they lay sprawled on their backs looking up at the canyon walls, the sun dried pearly drops of water off their skin. Canyon wrens and swallows dived overhead, and bees darted through the sun's hot beams while wispy gauze clouds drifted across the narrow patch of sky visible above the canyon rim.

Just as Beverly was thinking about grabbing her clothes and dashing off into the bushes to dress, Flash leaned across her. His hands brought her face toward his and he kissed her gently and sweetly. She was surprised by his gracefulness, something she never expected from the crude and often surly boatman. In the Real World—and maybe on the river as well—Flash and she were hardly couple material. Not exactly Romeo and Juliet. Or even Ozzie and Harriet. She didn't see True Love in the cards for them. But there was always the possibility of True Lust. Her wobbly loyalties to Steve evaporated into the steamy air, and she kissed Flash back.

He grinned wickedly.

Later, when they lay sprawled and spent on the sand, he asked if she was OK.

"I am very OK. I am fantastically OK." She propped herself up on her elbows. "So, was that the experiment?"

"Yup. I've been thinking about doing that for years. You are really something, ma'am. Jesus H. Christ. Christ on a cracker!"

He leaped to his feet and dashed screaming into the water. Beverly plunged in after him. The icy water left her sweaty skin feeling rubbery and cool. But even as she shivered in the river, a hot, achy place within her still throbbed and pulsed with a pleasant memory all its own.

They soon slogged their way out of the water, put their clothes back on, clambered into the raft, and shoved off. As they floated downriver, Flash put his headset on and hummed along with the Grateful Dead while Beverly enjoyed the otherwise peaceful silence and the late afternoon sun's warmth on her uplifted face. She thought back to his ardor and grinned. It was nice to know that somebody besides Steve thought she was worthy of carnal engagement, even if that someone was Flash. She tried to feel guilty about being unfaithful to Steve, but it didn't work. She knew he'd been unfaithful to her countless times over the years. The fabric that had held their relationship together for so long was badly frayed and in danger of unraveling completely. She still loved him—sort of—but she wondered if he was capable of loving anyone as much as he loved himself.

Just above Big Joe Rapids, Flash beached his raft alongside the other boats, and they joined their party. Nobody asked Flash or Beverly where they'd been. Nobody even made jokes or winked at them. She was relieved. There was a good side to River Rat manners.

In the morning, camp came slowly to life. Like butterflies crawling out of their chrysalises, the river runners left their sleeping bags and tents and converged on the campfire for a breakfast of huevos rancheros and frijoles. After breakfast, Beverly returned to her campsite to pack her gear.

Flash arrived to help. "Put up a tent, did you? It was a pretty nice evening down on the beach. Not cold at all. You missed a fabulous meteor shower."

"I'm not surprised. But this place is crawling with mice. I'd rather they didn't walk all over my face."

"True, true. Say, Jack wants to take your boat through Big Joe."

"What, you guys think I can't run Big Joe? I've done these rapids a dozen times."

He shook his head. "That's not it. He just wants to give it a try."

She stared at him and considered asking him why he or one of the other men couldn't lend Jack a boat. But she stopped herself. It was important to keep the peace on the river. Of course, as usual, that was a woman's job, not a man's. She reminded herself that Big Joe was a great ride even if you weren't rowing it. There would be plenty of other rapids to run.

"Do you want to ride with me again?" he asked, pushing his glasses up his nose.

Beverly certainly didn't want to ride with Jack. She'd kept her distance from him since his attempt to foist cocaine on her. "OK," she said.

Flash hoisted her river bag onto his shoulder and picked his way down the steep bank to the wide stretch of sandy beach and his raft. Beverly followed with the rest of her gear, clambered into his raft, and sat down on the forward pontoon.

He shoved the raft into the river and settled onto his rowing perch. The main current swiftly ferried them to the top of the rapids, where it went into high gear. The boat began bouncing up and down and rocking side to side, first gently, then violently as it plied the frothing rapids. Water poured over the pontoons. The prow of the boat rose high into the air, and the swift current catapulted the raft forward into wild whitewater. They screamed as the waves beat at the raft and drenched them with frigid water. Walls of churning water rose up on all sides of the raft, and Beverly tightened her grasp on the straps wrapped around the transverse pontoon. Huge waves blocked out the sky and the shore as the raft dived down into a hole and popped almost straight up out of it, threatening to hurl the rafters out of the boat or flip over backward on top of them. But the raft stuck to the top of the wave, and Beverly stuck to her pontoon, and Flash stuck to his tractor seat. After an eternal minute on the wave's pinnacle, the raft slid swiftly down the wave into the roiling whitewater. He hacked at the tumult with his oars to keep the boat from spinning, and his bow pointed straight ahead. Again, the raft rose up almost vertically into the air, then slapped down on the boiling water. A whirlpool at the base of a huge rock threatened to suck the rafters inside its maw. Flash swore, and half-standing, dug into the water with all his might and pulled the raft away from the rock. Beverly hung on with white knuckles. Water poured over the pontoons, and the raft tipped every which way at once. But soon enough, the water-weighted but upright craft slipped onto a rolling tongue of current and trotted into the calm waters below the Big Joe rapids. Flash groaned and dropped his oars into the gentle flow.

"Pretty good run, Mr. Boatman," Beverly grinned.

"Pretty good? Hell, it was brilliant."

Late that night, as Beverly lay in her tent, reading by lantern light, she heard someone approach.

"Knock, knock," a male voice said.

She groaned. "Who's there?"

"Orange."

"Orange who?"

"Orange you glad it's me?"

"Ayiiiii! Come on in, Flash."

He zipped open the tent flap, clambered inside on his hands and knees, and began to undo the zipper on Beverly's sleeping bag. She swatted him with her paperback. "Whoa!"

"You said to come in," he protested. "I'm just following orders, ma'am."

Four

With the moonglow tinting the riverine vegetation a light indigo, agent Frank Tollwut made his way downstream along the
riverbank. He didn't need to use his penlight. The moonlight
was so strong he could read his watch. The rendezvous was set
for 4:30 a.m., and it was now 4:15. When he caught sight of the
River Rats' beached rafts, dories, and several prone bodies in
sleeping bags clustered around the last embers of a campfire, he
quietly turned and walked back upstream, away from the camp.
Pausing under a cottonwood, he smoked a cigarette and waited.
Soon, he heard footfalls. Someone was coming his way. He
dropped the cigarette into the sand, crushed it out with the toe
of his boot, and stepped back into the shadows to make sure the
person approaching him was the right guy.

Five

Flash was gone when Beverly awoke the next morning. She crawled out of her tent and surveyed the camp. At the kitchen table, Lavonne was pouring a generous amount of Bailey's into her coffee cup, while her husband tipped a rum bottle into his. Ah, Day Four, Beverly thought. They were right on schedule for attitude adjustments. It always took a few days on the river for everyone to loosen up, and the normally tee-totaling Mormons were proving they were no exception.

Beverly's mind-set, too, had experienced a transformation after just three days on the river. Her usual worries—the store, unpaid bills, letters she'd forgotten to write, her houseplants, her chickens, Ricky's welfare, her relationship with Steve—all seemed like ancient history in a far-off world. Even the terror of the feds' bizarre campaign of harassment, which in the previous months had barely left her thoughts for more than a minute or two, was beginning to subside like the remnants of a bad dream. The river had become her only reality. All her days on the Yampa, whether yesterday, last year, or five years ago, were there together, like a class reunion. There was no place but the river. No time but river time.

She fetched her breakfast of eggs Benedict with asparagus and perched on a log next to Abe, Andrea and Flash.

"I have to tell you guys something," Andrea spoke up. "Early this morning, before dawn, I went upriver to pee. I was hunkered down in some willows when I heard voices. It was Jack and another guy. I think he was from that party behind us. He said something to Jack like, 'What do you mean, she didn't take a toot?' And Jack said, 'None of 'em did, sir. I really tried.' 'Well, try it again,' the guy said angrily. 'We got a lot riding on this, and we're counting on you. If you want us to do our part for you, you've got to come through for us.'"

A stone landed in the pit of Beverly's stomach.

Flash slammed his plate down on the log and jumped up. "I'm going to maim the bastard!" he yelled, looking around the camp in vain for Jack.

Andrea and Beverly grabbed him, and their half-eaten food toppled into the sand. "I have a better idea," Andrea said.

The day remained overcast. Although the scent of ozone lingered in the air, no serious showers fell on the rafters. In slow stretches of the river, beaver coursed the shallows near thickets of willow, their tails etching thin wakes on the water's glassy surface. More and more Canada geese appeared on the sandbars, waddling along the grassy banks. When they caught sight of the boats, they took flight, honking loudly to protest the human invasion as they flew back upriver.

Beverly and Doc saw a hen hastily duck down in the grasses along the riverbank.

"I'll bet she's sitting on a clutch of eggs," Beverly said.

"It's the right time. The chicks will be hatching soon," Doc said.

In a long stretch of placid water, the women lay back on the pontoons and let the river guide their raft downstream.

"Andrea told me you're being hassled by some feds," Doc said. "But maybe you'd rather not talk about it."

Beverly sighed. "Even though you and I only met the other day in Vernal, I feel like we've been pals for years."

"Ditto," Doc said.

"I don't mind telling you about it. Especially since it looks like the bastards are interfering with our river trip, which is to say, they're invading your privacy as well as mine."

She told Doc about customs' making life difficult for her since she'd protested their destruction of her retablo shipment.

"That's hideous. How can you stand it?" Doc asked.

"To tell you the truth, I can't. Privacy is one of those things you take for granted until you're deprived of it. But what's even harder is the aloneness of being harassed. You find you can't tell many people what's going on because it sounds so loopy, and you soon learn they don't want to hear about it. I think it scares them. People I have considered friends for decades know I'm not mixed up in anything like drugs or smuggling. They say the feds have to know that, too, and they wouldn't waste time and money following me around like I claim they are. But when I ask my friends if they think I'm nuts, they say no, absolutely not. They tell me to ignore it. And that, of course, is an admission they believe something is going on. Some of these people are lawyers, for chrissakes. Or old peaceniks. Liberals. Can you believe that?"

"Sure. People need to believe government and the legal system work. Lawyers especially. Others of us know the system has huge flaws in it. There's not much an individual can do to protect herself in the face of government abuse. What's happening to you is admittedly bizarre, but I believe you."

"I just want them to leave me alone. Or I want to be somewhere where they can't ever hassle me again."

"I saw those guys standing there on the ramp at Deer Lodge, dressed in their identical rain gear on a cloudless day, and I thought, hmmm, feds. What are they doing on the river? Pretending they're back on the Mekong? I hate what those macho, power-hungry, paranoid assholes have done to countries like Panama, Chile, Grenada, Vietnam, Cambodia, and the United States, too. This may not be the same agency, but it's the same mind-set. I'll help you. I'm going back to Boston next month, and I know somebody who might be able to get us some info. God, I hate those assholes. Those . . . COCKSUCKERS!"

A flock of ducks exploded out of a nearby marsh and took flight, quacking.

"This thing with Jack is pretty weird, but I think our plan is terrific," Doc said. "I have to warn you, though. Don't believe everything you see me doing, OK?"

"OK, but don't do anything that's going to get you in trouble. Not here on the river, not in Boston. Promise?"

"Dahlin', I swear!" Doc laughed.

At lunchtime, they beached the boats on a sandbar just beyond Harding Hole, and Doc disappeared into the brush with Jack. From time to time, Beverly heard raucous laughter. When Jack and Doc came out of the willows, they were arm in arm. At over six feet, she was nearly a head taller than he, but that made it easier for him to look down the front of her swimsuit.

"Can Jack come on our boat?" Doc asked in a phony little-girl voice.

"Sure," Beverly replied, doing her best not to burst out laughing.

The river runners packed their picnic gear into the boats and shoved off. A half-week of warm weather had swollen the river with snow melt, and the flow was increasingly swift. By early afternoon, they'd entered a realm of red sandstone. Doc and Jack giggled and huddled together in the bow of the raft. Like a good gondolier, Beverly ignored their cuddling and cooing and instead lost herself in the canyon's majestic scenery. In the late afternoon, when they reached the campsite at Laddie Park, Jack fell all over himself trying to be helpful as the women unloaded the boat. He offered to put up Doc's tent.

"You know what, honey?" she said. "Actually, I could really use a little drink. Could you fix me one?"

Obediently, Jack rushed off toward his cooler. In a flash, he was back and handed her a large plastic cup full of something with ice in it. She took a sip and patted his cheek. "Wunnerful. Just wunnerful, dahlin'."

Over dinner, Doc continued to knock back whatever hard

liquor concoctions Jack fixed for her. She became louder and louder. She weaved around the campsite, flailing her long arms and stumbling dangerously close to the campfire. "Cocksuck-aaaaaaaaaaaahs!" she yelled into the moonlit night, throwing her head back and laughing wildly.

Abe pulled her down next to him and put his arm around her. Then Jack sat down on the other side of her and snuggled close. She leaned against him, her head bobbling and collapsing on his chest. Suddenly, she stood up and walked off into the dark on unsteady legs, her drink in one hand. Jack got up to follow her, but she waved him back. "Goin' to powder mah nose, dahlin'. You just wait right heah."

"The drunker Doc gets, the more Dallas she becomes," Flash observed.

Andrea laughed. "She's always been like that."

Soon Doc was back. Clutching her drink, she sat down clumsily between Abe and Jack on their log. "Ladies and gennelmen," she announced, waving her drink around in the air. "Jack here has a little something special for our dessert. Doncha, honey."

"I do?"

"Sure thang, sugar pie! You know that li'l ole bag of candy powder you had the other night?"

"Oh, that. Sure."

"Well now, Jack, honey?" Doc said, her fingers digging at the flap on his shirt pocket, as she fell across him and planted a smooch on his cheek. "We just weren't in the mooooood the other night. But maybe—jus' maaaaaaaaybe—we are in the mood tonight." She stood up on unsteady legs, holding out a clear plastic packet that she waved around in the firelight for all to see. Then she began a little dance, twirling the packet overhead.

Jack jumped up and frantically tried to grab the baggie out of her hands. But Doc's arms were too long for him, and she easily danced out of his reach. With a clumsy flourish, she opened the

Ziploc bag. Pirouetting around the fire circle, she pulled out pinches of the white powder and strewed it over everybody's heads.

"Noooooo, Doc, noooooo," Jack cried as he tried to grab the bag from her.

She twirled out of his reach. "Ah am Tinker Bell, and you are nevah-evah goin' to grow up," she crooned as she sprinkled white dust on Abe's and Andrea's heads. She danced over to Flash, who tipped his head back and stuck his tongue out. She drizzled some of the powder on his tongue and more on his head. Jack got behind Doc and fought to pull her arms down. She struggled with him, then stumbled on a log and pitched forward. Abe grabbed her before she fell into the flames, and the two of them tumbled backward onto the sand, out of harm's way. The baggie had fallen out of Doc's hands during the struggle and landed in the middle of the fire. In seconds, it shriveled into a blob of goo on a burning log. The white powder turned brown and dissolved into the flames.

Jack howled and grabbed his head. "Noooooooo," he yelled. "Ohhhhh, noooooooh. Oh, my God, oh, I am done for. I am finished. I am dead meat. Oh, shit. Oh, God. Oh, fuuuuuuuuck!" Holding his head and moaning, he wandered off into the dark.

Doc lay half-sprawled across Abe's lap. A big grin spread across her face like a beam of morning light. She got up and dusted herself off. "Is he gone?"

"I'd say he's real gone," Flash said. "Jesus H. Christ, Doc, I can't believe you burned up a few thousand dollars worth of toot. "What if it was good stuff? What if it was really *great* stuff? We'll never know."

She pulled a pinch of white powder from Flash's hair and held it under his nose. "Care to snort a little Bisquick? Some drug connoisseur you are."

"Bisquick? So where's the real stuff?"

"In a good place. Aren't those brownies done yet? I'm famished."

Andrea lifted the lid off the Dutch oven and cut the brownies. "I thought you had lost it, Doc. Wasn't our plan for you to sneak into his tent and switch the fake coke for the real thing?"

"It wasn't in his tent. Believe me, I looked. Every time I went off to water my drink, I went through another part of his gear. Then I realized his little baggie was in his shirt-pocket all the time. He never let it out of his sight. So I had to change the plan a little."

"How'd you make the switch?" Beverly asked.

"Oh, well," she said, looking at the ground and scratching her nose. "An old boyfriend of mine taught me how to pick pockets, a little skill he picked up while in government service. None of you saw me pull the baggie out of his shirt pocket?"

"When did you do it?" Beverly asked.

"Just before I went off to powder mah nose that last time, honey bun," she laughed. "Then I got my own baggie with the Bisquick and aspirin concoction I made this morning and faked pulling it out of his pocket."

"Fantastic, Doc," Abe said, hugging her.

"But I thought I'd had it when I stumbled and nearly went into the fire. If you hadn't grabbed me when you did . . ." Doc leaned over and kissed Abe's cheek.

"You mean that wasn't part of your plan?" Darryl asked.

"No, that was for real. Way too for real. Now what do we do about Jack? The guy is out of his mind about losing the coke."

"I don't feel sorry for him," Lavonne announced. "I think it's rotten to set up your friends like that. What did any of us ever do to him?"

"What do you mean, set us up? What are you talking about, Lavonne?" Darryl asked.

"God, were you born yesterday? There's creeps following us.

The ones that were at Deer Lodge, the guys in the flashy matching clothes. Jack's gone upriver a couple of times to talk to them. I saw one of them give him that baggie of white stuff at Deer Lodge while we were rigging up. They met over there by the toidies."

"Why didn't you tell me?"

"You never listen to what I say. You think I'm a total ding-a-ling. So I just thought I'd wait and see if you'd be the last one to notice what was going on. And you were." She marched off toward their tent.

Beverly watched the fire slowly die as, one by one, her friends drifted off to their bedrolls. Darkness slowly overcame the campsite, and the moonless sky filled with a million sparks of light. A chorus of coyotes began to yip and howl, their calls echoing off the canyon walls. Beverly loved listening to coyotes. God's dogs, the Navajos call them.

When the fire's last embers had cooled into ash, she went to her tent. As she was crawling into her sleeping bag, she heard someone approach. "I have a headache," she called out.

Doc laughed. "Me, too, Bev. I was just coming to see if I could borrow some flashlight batteries from you."

"Ooops, Doc. I'll get them."

Six

Day Five dawned brilliant and noisy, with dozens of birds tweeting and trilling around Beverly's tent. They were so manic and giddy they made her smile. The sun steadily edged up over the canyon rim, suffusing the cool morning with brilliant white light. Silver BBs of moisture from an overnight drizzle glistened on leaves, logs, river rocks, boats, kitchen gear, and the tarp covering a heap of firewood. She followed the trails of footprints in the damp sand that converged on the campfire, where Flash was putting the finishing touches on a pot of coffee. He poured cold water into the coffeepot to settle the grounds and filled everyone's outstretched mugs with steamy brew.

"He's gone, guys," Abe announced.

"Jack?" Beverly said, rubbing the sleep out of her eyes. "Gone where?"

"Who cares?" Abe replied. "Maybe he's joined up with his friends, the neons."

Doc spoke up. "Nope, he's gone home. After everybody went to bed last night, I went over to his tent and told him he'd been had. I offered to give him back the coke, but he didn't want it. Said he'd tell the guy who gave it to him it had burned up in the fire. He said we ought to enjoy it; he owed it to us. I asked him who put him up to this. He didn't want to tell me, but with a little friendly persuasion . . . "

Abe shook his head. "Yeah, Doc? Go on."

"He was in a financial jam with his ex, needed some quick cash, and was arrested in a Vernal bar for selling drugs to an undercover cop, a federal cop. He was about to go to trial and was facing time because of some priors, but then the feds offered him a deal if he'd get himself invited on our trip and feed us coke. He's feeling pretty low, guys. Sure he fucked up royally, but that's no reason to turn on his friends. He's not a bad person, really. They've got him by the balls. He said he was going to walk home and spend the time thinking about what to do next."

Beverly muttered under her breath. "I thought they'd leave us alone on the river. Wrong."

"This has something to do with the people harassing you back in Albuquerque, doesn't it, Bev?" Abe asked.

"What do you think?"

He shrugged. "If so, somebody with a lot of pull is going to a helluva lot of trouble to hassle you. And using Jack stinks."

"I agree," she said, sipping coffee and studying the fire in front of her. "None of it makes any sense.

Andrea spoke up. "How is Jack going to get home?"

"He can do it," Abe said. "If he's got water, food, good shoes, and a decent pack. The guy's a mountaineer, you know, and he knows this country pretty well. He could track back to Mantle Ranch and take that road out or maybe hook up with the Echo Park road or hike back to Deer Lodge. It's not exactly a stroll. Maybe forty, fifty miles. But it's not that big a deal for a guy like Jack in this mild weather."

"I gave him my Evian," Doc said.

Flash wailed. "Oh, no. Not your last bottle of Evian! How could you?"

She put her hand on his shoulder. "It wasn't really my last bottle. But he thought it was."

The men prepared breakfast, sourdough crepes filled with sliced strawberries. "Eat 'til you puke!" Abe commanded cheerfully as he handed out plates.

"A few more days of River Rat fare, and we're all going to come down with gout," Doc said, digging a fork into her crepes.

· · · · ·

They left Laddie Park and drifted downstream toward the treacherous Warm Springs Rapids. The river was deceptively placid, a tea-colored mirror painted with the reflections of the cloudless sky, leafy banks thick with box elders, tall grasses, and graceful willows dipping their tips in the slow-moving river. The water's glassy surface was rippled only when a fish jumped or a beaver trailed his wake across it. A blue heron fished the shallows, and when it saw the boaters drifting its way, it would lift its lanky body into reluctant flight and head downstream. They flushed it several times before it had the sense to fly upstream and be rid of them forever. Beverly was half asleep at her oars when she was jarred awake by a pair of Muscovy ducks that quacked in alarm and burst into flight, their wings beating madly at the still air. A bit further downstream, Canadian geese parents strolling on a sandbar with more than a dozen fluffy gray-and-yellow goslings in tow frantically herded their offspring into tall grass at the raft's approach. Only the adults' black-and-white periscoping heads gave away their hiding place.

The serenity of the river didn't last long. The current strengthened, and a distant roar announced the Warm Springs Rapids. Above the falls, Beverly and Doc tied up their raft on the right bank and scrambled over elephantine boulders to a spot that overlooked the main part of the rapids, a half-block-long stretch of boiling water where massive, back-washing waves bordered deep craters. Toward the bottom of the rapids, stretches of shallow water rushed over jagged, boat-shredding rocks. Beverly studied the violent, churning river and considered how she would make a run. Even if she had wanted to run Warm Springs, however, the men wouldn't have allowed it. Doc, Andrea, Flash, and Lavonne joined her on the overlook.

"Oooooh, it looks hairy," Doc said above the roar of the water.

"It is," Beverly said. "But it's not impossible. Basically, this is a run that takes awesome oar power, some fast moves, perfect timing, and a lot of luck."

Andrea grimaced. "It's evil," she said with a shudder and turned her back on the river that had once nearly cost her and Abe their lives.

Doc suddenly jumped to her feet and pointed upstream. "Here comes Abe."

A hundred yards upriver, a tiny toy man in his tiny toy boat paused on the brink of a maelstrom of raging water. Andrea turned ashen. She took a deep drag on the joint she, Flash, and Doc were sharing.

Beverly held her breath as Abe's dory plunged into the mayhem, dipped out of sight, then popped up and rode a mad swirl of white foam. His oars flailing and his dory tipped at a dangerous angle, he surfed the edge of a massive crater. Waves poured over his down side, threatening to swamp him. But he righted the boat, disappeared into the lower part of the hole, shot up into the air, and slammed through the narrows between two sharp boulders in the middle of the river.

"Hard right! Hard right!" Flash yelled above the rapids' roar.

Although he couldn't hear Flash, Abe whisked the bow around toward the right, scraped past a jutting rock on his left, and tumbled safely through a shallow, obstacle-strewn gap into shallows where the current dissipated.

"Awright, Abe!" Flash punched the air with his fist.

Just upstream from where Warm Springs Creek spilled into the river, Abe tethered the dory and collapsed on the sandy shore.

"Here comes Darryl!" Lavonne squealed above the water's roar as her husband's dory eased across the top of the rapids. In a windmill of flying oars, he cleared the hole farther to the right than Abe, but pulled back toward it as the current drew him too close to a massive sharp-edged rock on the left. For several long seconds, he seemed suspended in the current until he was suddenly propelled forward by an avalanche of water that poured through a gap between two whirlpools. Chopping madly at the water to position himself as his dory rocked wildly from side to side, he zipped through a space in the toothy jaws and made for the shore.

Lavonne screamed, clapping and jumping up and down like a cheerleader. She skittered down the rocks, and when Darryl beached his dory, she threw her arms around him and gave him a hero's welcome.

Abe rejoined the party on the overlook.

"Dynamite runs," Flash yelled. "Picture book!" He draped his arms over Abe's shoulders, and they made their way back over the boulders to the top of the rapids where the two remaining boats awaited them. A few minutes later, Doc nudged Beverly with her beer can and pointed upstream. The gray rubber prow of their raft came slowly into view at the top of the rapids, Captain Abe at the helm. As they held their breath, he deftly repeated his first run, while the spectators cheered.

Now it was Flash's turn. Doc and Beverly sucked in their breath as his raft disappeared into the hole, only to be spat out like a wad of yellow bubble gum. His oars twirling, Flash beat his way in and out of the foam, away from chiseled boulders and the minefield of jagged rocks toward the bottom of the rapids that stretched across the river like teeth. In the clear, he made for the shallows. Doc and Beverly hurried over the boulders to help him tie up next to the other boats.

Andrea opened the cooler on Abe's dory and fished out cold beers for everyone. "Flash, baby, you look like a hound that's just chased a jackrabbit over forty miles of desert," she said with a laugh.

Flash sucked hungrily at the beer. "Jeez, I thought I was done for when that hole grabbed my bow and spun me around like a rag doll."

The boatmen were soon engaged in a serious Monday morning quarterbacking session. Lavonne and Darryl wandered off to hunt for arrowheads while the rest of the rafters elected to take a bath. Andrea and Flash stayed to wash their hair where Warm Springs Creek flowed into the Yampa just below the rapids, while Doc and Beverly went up the creek to a bathing spot beneath a thick canopy of box elders where lukewarm water bubbled out of the ground to form a shallow pool.

Doc and Beverly stripped off their sweaty clothes and immersed themselves. For days, their bathing had consisted of furtive dips into the icy, muddy river. The clear warm pool was a vast improvement. Beverly lay back and let the warm water course over and around her milk-white body.

"God, Doc, I feel like a Thanksgiving turkey." She plucked a fistful of watercress that grew along the edge of the creek and sprinkled it over herself. "Complete with garnish."

Suddenly they heard somebody crashing through the brush that rimmed the creek. Beverly sat up and attempted to cover herself with her hands.

"What have we here, ladies? May I join you?" a familiar voice boomed out. Without waiting for an answer, Abe entered the bower, peeled off his clothes, and waded into the pool. They frolicked in the shallow water like sea lion pups until they tired, then sat on a tree branch that crossed the stream, dangling their feet in the warm water and enjoying the hot sun's play on their naked bodies. Suddenly, they heard the clatter of an approaching helicopter.

"Nobody's supposed to be over this canyon in any kind of aircraft unless it's a rescue situation," Abe yelled above the din.

"I think it's more like a Peeping Tom situation." Doc pointed to the red and white craft that hovered some seventy feet above them, whipping the surrounding vegetation into a green frenzy. In unison, the trio stood up, bent over, and shined their bare bottoms up at the helicopter. Its rotor blades chattering loudly, the helicopter rose swiftly, banked, and disappeared into the cover of trees on the river's far side.

"Boy, that pisses me off," Abe said. "Did either of you get his ID numbers?"

Both women shook their heads in dismay.

"Damn!" Abe said. "Me neither. Well, maybe somebody down by the boats did. I'm going to report the sonofabitch."

They put their clothes on and made their way back to the boat landing, where Flash and Andrea stood at the river's edge, sudsing their heads with Dr. Bonner's soap and dumping bucketsful of clear creek water over each other to rinse off. They, too, had mooned the helicopter, but neither had thought to get its registration number.

Doc, Abe, and Beverly decided to wash their hair in the Yampa. Abe clambered aboard his dory to get another bail bucket. Standing in the dory, he glanced upstream and yelled. "Holy shit! There's a dude in the rapids! Flash, let's go!"

Abe threw on a life jacket as Flash hopped on board the dory, his head full of soap, and one arm half in a life jacket. Andrea and Beverly shoved the dory into the river while Abe, at the oars, stroked it into the channel.

Upriver, an overturned black and orange raft banged against the rocky right bank in an eddy, while just below the first big boulder, the river tossed a man in a yellow life jacket around in the churning water like a sliver of driftwood, his arms and legs flailing as the angry water cartwheeled him downstream.

Abe pulled hard upstream in the eddy that ran along the left bank, then pushed the dory out into the rock-strewn flow. He drew his boat as close to the deep current as he could get without being swept downstream and wedged it against a boulder bordering the main flume. Rushing water pummeled the dory against the rocks and fought to loosen it from its rocky mooring.

On the upstream side of the bow, Flash positioned himself to intercept the man in the life jacket as the flow carried him past. When the inert body bobbed by the boat, he leaned far out over the water and grabbed the man by his jacket just as Abe dropped his oars and grabbed Flash by his. The dory rocked wildly from side to side as Flash strained to hang on to the man and Abe hung on to Flash. Then, in what seemed like a surge of power, the two men yanked the limp and bleeding man into the boat.

As soon as Doc saw that Abe and Flash had him aboard, she loped across the boulders to the beached raft where, tossing things wildly aside, she dug out her medical kit, a sleeping bag, and some warm clothes.

In the dory, Flash held the man in his arms and lifted his jaw forward to open his airway while Abe pulled hard to get the boat back to shore. As soon as the dory neared the landing, Andrea plunged into the river up to her chest, grabbed the bowline that was half draped over the side of the boat, and threw it ashore to Doc and Beverly. They caught the line and reeled the boat onto the beach.

"Clear a space," Doc yelled, and the women hastily kicked rocks out of the way. Doc waded into the river to help Abe and Flash lift the man off the dory. "Gently, gently," she cautioned. "He's sure to have some serious injuries."

They carefully laid the man on his back.

Doc tucked the sleeping bag around the man and bent over him. He trembled and shook, tossing his head from side to side as Doc lifted his jaw forward and pulled his tongue out of the back of his throat. Suddenly a gush of water and vomit spurted out of his mouth. Then another. And another. Doc carefully rolled him onto his side. He vomited again, coughing and gagging. Then he began to groan and mumble. His legs jerked spasmodically, and his head rolled from side to side.

"Take it easy," Doc said, patting him gently on the chest. "You're OK. I'm a doctor, and you're going to be OK."

His eyes were wide with terror, and he flailed his arms and legs about frantically.

"Give me a hand, guys!" Doc called out. She ducked the man's wildly swinging arms and tried to pin them down. Abe and Andrea held him by his shoulders, while Flash and Beverly tried to keep his legs still. He began to call out.

"What's he saying?" Doc said. "Beverly, is that Spanish?"

He yelled out again, something that sounded to Beverly like *"¡Suéltame! ¡Fuera!"*

"It's hard to hear over the rumble from the rapids, but I'm fairly certain he's saying 'Let me go! Get away!'"

Beverly knelt beside the man. *"Cálmese. Cálmese."* She gently placed her palm on his blood-streaked, broad, brown forehead. *"Estamos para ayudarle*—we're here to help you."

The man blinked his eyes and looked at the circle of faces around him. Although he was still shaking, he quit fighting after Beverly spoke to him in Spanish. She told him the woman checking him out was a doctor. Breathing in less panic now, but still coughing and gagging, the man focused on Doc, his large, black eyes wide with interest.

Now that he was calmer, Beverly looked at him more carefully. He was short, husky, his skin a sun-darkened chocolate hue, and his hair thick, straight, and black. Blood poured from an angry gash at his hairline, and cuts on his hands, arms and legs were bleeding freely. "My God, he's an Andean Indian," she said.

Doc checked out the bones in his arms and legs, paying particular attention to his left wrist, which was already swollen and purple with bruising, "Do you know where you are? Do you know what happened?" she asked.

The man didn't respond. He kept looking into Doc's big blue eyes, taking in her long, blond hair draped over his chest. When she repeated her question, he mumbled something. Doc shook her head, uncomprehending. "Beverly, ask him if he knows where he is. I'm worried about a serious head injury. Let's see how clear he is."

Beverly spoke into his ear. *"Señor, ¿sabe usted dónde está? ¿Sabe lo que le ha pasado?"*

"Sí," the man said, smiling faintly. Then he spoke softly in a high, lilting Andean Spanish as he gazed up at Doc. *"Me ahogué y ahora estoy en la Gloria. Y ésta es la ángel que a mí me toca."* Beverly laughed and sat back on her heels.

"What did he say? What did he say?" everybody asked.

"He says he knows where he is. He drowned and went to heaven, and Doc's the angel who's been assigned to him."

"Guess again, dude," Doc laughed.

She finished her examination and daubed at the man's cuts with a cotton swab dipped in antiseptic. Suddenly there was a clattering on nearby rocks, and two men ran up.

"Stand back," a tall man with a brushy, reddish moustache commanded, shoving his way past the rafters. "You, too, lady," he said to Doc. She looked up at him briefly but kept tending the cut on the injured man's forehead.

"I said get out of the way!" the man said angrily, grabbing at Doc's shoulder.

"I'm a doctor. Take your hands off me."

"Oh, sorry," he said and quickly backed off. "This is one of my men. Is he OK?"

"That's what I'm trying to determine," she replied. "Why don't you have a seat in the waiting room, and I'll be right with you."

Abe steered the man firmly by his shoulder over to a spot away from where Doc was working. "Let's have a little talk."

The rest of the wounded man's party, dressed in neon orange uniforms with navy blue caps, joined Abe's confab with their leader, who introduced himself as Frank.

Doc asked Beverly to relay the laundry list of the man's injuries to him in Spanish: a probable concussion, a broken left wrist, bruised ribs, and at least two cuts that needed stitches—the one on his forehead and a nasty gash on the side of his right knee. He was also badly bruised on his back and legs.

As she began, the man interrupted her translation. "No, is OK," he said with a heavy accent. "I understand. Is nothing too bad."

"Well, those cuts need to be stitched up pretty soon," Doc said. "And just to be on the safe side, you should have a complete set of X-rays right away. We're only a few miles from Echo Park, where there's a ranger station, a road out, and maybe a phone."

"You come with me, no?" the man said. "We only have a medic, and he is not too beautiful like you."

"Sorry," Doc said. "I'm sure your medic's capable, and you'll be just fine."

One of the neons, a sandy-haired, lanky guy almost as tall as Doc, approached carrying a sleeping bag, some warm clothes, and a first-aid kit. He knelt down by Doc. "Hi. I'm Tim. Uh, I'm a medic. Can I give you a hand?"

"Sure," she said, flashing him her Miss America smile. "Let's wrap this guy up."

Andrea and Beverly planted sloppy kisses on Flash's cheeks.

"What a hero," Andrea said. "That was a terrific save."

"What an asshole," Flash said. "That dork doesn't know shit about rafting, but Frank, the 'leader,' let him do it anyway, because the guy's some important visitor from Peru. He got ahead of the others and didn't stop to look at the rapids like he was supposed to before shooting 'em. Abe says he saw him lose it right at the top. He took a total header over the hole and was out of his boat even before he got to the first washer. It's a wonder his brains aren't spread out all over that rock. God, I sure could use a brew."

Beverly popped open a beer, wandered off by herself, and sat on a rock overlooking the rapids. Her thoughts churned as the wild water below beat against the rocks in an endless battle. The injured man was Peruvian. Did this, too, have something to do with her? Her shoulders felt like they'd been weighted down with pig iron.

Suddenly her pals joined her.

"They're gonna go get the Peruvian's raft," Flash said.

The nose of one of the neons' rafts was soon inching across the top of the rapids.

"Hey," Darryl said, jumping to his feet. "It's Abe."

In the raft were two blue-hatted neons, one in the bow, one in the stern, but Abe was at the oars. He took the plunge half-sideways, and the boat nosed up out of the first dip. Then he went around the big rock on the right, staying on the rim, the raft nearly on its side. With the two passengers high-siding it, they kept the raft from being swamped on its low side as it dived into the bottom of the hole and shot into the air. Abe then pointed the raft's nose toward the first of the two sharp rock sisters. Behind the big boulder, the Peruvian's overturned raft bobbed in an eddy. The man in the stern of Abe's raft crawled atop the baggage. As Abe skidded on his right pontoon around the big rock, the man sprang into the air and landed on the overturned raft.

The onshore crowd went wild. "Jesus H. Christ!" Flash screamed. "This is better than the circus."

Abe finished his run in textbook fashion and rowed the raft into shore. Then he and his other passenger joined the crowd on the boulders to watch the man on the overturned raft.

From his backpack the man took out a long rope with what appeared to be a hook tied to one end. Balancing with his legs apart on the bouncing raft, he swung the doubled-up rope over his head a number of times and flung the tethered hook high out over the churning water into a thicket of trees on the far left bank. He tugged hard at the line, and it seemed to hold fast. Then he took something metallic out of his backpack and tied it to the rope.

"He's got a come-along," Flash said just as the man began to winch the boat and himself toward shore.

Once he got the boat into the shallows near the top of the rapids, the man hopped onto the narrow bank, pulled the raft in, and flipped it upright.

"Now walk it upstream to where you can put in," Flash coached.

As if he could hear Flash, the man walked upriver along the narrow shore, pulling the raft behind him, and disappeared around the bend. Some minutes later, the black and orange raft, followed by the neons' two remaining rafts, nosed across the top of the rapids. One by one, the trio plunged down the liquid precipice into boiling water and made identical near-perfect runs, about twenty feet apart. The last of the rafts pulled to shore and beached while the two others continued on down the river, neatly avoiding the sharp boulder—the Surprise—beyond the bottom of the rapids. They soon rounded a bend in the river and disappeared from sight.

Doc and the medic helped the bandaged man sit up. Then, with a cross-hand carry, they settled him carefully onto a cargo-net sling stretched across the stern of the neons' raft. They cradled his head with a life jacket, wrapped a sleeping bag around him, and shaded him with towels.

Then the medic, Frank, and the boatman shook hands with Doc and Abe, boarded their raft, and shoved off, following the rest of their party downstream.

Seven

The seriousness of the near drowning had sobered the River Rats. They floated down the river in near silence and beached at the Box Elder campground.

It was the women's night to cook, and they heated up tamales in Beverly's infamous homemade *chile colorado.* The men adjourned to lawn chairs down by the boats. Their backs to the fire and the women, they sipped margaritas and snacked on guacamole and tortilla chips.

"They can't bear to witness the travesties of our campfire cooking," Andrea said.

When dinner was ready, everyone wolfed down the food, having, as Flash put it, "mouthgasms." Then they drank the dessert Lavonne prepared—black Russians.

After dinner they sat around the campfire. "So who are those guys, Abe?" Beverly asked.

"Well, surprise, surprise, they're feds, dear. The leader told me they work at the Post Office in Longmont, Colorado," Abe said with a wry grin.

"Oh, sure," Beverly said. "And they're down here practicing what? Express deliveries?"

Abe shrugged.

"You know, maybe we should have told them about Jack," Doc said. "So they could tell the park service at Echo Park to call his family or go look for him."

"I did tell Frank, the leader," Abe said. "Sort of. He asked me if we were missing somebody from our party. I said yeah. One of the guys had a little disagreement with his girlfriend, and he decided to take our Sport-yak and head downriver ahead of us."

"What's a Sport-yak?" Doc asked.

"It's a little orange plastic tub you can float in. We could have had one underneath a tarp. They're not that big." Abe grinned. "Frank seemed pretty upset, and he asked if Jack had taken all his gear with him. Oh yeah, I said. We told Jack he might sink the yak with all that stuff, but he didn't care."

"Do you think he believed you?" Doc asked.

"Maybe. I thought I'd send them off track. Jack probably needs a little time to think things over before he has to deal with those guys again. He'll be all right. I'll have a talk with him when we get home."

When the fire died down and they'd hit the bottom of the Kahlua bottle, they headed toward their bedrolls one by one. Beverly was lying in her tent reading when she heard someone outside.

"Is anybody home?" Flash whispered.

She slipped out of the sleeping bag and unzipped the tent flap. Flash crawled in and lay down beside her.

"Oooooh la la, eau d'Off. My favorite cologne," he said, sniffing the insect repellent Beverly had sprayed on her arms and legs. He slid closer and reached for the hem of her T-shirt.

Eight

The next morning's float was slow and easy. The final campsite, Jones Hole, was only eight miles downstream. The party soon arrived at the confluence of the Yampa and the Green River. Beverly guided her raft around a sandbar into the wider, more swiftly flowing Green. Suddenly, three paddle rafts full of loud, boisterous teenagers zipped past her bow, their radio blaring a reggae tune, their adult leaders looking tired and resigned.

Doc moaned. "I guess we're approaching 'civilization.'"

"Indeed." Beverly pointed to a cluster of car campers parked along the left shore at Echo Park.

Abe docked his dory. While the other boats tied up one by one, he walked across a wide, grassy meadow to the ranger's cabin. Andrea put up the Perrier umbrella, took out sandwich fixings, and began to take lunch orders.

Abe returned in a few minutes, and the River Rats pestered him with questions.

"The parkie told me he had been gone for a couple of days and was just driving up to his cabin yesterday afternoon when he saw a helicopter taking off. White with a red stripe—not one of the Park Service's. Sounds like the one we mooned. The parkie thought the rafters in the orange suits were some kind of government outfit. They told him they'd radioed for the helicopter to take the injured man, a Peruvian general, to a hospital in Salt Lake. What a bunch of rotten liars. The helicopter was in the canyon buzzing us before the guy fell into the rapids."

"Did you ask him if he'd seen Jack?" Doc asked.

Abe peered over the top of his sunglasses at her and smiled. "Yup, I did. On his way out the other day, he picked up Jack on the Echo Park road near Cottonwood Creek and took him to Dinosaur National Monument."

"Was he OK?" she asked.

"The parkie said he was fine, but a little hungry and thirsty. He gave Jack a sandwich and an apple and refilled his Evian bottle." Abe chuckled. "He'll probably have that Evian bottle stuffed and hang it on his wall."

In the late afternoon, the River Rats arrived at Jones Hole and set up camp in the first campsite in a grove of trees. Just as their dinner, an elk meat stew, was beginning to bubble, the neons walked into camp, approaching from downstream. The day's uniform was black sweat pants and snug white T-shirts that advertised "Hard-Rock Café," "Carlos O'Brian's," and other famous bars. Beverly stopped cutting up broccoli for the stew and stared. Her heart beat wildly; she felt like a rabbit cornered by a coyote.

Frank Tollwut strode up to Abe. "We'd like to thank you for giving us a hand back there. We thought you might like to join us for dinner. We've got some Ramen noodles and tuna fish and a bottle of whiskey. But, uh, it looks like you've already got something going."

The other men in Frank's party gathered around the fire and stared hungrily at the stew pot. "God, that smells like real food," one said.

"Yeah, *real* food," the others chimed in.

"Well, hell," Abe said. "I guess we could potluck it." He looked around at the rest of the group. Nobody said anything.

When the collective silence became embarrassing, Andrea spoke up. "Sure. Why don't you guys bring your noodles over, and we can use the stew as a sauce to put over them."

"Thank you, ma'am!" exclaimed a wavy-haired Chicano. "I'll go get the noodles."

Frank nodded his assent, and the man took off for their downstream camp at a half run.

Flash grumbled under his breath. "Fuckin' mooches."

The gathering was like a bad cocktail party. The River Rats sat silently in their lawn chairs or on the picnic tables, while their guests, the Longmont Post Office crew, stood around the camp stiffly. Their bulging arms crossed over muscled chests, they stared like starved wolves at the pots of cooking food. When Andrea offered them drinks, they waited for Frank's nod before they accepted. She handed out margaritas, and Doc set out the salsa and chips. The men attacked the drinks and snacks.

Flash broke the ice. "So where'd you learn tricks like jumping onto overturned boats?" he asked Mickey, a short man whose muscular torso strained the seams of his T-shirt.

He smiled. "Special Forces."

"That was before he joined the post office, of course," Frank interjected.

"Of course," Abe said.

Andrea's and Beverly's eyes met, and they put their heads down to stifle their shared need to guffaw loudly.

The dinner disappeared quickly while the men rehashed their Warm Springs runs. The women sat by themselves, picking at the remains of their dinners in silence. When all the food was gone, each member of the River Rat party washed his or her plate and silverware. The visitors followed suit but made no moves to leave.

Frank pulled a small camera out of a pouch at his waist. "General Ramos asked me to take a picture of his rescuers. Oh, and I have a little present for you all. Maybe we could call it a 'toke' of our appreciation!"

He laughed at his own little joke and pulled a small plastic bag out of his pouch. Mickey, the Special Forces veteran, produced a small clay pipe from his pocket, and Frank handed him the plastic bag. He filled the pipe with a dark brown substance and lit it. A thick, sweet scent filled the air, overwhelming the smell of campfire smoke. Mickey drew on the pipe several times. Then he tried to hand it to Flash, who was standing next to him. Beverly held her breath.

Flash put up a hand. "Pass."

She exhaled.

Mickey offered the pipe around, but all of the River Rats followed Flash's lead, refusing to touch it. Each of Frank's men in turn took hits off the pipe.

"Can't believe you guys don't want to try this," Frank said. "It's hash. When was the last time you saw honest-to-God hash? Straight from the Beqaa Valley. Best there is."

He handed the camera to Mickey and walked over to Doc and Beverly. "Let's take a few pictures for Ramos." Settling the little pipe into a corner of his mouth, Frank put his arms around the women's shoulders and attempted to pivot them to face the camera. In unison, they ducked out of his grasp and turned their backs to the camera before Mickey could get off a shot. He put the camera down and looked toward Frank for direction. The leader's mouth was frozen in a Simon Legree smile.

"Maybe we should call it a night," Andrea said, busily gathering up the paper cups and trash that littered the tops of the picnic tables. "I don't know about the rest of you, but I'm bushed."

"Hope you don't mind," Abe said to Frank. "But we really are a little tired. It's been a big day."

"No problem," Frank said stiffly. He nodded toward his men and picked up their bottle of Lord Calvert, which nobody had touched. With murmured thanks, the Longmont Post Office crew slipped into the night.

Once they were out of earshot, Abe turned to Beverly. "I know what you're thinking."

"Murderous thoughts, that's what. I'm fed up with this sick

bullshit. *Federales* staging a frontal assault on our private river trip with government-supplied cocaine, helicopter, hash. What the hell is going on? If I had any nerve, I'd steal their patch kits and poke holes in their rafts."

"They'd just call in a helicopter for a resupply," Andrea said. "What a bunch of creeps."

When Beverly retired to her tent, she found she was too angry to sleep. She tried reading, but that didn't work, either. After tossing and turning for what seemed like an eternity, she put her clothes back on and paid a visit to Flash's tent. Maybe a bit of exercise would help her get to sleep.

Nine

The next morning, while Andrea stayed in camp to read, the rest of the group explored Jones Creek. They traversed a broad, grassy meadow where mule deer were grazing, then followed a trail along the rushing trout stream that led up a narrow canyon into the mountains. On either side of the divide, steep, bare walls of rock stood guard beneath a hot sun, while along the creek banks, leafy box elders provided shade and cooler temperatures. Birds, dragonflies, and butterflies darted low over the fast-moving water, and furry orange caterpillars inched across the packed-earth trail.

A couple of miles upstream, the hikers turned onto a well-worn path that led to the base of a pink sandstone cliff where prehistoric canyon visitors, using vermilion, had painted mysterious figures on the rock wall: three husky warriors, a big-horned sheep with horns that resembled feathers sweeping back from the top of its head, a coyote-like animal with big ears and a curved tail.

The pictographs, the lushness of the canyon, and its abundant fish and game led Beverly to ponder the likelihood that Jones had been as popular a spot with prehistoric peoples as it was with contemporary ones. She could imagine that maybe one fine summer day centuries ago, a group of people had beached their buffalo-hide boats where the river meets the creek and, like present-day river runners, took a hike up the canyon. There something inspired them to paint the figures on the canyon wall—a hunt, a special ceremony, an encounter with people from another tribe. Beverly considered adding her own pictograph to the mural in commemoration of her tribe's encounter with people from another tribe—the enemy. Fawns beset by snarling wolves might be appropriate imagery.

Toward midday, the River Rats walked back downstream, stopping for a picnic lunch where a small stream, Ely Creek, joined the more robust and tumultuous Jones Creek. Following a communal snooze on the bank, they hiked up Ely to a waterfall, where a clear stream tumbled over sand-colored rocks about twenty feet high. Shedding their clothes, they bathed beneath the waterfall, its cool water beating down on their skins like a pulsing shower to wash away sweat and grit.

As the sun began to slip behind the canyon walls, they dressed and walked downhill. When they walked into camp, Andrea greeted them. "You missed a visitor," she said.

"Yeah?" Abe said. "Who?"

"One of the mailmen—the one who looks like the Michelin man."

"Mickey," Flash said, "the Special Forces guy."

Andrea nodded.

"So what did he have to say?" Abe asked.

"Nothing. He was going through our gear."

"What?" Abe yelped. "I'm going to kill the sonofabitch! That's going waaaay too far."

"Well, you're too late, honey," Andrea said, taking a sip of her beer. "The Longmont Post Office has decamped."

She related the day's events. "I spent the morning reading in my tent to avoid the bugs. Then I walked upstream to stretch my legs a bit. As I was coming back into camp, I saw Mickey slip into Beverly's tent. I hid behind a tree and watched. He went through everyone's tents and gear, then the dry boxes, coolers, and lockers in the dories. He was meticulous, and he carefully put things back the way they had been. I don't think he took anything. He wasn't here more than fifteen minutes total. I thought about yelling at him, but I was more interested in seeing what he was up to."

"I would have murdered the son of a bitch," Abe said angrily.

"Yeah, right," Doc said. "Up against a Special Forces guy, a trained killer, with what? Your Swiss Army knife?"

Andrea continued. "When I saw he was leaving, I stepped out from behind the tree. He saw me and froze. We stood staring at each other for what seemed like hours until I asked him if he'd found what he was looking for. I was pissed off, but I was also scared. I was by myself, and I didn't know when you guys were coming back."

Abe put his arms around his wife, squeezed her against his chest, and kissed the top of her head. "You did just fine, babe."

"He didn't say a thing," Andrea went on. "He just gave me this smug look, like this was all a jolly joke. Then he walked out of camp. A little while later, through the trees, I saw him and the others load their rafts and shove off."

"Good riddance," Doc said. "I'll bet you money he didn't find the toot, if that's what he was after."

She walked off, and in a few minutes, she was back, triumphantly waving a Ziploc bag filled with white powder.

"So where'd you hide it?" Flash asked.

"The shitter," she said brightly.

"Yeeeeeaaaaaack!" everyone said in unison.

"It's not called shit for nothing!" She grinned. "And it wasn't exactly in the shitter. It was under the rocket box. In a couple of layers of plastic."

"How about your dope?" Abe asked Flash.

"Got it right here," he replied, patting the pocket of his shorts. "Don't leave home without it."

"I don't mean to be paranoid," Doc said, "but this drug business is getting too weird for me. Those guys seem to be intent upon foisting drugs on us. How do we know Mickey didn't plant drugs in our gear?"

"What a wonderful idea," Flash said.

"Wrong, Flash," said Andrea. "They could have a drug dog waiting for us at the take-out ramp."

"Or they could come back with their helicopter," Abe said.

"Everybody should go through their stuff and make sure Mickey didn't leave us any little presents," Doc said.

They adjourned to their tents while Abe and Andrea checked the boats and the rest of the camp gear for contraband.

Beverly dumped the contents of her duffel bag on the floor of her tent and wasn't surprised when she found a plastic baggie with hash and a familiar-looking pipe wrapped in one of her dirty T-shirts at the bottom of the heap. Holding the bag by a corner as if it were a dead rat, she crawled out of the tent, roaring like an enraged lioness. Everyone came running.

"Jesus H. Christ," Abe said when he saw the hash and hash pipe.

"Yeah, praise Jesus!" Flash said. "Let's fire 'er up!"

"Wrong," Doc said. She took the plastic bag from Beverly and gave her a hug. "Group, I think it's time we had a little ceremony to thank the river goddess for the great, safe trip we've had so far. Gather 'round, everybody."

Everyone joined Doc at the river's edge, where she opened the bag of hash and tossed its contents far out into the river, together with the little pipe.

Too late, Flash grabbed for Doc's hand. "Doc, noooo!"

Then she opened the baggie that held Jack's cocaine and leaned out over the water.

"Doc! Don't!" Flash wailed as she emptied the fine white powder into the current.

Abe shook his head sadly. Flash held his head and groaned loudly, like a dying bull elephant.

"Somebody downstream is going to have a hell of an alfalfa crop," Abe said.

"Can I lick out the baggie?" Flash asked Doc wistfully.

"No, we're going to burn the baggies." She draped an arm around his waist, drew him close, and pecked him on the cheek. Seconds later, she held another plastic bag out over the river and tipped it upside down. Shreds of dry leaves rained down on the swift-moving water and floated away.

A panic-stricken Flash anxiously patted the pockets of his shorts. "Doc, tell me that wasn't my dope you just dumped into the river. Pleeeease!"

"There are occasions that call for serious sacrifice. And this is one of them. The river goddess will reward you for your wonderful offering. She will shower you with chi."

He shut his eyes and moaned. "My dope! My beautiful home-grown dope! Ohhhhh, Doc, I'm in terrible pain. I think I'm gonna die. Could you spare me a Percocet?"

"Sorry, I'm off duty," she said, patting him on the cheek. "You'll live."

Lavonne stared at the river in the fading light, her face flushed a deep pink. "What right do those people have going through our stuff and planting drugs on us? This is outrageous. I think we should tell our congressmen about those guys."

Beverly shook her head. "That's how this whole thing started. I complained to my congressman. And look what happened. I don't think there's anything we can do about them."

"Well, I'm elated they're gone," Doc said. "Creeps, cretins."

Then with one voice, the River Rats yelled in unison, "Cooooooooooooockkssssssuuuuuuucckers!"

Ten

From behind a tree, Mickey watched the River Rats' gathering on the river's edge. He shook his head in dismay when the tall blonde emptied the drugs into the river. Government supplied or not, what a waste of good shit, he thought. It had been Mickey's bad luck that one of the women caught him in their camp. Bad intel, vato. Gets you every time. He thought he'd seen all the river runners head up the trail that morning, but he'd missed one. He chastised himself. Next time, do a head count, *pendejo*.

Quietly and carefully, Mickey slipped out of the Jones Hole campground and made his way along the shoreline toward the beach a mile downstream, where Frank and the others had set up camp for the night. He moved swiftly through the brush in the day's last light. Time was of the essence. The local sheriff, Utah state cops, a couple of customs guys from Albuquerque, and a contingent of media people were set to converge on the Dinosaur boat ramp the following afternoon for a big bust when Beverly's party pulled in. Frank had better get on the horn quickly and call off the raid. No drugs, no drug bust.

Mickey gritted his teeth. He dreaded having to tell his boss the bad news: the fat chick had found the hash in her gear, and the party appeared to have gotten rid of all the drugs. He didn't think she'd notice the baggie in the bottom of her duffel among her dirty clothes. Frank and his old army buddy in Albuquerque, Zoffke, the customs SAC, were going to be mighty sore that in spite of weeks of prep time and careful interagency coordination, their headline grabber was a complete *fracaso*.

At times like these, Mickey thought, it was better to be a grunt. Let the *jefes* take the flack. Somebody with some pull—

Zoffke or maybe somebody even higher up—was after the fat chick and her friends big time. Mickey didn't give a rat's ass. He'd had a great time on the river. His only regret was not having had a chance to put the *movidas* on the blonde.

Eleven

The River Rats invited Susan, the Jones Hole park ranger, to join them for their last dinner on the river. She hesitated at first, but when Abe recited the menu—grilled prime rib, baked potatoes, spinach soufflé, sourdough biscuits, and a fruit medley for dessert—she cocked an eye at Abe and Flash. "Are you guys the River Rats? I mean, *the* River Rats?"

They looked at one another and grinned proudly. "Yes, ma'am. We is they. Or, uh, they is us," Flash said.

"Far out. I've been hearing about you guys for years."

The men beamed.

"But I'll have dinner with you anyway. Especially since it's not Ramen noodles, tuna fish, granola, or peanut butter. That seems to be what most people on the river eat. I'll bring a little something special along, too. A contribution to the repast."

She arrived for dinner carrying a small cooler that she set down beside the picnic table. Behind Andrea's back, Abe whispered to Beverly. "If it's another goddamned controlled substance, I'm getting in my boat and hauling ass."

The dinner was accompanied by the last of the wine, three bottles of an '82 Châteauneuf du Pape Vieux Télégraphe. When it was dessert time, the ranger reached for her cooler, and with a flourish, she drew out a couple of pints of Ben and Jerry's Cherry Garcia ice cream. Flash clutched at his heart and fell backward off the bench in a feigned faint. Recovering quickly, he asked Ranger Susan to marry him.

The River Rats got an early start the next morning after a pick-up breakfast. They had a long day ahead and hoped to miss the bad winds that often crossed the flat stretches at Island Park.

When they emerged from the canyon, there was only a slight wind coming across the low plains.

"We're in luck," Beverly explained to Doc. "There have been trips through this stretch when I've pulled against the wind with all my might for hours, wearing my hands raw and getting nowhere fast. The absence of wind today is a gift from the river goddess."

"I knew she'd appreciate our sacrifices to her," Doc said. "I'd say the river looks higher than it was yesterday, but that would be a bad joke."

Beverly groaned.

In record time, the four boats reached the Rainbow Park stretch of the Green. Here the river was alive with day trippers, plying the water in a variety of vessels and picnicking along the cliffs overlooking the rapids.

Ahead of Doc and Beverly, Abe and Darryl's dories rode roller-coaster waves, their bows pointed skyward when they topped the crests, their sterns flashing like white-tailed deer at those behind them when they disappeared into the troughs.

"Hang on, Doc!" Beverly yelled as their raft began to bounce every which way at once. She dug her oars in hard to keep the boat straight as the current rocketed them into tumultuous whitewater. Huge waves curled over the pontoons, slapping the women's faces and threatening to fill the bottom of their raft with icy, murky river water. Doc bailed hard, quickly scooping up buckets full of muddy water and dumping it overboard. In short order, they ran a series of rollicking rapids—Moonshine, SOB, and Schoolboy. The raft churned with activity, Beverly hacking at the river with her oars to steer a safe course between menacing rocks, Doc bailing fast as the river water sloshed in over the pontoons. Soon, however, the last bit of rapids spat the raft into a churning current that quickly subsided into mild riffles. Beverly dropped her oars and shook the water from her head.

"Outstanding job," Doc said, tossing a bucketful of water overboard. "That was maybe the best ride of the trip."

"I thought we were goners for sure a couple of times. But I was determined I wouldn't dump us so late in the game. Wow, what a rush. I'd forgotten what a great ride Split Mountain is."

Rounding a bend, they saw the Goodyears and the Yeateses, in their birthday suits, stewing like cartoon missionaries in a bright-green, rock-rimmed hot springs pool at the river's edge. They docked their raft alongside the dories, as did Flash, stripped off their clothes, and carefully eased down into the steaming pool's hot water. Lying back, they gazed up at the cerulean sky, sipped beers, and rehashed the day's runs.

Too soon it was time to get back into their clothes and boats for the last stretch of the river and the take-out near Dinosaur. Beverly rowed the final stretch of the trip, feeling sad and somber and in no hurry to get to the boat ramp.

Doc noticed her mood. "You look like you just lost your best friend, Bev."

She nodded. "Maybe I have. The river really is my friend, a wonderful, special one. I already miss it and all of you. The trip's not quite over, and I'm already bummed out. The business with the hash was the last straw. I'm still shaking from finding that stuff—whether from fear or rage, or both, I don't know. It's all too weird. Now I have to go home to the real world and probably more bullshit from the feds."

"Maybe they've had enough fun for awhile and they're ready to go back to chasing real criminals. We outsmarted them twice, and we can do it again. In spite of all the stupid stuff they tried, we had a great trip, didn't we?

"Yeah, I guess so."

"Hey, buck up. You're a lot stronger than you think, and we're with you, all of us. We saw what went on back there with those jerks. I wouldn't have believed it if I hadn't been there. Absolutely astonishing. What do you think their all-expenses-paid jaunt cost us taxpayers? Helicopters. Their new, top-of-the-line river-running gear. Their cute, matching outfits. I don't know what we can do to help you, but we'll do something. You don't have to go through this alone."

"I don't want anybody to get hassled because of me, Doc. It's my problem. These are not nice people, and they seem to be able to do whatever they want to those they decide to pick on."

"I *want* to help you, and I *will* help you. And I know the others feel the same way. Trust us. And if you can think of ways we can help you, call on us. Promise?"

Beverly nodded and turned back to her oars with a heavy heart.

Soon the raft rounded the last corner, and the take-out came into view. She rowed across the current and eased the raft onto the boat ramp, where the rest of the River Rats were waiting.

BOOK THREE

One

June 1988

The drive back to Albuquerque from Abe and Andrea's house in northwestern Colorado took a full day. To pass the time as she meandered south along the Rockies' western slope, Beverly sang mariachi songs along with Linda Ronstadt tapes, lost herself in the spectacular Colorado scenery, and munched on Cheetos and apples. Ordinarily, she didn't mind a long drive by herself. But it was hot. The late spring heat hovered above the hood of Steve's pickup in shimmering waves, and by late afternoon, her bleary eyes were seeing too many mirages on the road ahead. The old cooling tricks of spritzing water from a spray bottle on her shirt now and then and driving with the windows down tempered the heat somewhat, but she still felt as if she were driving an oven. Oh for some air conditioning!

When Beverly wasn't competing with Linda for the high notes during the sixteen-hour drive, her thoughts invariably traveled back to the river. It had been a wonderful trip—great company, optimal weather and river conditions, grand scenery, outstanding food and wine. And great sex. But she couldn't keep her thoughts focused on the positive rather than the negative experiences. Over and over again, her errant mind played the reel of the encounters with Jack and the Longmont Post Office, leaving her furious and dejected. If she couldn't liberate herself from customs' clutches in the wilds of northwestern Colorado, where and how would she ever lose the bastards?

As she neared Albuquerque, a Southwestern sunset surrounded her like a 360-degree movie. In her rearview mirror, a red sun slid below mesas and mountains in a blast of color, turning the western sky cassava yellow, then cantaloupe orange, and finally, before darkness descended, the red-orange of a Persian melon. The world around her vibrated with color, and she wanted the astonishingly beautiful sight to last forever. Alas, the show was ephemeral, and in minutes, the tropical colors evanesced into gray shadows with only a narrow band of red limning the western horizon. Ahead of her, to the east, the majestic Sandía mountains rose ten thousand feet high, and in the day's last light, they flushed their famous watermelon pink, then deepened into a plum purple before flattening into black cutouts fronting a blueberry sky.

She rounded a curve and crested the high desert's last rise. Ahead lay the Rio Grande Valley, which ran north-south at the foot of the Sandías. Evening fell quickly on the valley, and the flickering lights of a half dozen little towns and pueblos soon speckled dark swaths of cottonwoods. To the south, a band of bright lights sloped down from the Sandías, indicating the sprawl of Albuquerque, while to the northeast, a glimmer of light above the horizon indicated Santa Fe in the distance.

She crossed the Rio Grande, now gorged with spring runoff, and turned south on the old highway that rolled through the town of Bernalillo, then paralleled the river into Albuquerque's North Valley, where it became Fourth Street.

For Beverly, descending into the lush and verdant valley after a long journey through the parched, sun-baked Southwestern *altiplano* was like enveloping herself in a luxurious mantle of green. Soon she reached her neighborhood, where towering elm trees, her lawn, the old apple tree that shaded the front yard, and the myriad plant life that lined the irrigation ditch alongside her property exhaled a cool, welcoming moisture into the air. Frogs, crickets, cicadas, katydids, and the neighbors' dogs chorused a welcome. Even her rooster, Hahn Solo, got in on the act, with an arpeggio of raucous cawing. Beverly got out of the truck and stretched.

She was anxious for a hot shower and an early bed, but first, she wanted to check on Ricky. When she looked across the street, she saw him wearing his Batman mask and cape, slumbering in his wheelchair on the porch, with Pooh beside him, and decided not to disturb them.

The minute she opened the door to her home, she knew something was amiss. It wasn't just the heavy, musty air of an overstuffed house that had been shut up in the June heat for nine days. There was something else, something that was making the little hairs at the back of her neck tingle. Ready to bolt out the front door at the first sign of an intruder, she quickly checked the living room, the kitchen, each of the bedrooms, and the bath. The few pawnables she owned—a cheap stereo, a short-wave radio, a ten-year-old TV, and a toaster oven, as well as her modest cache of well-hidden jewelry and an old sock full of quarters for the laundromat—were still in place, making it unlikely thieves had visited.

On closer inspection, however, she found that nearly everything in the house had been disturbed. In the bedroom, piles of folded clothes in the closet and bureau drawers had fallen over. The books, shoes, knickknacks on top of the bureau and her bedside table—everything was slightly out of place. The lid to the Chippewa porcupine quill box that Magdalena had given Beverly for her eighth birthday had been clumsily replaced and the box's contents jumbled. In her spare bedroom, the heaps of papers on her desk and on the floor beside her chair were out of alignment, and the closet door was half open. In the kitchen, the cabinet doors and drawers were slightly askew, as were the doors to the pie safe in the dining area. She opened one of the kitchen cupboards. The boxes of tea, herbs, spices, and other items had been moved around.

As she checked her house, she tried to tell herself she was imagining things. To the casual viewer, the house didn't look like anyone had trashed it. But Beverly knew her own order—the order within her chaos—and this wasn't it. Somebody had invaded her house. And that unknown someone had been after an unknown something. Money? Valuables? They had searched for it carefully and thoroughly. But what were they looking for?

A glance into the bathroom provided a clue. As she'd raced around the house packing to go on the river trip, she had tipped over a can of Ajax, leaving a little pyramid of white powder on the bathroom floor. Although she had put away the Ajax can, in her haste she had left the powder on the floor, to be swept up when she came back. Now, she clearly saw that two fingers had swiped through the small heap of cleanser.

Drugs. Maybe the intruders had been after drugs. If so, it had been a wasted effort. Beverly didn't have anything more exotic than aspirin in her house.

Quaking with anger, she headed for her kitchen. Here a more meticulous inspection revealed that everything in the category of "white powder" had been especially disturbed: the baking powder, the powdered sugar, the laundry detergent, the flour, the corn starch, and the baking soda in the refrigerator. All the canisters and boxes had been opened and clumsily resealed. Her two salt shakers—the one on the dining room table and the one on the shelf above the stove—had both been emptied, and some salt had spilled.

Beverly was furious. "Goddamn it!" she yelled. She was seriously entertaining the idea of getting in the truck and heading back to the Yampa River forever when the phone rang. "Hello!" she barked into the phone.

"Jesus, Beverly, bite my head off, will you?" Danny Pieri, a Peace Corps friend, was calling from New York City.

"Gosh, Danny, it's you. I'm sorry if I was surly."

"Surly? You were downright vicious. I guess I've caught you in a . . . mood."

"Yes, you have. I just got home and discovered somebody broke into my house while I was gone. I'm livid!"

"What did they take?"

"The salt out of my salt shakers. I've never been so pissed off."

"Bev? Are you OK?"

"No!"

"The salt out of your salt shakers?"

"It's a long story. If I start to tell you about it now, you'll think I've lost all my marbles. Let's talk about something else. How are you? How's Nancy? How's New York City?"

As Beverly and her friend conversed, the phone clicked occasionally, and the hollow echo of their voices made conversation difficult.

"What's with your phone, Bev?"

She groaned. "It may be related to the salt shakers."

"Ooooooookkaaaaaayyy."

"I'll tell you about it another day."

The connection suddenly improved.

"You're finally home. I've been trying to reach you for days."

"I was up in northwestern Colorado on a river trip."

"Oh, yeah, your annual floating beer-bust with Abe and the crew. How is the old guy?"

"No older than you, Danny. He's fine, Andrea's fine. I'm not so fine."

"Hmmm. Maybe we should talk about that, like in person. Can I mooch off you for a few days?"

"Sure. What's up?"

"Well, Nancy and I want to move back to New Mexico, and I'm coming out to job hunt. We've had it with New York. There was a dead person in front of our building yesterday morning, a diabetic street lady. Nobody came to pick up the body until two hours after we called the police. That was the last straw. Nancy's busy with her AIDS research team, so it'll just be me for now."

"It'll be great to have you here. Then I can tell you about what's been happening."

"Are you going to call the cops about the break-in, Bev?"

"I don't see the point. I don't think the intruders took anything other than the salt. The cops will think I'm looney tunes if I tell them that."

"I suppose you're right. Well, take a hot bath and a sleeping pill, if you've got one handy. I'll be there in a week. We can talk about it then."

Beverly felt better after she talked to Danny. She felt even better after she soaked in the bathtub for nearly an hour. The invasion of her house and the thought that someone had pawed though her things—her underwear drawer, for God's sake!—made her feel grimy and unclean. The only consoling thought was the possibility that whoever had scooped up the Ajax from the bathroom floor might have tried to taste it, or better yet, snort it.

After her bath, she put the air cooler on high, double-checked the locks on the doors and windows, and went to bed. Unpacking and cleaning her river gear could wait until morning. She was exhausted.

Unfortunately, she didn't have a sleeping pill. She spent a terrible night, tossing and turning, unable to lose herself in the narcotic of slumber. Then, toward dawn, she had a terrifying dream. She was sitting by the river at Jones Hole, alone, with no one else in sight. Suddenly, a man who looked like an old Hitler, with greasy white hair and a florid face, emerged from bushes along the path beside the river. Wearing a dirty cowboy shirt and shiny navy blue pants, he strode down the path toward her, his mouth twisted in an evil sneer. When he got closer, she saw he had a dagger in his hand. She tried to run away, but her legs wouldn't work. She tried to scream for help, but nothing came out of her mouth. She was frozen, speechless, and terrified. Then she saw Steve sitting on a rock nearby. She waved her arms frantically and squeaked out a call for help.

He shook his head tiredly. "You're exaggerating, Beverly. That man's not going to hurt you."

But the ugly man kept coming toward her, the sun glinting off the knife in his fist.

Steve yawned, picked up his tennis racket, and walked off.

Beverly tried to call out to him, but her voice didn't work. She tried harder to get away, but her feet were cemented to the ground. The man raised the knife over his head and just as he was about to plunge it into her, she woke up.

She sat up in bed, her heart pounding, and her legs aching terribly. Her cotton shift and the sheet beneath her were damp with sweat. For what seemed like hours, she lay curled in a tangle of bedding, trying to calm her terror.

Slowly, the dawn's pale light seeped through the shutters of her bedroom window, transforming scary, murky shadows and shapes into friendly, familiar objects—the fluttering leaves of the quince bush outside the bedroom window, the bedposts draped with her clothes and bead necklaces, Magdalena's porcupine quill box atop the chest of drawers. From the back yard, she heard Hahn Solo caw a boisterous welcome to the new day. She wished she could be as bold and cheery. By now she had stopped shaking, but all her muscles still ached. Her entire body felt worn out and flaccid as old elastic, as if she were coming out of another bout of dengue, the debilitating malaria-like fever she'd had twice during her Peace Corps service.

Determined to overcome the nightmare's terror, she swung her legs out of bed, threw on a T-shirt, shorts, and flip-flops, and walked out into the morning's coolness to feed her turkeys and chickens. When she got to the chicken coop, she discovered her birds were nearly out of feed.

"Sorry, girls, and you too, Hahn," she apologized. "Breakfast: Coming soon to a chicken feeder near you."

The day before Beverly left for the river, she'd bought a couple of bags of hen scratch, but in her haste, she forgot to move them from the trunk of the Dumpster to the coop for Doña Lupe, who was bird-sitting for her.

When she unlocked the Dumpster's trunk and raised the heavy hatchback, the lining flopped down onto the feed sacks. All the buttons that had fastened it to the door were gone. In fact all the car's interior linings had been torn from the frame and sloppily put back in place. The feed sacks had been slit open, and mixed grains were spilled all over the trunk. The ashtray, which Beverly used only as a file for bank receipts, lay on the floor in front of the passenger seat, and the papers that had been in it were strewn about the car like oversize confetti.

She slammed the car doors shut, stomped into the house, and dialed Steve's home number. On the twentieth ring, he picked up the phone. When he heard her voice, he groaned loudly. "Why on earth are you calling me in the middle of the night, Beverly?"

"Somebody rifled and trashed my house while I was gone, and there's chicken feed scattered all over my car!" she bellowed into the phone.

"Calm down. Calm down. I can't understand you when you're frothing at the mouth."

"How do you know I'm frothing? This is a telephone, not a TV."

"I have a visual image based on years of experience. Now slow down and tell me what happened. Start at the beginning and proceed slowly and cogently."

She did as Steve asked. "This is a fucking invasion of my privacy," she said with a slow burn.

"I understand. Truly I do. I suggest you file a police report."

"Right. 'Officer, somebody broke into my house and stole two fingers of Ajax from the bathroom floor and emptied all my salt shakers and slit my feed sacks open.'"

"Don't be glib. Tell them about your car being vandalized while you were gone. Tell them you believe someone broke into your house, but you have not determined what, if anything, is missing, and try to make as much sense as you possibly can."

"I don't make any sense. I know that's what you think." She was on the verge of tears.

"That's not what I meant. I keep telling you, I believe you totally. Well, almost totally."

"Why should I bother with a police report?"

"Because if more stuff like this happens, and if someday you catch somebody at it, there will be a record. Understand?"

"Yeah, I understand." She mumbled her thanks, hung up, and phoned the Albuquerque Police Department. The dispatcher said she'd send someone out.

Looking across the street at Doña Lupe's porch, she saw Ricky sitting upright in his wheelchair, Pooh beside him. "I'll be right over," she shouted.

Back inside her house, she hunted up the presents she'd bought for Ricky and his foster mother on her trip and hastily wrapped them in bits of recycled Christmas paper.

When she hopped onto Doña Lupe's porch with her gifts, Pooh raised her head and thumped her tail listlessly a couple of times. Ricky was not smiling. Beverly assumed he was mad at her for not coming over the minute she got home. "I'm sorry, guy," she said apologetically, kissing his cheek. "I got in late last night, and I didn't come to visit because I didn't want to wake you."

"Uuuuuuhhhhnnnn!" Ricky said, agitated, waving his arms and squirming in his chair. Noting the strain in his neck muscles, she knew he was upset. It was times like these when she wished he could talk. The boy looked at her intently through his thick glasses.

"And then I got a long distance call from New York. I was pretty angry. It looks like somebody broke into my house while I was gone."

"Nuuuuuhrrrrunnnng!" Ricky groaned, twisting in his chair.

"Yeah. Can you believe that? They went through all my drawers and cupboards. The freezer. My tool box. My sewing kit. Everything. They didn't steal anything, but they snooped through my personal stuff. Like my jewelry box and my underwear drawer. I am really frosted. And then my car. They ripped out the lining of the Dumpster and slashed open the feed sacks."

"Aaaaaahrrraaagh," Ricky moaned.

"So what can I do? Steve told me to call the cops and make a report, so I'm doing that. A lot of good it'll do. But, hey, how've you been, guy? I missed you. It was a great trip. I took pictures for you."

"Naaaarrrrgh!" Ricky said, his head rolling to one side.

"Ricky, are you trying to tell me something?"

"Yunggh. Naaaaaahhhhhrrrrll!"

"You saw them! You saw the guys who went into my house!"

"Yaaaaagggh. Puuuuuuhh."

"You saw them, and so did Pooh. Jesus!"

Just then an APD squad car pulled up in front of Beverly's house. She told Ricky she'd be right back and trotted across the street to talk to the policeman. She showed him the damage to the Dumpster. He took notes, but she could tell he was annoyed at being bothered by something so trivial.

"A number of things in my have been disturbed, but so far, nothing seems to be missing," she told the officer. She didn't mention the salt or the Ajax, bearing in mind Steve's admonition to make sense.

The policeman grunted and didn't ask for details. After he'd walked around the house and checked the locks, he said, "No signs of forced entry, ma'am."

"But someone was in the house for sure, she said. "The kid across the street saw them."

The policeman raised his eyebrows a few notches. "Oh yeah? Did he get a license number or anything?"

"Well, he can't talk. It's the kid in the wheelchair over there." She nodded across the street to Ricky on Doña Lupe's porch.

"Oh," the policeman said. Then he looked at Beverly with his eyes screwed half shut and his head tilted to one side. "So if he can't talk, how do you know he saw something?"

"Well, I can kind of communicate with him. Do you want to talk to him?"

"Lady, I don't have time. What's the matter with him anyway?"

"Nobody really knows. It seems to be a syndrome that affects Native American and Chicano kids. But nobody's interested in studying it."

"Huh," the cop said. He wrote some things down on the report, then handed Beverly his clipboard and a pen. "Sign here."

She glanced at the report form. The policeman's scrawl was brief and illegible. She signed her name in the box labeled "victim." The cop got back in his squad car and drove off.

Beverly walked back across the street, and Doña Lupe came out of her house to say hello. "Richard sure miss you," she said, wiping her hands on her apron, whisking a stray strand of gray hair back from her crinkled parchment face. "Every day he out here watching your house, looking for you. I tell him every day how many more days before you coming back."

For the time being, Beverly decided not to mention the break-in to Doña Lupe. It would only upset her. She thanked the elderly woman for taking care of her birds. "I hope they didn't give you any trouble. And I hope you got some eggs."

"Oh, they no trouble. Those turkeys, they sure eat a lot. The chickens, they give me egg every day. Pink, blue, green, like Easter. They so pretty. Richard love to eat chicken egg."

Doña Lupe refused the money Beverly tried to give her for taking care of the poultry, as she knew she would. But she did accept the present Beverly had bought for her in Colorado. Smiling shyly, she slowly and carefully unwrapped a clear plastic dome that depicted an alpine village scene and showered snow when she shook it. On the base it said "Vail, Colorado." And on the underside a sticker read, "Made In Taiwan."

"For my collection. Now I got twenty-six." Doña Lupe laughed. Beverly smiled. Her present was a hit.

Clawing at the loosely fastened Christmas paper on his gift, Ricky unwrapped an oversized red T-shirt with "Colorado" emblazoned on it in large white letters. He held up the shirt with his gnarled shaking hands and smiled broadly while Pooh beat her tail on the porch in approval. "Thhhh yuuuhhhhhh."

"You're welcome. Hope it fits." Beverly leaned over Ricky's chair and gave him a big hug. "I have to get going. I'm already late for opening the store. I appreciate you and Pooh taking care of my house. I know you did your best." She squeezed his hand and ruffled the dog's ears.

Two

The next week was a busy one. Lucille took a few days off to go camping. In between waiting on customers, Beverly tackled the mound of paperwork that had piled up in her absence. She came home late and left early for the store. It was sultry in Albuquerque as the summer rainy season approached. Clouds gathered every afternoon, promising rain, but only a few drops fell. In the unusually high humidity, the store's evaporative cooler merely stirred the hot, soggy air. By day's end, she was sweaty, tired, and cranky.

To add to her discomfort, military-looking young people came into the store nearly every day. They'd stay a half hour, forty minutes, wasting her time. They never bought anything. Invariably, they asked where her pre-Columbian art was and insinuated she was a smuggler of national patrimony goods stolen from helpless third world peoples. She'd sit at the front desk writing a letter or working on bookkeeping, ignoring them as best she could while they rooted through her inventory like pigs hunting for truffles.

One day she caught a young man with a buzz cut taking photographs of the pottery shelf. She flashed him a big, phony smile. "I'm sorry. We don't allow photography."

"Why not?" he huffed.

"It's store policy," she said, still smiling.

"But why?"

She shrugged. "It's the owner's policy. I just work here."

The man snorted and started to say something, then stopped himself, slung the camera over his shoulder, and strode angrily out the door.

Late one afternoon after closing, she drove to the airport to meet Danny Pieri.

"You look tired," he said when she greeted him at the gate. "Let's go have a drink and watch the sun light up the Sandías."

When Danny hoisted his suitcase into the trunk of the Dumpster, he saw the lining was duct-taped to the hatchback. "What happened?" he asked.

"Buy me a big margarita and I'll tell you all about it," she said.

They drove to the Monte Vista Fire Station, a restaurant near the university. Over drinks on the upstairs terrace, she told him about the rafting expedition. Before long, she began to focus on the weird aspects of the trip: Jack and the cocaine, the helicopter, the Longmont Post Office.

"Then when I got home, I found my house had been broken into. Everything that could be classified as white powder was messed with."

"Ah, the stolen table salt."

"Whoever it was tore the lining out of my car and slit the feed sacks that were in it, no doubt hot on the trail of more Ajax or salt. And every day paramilitary teenagers plague my store with stupid and offensive questions." Tears streamed down her cheeks.

Danny took her hands in his. "Somebody's harassing you and that's bad enough. But you're also dealing with the inevitable letdown from your river trip. A friend of mine has a theory about the physics of vacations."

"Explain."

"OK. When you're on a wonderful, relaxing vacation somewhere, you're in this wavelike pattern." He took a pen from his pocket and drew a rolling wave on his cocktail napkin. "Then when you get back into the city and you resume your normal, hectic kind of daily routine, dealing with a million people, noise, telephone calls, traffic, you're in *this* kind of pattern." He drew a jagged-edged up-and-down line. "The two patterns—the rolling motion and the jagged one—don't mesh. It takes a while for you to kind of ease out of one and into the other. And in the meantime, you're disoriented and bummed out."

"Interesting. On the river, most people take a few days to simmer down and get into the groove of things," she said, drying her eyes. "We call Day Four 'attitude adjustment day.'"

Danny nodded and doodled on the cocktail napkin. "You've come back from a wonderful, relaxing vacation, albeit one with intrusions, and back here, you have visits from people who threaten you and your business, so the clash of opposing patterns is particularly disturbing. I don't know if this is helpful."

"Yeah, it is. I've really been miserable since I got back—and not just because of the break-in and the cretins snooping around the shop. But until now, I haven't understood why. The physics of vacations. Thank you, Doctor. I'll bear this in mind."

"Allow me to prescribe another margarita and I'll tell you something else that occurs to me. Maybe the people coming into your store are customs trainees. From what you tell me, they're young and stupid, they have a certain look, and they all ask the same dumb questions."

"Hmmm. And I'm their guinea pig. Great."

The next day, after Danny interviewed for jobs in Albuquerque he drove up to Santa Fe in a rental car to spend a few days talking to people in real estate. When he returned, he and Beverly went out for dinner at Sadie's, a Mexican restaurant housed in a bowling alley. The hostess recognized Beverly and gave them one of the choice tables, a booth with a view of the lanes below.

"I'm impressed," Danny said, as they slid across the cracked orange vinyl seats and rested their elbows on the tacky Formica-topped table.

"Stick with me, guy. This is my town."

With the sound of rumbling bowling balls and crashing pins in the background, Danny talked about his interviews. "It's going to be difficult to land a good job, but I'm confident I'll find one eventually. I have to tell you something, Bev," Danny said, leaning across the table and lowering his voice. "There is definitely something weird going on. See that guy two tables over? The balding one with the Boston Blackie mustache?"

Beverly casually turned. "You mean the cool postadolescent dude in the white T-shirt?"

"Yes. Well, I saw him about five times in Santa Fe. He sat near me twice at lunch, he was behind me in the pharmacy yesterday when I went to buy some sunscreen, and I saw him hanging out on a park bench when I was walking around the plaza."

"Hmmm. He doesn't look like your type."

Danny laughed. "No, he's not. Sometimes he has the mustache; sometimes he doesn't. Once he was wearing gold-rimmed glasses, a short-sleeved shirt, a tie, and one of those canvas Tilly hats. Another time he was in street-person gear, a greasy T-shirt and jeans and a dirty backpack. But it's the same guy. I'm tempted to go over there and deck him."

"Look at that sewer pipe neck of his. He'd probably crunch you like a tortilla chip."

"He's not the only bizarre thing that happened in Santa Fe. My first morning in town, when I was walking down Otero Street, I turned around and saw the couple that sat next to me on the plane from Dallas walking behind me. When I said hello to them, they looked at me really weird, like they'd never seen me before.

So I said, 'You were on the plane with me from Dallas.' And the guy said, 'No, you must be mistaken. We're from Denver.' I swear it was the same couple. I remembered them because of the guy's horrible wig. I mean, it looked like a road-kill squirrel glued to the top of his head.

"And that's not all. The next morning, when I was sitting by the fountain in Sena Plaza, reading a paper and drinking coffee, a woman wearing a neck brace took my picture several times.

Later she was sitting in a car next to mine when I came out of a job interview on the other side of town. What's going on?"

"You think I understand it? Their harassing you makes me especially mad. If the customs guys have a beef with me for making complaints to Congress or for helping Pancha, then why don't they say so? But to do all this weird stuff to my friends is too much."

"They're bullies, Beverly. Let's go over and confront that guy right now."

They looked at the table where the man had been sitting, but he was gone. Just then, the waitress arrived with their guaco chicken taco dinners.

Three

A week later, Beverly was sitting alone at the front desk at La Ñapa when the postman dropped by a bundle of mail. A postcard featuring an oversized jackrabbit with antlers, the mythical jack-alope, topped the pile. Beverly read it first.

"I'm still waiting for the river goddess to shower me with chi. Miss you. XXX Flash. P.S. If you write, sign it Auntie Bev or my old lady will get all snarky on me."

Flash and his old ladies, Beverly laughed to herself. The man survives on the largesse of women with hearts of gold.

Next, a fat envelope caught her eye. It had a Boston postmark but no return address. As usual, the envelope had been opened and resealed. After she read a few lines of the unsigned type-written letter, she realized it was from Doc's contact in Boston.

```
CONFIDENTIAL MEMO
To: Ms. Beverly Parmentier

As requested by your associate, who wishes to
remain unnamed, we made some inquiries on your
behalf. The information is not readily available
to the general public, but our contacts in the law
enforcement community have been most helpful. At
this time, we are able to provide you with the
following information, which we hope will be of
assistance to you and your attorneys in preparing
the appropriate legal action:
   1. Neither you nor your business, La Ñapa, is
listed in the TECS computer—Treasury's data bank
of persons suspected of smuggling, drug running,
and other illegal activities. Our contacts
```

conclude that any law enforcement interest in you and your business may be ancillary to another investigation of which you are not a target. It is also possible the interference by local law enforcement personnel in your personal and professional affairs may be of a rogue or retaliatory nature.

2. Many in the national law enforcement community believe the United States Customs Service is seeking to expand its law enforcement mandate beyond border and port areas. Customs' role in the War on Drugs as well as in the Cultural Patrimony Initiative (see below) have provided opportunities to USCS to request and obtain special investigative and enforcement powers from Congress. For example, the surreptitious opening of U.S.-originated as well as foreign-originated mail, packages, freight, and travelers' luggage is now within the purview of USCS.

3. The CP Initiative is generally regarded by administration critics as an ameliorative gesture toward those countries the United States is pressuring on drug and "democracy" issues: El Salvador, Bolivia, Guatemala, and Colombia. The U.S.'s propaganda arm, the United States Information Service, works in concert with countries to identify items deemed worthy of the designation "national patrimony," and Congress passes laws proscribing the importation of those items into the United States. USCS investigates and prosecutes persons violating those laws.

4. USCS trains agents in Albuquerque at the Department of Energy's All Agency Training Academy based at Kirtland Air Force Base. The training

program, managed by Schlachthof International, a multinational security firm, usually involves eighty or so trainees at a time. Emphasis is placed on improving agents' language and cultural skills vis-á-vis Central and South America. Some language training takes place in Antigua, Guatemala, and Quito, Ecuador. Trainees also receive general instruction in weapons and investigation and surveillance techniques (including photography and wiretapping). The training program, in which local USCS Office of Enforcement personnel sometimes serve as instructors, strives to maintain a low profile. However, Schlachthof has been the object of a number of well-publicized lawsuits, chiefly discrimination suits filed by female employees of AATA and unfair competition actions filed by competitors, which allege that SI has bribed customs officials to obtain the lucrative training contracts. Several years ago, the DOE's Inspector General ordered SI to get rid of its large stockpile of wiretapping equipment, but to date they have not done so.

5. Since the mid-eighties, USCS has been criticized for heavy-handedness in its dealings with airlines, airports, general aviation, importers, other law enforcement agencies, and its own personnel. At the same time, there is thought to be wide-scale corruption among USCS agents. Border-state officials may be accepting payoffs and/or favors from drug smugglers. For example, although the El Paso port is known to be one of the most active for drug smuggling, customs has reported no major seizures of cocaine for more than two years. Agency employees who report

suspicious activities or incidents of corruption
are demoted and/or transferred to undesirable
postings, or pressured to take early retirement.
Oversight of the USCS, charged to the House Ways
and Means Subcommittee on Trade as well as the
Department of the Treasury's Inspector General's
office, is weak and ineffectual.

We hope that the above has been informative, and
if possible, we will provide you with additional
information in the near future. Feel free to
contact us through your associate if we can be
of further assistance.

Beverly read the letter a second time. She was into her third read
when a woman cleared her throat. Like Miss Muffet when the
spider suddenly landed on her tuffet, she leaped off her stool. A
customer was standing in front of the sales desk holding an embroidered dress and a credit card. Beverly apologized, processed
the card, and wrapped the dress in tissue paper.

The information provided by Doc's contact was a lot to digest.
It helped her understand some of what was going on at customs
in a large sense and provided clues to why they might have ini-
tially placed her and her business under surveillance. But what
the letter didn't explain was customs' persistence.

Four

In his office three floors above the downtown Albuquerque post office, Ray Zoffke read a photocopy of the mysterious letter to Beverly Parmentier from Boston. He slammed his fist down hard on his desk. "Goddamn it!" he groused. "Whoever is behind this is butting into my business, and I don't like it one bit. I guess I could call the Office of Enforcement in Boston to see if we can track down the letter writer, but I have nothing to go on. None of those idiot trainees inspecting Beverly's mail had enough sense to check it for fingerprints before they sent it back to the post office to deliver. I just can't believe this. Few people know the TECS database exists. It's supposed to be top secret."

The letter unnerved Zoffke. Whoever had written it had some inside dope on the agency. He briefly considered filing charges against Beverly to find out who had gotten the TECS information. But then she'd know he'd been reading her mail, and she'd bitch to Congressman Ovni again.

Zoffke read on. "Information. . .which we hope will assist you and your attorneys in preparing the appropriate legal action."

Does she actually think she can sue customs? Zoffke scoffed. But he had to wonder what she was up to. Who the hell was helping her? Attorneys, plural? He knew about Steve Bronstein. But he was no threat. The guy didn't care about anything but his own damn career. Maybe she had something else going on.

He slapped his palm down on the photocopied report. "That bitch is a major pain in the ass," he muttered to himself. Zoffke knew her latest salvo, alerting her import store buddies to customs trainee visits, could stir up a hornet's nest. If the importers realized their stores were being used for surveillance practice and got together to file a complaint, it could cause big problems.

They'd get some goddamn crybaby liberal journalist to pitch a fit in the papers. Then Eistopf would want to know whose idea it was. Well, Zoffke still thought it was a good plan. Surely none of those shopkeepers noticed the AATA kids until Beverly started calling them. And she had the nerve to call agency men Nazis!

He balled up the report and attempted to pitch it into a wastebasket in a corner of his office. The crumpled paper flew a few feet, then fell to the floor where it lay like a used Kleenex.

Ray Zoffke knew about Nazis. His long-gone, son-of-a-bitch wife-and-kid-beating father had been a real one, a lieutenant in the SS. Her cavalier pejorative made his blood boil.

Then there were those goddamn photographs she took of him and his friends at Delgado's. She could cause big trouble with those. Had the film really been destroyed like she told her birthday pals over the phone?

To be on the safe side, Zoffke and Elroy had paid a visit to her house when she was out of town. They'd looked high and low for the photos, with no luck, and were also unsuccessful in finding any drugs in her place. If it hadn't been for that damn kid in the wheelchair and his vicious little mutt that attacked him while they were going through her car, they would surely have found something. He didn't trust Beverly one bit. She was sneaky. Everybody has something to hide, and he was damn certain Parmentier was no different.

She needs to be taught a lesson, Zoffke thought. If I can nail her with something good, she'll be seriously compromised, and nobody will listen to any accusations she makes about me. Or she'll be willing to work out a deal.

Zoffke had turned his attention back to his paperwork when the telephone rang. His boss, Rupert Eistopf, wanted an update on the Operation Pillage task force. "We haven't heard from you for a while on this, Ray," Eistopf said.

Zoffke squirmed. "I'm a little behind in my reports, sir, but we're making progress. Especially now with the added manpower from the AATA trainees, who are gathering information on local importers, we're learning more every day about the smuggling ring here in New Mexico."

"Did you ever get a warrant to nail that importer who interfered with your raid?"

"Not yet. We're still working on it. But it turns out she's involved in drugs as well as pre-Columbian."

"No kidding?"

"We had a tip-off, and when she was out of town, we did a little black bag job on her house."

"Shut up, Ray. I don't want to hear about that kind of thing."

"We got a small amount of coke, but I don't think it's enough for a warrant."

"I said, shut up."

"OK, OK. She was up in northwestern Colorado a couple of weeks ago on a river trip, and we think she was actually making a delivery to some of her old connections. We put some guys on the river with her and her pals to try to collect evidence, but they got wise to us. We think they hid the drugs somewhere in the canyon to pick up later."

"You *think* she's involved in drugs. You *think* she was making a sale. You *think* she stashed drugs somewhere. 'Think' doesn't cut it, Ray. Evidence does. I need hard evidence, something the prosecutor can take to a grand jury."

Eistopf's voice became angrier. "You've got a lot of manpower, and you're going through a lot of dough, Ray. Don't forget, I have to justify these expenditures higher up the food chain, and you have to explain them to me. I want to see some action. And I want to see some results."

"Believe me, I do, too," Zoffke said, wiping a hand across his sweaty brow. "We're working on it. I've got my best people on this."

Five

Shortly after Lucille returned from her camping trip, she phoned Beverly at La Ñapa.

"I have some news," she said. "I hope you won't be mad at me. My grandpa is offering to pay my tuition and living expenses so I can attend school full time and finish my degree next year. Summer school starts in a few weeks, and if you can find somebody soon to replace me, I'd like to enroll."

Beverly wasn't completely surprised. Lucille was brilliant, in her own daffy way, and science was her thing, not the import business. "Of course I'm sorry to lose you. You've done a wonderful job. But I understand completely. This is a terrific break for you."

She was trying to sound cheerful, but the news dismayed her. It would be hard to find and train someone quickly, especially someone as dependable, hardworking, and pleasant as Lucille.

"I can still help out during vacations," Lucille said. "And I'll help you train the new person, OK?"

Beverly immediately called other retailers to see if they knew of anyone looking for work. Within two days, a young woman named Sherrell Stahnick came by the store when Beverly was out. She chatted with Lucille and left a résumé that looked pretty good. Sherry had graduated from a college in Texas with a degree in international business, had several years of retail experience, and was fluent in Spanish. Moreover, Lucille said she seemed bright and personable.

Beverly checked out Sherry's references. One was Stacey Rose, an importer Beverly knew slightly who had employed her for a few weeks in Santa Fe. Stacey's gem-importing business had something of a clouded reputation, thanks to a former partner who'd slipped some cocaine into a shipment of Brazilian tour-malines, but word was Stacey had not been involved, and the business had recovered.

"Sherry's smart, she catches on quickly, and she seems reliable and honest," Stacey said. "Her references in Texas checked out, and her past employers thought highly of her. I would have kept her on, but she didn't want to work full time, and I need a full-time person here. I think you'll be pretty happy with her."

Beverly invited Sherry for an interview. She arrived the next morning wearing a low-cut peasant blouse, a calf-length skirt of striped Guatemalan fabric, and a mouth of blood-red lipstick.

"So where did you learn your Spanish?" Beverly asked.

"I spent a summer in Guadalajara, and then I was at language school in Antigua for intensive Spanish," the young woman answered.

"*¿Qué tal estuvo?*"

"Huh?"

The question was a simple one—how had the program been. It was unlikely Sherry was as fluent in Spanish as she claimed, but then, Beverly only needed someone with a passing knowledge of the language. "What interests you about working here in the store?"

Sherry looked down at her sharp fingernails, painted the same vivid red as her mouth, then flicked her long chestnut hair back from her face.

"Well, I thought maybe I'd like to have my own clothing busi-ness some day. You know, design clothes and have them made in Guatemala or somewhere. This could be a good opportunity for me to learn all about the importing business. Y'all do a lot of im-porting?"

"Not a *lot,* but some. Importing clothing is a tough, compli-cated business. At times, I think it's not worth the hassles from customs."

Sherry flashed a toothy smile that had a bit of lipstick on it.

"I see from your résumé that you only worked for Stacy Rose for a few weeks. Can I ask why you left?"

"Oh, Stacey didn't have enough work for me. I need at least twenty hours a week."

Why would she lie about that? Beverly wondered. But maybe Sherry had quit for other reasons. She wouldn't be the first person to fudge a résumé.

Sherry was nice looking, her shiny hair pulled neatly back from her oval face and thick black Frida Kahlo eyebrows that nearly met over her wide brown eyes. Though she wasn't beautiful, she certainly was zaftig, her principal pair of attributes announcing themselves proudly at the neckline of her low-cut blouse.

Beverly described the responsibilities in detail, then asked if she thought she would enjoy the job and be willing to commit to at least a year.

"No problem," Sherry replied.

"Do you have any questions?"

"No, I'll do fine."

Beverly was somewhat put off by the inflated opinion Sherry seemed to have of herself, but she needed someone quickly. "You're hired," she told her.

Síx

Dave was on his hands and knees pulling weeds from the front flower beds at La Ñapa when Sherry Stahnick, AATA trainee, parked her vintage BMW, sauntered up the walkway, and went into the store. What was Sherry up to, Dave wondered? He waited a few minutes, then followed her in to check things out. Beverly introduced him to Sherry, her new salesgirl.

Dave was shocked, but he did an excellent job of not showing it. He wiped his dirt-caked hands on his jeans and shook Sherry's hand uneasily.

"I'm Sherry Stahnick," she said smugly. "And you're?"

"Dave. Dave Carney," he mumbled. "Nice to meet you."

He wandered into the back room, saying he was going to make coffee if anyone wanted some.

A couple of minutes later, Sherry walked into the kitchen and paused at Dave's elbow. Her broad smile stretched nearly ear to ear.

"Whose bright idea was this, Stahnick?" he hissed.

She leaned close to whisper in his ear. "Whose idea do you think it was? Zoffke's, of course."

He shoved the plastic filter holder into Beverly's new automatic coffee maker and flicked the machine's switch. "There's nothing going on here," he said in a low voice.

"We'll see about that," she whispered, standing so close to him he could feel her breath hot on his face. "Zoffke says she's just lying low for a while. Her and that Salvadoran guy and his pregnant manager."

The machine began to burble and spurt water into the filter.

"So I'm undercover to get the particulars. Then we'll bust 'em."

"Zoffke watches waaaaaaay too much TV," Dave muttered. "His

mind is fried. He should have talked to me before he sent you over here." He opened the cupboard above the coffee machine and got out a mug. "Want a cup, Ms. Stahnick?" he asked with a tight smile.

"No thanks, Dave," she said. She tugged her blouse down and looked up at him from beneath her prominent eyebrows. "Coffee causes breast cancer."

"It doesn't either," he said, eyeing her swelling chest as she took a deep breath and tossed her hair back over her shoulder. "Hey!" he yelled loudly toward the front of the store. "Coffee's on. Anyone want a cup?"

"Later, thanks." Beverly yelled back.

"I think we ought to have a little talk," Dave said. "But not here."

"How about my place?" she said, leaning across him to fill a glass with water from the tap. "I live over by the university."

Dave closed his eyes and shook his head tiredly. "Stahnick, the place is García's on Central. The last booth on the right in the front room. The time is seventeen thirty hours. Today. Be there."

He knocked back his coffee, plunked the mug down beside the coffeemaker, and began to speak in a barely audible voice. "When you are here, Stahnick, or if you meet me in the hamburger palace across the street or run into me at the post office, you will at all times follow procedure. I am a dumb-fuck gardener, and you are a bimbo store clerk, and we don't know each other except as such. Got that?"

She clenched her teeth, and her mouth puckered into a tight red seam. "Yes, *sir*," she hissed.

Dave smiled, grabbed his cap and garden gloves off the counter. "Good," he said and pointed to the coffee cup. "Now wash that."

Without waiting for her response, he jerked the cap down on his head and left through the back door.

Dave arrived at García's fifteen minutes before his appointment with Sherry. He sat in a booth in the far corner of the restaurant beneath a mirror, sipping a steaming cup of coffee, and watching the waitresses swirl around the tables with coffee pots in a constant surveillance mode. The old girls with their big hair, short skirts, frilly Mexican blouses, and sparkly nail polish that matched their sparkly eye shadow, were a cheerful and chatty lot, calling the customers they didn't know "hon" and greeting the regulars by name in English or Spanish. In a whirlwind of tireless activity, they took orders, delivered steaming platters of Mexican food, and picked up empty dishes.

A six-foot-long rattlesnake skin on the wall above the glass case that held pies and *pan dulce,* plastic *ristras* of green and red chile around the door frames, sequined Mexican sombreros, dolls and clowns on the wall over the lunch counter, and laminated hand-lettered signs advertising the specialties *de la casa* constituted García's permanent décor. A riot of bright-colored paper decorations, reflective of the season, filled the restaurant's remaining wall and ceiling space. Although it was June, Dave assumed the current theme was Easter. Piñatas of bright yellow chicks, Big Bird, pink bunny rabbits, a fuchsia Miss Piggy, and oversize Easter eggs swung from the ceiling, connected by swags of tufted crepe paper in pastel hues. The low-slung lunch counter, occupied by a permanent coterie of *viejitos,* old guys, was decorated with baskets of day-glo plastic eggs set in shrill green shredded cellophane.

García's was Dave's favorite lunchtime restaurant. Although the coffee was wimpy, the food was good, plentiful, and cheap.

While he waited for Sherry, he thought back to his exchange with her in La Ñapa. Maybe he had pulled rank on her a little too hard and fast. After all, she was just a kid, a trainee. But she had a helluva lot to learn, she was a smart-ass, and Dave was goddamned if he was going to let her blow his cover at Beverly's. He had his raise and pension to protect, by God.

Suddenly, all the heads in the restaurant were turning toward someone who had just come in. Dave wasn't surprised when Sherry came into view, swinging her hips and tits through a gauntlet of old-fart admirers as she made her way toward him. He looked at his watch. She was right on time.

She plunked her large leather purse down on the table and slid onto the bench opposite him. He could see she was pissed off. Time for a little fence mending, he thought. He needed her co-operation. "I think I owe you an apology, Ms. Stahnick."

She shrugged and flipped her hair back from her face.

"You know, I've been in the agency . . . with the firm," he corrected himself, "for a long time. Twenty-two years, in fact. And sometimes I simply forget things have changed. And not only with the . . . firm . . . but here in the United States as well. I was in the field—in the *selva*—for almost three years. Got back just a few months ago. It takes a while to readjust."

"Where's Selva?" she asked as she looked around for a passing waitress, who quickly appeared. Sherry ordered a cup of decaf.

Dave hesitated. These trainees were supposed to be fluent in Spanish, and this kid didn't recognize the word for jungle? "In the jungle. Peru."

"Huh," she said, reaching across the table for a little plastic cup of nondairy creamer. She peeled back the foil seal with her long fingernails, and imitation cream spurted down the front of her red silk blouse. "Fuck!" she exclaimed loudly, grabbing a paper napkin and brushing madly at the wet spots on her chest.

The entire lunch counter of *viejitos* turned toward her.

Dave closed his eyes and took a deep breath. "What I'm trying to say is . . ."

She interrupted him. "Yeah, I know what you're trying to say. You're not used to working undercover with broads."

Dave took a slow sip of ice water.

Sherry continued. "Lita, one of our trainers at AATA—you probably don't know her, she's retired Secret Service—Lita gave us women a lecture about all the macho bullshit we're going to run into in law enforcement."

"Keep your voice down," Dave said, looking around to see if anyone was listening. Negative.

Sherry followed his gaze around the restaurant and seemed genuinely chagrined to have spoken too loudly. "Sorry," she whispered.

"Look," he said. "I truly did not intend to offend you this afternoon. I guess I was just a little surprised that I wasn't consulted beforehand."

Sherry flicked her hair back from her face and tucked a strand behind her ear. "Zoffke is giving this investigation top priority. And Washington has given him the go-ahead to use AATA manpower. We've got Beverly covered like a blanket. And the other New Mexico based importers, too."

Dave shook his head. "I hate to tell you this, Stahnick, but the cultural patrimony thing is a crock. A make-work project. I've seen it a million times. It's politics, a trade-off to countries like Bolivia, El Salvador, and Guatemala if they'll cooperate with us on drug-interdiction efforts and tone down their death-squad activities. I seriously doubt there's any major trafficking in artifacts here in New Mexico by two-bit importers like Beverly, or anybody else, for that matter. Think about it. If it were true, where's the stuff?"

Sherry sniffed. "It's in private collections. We have some undercover guys gathering info on the major collectors now. And you should see all the stuff we confiscated from Galería Galo."

"I heard it was mostly folk art, jewelry, and religious art," Dave said. "And all there was in the way of pre-Columbian stuff was a couple of Colima dogs that are probably fakes. Then Zoffke, looking for his name in lights, tells the newspapers he nabbed a quarter-million dollars worth of valuable pre-Columbian artifacts." He shook his head in disgust.

"That's right," Sherry said defensively. "He was including the religious art in that figure. We think it was stolen from churches. We're sure Beverly and Pancha hid the important pre-Columbian."

"Think about it, Stahnick. Here we are, expending all our time and resources on an importer who makes one or two entries a year for a total of less than ten grand, all the shit small enough to X-ray. Nothing's ever been found in her shipments, her inventory, her luggage, her mail, her bank accounts, or her house. She drives a fifteen-year-old car and lives like a bag lady. But here we are, dedicating significant agency resources to monitoring her. And now we've got not one but two people hanging around her store. In the meantime, a half-mile away from La Ñapa, one of the biggest heroin importers in the country openly does business from his adobe palace in the South Valley like he was running a 7-Eleven. And five blocks from here, in Old Town, there's a guy who's been selling every drug under the sun for forty years. Forty years! You gotta wonder."

"So who's the big South Valley dealer?" Sherry asked, raising her eyebrows. "I haven't heard about this."

Maybe I should shut up, Dave thought. But fuck it. It was time this kid to got clued in on a few realities. "It's a DEA deal," he told Sherry. "But we oughta be in on it. I think the shit's coming across the border in produce trucks, right under our noses. And by shit, I mean pure Mexican brown and coke, not weed. Pre-Columbian artifacts come in through Miami, New York, Houston, and L.A.—where the money and the collectors are and the big auction houses that sell the stuff for megabucks. New Mexico is an insignificant market for artifacts. Drugs are what we ought to have our eyes on here. Some of our own guys have to be involved. But are we taking a good look at our agents' bank accounts and lifestyles? No, we're not. Because we're busy beating up on pregnant women and penny ante shopkeepers. Because Zoffke and the U.S. attorney are hot to be errand boys for the administration's political agenda. And pregnant women and penniless importers are a lot easier to pick on than drug dealers who'll blow you away in a flash if you look at them cross-eyed."

Dave came up for air and took a deep breath. The girl was watching a fly on the wall. Had she heard any of what he'd said? Who the fuck cared? It was something he had to get off his chest. "Can I ask you something, Stahnick?"

"Sure, Dave," she replied, blinking her eyes slowly, her long eyelashes brushing her cheeks.

"Is Zoffke pissed at Beverly about something? I mean, she wrote Congressman Ovni complaining about the airport guys busting up her stuff. But does he have some special beef with her?"

"Well, she called him a Nazi," Sherry replied.

"Like in a letter? Like to Ovni?"

Sherry looked at him in exasperation. "No, not in a letter. She calls him that all the time on the phone, at restaurants in Santa Fe where she eats with her friends, and over at her lawyer's. She says the whole agency's a bunch of Nazis."

"At her lawyer's?" he asked innocently. "Was somebody over there in his office?"

"No, Elroy taped them from the lawyer's parking lot. Piece of cake. Her lawyer friend's desk is in front of a window overlooking the lot, and that's where they were talking. Elroy didn't even have to get out of the van."

"Who's Elroy?"

"Elroy Hardin, that skinny ex-Army kid with the frizzy blond hair. Haven't you seen him over at the task force office? He's part of the Operation Pillage team, too, you know."

"Oh, yeah. Of course, AATA's electronics whiz kid. Zoffke's pet." He looked at his watch. "Oh, boy. It's after six. I've got choir practice at church at seven. I gotta run, Stahnick." He patted her hand. "I hope you can forgive my rudeness this afternoon," he said looking directly into her eyes with a puppy dog sincerity that usually melted women's hearts.

"No problem," she said, whisking her hair back.

"I hope we've cleared the air a little here," he said, letting his hand linger on hers. "I want you to know I'm happy working with you on this case, and I hope you'll let me know if there's any way I can help you, OK?"

"OK," she said. She reached for her purse and slid out of the booth. Dave watched her saunter out the front door, giving the old guys at the counter another cheap thrill.

He pointed his bicycle uphill toward the sanctuary of home and family. As he pedaled through the light early-evening traffic, he thought back to his conversation with Sherry. Jeeze, it was stupid to have been so candid with Stahnick. He could get in big trouble, wagging his tongue about the agency. But it sure felt good to get a few things off his chest. Customs wasn't the same agency he'd joined after Nam. He was glad to be getting out. With people like Zoffke in charge, anything could happen. He was a Nazi. Beverly had that right. Maybe that's why he had his dick in a wringer about her. Zoffke was sensitive about being born in Germany. So he'd exchanged his German accent for a Southern one, and made a point of turning on the charm around Jews. But his true colors were as obvious as if he had a swastika tattooed on his fat forehead.

Dave hated the sonofabitch and the ugly-cop attitudes he brought to law enforcement. A lot of guys did, but there wasn't anything anyone could do. Especially now with an agency chief like von Geier, another asshole Nazi.

Sherry and those baby feds are too much, Dave told himself. What the fuck were they doing up there at AATA? Detailing the entire colony of New Mexican importers. Eighty trainees all over a dozen mom and pop operations. Brilliant! Sending a radioman to tape Beverly's conversation with her lawyer. That wasn't just stupid; it was goddamn felonious. In New Mexico nobody much cared, but in New York or L.A., the leftwingers would go apeshit.

Sherry's most shocking information, however, was about Lita. Well, well, Dave muttered to himself as he worked harder to gain the top of a hill. So Lita was on staff at AATA. That was news to him, big news. He hadn't seen her in, what, ten years? The last he knew, she was on a Secret Service detail guarding Ferdinand and Imelda Marcos in Hawaii, and from time to time, the VP or the First Lady. Rough.

Lita and Dave had entered the agency together, but after a few years, she switched to Secret Service. So Sherry didn't think he knew Lita. Ha! He knew things about Mary Elizabeth Lanier Liebling that maybe she herself didn't know. Like the exact location of a really interesting little kidney-shaped mole, one you couldn't see unless the light was good, you were in a prime position, and Lita's ankles were up around her ears.

Dave's heart ached when he thought about Lita. She was the love of his life, the most brilliant, beautiful, and complex woman he'd ever known. Her long, swaying, white-blond hair, soft as silk floss. Brown onyx eyes, big as an owl's and as keen. Lita could spot a flea at thirty meters and hit it with one quick shot. A body with more tight curves than a Colombian highway. Knockers like ivory satin pillows stuffed with down. A woman with a quick mind and a lascivious nature. And Dave had blown his chances with her. Getting it on with a ditsy file clerk in the cloakroom when somebody was bound to walk in. And that somebody had been Lita. Not two days after they'd been talking about getting married, once Dave had divorced Paulette, of course. The next day, Lita requested the transfer to Secret Service. Dave couldn't think of a better person to give the female trainees a talk about macho fuckheads.

His chest felt as if it were filling with rocks as he rode his bike homeward along Albuquerque's elm-lined streets, thinking about Lita.

Seven

One cool fall morning, Zoffke was hanging his jacket on the coat rack in his office when his secretary buzzed him.

"A Mr. Elías Lechuga for you on line two, sir. Do you want me to take a message?"

Zoffke felt a stab in his gut. "No, I'll take the call."

He picked up the telephone. "Zoffke here. Can I help you?"

"Ray, my man! What's the *qué pasó?*"

Zoffke waited until he heard Melissa click off the line, then he spat into the phone. "I told you to never call me here."

"We haven't heard from you in a while, guy."

"I'll call your mobile in fifteen minutes."

Zoffke slammed down the receiver, put his jacket back on, and left his office, telling Melissa he was going over to the task force office in Old Town for some papers he'd forgotten. His engine roaring, he drove his baby-blue Lincoln Continental out of the parking garage below the Federal Office Building and sped west on Central Avenue to a public phone in front of a gas station. Making certain no one familiar was around, he dialed Lechuga's mobile phone.

"Don't you ever do that again!" he thundered when Lechuga answered.

"Like I said, we haven't heard from you in a while, Ray. I was just checking up on my investment. How's the *ranfla* running?"

"The what?"

"The *ranfla,* man—your baby-blue ride."

"Get to the point, Lechuga."

"*In-for-ma-ci-ón, hombre.* We want our money's worth."

Zoffke cleared his throat and looked both ways up and down

Central. "The Deming aerostat is going to be down all next week for maintenance, until the twenty-first."

"You mean the computer?"

Zoffke shook his head in disgust. "The radar balloon," he said. "It's that huge balloon that hovers over the border near Deming. It's how we track border airplane traffic."

"Hey, great talking to you, Ray. Hope you're enjoying the car."

Eight

On a Saturday night in early October, Beverly sat at her dining room table with a pen and paper. She'd finally summoned the nerve to write Magdalena and accept her offer to pay for a good attorney. It was a letter she'd been mentally working on for weeks. While she tried to write, Ricky and Pooh were watching a Batman video in the living room. The phone rang, shattering her concentration. It was Beverly's dad calling from northern Michigan. It took her a few minutes to understand what he was trying to say. Finally, he stammered out the awful news.

"Magdalena died in New York this morning."

Beverly felt like somebody had kicked her in the stomach. Mag, dead?

"No one knew she had liver cancer. If she'd only told us," he said, "maybe we could have done something for her."

"I can't believe this, Dad. I was just writing her a letter."

"She called me last week, and she never said a thing about being ill. She sounded a little weak, but I thought maybe she had the flu or something. We laughed and talked about a new play on Broadway and made plans to spend New Year's Eve together here in Mill Harbor."

Beverly could barely breathe. "Well, maybe that's the way she wanted you to remember her—upbeat, on the move—not ill and helpless."

"The funeral will be Thursday at the new St. Jude's. Can you come?"

"Of course," she said, hoping she could borrow the airfare from Steve.

When she hung up the phone, she collapsed onto the sofa,

sobbing. Ricky reached for her hand and held it tightly while Pooh jumped onto her lap to lick her teary face.

Later, for what seemed like endless hours, she lay in bed trying to absorb the news. It was only weeks since they'd been together in Mexico, right? Beverly would miss her aunt terribly. As far back as she could remember, Magdalena had been her special pal. Someone she could always count on, her mentor, her rock, her anchor in the storm. One of the few people who'd encouraged her to make something of her life. And one of the few who'd offered to help her deal with the feds. Now Mag was gone. There was a crater in Beverly's life the size of Wyoming.

Steve loaned Beverly the airfare to Mill Harbor, her hometown on Michigan's Upper Peninsula. She flew from Albuquerque to O'Hare and then got on a puddle jumper that stopped in Milwaukee and Green Bay. On the last leg to Escanaba, an hour's drive from Mill Harbor, she was one of only two passengers. The other was a petite dark-haired woman in a floral dress and a fur stole. She had been on the plane from Albuquerque to Chicago, too. A coincidence?

It was always strange to be back in the Upper Peninsula. Since New Mexico had become Beverly's home and frame of reference, things she'd never noticed when growing up in the U.P. now seemed exotic to her—the abundance of green, the endless pines, the broad expanse of Lake Michigan, the humidity, the dead deer beside the highway. Driving past old, familiar buildings like the limestone Congregational church, the turreted red brick Carnegie Library, the abandoned roundhouse in the railroad yard, was like leafing through a sepia-toned magazine, its pages yellowed and brittle with age. The innovations since her last visit—new supermarkets, gas stations, a monstrous Wal-Mart, the half-mile-long paper factory, a slick, four-lane highway that bypassed the old mill towns—had a cartoon-like phony quality to them, as if they had been set into the familiar landscape with computer imaging.

To Beverly's way of thinking, the new St. Jude's Catholic Church, an ugly cement-block and steel-beamed pentagonal building, had been plopped down like a UFO on an asphalt parking lot. Beside it stood the old peaked-roof brick church, where, as children, she and her grade-school classmates had spent countless hours imprisoned in its dark, dank, incense-smothered interior singing dirges at funeral masses for parishioners. The archdiocese had condemned the hundred-year-old building and wanted to tear it down, but parishioners had protested.

A pompous Irish priest presided over Magdalena's funeral, droning the standard prayers without emotion—or, Beverly thought, sincerity. The loyal Catholics in the crowd probably found the service lovely. It had all the requisite parts: homilies read by family members, some OK organ music, beautiful bouquets of flowers on the altar and atop the closed rose-colored metal casket. But Beverly, a devout and practicing *nada,* hated the place, and considered it hollow rather than hallowed. Mag and Beverly had always agreed the Catholic Church was possibly the most morally bankrupt institution on the face of the earth.

In the worst way, Beverly wanted to flee the church. If Magdalena had been present, in some form other than as a corpse, she and Beverly would have slipped out of the building and headed for the nearest bar to enjoy a few beers and maybe a game of pool.

But Magdalena wasn't there. Tears flowed down Beverly's face like rainwater on a bay window.

As the service dragged on, she looked around and noted that everyone else seemed to be engrossed in the service. Then, out of the corner of her eye, she saw a figure standing at the church door—a dark-haired woman wearing a pillbox hat with a veil and a fur stole over a dark green suit. She stared hard. It was the same woman who had been on the planes from Albuquerque to Escanaba.

She nudged the man next to her—Murray, Magdalena's attorney and the only friend who had come from New York for the funeral. "Do you recognize that woman at the back of the church?" she whispered.

When he turned around to look, the woman immediately slipped out the door.

"Nobody I recognize," he said. "And I think I know Magdalena's circle pretty well."

Beverly's mother, a plump, bespectacled woman in a worn cloth coat who was seated across the aisle from Beverly, glared at her as she walked quickly down the aisle to the exit. Outside, the woman was nowhere in sight. Beverly stopped and wrapped her arms around herself against the sharp chill wind. The chances that the dark-haired woman knew Magdalena were slim. The chances she had just happened by the church were even slimmer. Beverly stood in the parking lot with her back to the ugly church and the penetrating November gusts and cried hot, angry tears.

Following the funeral, family and friends reassembled at the new Howard Johnson's on the edge of town for lunch. Murray sat next to Beverly. From her perch at the head of the table, Beverly's mother glowered at him with sharp disapproval whenever he honked into his cloth napkin or shoved a whole roll into his mouth. He ate noisily. He talked with his mouth full. His appetite was astonishing. But he was funny and irreverent, and Beverly could see why he had been a friend of Magdalena's. His eyes misted over every time anyone mentioned her name.

"You and I have to have a little talk," he said as he plunged his fork into a sagging piece of lemon meringue pie.

"Sure," Beverly said, sipping her dessert, a double Scotch on the rocks.

"Meet me in the coffee shop here tomorrow morning, OK? Say ten o'clock. I've got a plane to catch."

That afternoon and late into the evening, Beverly sat around the kitchen table at home with some of her family. Her father told stories about some of Magdalena's wild capers, and everyone got drunk.

She woke up the next morning with a cottony mouth and such a pounding headache that she nearly forgot about her date with Murray. Fortunately, his hotel was just a short walk from her parents' house.

Murray pulled out a chair for her when she approached his table. "Sit down," he said.

She propped up her sore head with her hands, leaning on the table with her elbows for support.

He laughed. "Scotch, huh?"

"Scotch, Bailey's, Chianti, slivovitz, Boone's Apple Farm Wine. I think I'm going to die."

"Well, I hope you'll put me in your will first."

She looked at him quizzically. "How come?"

"Your Aunt Magdalena thought a lot of you."

"Yeah," Beverly said, getting teary-eyed once again. "And she meant a lot to me. She was a real inspiration to me, Murray. Even though I didn't see her but once in a blue moon, she always made me feel special. She thought I could be somebody. And that helped me think that maybe I *could* be somebody. Around here women are doormats. They're some guy's daughter, sister, wife. They're not anybody on their own. And most of them don't want to be.

"When I was in grade school, the nuns would ask us what we wanted to be when we grew up. All the other girls would say they wanted to be mommies or nuns or maybe nurses. But me? I once made the mistake of saying I wanted to be a sailor and join the merchant marine. After that, when I walked down the hall at school, the kids always yelled ship ahoy! or they called me

Captain Ahab. It was awful. For years, Magdalena was the only woman I knew who had gotten out and away and done something with her life. From the earliest time I can remember, she gave me books and paints and sent me postcards from exotic places. She told me I was smart and I could do anything I wanted, when the rest of my family was telling me I was weird and ugly and stupid and I would never catch a husband. And they still think that. I've failed at the only thing in life I was supposed to do. And they're scared to death I'm going to embarrass them. Which I suppose I do on a regular basis."

"Oh, it can't be that bad," Murray said.

"Oh yeah? My mother has everybody's picture on the piano but mine. There must be fifty frames filled with pictures of her beautiful, smiling children and grandchildren littering the top of her baby grand, a pictorial manifestation of her own personal contribution to the population explosion. But no *moi.*"

"Don't feel too sorry for yourself, dear. I have terrific news for you. Magdalena left you some money."

Beverly sat up. "She did? Enough to pay for the plane ticket to her funeral, I hope. I had to borrow money for the fare."

Murray laughed. "Enough to buy a plane, sweetheart."

Beverly stared at him. "What?"

"Yeah," Murray laughed. "You heard me. You wanna buy a plane? You can buy a plane. Magdalena left you more than $900,000."

The elbow propping up her chin slid across the Formica tabletop, her poor, sore bowling ball of a head bobbed, she lost her balance, and the fragile-looking ice-cream-parlor chair she was sitting on tipped over. The next thing she knew, she was sprawled on the restaurant floor, and Murray and the waitress, an elderly lady with a pleasant, floury face, were helping her up. The entire dining room stared as Beverly stumbled to her feet and sat down carefully.

She turned to the waitress. "I think I'll have a Bloody Mary. Extra Tabasco sauce, please. And an English muffin."

The elderly waitress seemed a little shocked, but she went to fill the order.

The Bloody Mary was horrible at first—metallic, bitter. But its taste improved quickly. Soon she felt better. "I don't make a habit of drinking these for breakfast," she told Murray. "However, I now understand their appeal. *Un pelo del perro que me mordió.*"

"Translation?"

"A hair of the dog that bit me."

Murray laughed.

"I didn't know Magdalena had much money," Beverly said.

"Not many people did. I was a little shocked myself when we worked out the revisions to her will some months ago."

"Where did the money come from?"

"It's totally legitimate, if that's what you want to know. In the early days, before she became an editor at Harper's, she worked for a brokerage house. Typing, you know. That was all they let women do back then. But Magdalena was no dummy. She learned the trade. And on the QT, she bought and sold. She paid attention. She networked. And quietly, she invested. She also played a mean game of poker."

"Yeah, I know," Beverly laughed. "When she'd come home to the U.P., she'd play with the local poker hotshots—the chief surgeon at the hospital, the golf pro, the Lutheran minister. She beat them so badly that after a while they wouldn't play with her any more. My mother wouldn't allow card games at our house if Mag was involved. She considered her sister-in-law's poker playing for money unladylike. 'What will people say about our family?' she'd whine. She once told Magdalena to lose a game now and then so she wouldn't upset the men. Mag thought that was a lousy idea. 'Never lose when you can win,' she told me. 'Never.'"

"Well, poker helped her build her stock portfolio," Murray explained. "She was shrewd about who she played with. They may have lost to her, but they weren't losers. She sometimes took her winnings in stock from the guys she beat. She was big on electronics, telecommunications, and auto parts."

"Auto parts?"

"When she saw the post Vietnam War recession coming, she bought into a chain of auto-parts stores, figuring when things got tight, people would be keep fixing up their old clunkers instead of buying new cars. And she was right. Your aunt had some real talent for investing. She could have made even more, but I don't think money interested her all that much."

As Murray and Beverly talked, her mind kept wandering back to his extraordinary piece of news. Beverly rich? It was incomprehensible.

"Did Magdalena give *everybody* in my family $900,000?"

"No," he laughed. "She died a wealthy woman, but not that wealthy. Each of your siblings gets $10,000. And your father gets $50,000. I'll call them about it later. She also bought your parents a first-class, all-expenses-paid trip to New York and London, complete with theater tickets."

"I hope it's nonrefundable. My mother will want to cash it in so they can buy new storm windows."

Murray laughed and shook his head. "It *is* a nonrefundable trip. How did you guess?"

"I know my mother. She and my father haven't had any fun in years, and I doubt she wants to break the habit now. God, Murray, is my family going to be pissed that Magdalena gave me so much?"

"Who says you have to tell them?"

"True," she said, taking a sip of her Bloody Mary. "They never come to New Mexico. So who's to know?"

"Right," Murray replied, cramming half a blueberry muffin into his mouth. Crumbs cascaded down the front of his shirt, adding more debris to the already littered table. "It's going to be a month or so before you receive the funds. I'll be in touch."

Beverly walked home slowly, a fine rain dripping down her face and seeping through her wool ruana. Although it was nearly noon, a bank of fog hung low over the pines and the grimy tarpaper and cement-block buildings of downtown Mill Harbor. In the dim gray light, Beverly stumbled more than once on the uneven sidewalk that was tipped every which way where elm roots had pushed up the cement slabs.

Engulfed in an alcohol-induced mental fog, and with a throbbing head, she found she couldn't absorb the enormity of this change in her life. Maybe the hangover had rendered her incapable of thinking clearly about anything, even terrific news. She didn't feel particularly elated or excited about Murray's news. The initial shock had worn off and was replaced with numbness.

When she got home, she went upstairs to her narrow childhood bed under the eaves and slept for the rest of the day.

The next morning, her sister drove her to Escanaba airport, where she boarded the small plane to O'Hare. Her flight was delayed in Milwaukee by a mechanical problem, and by the time she landed in Chicago, the last plane had already left for Albuquerque. When Beverly requested a hotel voucher, the airline representative responded with a Gallic shrug. "You're on your own," he said.

Faced with the prospect of spending a night in a plastic chair at O'Hare or spending more than a hundred dollars she didn't yet have on a hotel room, she called Patty Siegal, a Peace Corps friend who lived in Chicago. Perhaps she and her husband, Jason, would provide Beverly with a berth somewhere in their twenty-room bungalow on Sheridan Road in Evanston.

An hour later, an airport shuttle deposited Beverly on her

friends' doorstep just as Jason was getting home from his downtown brokerage.

In a spacious, high-ceilinged living room hung with bright-colored Mexican tapestries, Patty, Jason, and Beverly sipped sherry in front of a roaring fire and talked old times and old friends. Beverly told them about Magdalena's bequest. It seemed OK to tell the Siegals, who had more money than God or possibly even the Pope. Nine hundred thousand dollars was probably chump change to them.

"I'd be happy to help you invest," Jason offered. "IRAs, tax planning, annuities, estate planning, there's a lot to think about."

"If it really happens, I'll be in touch with you. I'll believe the money is real when I have cold, hard cash in my hand. It's still such a shock."

Patty threw together a veal marsala dinner with about as much apparent effort as it took Beverly to make toast, and Jason opened a bottle of champagne to celebrate her good fortune.

"Here's to Magdalena," Beverly said, raising her glass, her eyes misty as she drank.

That night, for what seemed like hours, Beverly lay awake beneath crisp percale sheets and a feather comforter on a bed the size of her living room. She stared out the windows of the Siegals' guestroom at the lights of ships traversing Lake Michigan, and wondered how Magdalena's money was going to change her life. What would it be like to be rich enough not to have to first run her desires through the can-I-afford-it edit?

Some things wouldn't change, she told herself. Not even a billion dollars would transform her into a fabulous hostess like Patty. And even if she had the money, she'd never choose to live in a huge house like the Siegals'. Except for the absence of Prince Charming, and the feds' ongoing harassment, she liked her life in New Mexico the way it was. The store, her friends, her funky little adobe house in the valley with its apple trees and chicken coop, her buying trips to Latin America, and her river trips. She could use some new clothes, a new suitcase, and a replacement for her geriatric vacuum cleaner. She might buy something her guests could sit on that was more comfortable than the foam-covered Taos sofa she'd crafted out of two-by-fours. Maybe she'd splurge on a set of matched dishes to replace her chipped, flea-market Fiestaware. Once in a while she'd spend more than five dollars on a bottle of wine. She might even go south in winter to a warm beach or take a trip somewhere she'd always wanted to go—the Galápagos, Kenya, the Caribbean. But no diamonds, no designer clothes, no social climbing. Mag would hate that. And that wasn't Beverly's style.

At least she wouldn't be staying awake nights any more, worrying about how to pay the mortgage and the rent for La Ñapa and the phone bill, especially if she got sick. Magdalena's money was going to take care of her the way the elusive Prince Charming never would. If she were careful, with the help of Jason's financial advice, she'd have an income for the rest of her life. There'd be money left over to give away, and she could help Ricky. Yahoo!

As she tried to imagine her future, she was haunted by one question. What would Magdalena have wanted her to do with her bequest—beyond taking care of the basics? Give it away? Spend it wildly? When it came to her, she laughed out loud. Magdalena would want her to get first-rate legal help to fight the feds. Well, that wasn't a bad idea. The bastards weren't showing any signs of going away.

Beverly declined Patty's offer to drive her to O'Hare and insisted on taking a cab. Jason called the limo company they had used for years. The car arrived promptly at 8 a.m. Sunday, and the Siegals came downstairs in their bathrobes to see Beverly off.

They hugged good-bye, and she sped away with a wave through the back window of the limo.

"So where you from?" the driver asked, eyeing Beverly in his rearview mirror.

The man gave her the willies. He stared at her through the thick panes of his eyeglasses like a Peeping Tom at a bathroom window. His limo driver's cap was perched like a cloth butterfly on a head that was the same size, shape, and color as a basketball. Thatches of furry orange hair stuck out from under the hat, and more orange hair covered the huge hands that gripped the steering wheel as if it were a ring of piano wire.

"New Mexico," Beverly mumbled.

"Oh yeah? You don't talk like you're from New Mexico."

"Well, actually, I'm from the U.P.—Upper Michigan."

"Lemme guess, Mill Harbor." He looked in the mirror again and flashed her an open-mouthed grin crammed with shark teeth.

"No," she said in a panic. "Bayfield."

She took a magazine out of her carry-on bag and held it in front of her face to fend off the driver's attempts at conversation, mentally urging the car to go faster. When they pulled up in front of the airport terminal, she slipped out of the back seat with her luggage before he opened his door and tossed thirty bucks at him over the front seat.

At the gate, she sat in a corner as far away from other passengers as possible, her bag and purse on the adjacent seats so no one could sit next to her, her face hidden behind her magazine. She didn't want to see anyone she'd seen before, and she didn't want to see anyone she might see again. On the plane, she ordered three glasses of wine and read a copy of *Esquire* cover to cover, ignoring the scowls of the pimply man next to her, who was reading a Bible with his finger.

· · · · ·

At the end of a sunny day in early December, Beverly opened her mailbox and retrieved a half dozen pieces of mail. One envelope bore the return address of Murray J. Silverberg, attorney-at-law. Her heart began to pound, resonating in her chest like a Pueblo Indian drum. She sat down on the stoop of her porch, opened the envelope, and withdrew a piece of green paper. For what seemed like ages, she stared at the check until the numbers began to dance.

Intent upon the piece of paper she held in her hand, she didn't see Ricky until he pulled up beside her in his wheelchair, Pooh at his side. "Ricky, how did you get over here?" she asked.

The boy grinned with pride. Then he placed one of his twisted brown hands on hers. "Oooooooh kkkkkk?"

Beverly hugged him. "I'm fine, sweetheart. In fact, I am fabulous. That's why you came over here, isn't it? You saw me crying."

"Uhhhhhhhh," the boy nodded.

"I'm happy, Ricky. I am really, really happy! Sometimes people cry when they're happy, you know." She held the check in front of his thick glasses. "This is money, Rick. It's a *lot* of money. It's gonna buy you a motorized chair and a computer that talks, and it's gonna buy me, well, I don't know what it's gonna buy me. But we're rich!"

Brandishing the check, Beverly laughed and whooped and jumped up and down. Pooh danced on her hind legs, yipping and barking. Ricky threw his head back and howled.

Níne

The more Dave thought about it, the more he regretted expressing his feelings about the agency so candidly to Sherry. What would keep her from blabbing to Zoffke and screwing up his chances for promotion? The girl was green, and she was a conniver.

He embarked on a campaign to get on her good side but quick. Flattery was a good place to start. Sherrell Stahnick thought she was pretty, smart, and clever. When Dave began to pay attention to her, she thought it was smart and clever of him to notice her. He told her how great she looked. He complimented her clothes and her hairstyle. He praised a display she'd set up at the store. In no time, she developed a crush on him. His plan worked beautifully. She hung around when he was weeding at Beverly's, she'd bring him coffee and cookies, she'd sit next to him at task force meetings.

At his insistence, they barely spoke when they were at La Ñapa. Instead, they met at out-of-the-way coffeehouses near the university. Their heads together over steaming lattes, they discussed Beverly, Operation Pillage, AATA, agency politics. He marveled at how quickly she was able to analyze things. He told her she was going to be tops in her class at AATA. He even asked for her advice about gardening. Sherry had a ready opinion on everything and gave him plenty of advice. Much of what she had to say on any given subject, however, was generally stupid, wrong, or obvious.

Soon Sherry wanted to spend more time with Dave. He thought he could now count on her loyalty. One day he couldn't help himself. He stared deep into her eyes and told her his wife didn't understand him. Sherry invited him over to her house after work the next day. He wasn't surprised when she pressed the palm of her hand against his cock. With her other hand on the back of his neck, she drew his face into the warm ravine of her low-cut blouse and backed him into her bedroom.

After that, things got complicated. Everybody wanted more of Dave. Operation Pillage wanted detailed reports on Beverly, and because Dave was a senior member of the task force, Zoffke wanted him to analyze other agents' reports as well. Beverly wanted her rose bushes and watering systems winterized and the tangles of her iris bulbs dug up. Dave's wife complained he was never home and never paid any attention to her or their daughters. And Sherry wanted more and more of his time—and his dick. The woman had the staying power of a steeplechase jockey, and she rode him like one, leaving him sore and bruised and limp. She was getting insistent, she was getting careless, and she was getting out of hand.

He had to break things off with her. He'd appeal to her female compassion and solidarity, pleading he was a married man with a wife and two daughters, and surely she'd understand they needed him.

They met at the tire store office one morning when everyone else on the task force was at a meeting downtown. They sat on the edge of the receptionist's desk and held hands. Dave took a deep breath and moved into his family-man spiel. Sherry dropped her head, and her hair fell forward alongside her face like sheets of rain. She raised her eyes to his, and he saw they were misty. Just as he was getting to the part about how much his teenage daughters needed him, Sherry put a finger to his lips and stood up. Taking him gently but firmly by the hand, she led him into the small, closet-like room where the task force's Xerox machine and office supplies were kept and kicked the door shut.

Dave's resolve melted like butter between her hot, heaving breasts. In seconds, he had her blouse and bra down over her ribs and her skirt up around her waist, and Sherry had his pants and shorts down around his ankles. He hoisted her up onto the Xerox machine and tugged her panties off her legs with his teeth. Sherry grabbed his dick, holding it with both hands like it was a loaded .38. Then they heard the alarm pad beep as someone pressed in the five-digit code. They stared wide-eyed at each other and froze. A key clicked into the lock of the office door, the door opened, and someone in high heels tack-tacked across the wooden floor, coming in their direction. They grabbed for their clothes. The door to the Xerox room opened just as Dave was zipping up his pants and Sherry was jerking down her skirt.

Dave's former girlfriend, Lita, a sheaf of papers in her hand, stood in the door frame. She eyed Sherry and Dave as they fumbled with their clothing. "Well, well," she said, "some things never change, do they, Dave? Do we have something about closets? And bimbos?" she added, eyeing Sherry.

Dave closed his eyes and leaned against the Xerox machine. Sherry tried to leave the room, but Lita stopped her with a stiff arm to the chest. "Stahnick," she said sweetly, "aren't you forgetting something?"

Sherry looked up at her with wounded Bambi eyes. Lita pointed to a wad of black nylon on the floor beside the Xerox machine. "Your knickers, Stahnick," she said. "Don't tell me—he took them off you with his teeth."

Sherry scooped up the panties and fled the office.

"Now, Mr. Carney," Lita said, "if you don't mind, I have some copying to do."

Ten

By Christmas, Sherry had been working for Beverly for almost six months. As she puttered around the store one morning, straightening piles of sweaters on the shelves, she mused about her assignment at La Ñapa. It was an OK job, but a lot of the time it was reeeaaally boring, like just then. She hated cleaning up after customers! They were such slobs! And after all, law enforcement was her profession, not retail. But she had to win Beverly's trust. If she came across as reliable and a good salesperson, maybe Beverly would let down her guard. If only Sherry could find out how she smuggled her pre-Columbian stuff and where she hid her dope, she'd score major points with Zoffke. He said Beverly was clever, but he had it on good authority she was both a user and a dealer.

When Beverly met with suppliers at the store, often before or after store hours, Sherry was on hand to see what she was buying. She was especially on the lookout for pre-Colombian. One day a couple tried to sell Beverly some archaeological items from Peru, and she shooed them out of the store.

Excitedly, Sherry waited until Beverly left for the post office, then she called Dave on his mobile phone. "Maybe she sent those two off because I'm here," she told him. "Maybe they're going to meet somewhere else later. I'd better report it to Zoffke right away."

Acting on a hunch, Dave asked Sherry to describe the couple to him.

"The woman's mid-thirties, has snarly red hair, and she's kind of tubby and whiney," Sherry said.

"And the guy has shoulder-length greasy black hair and looks like he's asleep?"

"Yeah," Sherry said. "How'd you know? Are they big dealers?"

Dave sighed deeply. "Don't mention them to Zoffke. They're ours."

"What? They look like hippies to me. They're staying in a really grungy motel near here on West Central."

"We call it camouflage, Sherry," Dave said, rolling his eyes. "Thanks for calling me. Keep up the good work."

Sherry was adept at eavesdropping, covering Beverly's conversations on the phone and with friends who dropped by the store. She kept an eye on incoming as well as outgoing mail and UPS deliveries. She thought maybe Beverly had a P.O. box somewhere because noteworthy mail so rarely showed up. When it did, she'd open it before Beverly saw it, then apologize because she'd opened it by mistake.

"Watch how she handles her cash," Dave advised. "A lot of retailers pocket their cash sales to avoid reporting the income."

"Maybe I've missed it, but I've never seen her dipping into the till or buying things with cash. And I've never seen anyone so anal about their checkbook. Shitfire! At the end of every month, she spends hours matching up the deposits with the sales reports we fill out every day. It has to be to the penny before she'll send the figures to her bookkeeper."

On the surface, it looked to Sherry as if Beverly had built up a nice little business. She put in long hours, she was smart about what she bought, she kept good records, and she spoke Spanish so fluently Sherry could scarcely understand a word of it. She handled difficult customers with good humor and dealt kindly with crazy street people who sometimes wandered in.

"I hate to admit it, but she's actually great to work for," she told Dave. "She does the disagreeable shit, like cleaning the bathroom and taking out the garbage. And she is superb at sales. That woman could sell ice to Eskimos. But I'm damned if she's going to fool me into complacency. This place has to be a front. Zoffke says Beverly's lying low for a while, but sooner or later we'll get the goods on her. We have an important mission to fulfill for Operation Pillage. And I mean to succeed."

Dave sighed to himself. Oh, to be young again and soooo, soooo stupid.

Suspicious types rarely visited the store except for the AATA trainees. They came around almost every day and were so obvious Sherry wanted to scream at them. They might as well have worn T-shirts that said CUSTOMS in big red letters. They pissed Sherry off by leaving clothes on the floor of the changing room and disrupting the piles of clothing she'd just neatened. She considered reporting them to Lita, but there was the closet incident with Dave. Better not.

When Sherry and Beverly weren't busy, Sherry tried to ingratiate herself with her boss. They gossiped about customers and other storekeepers. Sometimes they talked politics. Not surprisingly, the woman was a pinko, who thought the United States had no business "meddling" in Latin countries' affairs, and she had nothing good to say about customs. Most of what she said about the agency pissed Sherry off, but she kept her mouth shut.

After Beverly came back from her aunt's funeral in October, she moped around the store and sat in her office a lot staring at the wall. She was quieter than usual, and she would get all misty-eyed whenever she talked about Magdalena. Then one day in early December, her mood changed dramatically. She came into the store like a dust devil, totally wound up. Sherry was tempted to ask her if she was on something. Speed? Coke? Angel dust? But Beverly's high didn't seem drug-induced.

All day long, Beverly walked around humming little tunes to herself, grinning like Garfield the cat. She spent a lot of time with customers and sold up a storm. When a couple of dopey AATA kids came into the store looking for striped antique textiles that Bolivia had recently listed as national patrimony, Beverly sold them new Ecuadorian neck scarves that had stripes in them. And when they left the store, she roared with laughter.

Something is definitely up, Sherry thought. Maybe after months of lying low, she's getting ready to make a move.

At the task force meeting that evening, Zoffke was in a dark mood. He pressured everyone to dig deeper, keep closer tabs on the New Mexican importers and storekeepers, compile lists of their visitors, watch their inventories, not let a single piece of mail get through to any of them without inspection, open every box, every package—U.S. mail, FedEx, UPS, DHL—whatever. In no uncertain terms, he let everybody know Parmentier and the artifact smuggling ring hadn't yet been busted because his bozo agents and the AATA kids weren't doing their jobs. He came down especially hard on Sherry, as if she weren't smart enough for the task or clever enough to see through Beverly.

Sherry was surprised and hurt when Zoffke picked on her. Tears welled up in her eyes, but she was damned if she was going to cry in front of everybody. She was doing a superb job watching Beverly, and Dave, a crackerjack undercover agent, thought she was, too. Zoffke was just an asshole.

When the meeting was over, Joe Scarafaggio cornered Sherry. "No matter what Zoffke said, you're doing a great job, kid."

"Thank you, Scary," she said. "That's very kind of you."

"I heard some things. Thought you might be interested."

"Oh, yeah? Like what?"

"Well, maybe Zoffke's in trouble, and that's why he was a little hard on you tonight. I heard the suits in Washington think he's blowing their cultural patrimony initiative by making them look bad with the press and the Guatemalans. Customs finally had to admit to the Guats that we didn't nab any significant Mayan artifacts in the raid on Galería Galo. No doubt he's under the gun for that."

"I don't care if his ass is in a sling. Picking on me, especially in front of everybody, was totally uncalled for."

"Yeah. I think he's even more frazzled than usual. Plus he's getting pressure from Washington on the drug interdiction front. It's been some time since we made any significant drug busts. A Texas congressman's calling for hearings into allegations of high-level customs corruption in the Southwest region."

"Wow."

"I scored some other bits of inside information from Herman Naranjo—Agent Orange—when we had a few margaritas last night. Let's you and me go have a drink, and I'll share my info with you."

Sherry hesitated a few seconds. Rumors were Scary was a wife beater and he had a bad reputation for the way he treated women.

But this could be a good opportunity, she told herself. She agreed to meet with Scary.

After work the next day, they drove to O'Blarney's, an uptown bar with Irish pub décor and plastic ferns. They hunkered down in a corner booth with brandy Alexanders, Sherry's favorite drink.

"Orange says that in early fall, the court ordered customs to return Galería Galo's goods, keeping only the few pre-Columbian artifacts. A lot of things like the wooden santos and folk art, and old paintings got heat damaged over the summer in the agency's El Paso warehouse. Galo's lawyer is talking about suing customs for the losses."

"Can they do that?" Sherry asked.

"Galo doesn't have the money to sue, and anyway, Zoffke says the agency is immune. He told Orange that since Beverly helped Pancha inventory the returned items, it's proof she's part of Galo's smuggling ring, and we ought to step up the surveillance on her. He wants her store and her house 'inspected' and then wired, and he wants a transponder on her car. After his third margarita, Orange told me he'd never seen anything like it. Zoffke wants Beverly bad. Orange said he was even thinking of suing her for libel for calling him a Nazi in her phone conversations."

"She calls all of us Nazis," Sherry said heatedly.

Scarafaggio shrugged. "Orange said that a couple of weeks later, Elroy picked up a tidbit from the tap on the phone in the Archibeques' apartment. Pancha's husband told his brother that Pancha found a group of Mayan jades packed in a basket in the pile of returned goods, and she gave them to Galo's attorney for safekeeping."

"Are they pre-Columbian?"

"You bet. And they're worth real money. They were probably the only valuable things in the store. Even if they were from Galo's private collection and not for sale, they could still be used as evidence. Zoffke went ballistic when he found out the people who went through the seized goods missed the jades."

"Didn't he go through the stuff, too?"

"Sure he did, but nobody dares remind him of that. Anyway, he called Deutsch, the lawyer, and told her that the judge said he could have the jades back. So Deutsch checked with the judge, who told her he had said no such thing. Zoffke's response? We'll get that lawyer bitch good one of these days."

"Can he do that? Go after Deutsch?"

"Not legally. But 'legal' never put the brakes on Ray Zoffke. Orange went on to tell me that by mistake, somebody also released an important customs file to Galo's lawyer, and Zoffke was hot about that, too."

"What was in it?" Sherry asked.

"Complaints to Zoffke from the Old Town postmaster and the post office in Santa Fe about how uneasy they are about allowing customs to open importers' mail and packages without paperwork."

"Can Deutsch make trouble for us with that stuff?"

"Naw, not really. What's she going to do?"

"I don't know, maybe go to the press?"

"Not in this town. The *Albuquerque Sentinel* is loyal to law enforcement. And the TV stations? If it doesn't fit into a few seconds' sound bite, we got nothing to worry about."

After several brandy Alexanders, Sherry was drunk. "Scary, I think I'd better be getting home."

"Aw, come on, kid. Let's grab some dinner and maybe cruise on back to my place."

"What's your wife going to say about that?"

"The wife and I are having a few problems," he explained. "So I'm crashing at an agency apartment on Montgomery. She doesn't understand how stressful my work is. But you do, don't you, kid? I'm willing to bet you know some great ways to work off stress."

"Gee, Scary, I'd love to, but I just can't. Not tonight." Sherry didn't really like Scarafaggio. He had googly eyes, and he was fat and hairy and weird. But the guy had his ear to the ground, and he could be useful to her. Most of the agents wouldn't even talk to trainees, much less let them in on things.

Later, as they sat in his car in front of Sherry's place, she let him cop a couple of feels. "If you're a good boy and keep me in the know, well, there might be more goodies in Mamma's cookie jar for you," she told him.

A few days later, Beverly told Sherry she was going on vacation to the Caribbean, someplace called St. Bard's, as soon as they'd taken inventory in January. Sherry waited until Beverly left to talk to her travel agent and called the tire store. Scary answered. "It looks like Beverly's going to make a major move," Sherry said excitedly. "She's going to the Caribbean. The lady who never has two nickels to rub together is going on a Caribbean vacation. She must have come into a little money."

"You've snagged some important information, babe," Scary said. "I'll pass it along to Zoffke."

Sherry was thrilled. This important bit of intel was just what she needed to convince Zoffke she was doing a good job. She called Dave on his mobile phone and suggested they have a drink to celebrate.

Scary hung up from Sherry's call and had a good laugh. What a bimbo that Sherry was. He'd known about Beverly's trip for a week.

Scary had been sitting in Zoffke's office when Elroy played a tape he'd picked up from Beverly's home phone. She was talking to her pals in Chi-town, the Siegals. She said she wanted to take a nice vacation after the Christmas rush. Her friends recommended St. Barth's, a little French protectorate in the Caribbean. The Siegals put her in touch with a fisherman and his wife on the island who rented beach houses.

Yeah, Beverly's come into a little money, all right, Scary mumbled. Sherry obviously didn't know about the check, but he knew the exact amount—$916,524.56. Scary had gleaned that little bit of info from a trainee who was going over Beverly's mail. "The fuckin' luck of some people," he groused. The check came from a New York lawyer. An accompanying letter said the money was a bequest from Magdalena Parmentier.

Scary found Zoffke's reaction to the news about Beverly's bucks weird.

"The money confirms my judgment that Beverly's a major player," Zoffke had told Scary.

Scary found it curious that his boss wasn't excited he'd been proved correct. In fact, he looked worried.

"I'll follow the money carefully," Scary volunteered. "See what she does with it, Ray."

Zoffke nodded. "Fine, but I want you to report directly—and only—to me."

True to his word, Scary notified Zoffke when Beverly deposited the check in a special savings account. A week later he called his boss again when she bought a cashier's check for $120,444.58 payable to the IRS.

Zoffke didn't seem too happy about that. "Just because she's declaring it doesn't mean she's not lying about its source," he said.

The way Scary heard it, Beverly had inherited the money from a rich aunt. A likely story. He didn't give a shit about Beverly or where her money came from. And he didn't care about Zoffke or whatever was bugging him. What he wanted was for Zoffke to let him go to St. Barth's with the guys who were going to tail Beverly on her vacation. He'd pay the extra for his wife to go along. The trip would be a good opportunity for him to get back in her good graces. She'd kicked him out of the house for knocking her around a little, and it wasn't making him look too good with the *jefes*. Everybody else was going to Barth's—Elroy, Zoffke, some guys from the El Paso office, even Melissa the receptionist. Everybody but Sherry and Dave. Scary was jazzed. Was this gonna be a big party or what? A couple of guys from San Juan were going to handle most of the surveillance, so Scary and the others could do their investigative work on the beaches and tennis courts.

Zoffke was the only one who took the trip seriously. He told the task force that Beverly suddenly had a large sum of unexplained cash. It looked as if she had sold off some of her hidden pre-Columbian collection. She was probably meeting someone on the island to make a buy, and she was probably going to stash some of the money offshore.

Sure, Scary wanted to say to Zoffke. After she declared it? But who cares. The island is supposed to be gorgeous—great restaurants, cheap booze, nude beaches. Scary figured he could ditch the wife now and then to hang out at the free skin show down by the water. He was primed for a great time.

Eleven

Although Magdalena's bequest meant Beverly didn't need to worry about having a good Christmas season at the store, she couldn't seem to switch gears yet into her new life as a person of means. Just like every other Christmas, she worked twelve-hour days, seven days a week. What sustained her through the holiday ordeal was the prospect of her trip to St. Barth's. As she waited on customers, rang up sales, packed boxes, and gift-wrapped packages, visions of white sand beaches lined with swaying palm trees played through her tired brain. The light at the end of the tunnel was tropical, sunny, and deliciously near.

Thanks to Magdalena, this Christmas she was able to lavish gifts on her friends. She sent new life jackets to each of the River Rats and gave alpaca sweaters to Lucille and Sherry, Pancha, Tom, and their new son, Pablito. She even had a present for Dave, an alpaca hat. He was reluctant to take it, but she forced it on him, and he actually wore it. She bought Steve a fancy tennis racket and eight tennis balls, one for each day of Hanukkah.

On Christmas morning, she wheeled the best gift of all onto Doña Lupe's porch and rang the bell. When Ricky came to the door, she presented him with a beribboned, motorized wheelchair complete with a speech synthesizer. The boy was ecstatic. They spent Christmas Day learning how to use the talking computer. He caught on quickly and they had a ball.

The next week, Beverly opted to spend New Year's Eve alone. It seemed like a time for reflection, rather than celebration. She built a fire, put a Mozart symphony on the stereo, poured herself a glass of real French Côtes du Rhone, and settled into the down pillows of her new sofa. As she watched flames lick the logs, she thought about the past year—the raid on Galo's, the horrifying experience of being harassed by people she didn't know for reasons she didn't fully comprehend, Magdalena's death, and her astonishing gift.

Now that she had some capital, Beverly wanted to hire Pancha to help in the business. She, Tom, and their baby were moving from Santa Fe to Albuquerque, where life was more affordable and they had relatives. Tom was going to work full time for his contractor friend, and Pancha said she was ready to go back to work for at least a few hours a week.

Beverly offered her a job at La Ñapa. "We'd make a good team. You're cautious, methodical, sensible, and thorough, and I'm impulsive, creative, and risk-taking. We'd balance each other out, don't you think? Working together, we could develop the best Latin American folk art gallery anywhere."

Pancha said she'd think about it. But Beverly knew she'd say yes.

Even if Pancha decided to decline the offer, some things were going to change at La Ñapa. Beverly's days of traveling to Central and South America, and even importing directly, were probably over. True, nobody had sent her a notice in the mail that said she couldn't travel south anymore, but with customs harassing her, it seemed too risky to make her annual buying trip to Latin America. For $5 and a bottle of Chivas Regal to the right guy, customs could have a kilo of cocaine put in her luggage and get her tossed into an Andean dungeon for the rest of her days.

Then there was the letter from Delia Quispe in Peru, Beverly's long-time supplier who had packed and shipped Dionisio's museum show to her.

Something strange is going on here in Lima. One night a couple of weeks ago, two men in a black Ford followed me across the city. They tried to pull me over in a deserted area near the airport, but I sped up *and kept going until I was in my own neighborhood, where everyone knows me. I stopped in a well-lit plaza near my house. Like in one of those old black and white American movies, the men got out of their car, flashed police badges in my face, and demanded I get out of my car. Were they really cops? You can probably buy a badge here for ten soles. `No, señores,' I said. They became angry. One of them tried to reach in through a window to unlock the car door, and Tupac, my faithful mutt, bit the man's hand. Then the cabrón drew a gun. I didn't know whether he was going to shoot Tupac or me or both of us. It was terrifying! The other guy, who had an American accent, ordered him to put the gun away. In the meantime, my neighbors and people in the street gathered around my car. They hissed and hooted at those guys until they got back in their car and drove away. I still have no idea what they wanted. It was awful. Nothing like that has ever happened to me before. I'm still having nightmares about it.*

Delia's story upset Beverly, and she couldn't help wondering if it was in some way related to her problems with customs. The presence of an authoritative American was noteworthy.

Moreover, it looked like a wave of harassment was washing over the entire Latin American importing community. Fellow importers told her about visits from police all over Latin America. The cops would come into their hotels and *pensiones* at night, saying they were from Interpol, and ask to see their passports. And when the importers were out of their rooms, cops would come to the hotels and demand the maids allow them into the importers' rooms, where they'd search their luggage. Weird gringos would cozy up to Beverly's colleagues in bars, wanting to accompany them on their buying trips to market towns. One woman told Beverly that she walked in on an African-American man in her Guatemalan hotel room as he was quizzing the chambermaid about her in broken Spanish.

"Oh, sorry to intrude," he said to the importer. "I'm just looking for my room. I'm here on business from U.S. customs in Washington. Once I find my room, would you like to have a drink with me?"

It broke Beverly's heart to quit importing for a while, but under the circumstances, it seemed like the safest course for her and her overseas suppliers. She had put years of hard work into building up reliable sources all over Latin America for top-quality weavings, pottery, and folk art. Artisan families had diligently kept her supplied with their best work and relied upon her orders for steady incomes. She felt she was deserting them, but she also didn't want them to be subjected to the kind of terror Delia had experienced. Habeas corpus was a joke in Latin America, especially for the poor Indians and mestizos who sold to her.

She wrote Delia and each family, explaining the circumstances. She hoped they would be able to sell their goods elsewhere until this thing blew over and provided them with the names of importers in Europe and the States who might become customers.

Beverly had already begun turning to stateside suppliers for her inventory, though their goods weren't the quality of hers, and the higher costs were cutting deeply into her profit margins.

Buying from other people still didn't free her from harassment. Packages of items she'd ordered from companies in the United States arrived showing signs of having been opened and rifled en route. Sometimes things were missing.

One day, a shipment arrived without a large whimsical clay pig she'd special ordered. Beverly called the shipper in Texas, who swore he had packed the pig himself and double-boxed it. Instead, the package contained an empty box, though the weight clearly indicated that something had been shipped. When she called UPS, they sent a young inspector over to the store.

"Ummmmm," he said as he looked over, under, and around the packing materials for the missing football-sized clay pig.

"This was just one of several boxes; all of them were opened en route," Beverly told him.

Sherry stood at her elbow, carefully observing the proceedings.

"Ummmm," the young man said.

"How can that be?" Beverly asked him.

"Wellllll," he replied, tugging nervously at an ear lobe. "We do reserve the right to open any box, you know."

"You do? Why would you open somebody's package?"

"Ohhhh, we might want to see if the item has been properly packed, if the declaration is right. And, of course, we're cooperating fully in the War on Drugs."

"Of course," Beverly said. "Does that mean you let people other than UPS personnel inspect packages? Like law enforcement people?"

"Sure."

Sherry began to interrupt the inspector. But Beverly slowly pressed her foot down on Sherry's toes, to shut her up.

"Ow!" she protested.

"So like who?" Beverly asked. "Local police? The DEA? Customs?"

"Yeahhhhh. Customs sometimes has guys standing at the bottom of the conveyer belt, and they tell us which packages they want to open. Or sometimes they ride with us in the trucks. It's important to stop drug shipments, you know. We're proud of our record of cooperation."

"I'm sure you are. But don't they need search warrants?"

"Wellllll, I guess not." The question seemed novel to him.

The inspector filled out a report form and had Beverly sign it. "I don't think UPS will pay for the missing pig because the shipper probably forgot to pack it. You'll have to work things out with your supplier."

Hours later, as Beverly was preparing to close up shop, she received a panicked call from the inspector.

"Ms. Parmentier?" he said, his voice wavering. "I . . . I made a terrible mistake. I told you something all wrong."

"Oh? UPS is going to pay for the missing pig after all. Good."

"Noooooo . . . no. We can't be held responsible for that. No . . . I mean . . . about who opens the boxes. It's never anybody but UPS personnel. Never anyone else. I . . . I misspoke!"

"No problem. I wasn't paying attention anyway." Beverly lied. She had just finished writing up a memo for her files about the inspector's visit. "But I do think your company ought to pay me for the clay pig that was taken out of the box en route."

"I'll do what I can."

A few days later, she received a terse letter from a UPS executive in Texas. "UPS absolutely reserves the right to open any package at any time for any reason. Such inspections are only carried out by qualified UPS personnel, never by anyone else. As for the missing inventory item, we regret to inform you that the company cannot be held responsible for your loss."

All packages coming to the store now arrived open and rifled, even a box of dainty things Sherry had ordered for herself from Victoria's Secret. She was outraged. "I can't believe this!" she wailed. "What right does anybody have to open my box?"

"What right does anybody have to open any box?" Beverly asked.

Sherry sniffed. "Well, but *this* box is personal."

"They're all personal."

Beverly tried her best to ignore the hassles and focus on her upcoming vacation. It occurred to her that she had to stop overnight en route to St. Barth's, so she decided to combine pleasure with a business trip to the capital of Latin America— Miami. Maybe some of the Central and South American émigrés might be interested in selling their Spanish colonial silver, paintings, furniture, *santos,* and vintage folk art for money they could use to buy items more useful in modern American life—

big-screen TVs and tractor lawnmowers, for example. If this gambit worked, it could be a good way of getting some high-class Latin American merchandise without the hassles of importing it. She ran an ad in the *Miami Herald,* and a number of people contacted her about things they'd like to sell.

Her friends, Danny and Nancy Pieri, who were finally moving back to Albuquerque from New York, were delighted to house-sit for Beverly. After the break-in while she was on the river, she didn't want to leave her house uninhabited. She wanted people she trusted staying there, people who wouldn't snort her Ajax or steal the salt out of her shakers.

Twelve

Beverly was both apprehensive and excited as she approached the car-rental agency counter at Miami International. Because it was Super Bowl weekend, the line was long and progressing slowly. Behind her stood a short, squat, Italian-looking man with kinky black hair sprouting from under his baseball cap. A nervous, pie-faced woman accompanied him. She was festooned with bad turquoise jewelry, and a stiff hairdo hugged her head like a leather bomber helmet. The couple had sat across the aisle from Beverly on both her flights: Albuquerque to Dallas and Dallas to Miami. She thought she'd seen the man around Albuquerque somewhere and his companion too. She smiled and said hello to them, but both ignored her.

The drive from the airport into Coral Gables, where she was staying, wasn't as difficult as Beverly had feared. She had never negotiated Miami by car. The detailed map she'd picked up at AAA before traveling provided some comfort, and Danny had given her tips on how to navigate the city. In no time, she had checked into a small, European-style hotel, the St. Jacques.

After placing calls to the people whose collections she planned to visit, she made her way to the hotel's lush interior courtyard and sat down at a table beneath flowering lime trees. The air was clear and refreshingly humid after she'd been cooped up all day in the desiccating stale air of airplanes and airports. She was elated to be out of Albuquerque's cold, snowy January, and with her year-end chores completed, she could enjoy the tropical warmth, scents, and colors of South Florida. "At last, I'm a free woman," she sighed with pleasure.

Sipping a tequila sunrise, she watched seagulls circling over-head in the pale twilight. Sunset colors played around her as she

wrote to friends. She signed her postcard to Flash "With fond re-
membrances, your loving Aunt Beverly" in a faint hope the signature would pass his girlfriend's inspection. Ah, the river. How
far away and long ago it seemed.

She looked up, and suddenly her good spirits evanesced into
the twilight. Sitting at a nearby table was the dowdy woman
from the airport. She was intently drinking an amber liquid,
her shiny red mouth waxing the glass rim with lipstick. She had
traded her hair helmet for a short mop of dirt-brown hair tortured into Tootsie-roll-sized tubes. Impossibly large turquoise-
nugget bracelets grasped her wrists, while a necklace of equally
implausible blue rocks and tacky silver foliage lay across her pink
polyester bosom—Albuquerque bad taste par excellence.

Beverly grabbed her postcards and purse, dashed a signature
onto the chit, and raced for the refuge of her room. For a long
time, she lay on the bed, staring at the ceiling, trying to convince
herself it was mere coincidence that the bad-hair lady was staying at her sixteen-room hotel. She was going to have company
on this trip, too. She snapped on the bedside lamp and punched
in Doc's telephone number in Utah.

"Thank you for using AT&T," the electronic operator intoned.

"Oh, you're welcome," Beverly said. "I love doing business
with you wonderful people."

Two young male voices laughed through the phone line. It
sounded as if they were in the room next door as well as on Beverly's telephone. A surge of anger ran through Beverly like an
electric current. Instead of screaming at the motherfuckers listening to her telephone conversation, she gathered her wits and
stayed cool.

She and Doc chatted briefly about the holidays as the telephone line buzzed with clicks and echoes.

"Is this a private conversation, darlin'?" Doc asked in her Texas
drawl.

"It's as private as our elk stew dinner at Jone's Hole," Beverly said, hoping Doc would catch on to her meaning.

Doc's tone changed. "Hmmmm," she mused. "Say, my brother said he'd talk to one of the Sulzbergers about your story, see if the *New York Times* wouldn't like to put an investigative reporter on it."

"Great!" Beverly said. But she was puzzled. Doc didn't have any brothers. Then she caught on to the game. "Is this the brother who writes for *Covert Action Quarterly?*"

Doc laughed and Beverly smiled. They were humming the same tune.

"No, this is the one who works for NPR in New York. You know, the Rhodes Scholar who dates the daughter of Robert Morgenthal, the D.A."

It was great to have friends like Doc.

As Beverly made her way around Miami, it was obvious that she had more company than the guys on the phone line and the woman with the bad hair. Bland young men with military haircuts followed her as she called on the people who'd answered her *Miami Herald* ad. When she came out of a house, a gallery, or the hotel, the snoop du jour would lean out of the window of his red, white, or blue Corsica and snap her photograph. When she was driving, the surveillance followed certain patterns. If she looked at the tail once too often in her rearview mirror, he'd turn off at the next intersection, only to reappear minutes later a few cars behind her. A telephone truck parked in a loading zone in front of the hotel never moved during the three days she spent in Coral Gables and never collected any parking tickets.

The day after she arrived, she found someone had rummaged through her room and her locked luggage, and rearranged her cosmetic kit. Whenever she left her room and headed for the elevator, she'd hear the door to the room next to hers open and close. No one ever appeared in the hallway. Every time she'd pass by, the unmistakable odor of marijuana wafting into the corridor from the mysterious room would nearly knock her over.

Some of Beverly's contacts wanted to sell tourist junk, ugly stuff, or things in poor condition, but some of the goods were high quality. From a man who had been a shipping company executive, she bought a small collection of charming nineteenth-century religious folk pieces—wooden *santos* and *nichos* and *retablos* painted on tin. A retired Peruvian diplomat sold her several small, carved wooden boxes, a pair of silver bowls, and an old silver and coral bead *rosario*. Relatives of his had a lovely inlaid writing desk, a *bargueño,* and were willing to part with it for a reasonable amount. And from an elderly Spanish woman, she bought an Andalusian trunk and several small ex-voto paintings from Mexico.

After she made arrangements to have her purchases packed and shipped by truck to Albuquerque, she called the store and left a message on the answering machine to alert Lucille that shipments were on the way. "I got some terrific stuff here in Miami. Remember, if anything arrives damaged, save the packing materials. Thanks again for helping out while I'm gone. *Bueno* bye!"

On her last day in Miami, she drove to an address on a shady street near the Hotel Fontainbleu and rang the doorbell of a pink-stuccoed town house. Señor Vargas, a small, natty man in a guayabera shirt and neatly creased white linen pants answered the door. He showed her to a comfortable old leather chair in his living room and offered her a glass of Perrier with lime. He had told her over the phone that he had some old Guatemalan furniture to sell. While she waited for her host to return with her drink, she looked around his living room. For someone who said that he had been a low-level clerk in Latin American embassies, he had exquisite and expensive taste. Fine old Cuzco paintings in gilded frames decorated the walls. Heavy, lustrous antique furniture from Peru and Central America sat like genteel aristocrats around the room. In the adjacent dining area, colonial silver cups and bowls gleamed from the center of a rosewood dining table. A valuable collection of Central and South American pre-Columbian artifacts filled floor to ceiling glass shelves along one whole wall of the living room: gold figurines, polychromed tripod bowls and vases, jade, rock crystal, and obsidian pendants, all museum quality.

On a table next to Beverly's armchair, she noticed a silver-framed photograph of her host shaking hands with someone who looked familiar. She picked up the frame and recognized George Herbert Walker Bush. The black-and-white picture had been taken in an office somewhere. The blinds were drawn. Apart from the photographer, the man and George Bush were alone.

Beverly put the photograph down carefully.

Her host returned with the Perrier. Crossing his legs and clasping his hands about his knees, he asked about her business. His intense black eyes and the sharp, almost accusatory edge to his questions made her uncomfortable. He seemed curious about her lack of interest in buying pre-Colombian art. "How could you not be interested in such exquisite work?" he asked, sweeping his arm around the room to indicate his collection.

"I don't think amateurs should be digging up pre-Colombian sites. They're destroying them and the information they contain," she said.

The man scoffed. "It's not amateurs digging up the sites," he said derisively. "And if we collectors don't preserve these exquisite works of art, they'll be gone forever. The peasants will use priceless vessels for target practice or as troughs for their swine. Let me show you something I doubt you can resist."

He disappeared into another room and came out carrying several large cardboard and glass display boxes. Proudly, he set them on the coffee table in front of her. "Mayan esoteric flints with warrior profiles. Have you ever seen such incredible knapping?"

"Not outside of a museum," Beverly said. "You're right. They are exquisite."

"And they can be yours, my dear. I recently acquired a large collection of them and have decided to deaccession a few. Fifty dollars each." He peered into her eyes, waiting for a response.

She shook her head. "Thank you. I'm really not interested."

The man's head snapped back in amazement. "What? These are worth many times that. You'll make a bundle on them."

"I'm not interested. I don't buy pre-Colombian art. I specified that in my newspaper ad. I appreciate your showing them to me, but I'm here to look at the Guatemalan furniture you said you had for sale."

The man pulled at the ends of his thin black moustache, ran a hand over his egg-smooth pate, and narrowed his eyes at her. "Don't be disingenuous with me."

She stood up. "There's no Guatemalan furniture for sale, is there?"

The man smiled icily. "I've decided not to sell it."

Beverly strode to the front door, flung it open, and walked out.

BOOK FOUR

One

January 1989

Less than a half hour after her touchdown at St. Barth's toy airport, Beverly, garbed in a T-shirt and shorts on a late January afternoon, was sitting on the front porch of a charming Caribbean cottage, sipping an orange juice she'd squeezed from fruit she picked up under her landlady's tree, gazing down a hillside of palm and mango trees to a half-moon bay of golden sand beaches and a French-blue sea merged with a sky the same color. Was she truly in the French West Indies and not simply hallucinating?

A little black-and-white cat named Domino, who came with the cottage, rubbed up against her bare legs, purring loudly and convincing her that he, if not all the tropical paradise surrounding her, was real.

Beverly sat on the porch for hours taking it all in, until darkness descended on the panorama and the twinkling lights of a billion stars lit up the night sky.

The next morning, she walked downhill to a small *supermarché* to buy groceries. The store was stocked with the usual American staples she never bought at home: cornflakes, Poptarts, Wonderbread, Oscar Mayer baloney. But she was pleased to find they also offered reasonably priced French cheeses, pâtés, locally baked baguettes and croissants, and French wines.

She was choosing salad fixings when a woman pushed her grocery cart past Beverly in the narrow aisle, nicked a corner of her *chariot* with a metallic bang, and without saying anything, paused to toss some limes into her cart. Beverly turned to glare at the rude woman, and her heart seized up. It was the woman with the cheap turquoise jewelry, the same one who had been at the Miami Airport and the hotel in Coral Gables.

She drew in a deep breath of courage and was about to assail the woman with a torrent of verbal abuse when she noticed the woman seemed drunk or otherwise stupefied. Her eyelids were puffy, and she'd tried unsuccessfully to cover up a shiner with pancake makeup. Beverly released her pent-up breath. The woman was too pitiful to hassle. Someone had used her as a punching bag, and her cart was full of little more than rum bottles, Coca-Cola, and limes.

Oblivious to her close call, the woman careened down the aisle to the checkout counter.

Beverly picked out a few more things, paid for her groceries, and left the store. Suddenly, not twenty feet away, a man leaned out of a nearby black Suzuki jeep with tinted windows and pointed a video camera at her. She looked behind her to see what he was filming and saw nothing but parked cars and garbage cans. Angrily, she flipped the man a middle finger, and he quickly drove off in a spurt of gravel.

It's a coincidence that woman's here, too, she tried to tell herself as she walked the five blocks uphill to her cottage. Maybe it's not the same woman. Maybe an outbreak of bad taste, Southwestern style, has swept New Mexico, Florida, and St. Barth's simultaneously. And the guy in the Suzuki jeep is documenting it for *Women's Wear Daily?*

Beverly was damned if anyone was going to ruin her longed-for vacation. She put away her groceries, got into her bathing suit, slathered herself with sunscreen, and walked back downhill to St. Jean Beach. Tossing her towel and paperback onto the sand, she went for a long walk, emptying her mind and worries into the endless shimmering ocean. The fine sand underfoot was gentle to her winter-softened soles, the sun warm on her bare back, and the seawater that lapped at her toes was just cool enough to be refreshing in the late morning heat.

For several hours, she alternated swimming laps in front of the beach with reading sessions in the shade of a sprawling sea grape tree in front of a small beachside hotel. The few people on the beach were quiet and kept to themselves. Even the young children, playing in the sand with shovels and buckets and chirping to one another and their parents in French, were well behaved and unobtrusive.

When the overhead sun became too strong, Beverly returned to her cottage, ate a salad, and retired to the hammock on the porch with her book and Domino, who jumped into the hammock with her. Soon they were both sound asleep.

When she awoke, the sun was slipping toward the horizon. She couldn't believe she had slept for nearly four hours. I could get used to this, she thought.

That evening, as she was enjoying a spaghetti putanesca dinner at a restaurant down the hill, the Palme d'Or, a slight young man walked up to her table, camera in hand, and asked her *en français* if he could take her picture. Beverly said no, but she was positive he clicked off several shots of her from across the room before he walked out of the restaurant. She asked the waitress who he was.

"Oh, that's René," she said. "He has a photo shop in Gustavia and takes paparazzo-type shots of the beautiful people in restaurants and clubs around the island. But I've never seen him in here before."

The next morning, while the island air still had a crispness to it, Beverly strolled down the St. Jean beach for more than a mile, then returned. She had nearly reached the sea grape tree where she had left her beach bag, when a short, balding, paunchy man in plaid bathing trunks jumped up from his beach towel and tried to strike up a conversation with her. She gave him a quick brush-off and kept walking.

An hour or so later, as she sat in the shade reading a Sara Peretsky novel, the same man flopped down on the sand next to her and invited her to go for a drink.

He seemed nice enough, but Beverly immediately pegged him for a Fed. He was deliberately making contact with her, and she knew she wasn't exactly a male magnet. She hesitated. Then, surprising herself, she accepted his offer, reasoning that if she had indeed been followed to St. Barth's by the *federales,* maybe it was time to turn the tables, time to start asking these guys some questions.

Over drinks in a nearby thatched roof bar, Jim Ross told Beverly he was a health care consultant in Puerto Rico. She soon discovered, however, he knew nothing about P.R., and he was unfamiliar with island health issues like dengue fever.

"So what kind of work do you do?" he asked her.

Beverly smiled sweetly. "I'm a Spanish teacher from Uvalde, Texas," she said with a light drawl.

Jim, taken aback by her answer, was at a loss for words.

Beverly thought he looked like he'd been hit in the face with a cow pie. This could be fun, she thought. "I do intensive language seminars for federal cops because their Spanish is so lousy," she added.

Jim turned lobster red, and she thought he was going to rupture himself.

He regained his composure and asked a few more questions. She wasn't surprised when apropos of nothing he broached the subject of pre-Columbian art and getting things across the border.

Now she knew for certain that he was a Fed. "What would a Spanish teacher from Texas know about those things?"

Before Jim could answer, a tall, thin young man with bright blue eyes beneath a furze of spiky blond hair came up to the table, greeted Ross, and sat down. He introduced himself to Beverly with a little bow as Les Klug.

"Beverly's a Spanish teacher from Texas," Jim told Les, who had to stop himself from laughing out loud.

Jim glared at his partner, then began asking Beverly about Mexico. Les, giggling like a schoolgirl, asked her if she'd ever been to WAX-a-kah.

"I think you mean Wah-HAH-ca," she said.

"Yeah," Les said. "I hear Pwerda Escondid-ah is great, and the place to stay there is the Hotel Santa Fe. Do you know the owners, a couple from New Mexico?"

Of course she knew the Hotel Santa Fe, although she wouldn't tell them that. That was where she and Magdalena had stayed. Its owners were old friends. They had a small import store in Santa Fe, and over the years, they'd done a little business with each other.

Beverly smiled. "I've only been to Santa Fe once, when I was fifteen," she lied.

Les started to laugh. Jim swatted him with his cocktail napkin and told him to shut up.

She got up to leave and Jim grabbed her arm. "We'd like you to join us for dinner," he said. "How about seven, at the Mayan Inn?"

"Sure," she said, lying again. She had no intention of having dinner with them.

She left the bar and walked back uphill to her little house, feeling lousy on a number of accounts. In spite of her bravado with Les and Jim, she was demoralized. Her wonderful vacation had been invaded by men from Mars, the war planet. Worse yet, her body was betraying her. She'd been having terrible cramps for months. Now there was unusual bleeding as well. She promised her uterus a visit to the gynecologist the minute she got home.

By the time she reached the top of the hill, it was raining, a gentle tropical shower that tapped a soft tattoo on her house's tin roof. With the little cat on her lap, she sat on the porch and watched the rainfall bathe the orange trees and hibiscus in her landlady's yard. Flowers and leaves bowed their heads to receive the blessing of moisture and bobbed up and down in a light breeze that swept rain across the hillside.

Twilight disappeared into low-hanging clouds, and soon, the shower's tempo increased. A steady rain beat loudly on the roof as if it were a kettledrum. Although Beverly, a desert dweller, was unaccustomed to serious rainstorms, she felt peaceful and cozy. She poured herself a glass of Beaujolais, decided on a dinner of guacamole and chips, and adjourned to a table by the open door with the food, wine, and a novel.

The cramps had subsided somewhat, but the last thing she felt like doing was walking five blocks downhill in a downpour to find a cab and pay $20 each way to have dinner. At a restaurant called the Mayan Inn, no less, with two guys who showed every sign of being *federales* trying to pin some pre-Columbian smuggling rap on her.

After a good night's sleep, Beverly felt better. She bummed a ride with her landlady, Madame LaFleur, into Gustavia, St. Barth's quaint, postage-stamp-sized capital city. While madame went shopping, Beverly sat on the post office steps writing postcards. Suddenly, the young photographer she'd seen at the Palme D'Or trotted up the steps. They were surprised to see each other. In her best high-school *français,* she greeted him.

"*Monsieur le Photographe!* Ah, I recognize you from the Palme d'Or, where you took my picture night before last."

He looked nervous. *"Mais non,* you must be mistaken, *mademoiselle.* I've never seen you before, and I have never taken your photograph." He ran down the steps and quickly disappeared.

His evasive answer gave Beverly an idea. Since she had time to kill, she decided to visit his shop. Madame LaFleur had pointed it out when they drove into town. It was only a half block away.

When she walked in, the photographer and a chunky man behind the counter looked as startled as raccoons caught in a garbage can on a moonless night.

"Where are the pictures you took of me Tuesday night?" she asked the photographer.

The two men spoke simultaneously. The photographer said, "I didn't take any photos Tuesday night." And his chubby friend said, "None of those photos turned out."

Beverly laughed all the way out the door, willing to bet the men didn't breathe again until after she was well out of sight. For all they knew, she was Mrs. Joe Bananas, and she was going to pull a Tommy gun out of her shopping bag and blow them away.

That afternoon, when she walked out of the water after a long swim off St. Jean Beach, Jim and Les were waiting for her by her towel. She was dismayed to see them.

Jim was annoyed. "So what happened to you last night?"

"Sorry, guys, I wasn't feeling well. My cottage doesn't have a phone, so I had no way to let you know."

"Yeah, sure you were sick," he said sarcastically.

As she walked a bit away from the men to shake the sand from her beach towel and dry off, she heard Les whisper. "She really was sick. Female stuff. I checked it out. Gross, man."

Beverly was enraged. Les had gone through her bathroom garbage! In the worst way, she wanted to kick both men in the balls and stomp their prone, writhing bodies into the sand of the St. Jean Beach. But revenge could be almost as sweet. She resolved to find out everything she could about these bastards and somehow make them sorry they'd ever invaded her privacy.

She put on a Pepsodent smile and walked back over to them. "How about a rain check?" she said.

Beverly spent the rest of the day on her porch, writing postcards and reading. Domino lay beside her chair on the cool cement floor. Soon, the sun was sliding rapidly toward the sea in a ball of molten gold that burnished the tops of the waves and gilded the seaside vegetation. She put down her pen, propped her feet up on a chair, and watched the day dissolve in a spectacle of shimmering color and light. When darkness spread like ink across the panorama of endless sea, she went inside to get ready for her dinner date.

At the appointed time, she walked into a pleasant upstairs restaurant in the center of Gustavia. Les rose to greet her at a table on the balcony.

"Jim had to take care of something, so he'll join us after dinner," he explained.

Beverly decided to get him drunk. "I hear this place serves dynamite martinis. We'll have doubles," she told the waiter. At the last minute, she changed her order to club soda, but Les stuck with a double martini. Halfway through his first martini, he was giggling. Beverly asked him about himself.

"I sell real estate in Manhattan."

"Oh, do you ever have any dealings with Will Simonson?" Simonson was a nosy "collector" who regularly visited importers all over the country, although he never bought anything. He told everyone he made his money selling Manhattan real estate. All Beverly's female colleagues thought he was a Fed; the men thought he was a cool guy.

Les laughed so hard he sputtered some of his drink on the tablecloth. "Naw, Simonson's uptown, and I'm downtown." He narrowed his eyes at her in a way that made her nervous, then broke into a sly smile. "I've been thinking of getting out of real estate and going to work for the *New York Times* or *Covert Action Quarterly* or National Public Radio, if I can't get a job with the attorney general, Robert Morgenthal."

Les folded his arms across his chest, smirked at Beverly, and waited for her reaction.

Beverly didn't flinch as he threw back parts of her conversation with Doc at her. Although she was seething, she coolly sipped her club soda and smirked back.

Les continued. "I love to travel to Latin America. I was there three times last year, on my frequent-flier miles."

"Yeah," Beverly said. "You New York real estate agents really rack up the miles."

He roared. "You know, I've been thinking about importing pre-Columbian art. Maybe you could give me some pointers."

"I don't know a thing about it, but I do know who you should talk to."

Les seemed to sober right up and took out a pad and pencil. "Who?"

"A couple of sleazeballs in Albuquerque, Ray Zoffke and Herman Naranjo."

Les laughed so loud that every head in the restaurant turned toward them. Then he shook his finger at Beverly. "You're baaaaaad!" he said.

Beverly had had enough. She was getting up to leave when Jim approached the table with a troupe of kids in their mid-twenties in tow. He glared at Les, who was obviously drunk.

"I'm sorry if Les has upset you. Please don't go." He took out his American Express card and paid for the drinks. "I've got a special treat lined up for you. These kids are crewing on a two-masted schooner that's anchored in the harbor. There's a party on board, and I was hoping you'd join us. Come on, Bev. It's going to be a lot of fun."

All during Jim's pleading, Beverly felt someone staring at her. She turned. One of his entourage, a beautiful, exotic girl with waist-length, reddish-brown hair and looks that combined the best features of the world's major racial groups, was eyeing Beverly as if she were good enough to eat. Yikes, Beverly thought, is this girl putting the *movidas* on me?

She noticed that all the men in the restaurant, even the gay ones, and most of the women couldn't keep their eyes off this stunning young woman who luxuriated in their attention like a preening Persian cat while keeping her focus on Beverly.

"I'm way too tired for a party," she said. "All I want to do is go home and slip under the sheets with a book. Have a nice time."

She fled down the stairs, heading toward a nearby taxi stand. The gorgeous young woman caught up with Beverly and slipped an arm around her shoulders. "I'm sooooo disappointed," she purred in a breathy voice. "I really wanted you to go to the party with us."

Beverly was unnerved. She'd never been hustled by a woman before. And she wondered what Jim and Les had planned for her. A Wesson-oil party aboard, complete with video cameras? Were they planning to shanghai her to Shanghai? No way was Beverly going aboard any boat with that crew.

She slipped out of the woman's grasp. "Thanks," she said. "But I'm just not up for it." She walked briskly toward the taxi stand.

Jim caught up with her. "Hey, Bev! Guess I won't go to the party either. Let me give you a ride home on my scooter."

Rather than pay $20 for a taxi ride, Beverly accepted his invitation. She wasn't yet beyond her parsimonious ways. Besides, there wasn't a taxi in sight, and she wanted to be home as soon as possible.

When Jim took the scooter keys out of his pocket, a set of VW keys with an orange St. Barth's Budget Rent-A-Car tag fell out of his pocket.

"The keys to my car back in San Juan," he said nervously as he scooped them up.

Jim drove the scooter right up to Beverly's casita. He seemed to have forgotten she hadn't told him where she was staying.

She got off the scooter. "So how did you know where my place was?"

Even in the half-light coming from a nearby street lamp, Beverly could see him turn bright red. "You told me about your rented house when we first met on the beach," he said.

They both knew he was lying.

Next day, Jim was waiting for Beverly on St. Jean Beach. Beverly glowered at him when he approached her. "Leave me alone. I know you guys are Feds, and you know I know, and goddamn it, I'm fed up!"

"OK, OK, come out to dinner with us and we can talk frankly," he said solemnly. "We're not the enemy. You'll see. It's your last night."

Beverly didn't believe Jim and Les were going to level with her about anything, and they were the last people she wanted to spend time with. But she hadn't taken photos of them. If she was ever going to get the outrageous violations of her privacy investigated, pictures of these guys would be helpful.

She let him convince her to accept the dinner offer, and they agreed to meet around eight at the Pizza Napoli at the far end of Gustavia harbor.

Shortly after dusk, with her camera in her purse, she walked down the hill to the main road, where an old black Peugeot taxi was idling beneath a large tree. The driver, heavy-set with thick glasses, a five-day-old beard, and a thatch of kinky black hair sticking out from under a vintage Brooklyn Dodgers cap, opened the taxi's back door. It was as if he had been waiting for her. He reminded her of someone, but she couldn't remember who. In French, she asked how much the fare to Gustavia would be.

"Whoa!" the driver yelped. "I don't speak no French."

His Brooklyn accent was thick as mascarpone. Beverly switched to English and asked him what the fare was to the Pizza Napoli.

"Six bucks," he said.

That was a third of the usual fare. She was immediately on guard, but wanting to be on time, she got in anyway.

He drove at a snail's pace, wandering all over the road, missing palm trees by inches as he gabbed and looked over his shoulder at her. He broached the subject of offshore banking. "It's a great way to free the bucks from Uncle Sam's mitts."

She didn't respond.

Then he wanted to talk about the island's "nooodie" beaches. She only answered his questions with grunts. Not soon enough, he delivered her to the pizzeria.

Her dinner dates nowhere in sight, Beverly perched on the edge of an oversize flowerpot to wait. After nearly twenty minutes, she gave her name to the maitre d' and told him she'd be sitting out on the dock behind the restaurant.

It was a clear night, the moon a faint fingernail paring against a black satin sky over the harbor. She watched the stars flicker like fireflies in and out of filmy passing clouds, listened to the sounds of gentle waves lapping at the boats moored in the harbor, and let her mind float out over the water. A half-hour later, she returned to the restaurant patio. The only person in sight was a young woman alone at a table set for four. She looked annoyed. And she looked wasted, as well, with glazed eyes and a bobbling head.

"Excuse me," Beverly said. "Have you seen two guys come in?"

"No. I'm waiting for a couple of guys myself, and they're an hour late, the jerks."

Beverly had a hunch. "Are their names Jim and Les?"

"Yeah. How did you know?"

Just then Beverly saw the two men approaching the patio entrance. "Look, here they come." Then she added hastily. "I know it's weird, and you don't know me, but I want to get their pictures. Help me if you can. Please."

The woman's eyes weren't focusing very well, but she smiled mischievously. "That sounds like fun."

"Sorry we're late, ladies," Les said. "We had trouble getting Jim's motor scooter going."

"You should have used his Budget VW then," Beverly said.

Les roared, and Jim scowled at him in reproof.

To Beverly's eye, the woman, whose name was Missy or Sissy or something cupcake like that, had a pretty face with a lot of miles on it. She said she was from somewhere in Virginia hunt country, but had also lived in Vail, Santa Barbara, and Fort Lauderdale.

"You forgot to mention that little eighteen-month stint in Texas," Les whispered to her.

She froze. "Who told you that?"

"Oh, a little bird," Les said.

"Shut up, Les," Jim said sternly.

They ordered margaritas and pizzas. When the waiter set their drinks on the table, Beverly whisked her camera out of her purse and quickly snapped shots that showed both men's faces clearly with the big drinks in front of them. Jim set his jaw. Les grinned nervously. The young woman clambered onto Jim's lap, threw her arms around him and mugged for the camera, while Beverly snapped off shots as fast as she could. Missy, clearly enjoying her role, began planting kisses all over Jim's face.

A crimson flush spread across his face, ears, and neck. "Cut it out," he ordered angrily.

"What's the matter, honey?" she said, patting his burning cheek. "Don't you like girls?"

"Why don't you beat it, slut," he said, swatting her hands away from his face, and practically tossing her back into her own chair. "We'd like to have a nice quiet dinner with Ms. Parmentier here."

She pouted. "You all seem to be forgetting that you invited me. You promised me some . . . candy," she said in a bratty voice. "And I'm not leaving 'til I get it." She knocked back the rest of her drink and sat tight.

Jim whipped out a thin black wallet that he snapped open in the woman's face. She blanched. In a flash, she leaped out of her chair and fled into the night.

When Beverly made a grab for Jim's little black wallet, Les caught her wrist in midair and let it go only after Jim had put it back into his pocket. The atmosphere at the table was tense. Just then, the waiter delivered their pizzas.

"Put mine in a carry-out box, please," Beverly said to the waiter. "I'm leaving."

While waiting for him to return with her pizza, she turned to the men. "So did you get a lot of top-secret information on your taxpayer-sponsored mission to St. Barth's?" she asked.

Jim bristled. "You've got some strange ideas, lady. I don't know where you got the idea Les and I are some kind of cops."

"You've got a short memory. Yesterday you admitted it. And a moment ago, you flashed a badge at that girl."

"Badge? What badge?" he scoffed. "We don't need no stinkin' badges. We're just a couple of guys down here on vacation. I'm a health care consultant, and Les is a real estate agent."

"Yeah, and I'm Princess Di," Beverly said. She took her pizza box from the waiter and turned to go. Jim grabbed her hand, but she jerked it away. "Get your hands off me, you fucking creep."

"Aren't you going to pay your share of the bill?" Jim asked.

"Hell no! First of all, you invited me. And furthermore, you're not paying the bill anyway. It's on the taxpayers. And believe me, I've already paid my share."

Beverly stomped out of the restaurant and headed down the road.

"You're not going to find a taxi," Jim sang out after her.

She knew he was probably right. But she didn't care if she had to walk the five miles home. After she had been walking for about a half hour, the taxi that had taken her into Gustavia drove up. Beverly groaned. It was the Brooklyn tree dodger again.

"Hop in," he said.

She hesitated.

"C'mon, it's a freebie. I'm on my way home."

He held open the front door of the cab, but Beverly got into the back seat, figuring she could make an escape if she had to. Her aching feet made her get into the taxi; her head was against the idea.

Looking in the rearview mirror, the driver asked whether she'd thought any more about stashing her money offshore. "I got an uncle in the Cosa Nostra. He parks his cash over in the Caymans. You know the Cosa Nostra?"

"Of course I do," Beverly said.

"So what do you know about the Cosa Nostra?"

He was looking in the rearview mirror so often now she was sure they were going to end up in the ocean. "It's a great pizzeria in downtown Escanaba, Michigan," she told him. "Except they don't deliver."

"Haw, haw!" he laughed.

Beverly got him to take her to the door of her cottage, declining his invitation to go for a drink and "have a little fun for a change." Not if you were the last man on earth, she thought.

The next morning, when Madame LaFleur dropped her off at St. Barth's airport, the taxi driver was at the coffee bar, talking to a red-haired Chicano who was clutching a couple of tennis rackets. She couldn't swear it was Herman Naranjo, whom she knew only from Pancha's description, but the man was wearing a Santa Fe Rodeo T-shirt and cowboy boots, and he looked New Mexican.

Two

A few days after Beverly's return from St. Barth's, she and Lucille met at the store. She had never seen the young woman so upset. The handsome six-board, eighteenth-century Andalusian trunk Beverly had shipped from Miami had arrived at La Ñapa with eight quarter-sized holes drilled in its sides. Lucille seemed to feel it was her fault somehow. Her face was creased in a worried frown, and her purple-rimmed glasses slid down her nose.

"It's not your fault. You didn't drill the trunk," Beverly said.

"But I feel responsible."

"You're not. But I'd sure as hell like to know who is."

In spite of someone's lame attempt to age the rims of the holes with colored wax or shoe polish, it was obvious they were new.

"I know they weren't there when I bought that trunk in Miami. I'm not blind," Beverly said.

"It's ruined!" Lucille said.

"No, but its value is certainly lessened. We'll have to get those holes plugged before we can put it out for sale."

"The holes matched the ones in the exterior packing, so whoever made them must have drilled right through the cardboard and the paper."

Beverly looked around the storeroom. "Where are the packing materials anyway?"

Lucille groaned. "I told Sherry you said not to throw them away. And I reminded her again after I saw there was damage to the trunk. But she pitched the stuff out anyway when I wasn't here."

"Ay, that woman! Nobody can tell her anything."

"She said there was too much junk in here, and she wanted to keep the place neat," Lucille said.

"Hmmm," Beverly said. "Since when is she a neat freak?"

The damage infuriated and depressed Beverly. It wasn't the result of any legitimate inspection of interstate commerce. It was a deliberate fuck-you message from the only people who had the huevos to intentionally damage a valuable antique: *federales.*

She retreated to her office, slumped into her desk chair, and contemplated filing a claim with the shipper. But without the wrappings, she couldn't prove the trunk had been drilled after she consigned it to the shipping company. Sherry did somebody a big favor when she ditched the packing materials. Why had she done that?

Everything Beverly had shipped from Miami arrived damaged. Other antiques had drill holes in them. The joinery on the *santos* and small furniture items had been pried apart, and the paper backing on the paintings had been slashed. It would take time and money to have a professional repair the vandalism.

Beverly's house sitters, Danny and Nancy, had problems with the telephone in her house while she was away.

"I'm sorry," Beverly said.

"Bev, it's not like you caused the problem. Ordinarily, it wouldn't have been a big deal," Nancy said. "But I was putting together a report for an international group working on an AIDS vaccine. I set up my fax machine, and at first, I had no problem sending and receiving faxes from the other grant participants in Mexico, France, Germany, and Japan. Then one day, none of my international calls would go through, whether I used your Sprint service, my AT&T long distance card, or Danny's MCI number.

"I called Sprint customer service, and they told me they were experiencing temporary problems in calling out of Santa Fe. 'I'm in Albuquerque,' I told them. 'I'll get right back to you,' the Sprint representative said, but he never did.

"I thought the problem might be in the fax switching device, so I disconnected it. Regular international calls still wouldn't go through. I could receive calls, but the connections were terrible. I asked several people in Albuquerque if they were having problems with their international calls. No one was. I couldn't wait for the problem with your phone to be worked out, so I moved to a temporary office."

Beverly made several angry calls to Sprint, getting a different person and a different answer every time. Then she wrote a letter to the chairman of the board of the company. A week later, she received a call from an area supervisor.

"Ms. Parmentier, we had difficulties with our satellite connections, but we have solved the problem, and you should have no more inconveniences with your long distance service, including international calls. We'd like to offer you a $10 credit for your trouble."

She wanted to tell him to put his ten bucks where the sun didn't shine. Instead, she thanked him graciously and accepted the credit.

Strange noises continued to disrupt Beverly's home and business phone calls. Exasperated, she requested a meeting with the head of US West security.

The phone company's main office in downtown Albuquerque reminded her of a World War II cement bunker. It took her some time to find the security office, which was unmarked and windowless. The head of security was a balding, priestly person who nodded sympathetically over his folded hands as she described the noises on the lines, the abrupt disconnections when she said anything negative about U.S. customs, and the blocking of international calls and faxes. Reluctantly, he agreed to send someone to inspect her phones.

The following day, a technician arrived at Beverly's house. She watched him put on a pair of headphones and futz around the house, sticking things into the phone jacks and nodding. After he left, heading for her store to repeat the inspection, she discovered the phones didn't work at all. She called the store from Doña Lupe's house to ask the tech to come back.

He apologized when he returned and fixed the problem in a few minutes. On his way out the door, he hesitated. "Ma'am? Did you know answering machines can be used as background microphones?"

Beverly suddenly felt cold, as if an icy north wind were sweeping through her house. "No, I didn't know that. Thank you for telling me."

The tech looked at the floor. "There's not much I can do about your phones. I'm sorry. I just do my job, you know."

Beverly nodded. "I understand."

Three

A couple of days after Joe Scarafaggio and the other customs agents returned to Albuquerque from St. Barth's, he and Sherry met at the agency apartment on Montgomery where he was staying again. Sherry was eager to hear how things had gone on the trip, and Scary was the only task force member who would tell her anything.

The apartment was a typical bachelor pad. Grimy, mismatched plaid sofas and chairs, and a ratty Naugahyde La-Z-Boy with a broken footpad slumped in front of a big-screen TV. A chipped coffee table in front of the TV, draped with a couple of socks and a bedroom slipper, appeared to serve primarily as a footrest. Half-empty beer bottles filled with cigarette butts and empty pizza boxes littered nearly every horizontal surface in the living room.

Sherry went into the kitchen to get a glass of water, but changed her mind when she saw the sink. Mired in its scummy pond was a fleet of half-sunk dirty dishes and coffee cups. The counters were dotted with chicken bones and fast food containers. The stench of garbage chased her back into the living room, which merely reeked like an old bar. She hoped she wouldn't have to find out what the bathroom smelled like.

Although the apartment grossed her out and she wanted to flee, Sherry reminded herself of her mission. She sat down next to Scary on the sofa in the living room and played with the hair that sprouted from the top of his half-unbuttoned shirt. "Did you guys get the goods on Beverly?" she asked.

Scary laughed and moved closer to her on the sofa. He leaned over and nuzzled her neck.

"Oooowwwww," she said, pushing him away. "You need a shave, Scary."

He ignored her and fumbled with the buttons on her furry mohair sweater. "Scaaaarrrrry," she protested, "someone could come in on us. Don't a lot of people have keys to this place?"

"Naaawww. Not that many. It's mostly used by the El Paso guys when they come to town."

"What if it's bugged?"

"It's not bugged. And nobody's gonna walk in on us. Don't you worry. Now why don't we go back in the bedroom and get a little more comfortable, huh?"

"Maybe later, honey. OK?" Sherry whispered, dropping her head so that her hair brushed softly against his hands, which she held just out of reach of her breasts. "Did you guys get her doing anything?"

"Plenty," Scary said sarcastically. "She read books, wrote postcards, walked on the beach, and swam laps for hours. That broad doesn't know how to have a good time. But the rest of us had a blast. That place is beeeyoooootyful, I mean to tell you. They've got terrific nightclubs and restaurants, and cheap booze. Our hotel had a pool and hot tubs. Three hundred a night for a single— even with a government discount. Agent Orange went ape over the grass tennis courts. He said they were as good as any he'd played on anywhere. The guy used to be a pro, you know. Then they've got this nude beach, kid. I have never seen so many loose jugs in my whole life. Not even in Vegas are you going to see skin like you see on that beach. I had to keep a towel on my crotch the whole time. And on the way down there, we got to go to the Super Bowl. Tickets right on the fifty-yard line. The guys in Miami showed us a good time."

"You went to the Super Bowl? I would have given anything— anything—to go to that game. I'm a lifelong Cowboys fan, you know. The Super Bowl, Miami, the Caribbean island. How come everyone else gets plum assignments while I'm stuck in that dump of a store?"

"You're paying your dues, kid. Later you get the job perks."

"So you guys didn't get Beverly doing anything?"

"No." Scary nuzzled her neck again.

She winced as his whiskers scraped her skin.

"The San Juan guys picked her up and tried a few things."

"What did they try, honey?"

"Oh, they tried to get her to talk about her pre-Colombian smuggling. And they tried to take pictures of her together with a girl who's done time for dealing coke. And they had an AATA kid hustle her."

Scary nibbled Sherry's ear and she squirmed. "Which kid? Do I know him?"

"Not him, sweetheart—her," he laughed. "What a doll. I mean, that babe is a walking wet dream. I'd put on a dress if it'd get me into the sack with her. I can't believe she's queer. She just hasn't had the right guy, that's all."

Sherry knew the woman Scary was referring to, the one everyone in the program called "The Amazon" behind her back. She was from Dutch Guyana, wherever that was. She spoke a lot of foreign languages, and she was pretty good looking. But so what? She had never put the moves on Sherry, but she'd hit on some of the other women. Maybe some of them had gone for it. In today's agency, you have to have all kinds, Sherry thought. Even dykes.

"So did she get Beverly into the sack?"

Scary laughed. "Beverly's not that way. I told the San Juan guys they had it all wrong. They should have tried a beach boy on her. But for some reason, Zoffke wanted to get pictures of her in bed with a woman. I think the whole thing was a bust. The San Juan guys were a couple of losers. Beverly had their number right away. She even photographed them. By the way, kid," Scary said, "Zoffke is very hot for you to get the pictures she took of those guys in St. Barth's. And the negs. He wants you to find out where she keeps her photographs."

"It's not like I haven't tried, Scary." She leaned away from his mouth. "When you told me to look for the pictures, I went through her purse and everything right away. I think she gave the roll to somebody else to get developed, then took some other rolls to the Fast Photo to get us off the track. I haven't seen the photos again after she showed them to Lucille, except for one she pinned up in her office. She cut a thing out of an insurance ad and pasted it onto the bottom of a photo of two guys and some blonde at a table full of drinks. It says, 'Know your agent.'"

"Har!" Scary laughed. "That Beverly, she should have been a comedian."

"It's not funny, Scary. If there's ever an investigation . . ."

He patted her knee, then tried to move his hand up her thigh. But her skirt was too tight across her legs for his hand to get very far. "Don't you worry. There isn't going to be any investigation. But you'll get big brownie points with Zoffke if you find those photos."

"I think she stashed them somewhere. I'll keep looking. I got the packing boxes ditched before she got back, just to be on the safe side. I asked Dave to come by in his truck late one night and pick them up. The Albuquerque garbage collection isn't the most reliable in the world, you know. Lucille was pissed, and so is Beverly. You'll tell Zoffke how I got rid of the packing materials, won't you, sweetie?"

"I'll make sure he knows, kid." Scary nudged his nose into the top of her sweater.

Sherry giggled and pushed his head away. "God, Scary, your nose is colder than a greyhound's."

Scary smiled and tried the maneuver again. She shoved him away more forcefully this time. An angry look crossed his face. Worried she'd rejected him too harshly, Sherry quickly kissed him, then rested her head on his shoulder.

"Why did Zoffke tell that AATA kid to drill Beverly's stuff and bust it up, Scary? It was some nice old stuff. There wasn't any pre-Columbian in the shipment."

"I know that, and you know that, and everyone knows that. But Zoffke really has it in for Beverly. He's out to bust her balls big time."

"Girls don't have balls, Scary," she reminded him.

He leaned his head against her breasts, and through her sweater she could feel his warm breath on her skin.

"I know that, and you know that, sweetheart. But Zoffke, I don't think he knows about girls."

Sherry giggled, and with her arms around the back of his neck, she pulled his face deeper into the top of her sweater. If she kept his mouth away from her face, she wouldn't have to inhale his stinky breath. "So what are you saying, Scary?" she asked, rubbing his furry head with her chin as he nosed into her cleavage. "You think Zoffke's queer?"

Scary sat up, knocking her jaw with the top of his head. "Don't you ever say that!" he barked into her face. His bad breath hit her like an explosion of rotten onions. "Not to me, not to anyone. Ever! You hear me?"

"Take it easy, Scary." Sherry rubbed her jaw where his head had struck her. "I hear you. I hear you!" His violent outburst shocked her.

"You've got a lot to learn," he said, frowning. Then, with a heavy sigh, he settled his face back into the top of her sweater. "What do you say we go climb in the sack now?"

She pushed him gently away. "Honey, I just can't. You're a married guy, and I . . . I have to get back to work. I'm supposed to be out buying office supplies. Beverly's going to be upset if I'm not back soon. She's going to talk to her lawyer friend again as soon as I get back. I think they're up to something. I have to go now. Really, honey."

Scary sat up and gave her a dirty look. "You better not be playing with me," he said, tightening his grasp on her breasts. "I don't like to play games."

He was hurting her, and the pain brought tears to her eyes. Sherry was frightened, but tried to make light of his threat. She patted his hands playfully. "Owww, Scary. Lighten up, babycakes. I'm not playing with you, Joseph," she said with the deepest sincerity she could muster, flickering her eyelashes at him several times for emphasis.

Scary relaxed his hands, but he didn't remove them from her breasts.

"You're feeling the peaches a little too rough, honey," she whispered, blowing her warm breath into his hair-tufted ear. "Momma's not going to let you into the fruit stand if you're going to bruise the merchandise, baby."

Fearing he might not be convinced of her sincerity, she held his face gently and gave him a long, lingering kiss, an enthusiastic mashing that left both of them a little breathless when they came up for air a couple of minutes later.

Sherry stood up and smoothed out her skirt. "I'll see you here again next week, OK?" she whispered.

He stretched his arms out across the back of the sofa, watched her gather up her things, and tugged at the crotch of his pants. "Damn," he grumbled. "The things a guy has to go through to get a little nookie."

At the door Sherry turned and blew him a kiss. When the door closed behind her, she tossed a handful of breath mints into her mouth. Eeeeeeaaack! Kissing Scary was worse than kissing a dog that'd been eating dead fish!

Several days later, Sherry was in the clothing room folding sweaters when the telephone rang. Beverly answered it. "You've got a phone call," she told her and went back to her paperwork.

Sherry approached the sales desk and picked up the telephone. "This is Sherrell Stahnick. How may I help you?"

"You cunt!"

She recognized Scary's voice. His anger came at her through the telephone line like a speeding Mack truck. "Excuse me?"

"What kind of game are you playing with me? Agent Orange tells me you've got a thing going with Dave. A hot thing."

Sherry felt icicles breaking in her stomach. "I, uh, . . ."

"I'll see you at your house in twenty minutes," Scary hissed.

"I'm at work right now, you know. Maybe you could come fix my washing machine later." Sherry put her hand over the mouthpiece and turned to Beverly. "It's the washing machine repairman. My machine broke down. I need to get it fixed."

She put the phone back to her ear.

"Now!" Scary yelled. "You get your ass on home right now!" Then he hung up.

Sherry put the telephone down. "The repairman says this is the only time he can look at the machine unless I want to wait three weeks. Would you mind terribly if I went home now?"

"No problem." Beverly said. "It's been a slow afternoon."

Sherry grabbed her purse and raced out the door.

Four

When Sherry didn't show up for a Wednesday night coffee date with Dave, he went to her house, a little one-bedroom frame stucco near the university where she lived alone. She never missed their dates. Her BMW was parked in the driveway, but there was no response when he knocked. Dave's sixth sense told him he should go in. He took out his picks and went through her lock in less time than it took his wife to find her house keys in her purse.

"Sherry?" he called out when he walked into her living room. "Sherry?"

He heard a faint groan from the bedroom. He walked to the open door. The young woman lay sprawled on her bed, a naked, broken doll, tangled in a mess of bedclothes. "Oh, fuck," Dave said. Somebody had beaten her badly and maybe done worse to her. Her face was a rotten plum of bruises and cuts. She was barely conscious, her breath labored, her eyes enveloped in purple puffballs. But she recognized Dave and began to cry.

He picked up the phone to call an ambulance, but Sherry groaned and waved for him to stop. "Call Lita," she managed to mutter through a swollen jaw and fat, bleeding lips.

Dave called AATA with an urgent message for Lita: come to Stahnick's on the double.

As a medic in Vietnam, he'd seen a lot of bloodied, ravaged bodies, a lot of suffering and death. But the carnage of war was usually impersonal and random, and when a soldier was killed or wounded, it was fate: the guy had been in the wrong place at the wrong time. He was certain the attack on Sherry had been neither random nor impersonal.

While he waited for Lita, he sat on the edge of Sherry's bed, sponging the blood from her battered face with wet towels, stroking her hair and talking softly to her. Within twenty minutes, he heard the front door open. Lita came into the bedroom and knelt down at the Sherry's bedside.

"Get out of here, Dave," Lita said.

He tensed. "If you think for one goddamn minute that I . . ."

"Shhhhh," she said gently. "Go wait in the living room. I want to talk to her alone." She put her hand on his shoulder. "Please."

A quarter of an hour later, Lita came out of the bedroom and closed the door. She dropped onto the sofa and didn't say anything for several minutes. At last, she spoke. "Go home, Dave. Go home to your wife and daughters and pray nobody ever does to them what that animal did to this kid."

He shook his head. "We need to get her to a hospital. She has a broken jaw, some busted teeth. She's in shock, and I'd guess there are other injuries too."

"More than you can imagine," Lita said.

She called the Air Force base hospital and made arrangements to take Sherry in a side entry. They wrapped her in blankets, and Dave carried her out to Lita's car. He sat in the back seat and held Sherry in his arms, talking to her in the low, tender voice he'd used with his daughters when they were babies.

After the ER personnel took over, Lita and Dave went to the hospital canteen. She sipped coffee and avoided looking directly at him.

"OK," he finally said in exasperation. "What the hell happened? Was it someone she knew? I'll tear his limbs off!"

She took another sip. "I'll take care of it. It's an AATA matter. You are to stay out of it and act like nothing has happened. You've done enough already."

Dave exploded. "Who the hell are you to tell me what to do?" he yelled, pounding the table with his fists. The dishes and flatware bounced and rattled. The cafeteria was suddenly silent. For what seemed like a very long time, Dave and Lita stared at each other like junkyard dogs in an alley.

When everyone else in the canteen resumed eating, Lita broke the silence. "I can't decide whether you're to blame for this. Sherry is old enough to know better, I should think. But you are definitely old enough to know better. It was really stupid of you to have an affair with her. Good God, a trainee."

"OK, I'll concede it was stupid of me. But how did that get her hurt like this?" Dave grabbed Lita's wrist. "Who hurt her? It's somebody I know, isn't it."

She jerked her hand away and picked up her coffee cup. "This will get handled through proper channels. Don't fuck up anything any more than you already have. You shut your mouth, you go about your business, and it's all going to get taken care of. Our way. Otherwise it's the local police, the newspapers, and hassles from upstairs. *Big* hassles from upstairs. This program needs to keep a very low profile. And I'll make sure it does."

He stared at the exit sign for a few seconds and said he understood. But that was to mollify Lita. He'd find out who had hurt Sherry and make mincemeat out of the son of a bitch. Maybe he'd have to bide his time before he got the opportunity to wreck the guy. But he knew all about biding his time. He'd had a lot of practice at it.

Back at Sherry's, Dave and Lita gathered up things she would need, put on her answering machine, and locked her house. Dave turned down Lita's offer of a lift and rode home slowly on his bicycle. He needed some time alone before he had to endure the cacophony of televisions, telephones, and temperamental teenagers.

The next day, Lita called Beverly, posing as a friend of Sherry's, to say the young woman had to go home to Texas suddenly. An illness in the family, and she'd be gone for a long time.

Truth was, Sherry was gone for good. When she left the hospital, she dropped out of the program.

Five

In Washington, Rupert Eistopf paced up and down in front of his large desk, ranging as far from it as his phone cord would allow. He was on a call to Ray Zoffke.

"Galo Rivas Griswold was here last week and signed the plea bargain," Zoffke announced, pride showing in his voice. "He pleaded guilty to one count of making false statements on an import document and agreed to pay customs a $10,000 fine."

"What false statement? You mean the packing list on the infamous box of rocks you claimed were valuable pre-Columbian artifacts? All you got was one count on the guy?"

"I did my best with the prosecutor, sir, but this was all we could get."

"What happened to the deportation order on Rivas?"

"I slipped it into the pile of documents for the judge to sign, as we'd discussed, but Rivas's lawyer found the order. I knew she might notice it, but I was hoping she wouldn't make a fuss about it. We timed the signing to shortly before she was set to fly to Colorado on a skiing vacation. But she squawked anyway. The judge pulled the order, and the lawyer still made her goddamn plane."

"I was counting on the deportation order to add a little juice to the plea bargain, Ray. Now we'll have to rewrite the press release for the Central American news media. I'm disappointed in you." Eistopf tried to contain his emotions, but his voice quavered with anger.

"We did our best, sir. Rivas signed the plea bargain, though. Isn't that important enough?"

"You don't get it," Eistopf said tiredly. "This isn't a puny little cultural patrimony bust. Rivas is a well-known left-winger, even if he is an important member of the Salvadoran oligarchy. Usually those guys are to the right of Genghis Khan. But Rivas and his commie pals are thwarting our democracy agenda in Central America. Plus Roberto D'Abuisson is one of Rivas's sworn enemies."

"The death squad guy?"

"Yeah. But we have to keep him happy. There are big elections coming up in Salvador, we want Rivas's party to go down in flames, and we need D'Abuisson's help."

"How does this figure in, if I may ask?"

"By painting Rivas as a big-time artifact smuggler, the central figure in a huge, international band of grave robbers plundering Salvador's national treasures, a felon the United States has deported, we embarrass Rivas's party. And we add one more log to the bonfire the administration is trying to build under the Salvadoran electorate to vote the right way."

"Well, we've certainly been trying hard to do our part, sir."

"To tell you the truth, I'm not satisfied with your work. More than two years of planning and the expenditure of a lot of agency money and manpower went into this thing. Rivas's plea bargain isn't much of a haul. Making false statements on an import document! That's a charge you could probably level at 99 percent of the shoppers getting off a Hong Kong flight."

"We're still investigating Rivas's smuggling ring, sir. We think it goes far beyond Rivas. Others are involved."

"Anything new on Parmentier? That damn woman keeps writing letters to her congressman and senators, claiming customs is harassing her. I hate dealing with congressional inquiries!"

"As a matter of fact, I do have news on that front. All of a sudden, Parmentier has nearly a million dollars in her bank account. A well-placed source says she sold off part of her pre-Columbian art collection. And before Rivas left New Mexico, he sold his remaining inventory and most of his personal collection to her.

Moreover, Rivas's manager, Pancha Archibeque, the woman I nailed in the raid, is going to work for Parmentier in Albuquerque. We consider this proof positive that Parmentier has been part of Rivas Griswold's smuggling ring. I'd like your go-ahead to continue surveillance on her, sir. I think something's about to break here."

Eistopf pursed his lips and stared out the window at the Washington Monument. It was interesting that Parmentier suddenly had a lot of funny money. He'd never given much credence to Zoffke's contention that the woman was involved in smuggling and drugs. But maybe Zoffke was on to something after all. Still, this was all such penny ante stuff. The SAC was a megalomaniac nutcase. Normally Eistopf wouldn't bother with this lower-echelon crap. But the nat-pat initiative was his baby, and—like it or not—Zoffke and his ATTA trainees were his babysitters.

"OK, Ray. Keep going for now. But I want results. I want bodies. I want convictions. Do you hear me?"

"You're coming in loud and clear, sir."

Six

Beverly rested her elbows on a pile of law journals on Steve's desk and told him about the people who followed her in Miami and her encounters with "Jim Ross" and "Les Klug" on St. Barth's. He listened quietly, folding and unfolding his hairy hands.

"Steve, I've had enough. I think it's time to turn the tables."

He leaned back in his chair and crossed his arms behind his head. She noted the light from an overhead florescent fixture flashed across his glasses, momentarily giving him Orphan Annie eyes she couldn't see into.

"I think you're exaggerating all this," he said.

"Exaggerating what? The weirdos on St. Barth's? The holes in that trunk? My rifled packages? Ask Lucille if I dreamed up the deliberate damage to my shipments."

"I'm not saying you're imagining it. I'm saying you're making too big a deal out of it. It's the federal government you're talking about. You can't go after the federal government, Beverly. They could really come down hard on you. Just live with it."

"I *have* been living with it, for a year now. There is a huge, nasty, black cloud hanging over me wherever I go, whatever I do, and it's raining bowling balls on my house, my business, my car, my phones, my friends, my business contacts, my whole life."

"You should expect trouble if you're doing business with Latin America."

"That's horse shit! I have been in this business for more than fifteen years, and I have never handled anything even remotely questionable. You know that, and so does customs. What's going on here? Our stupid government spends millions in Latin America to wean people from the drug trade. And here I am, running my own successful—if miniscule—foreign aid program. Who's throwing a wrench in the works? *Los mismos cabrones*—the same bastards. Go figure."

Steve spun his chair around to look out the window. "As I've said before, if you had money, there are a few things you could do. But you don't, so you have to live with it."

She hesitated. "Well, now that you mention it, I do have a little money. My Aunt Magdalena left me a small inheritance. That's how I paid for the St. Barth's trip. I'd like to hire you to work for me on this."

Steve sat up so suddenly that his chair nearly catapulted him across his paper-strewn desk. Beverly could see his pupils clearly now. They flashed dollar signs.

"Wonderful news, Bev. Now we're in business. Here's what I think you ought to do. Keep records."

"I've been doing that all along. I've written volumes about this crap. Dates, descriptions of the people, license plate numbers, synopses of what has happened. I made copies of everything and stashed the papers in safe places."

Steve nodded and continued. "Buy yourself a camera."

"I've done that, too, a point-and-shoot. I've taken a number of pictures of the creeps. Don't you remember? I gave you some to safeguard for me last May, photos of Zoffke with some Mexican lowlifes, and just last week, I gave your secretary pictures of the two guys who tried to hustle me on St. Barth's. I think those photographs are really important, don't you?"

Steve nodded again. "As for legal moves, maybe we should make a Freedom of Information Act request of customs to see what records they have on you. We should get your phones checked out. And I'll find you a private investigator to document the harassment and ascertain exactly who these people are. We need incontrovertible evidence that it's customs before we can take any legal action against them. And Jesus, Beverly, if you have money, why don't you buy yourself a decent car?"

"My car runs just fine. Why should I buy a new one? And what does that have to do with anything?"

Steve wagged his head and frowned his "you're hopeless" look at her. He tapped his fingertips together. "It's going to cost a couple of thousand dollars to get your phones checked out."

She gulped.

"And a PI will cost you about $500 a day plus expenses."

She coughed.

"I'll have some information about a PI for you in a few days."

Beverly walked slowly out of the office. She wondered whether she was doing the right thing, hiring Steve rather than an expert civil rights attorney, as Mag and Danny had suggested. She was stunned by how much it cost to hire professional investigators. Magdalena's money could evaporate in no time.

Seven

Steve arranged for an electronics expert to inspect Beverly's phones on a Sunday morning. She was careful never to mention the plan over the telephone, and Steve said he had been careful in making the arrangements with the tech, George Sherman, aka Sherlock. If customs got wind of their plans, they would pull out all evidence of wiretapping before his inspection.

Danny was at Beverly's house by 7 a.m. the Sunday Sherlock was due to arrive, so she could leave to meet the tech at the store. With Danny there, she figured nobody would be able to get in to remove any bugs if he saw a technician checking out the phones at La Ñapa.

Minutes after Beverly arrived at the store, a black Bronco with tinted windows and oversized tires rumbled into the parking lot. A short, stocky man introduced himself as George Sherman. When she shook his hand, Beverly thought every one of her fingers would snap in two. His hands were as large as dinner plates, and although he wasn't much taller than she was, he was as wide as he was high and built like a pallet of cinder blocks. His arms, thick as a fullback's thighs, stuck out at his sides, and his neck looked as if it was reinforced with rebar.

As Sherlock began to haul huge loads of equipment into the store, Beverly asked him where he'd learned his trade.

"In the Army. I've been sweeping embassies and military installations all over the world for a dozen years. I went private a couple of years ago." He made a quick survey of the store. "Listening devices are usually placed in open containers."

Beverly rolled her eyes. "I have hundreds in here: baskets, pots, little clay churches, pencil holders."

"Well, they'd put the bugs in something not likely to be moved often."

Wearing headphones and playing ear-blasting heavy metal to activate bugs, he roamed slowly over everything in the store with a listening device. He paid special attention to containers in hard-to-reach spots, like the tops of cabinets and the backs of shelves.

For a while, Beverly watched Sherlock's search, then retired to her office and her paperwork. His jarring music made it impossible to concentrate, and besides, she was doing mental gymnastics, dying to ask him what—if anything—he had found. When he went outside to inspect the incoming telephone lines, she followed him.

He opened the phone box on the side of the building and studied its contents. "How long has this box been here?" he asked.

"Maybe a year. The phone company gave me a new box when I had a second line installed for processing credit card sales."

"Hmmm," he said.

Sherlock finished sweeping the store in two hours, then followed Beverly to her house. While he repeated the inspection process, Danny and Beverly sat at the dining room table, sipping coffee.

"Can't say I think much of his taste in music," Danny shouted over the din.

"Could be worse. He could be a Barry Manilow fan."

When the racket would permit conversation, they discussed Ricky.

"I think it's becoming too hard for Doña Lupe to care for him," Beverly said. "She's well over sixty-five and increasingly frail. As loyal and loving as she is to Ricky, I bet she'd be relieved if we could find him a place in a group home. Her daughter in Belén wants her to move in with her family, but they don't have room for Ricky, too."

"Let's work on finding him a new home. Living alone with an elderly lady isn't an ideal situation. He's fourteen and needs to be with other kids."

"The talking computer has been a huge success. He loves it."

"While you were in St. Barth's, Nancy and I spent hours struggling to program it. The technology's not where it should be, but we have it mostly figured out. We were amazed at how fast he picks up things. That deep, Darth Vader voice he chose is kind of scary."

"He enjoys shocking people with it. He's a typical teenager in many ways."

"'That makes me want to barf!' was one of the first things he wanted to be able to say. We programmed the sentence into the computer and showed him a key he could press to activate it. He's a good speller, but it's hard to watch him painstakingly peck out each letter."

"He's got a good mind. Now that he can communicate better, his teachers are amazed at how much he picked up in school in all those years of not being able to talk."

"He seems to be doing well with his electric wheelchair, too."

"I'll say. He whizzes around the halls at school and at Doña Lupe's house and never nicks the walls or the furniture. At first, Pooh was scared to death of the chair, but now she rides around on Ricky's lap or in the basket at the back of the chair. They cut quite a figure zooming around the neighborhood—Ricky's Batman cape fluttering in the breeze, Pooh peering over his shoulder with her raggy ears flapping."

Sherlock began to pack up his gear. Beverly offered him a cup of coffee, and a seat at the dining table for a debriefing. She held her breath.

"Well, I didn't find any bugs at either the store or in your house. In the telephone box outside the store, however, I found evidence of a 'third wire,' an illegal tap. But it's been removed.

Someone has been listening in on the store's phones from less than a mile away. In all likelihood, there have been bugs in your store, but they're gone now. Maybe somebody found out you hired me to sweep the store and your house."

"Only Steve and my close friends, Danny and Nancy, knew about the sweep," Beverly said.

"Hmmm," Sherlock mused. "I'm about 90-percent certain there are taps on both your home and store phones, but I can't prove it. They're probably legal taps, done at the phone company. You're not supposed to be able to notice anything when your phone's been legally tapped, but I can sometimes tell."

"How?" Danny asked.

"I send a signal down the line and listen to its echo. A tapped line sounds different from a clean one, although to most people, the difference is imperceptible."

"Since all of this started, I've noticed a hollowness to the sound coming over the line, and there's a faint echo when people speak," Beverly said.

Sherlock nodded. "That's it. Your lines don't sound clean to me. I'm sorry I can't give you anything concrete, and I'm really sorry the third wire is gone. In all likelihood, that was illegal surveillance, maybe a way for customs to listen to your phone conversations before they got legal permission."

Danny spoke up. "Last summer when I was here in New Mexico job hunting, I had phone problems where I was staying in Santa Fe. When a call came in, after the person identified himself, it sounded as if someone in the next room picked up an extension, but the house only had one phone."

"That's an illegal tap. There's somebody close by listening in, maybe a block or two away. And that's pretty much what they do—they tap into the line and pick up an extension when a call comes in. Pretty crude job, though. If you can hear them that clearly, they must be rank amateurs."

"So how do I have a private telephone conversation with my lawyer? Or my gynecologist?" Beverly asked.

"Talk someplace other than on your phones. Also, it takes two seconds to put a bug back in. I'm sorry, Ms. Parmentier. All I can suggest are low-tech answers. You get yourself some quarters and use a different pay phone every time you make a call. And if you want to have a little fun, when you know someone's on your line, put the phone down, plug your ears, and blow a police whistle into the receiver. That'll fix 'em for a while."

"It just makes me feel all warm and fuzzy to know that the private telephone call is a thing of the past," Beverly said.

Sherlock shrugged. "That's technology for you. But as soon as somebody figures out one move, somebody else figures out a countermove."

Beverly took out her checkbook and paid him an amount equal to what she made in two months.

Eight

Dave was at Garcia's enjoying a bowl of *menudo* when his pager went off. The call was from a couple of ATTA trainees parked down the street from Beverly's house who were letting Dave know that Sherlock had just backed out of her driveway.

Beverly was no dummy. She had been careful in hiring Sherlock. She had only talked to him on pay phones, she had Steve Bronstein pay the deposit for the job, and she hadn't given any hints that she was calling in a tech to sweep her store, house, and phone lines. The lawyer had been less careful. He called Sherlock from his office to set up the deal, oblivious to the magic that Elroy had worked on his phone lines.

Dave had known about Sherlock for days. An Alcohol, Tobacco, and Firearms guy he sometimes jogged with, who knew he was undercover at La Ñapa, told him ATF had been keeping close watch on Sherlock and had heard he was doing a job for Beverly. ATF was about to indict him. He was one of the best wiremen around. But he liked the ponies, he nearly always bet on the wrong ones, and when he ran short of funds, he resorted to gunrunning to the wrong people in Mexico.

Before Elroy went to Zoffke with the news about Sherlock, Dave had already contacted the boss, suggesting he get rid of the bugs and the third wire AATA had installed at her store as part of a training exercise. Dave had never liked the idea of the illegal tap. Too easy to find, and once the *permiso* had come through to tap Beverly's phones legally, it had been unnecessary.

It gave him great pleasure to scoop Zoffke's "electronics wizard," whom he detested—not because he was swishy (who cared?)—but because he was an arrogant little prick and had no business tapping or taping a lawyer's conversations. A good lawman doesn't need to break the law to enforce it; at least, not usually.

Two days before Sherlock's visit, while Beverly and friends were at the movies with Ricky Sandoval—and a couple of AATA trainees—the cleanup crew visited her house and store. When the techs were unable to dig a bug out of the tower of a large pottery church that had sat for more than a year in a window facing Lomas Boulevard, Zoffke sent a trainee to the store the next day to buy it, at a cost of $400 to Operation Pillage.

Dave almost felt sorry for Beverly. She had made a smart move, hiring Sherlock. But the deck had been stacked against her, and now she was out more than $2,000.

He finished the last of his *menudo* and wiped the bowl clean with a flour tortilla. He should have gotten a few points for warning the task force about the impending sweep. But nobody noticed. Certainly not Zoffke, the gatekeeper to his promotion.

Nine

Steve Bronstein danced into his office, his hands high over his head as he snapped his fingers. His suitcoat and tie flapping, he twirled on the tips of his tassled loafers and pirouetted down the hall toward his secretary's desk.

Darleen looked up from her word processor. "Let me guess, Steve. You got a bit part in *Fiddler on the Roof.*"

"Wrong, wench. Nope, I am expressing joy at the distinct possibility that you—lucky soul that you are—may be resting your eyes upon the next assistant U.S. attorney for the state of New Mexico!"

"I guess you and the U.S. attorney had a nice meeting, Steve. Did you have any food—or did you just drink your breakfast?"

"Madame, I assure you I am the paragon of sobriety on this pivotal occasion in my career as a lion of the law. Had I been offered intoxicants, I would have judiciously declined them, all but the heady brew of discussing my brilliant future with Schwentzle."

"So is it a done deal?"

"Well, not exactly. But the carrot was definitely dangled. Schwentzle wanted to know all about my cases, who I'm representing these days. He said he'd been following my work, and he was impressed. His office is always on the lookout for rising stars. His former aide, Armando Mendoza, was there, too. You know him. He's from your old stomping grounds in Los Lunas. He's a private investigator now, and he's running for state senator.

"I hate to ruin your good news, Steve. I think somebody broke into the office last night."

"Really? This office? Jesus! What did they get?"

"Well, that's what's weird. None of the stuff you would expect a thief to take is missing, like our computers, fax machines, tele-phones, or our petty cash."

"So what makes you think somebody broke in here?"

"Well, first off, the dead bolt on the back door was wrecked. Then I noticed somebody spilled a Pepsi or something brown and sticky on my desk, and they moved a bunch of things around, like maybe when they were trying to clean up the mess. Then I found the locked files had been opened and the files jumbled."

"Oh, boy. Was anything missing?"

"I had to take an inventory. Unless I'm mistaken, things were taken from just one file: Beverly's."

"What's missing?"

"Her photographs. She gave you two packets of prints—one last spring and then another last month when she came back from the Caribbean. This is creepy."

"Well, take it easy. I don't think it's any big deal. I'm sure you just misplaced them. They're surely around here somewhere."

"No, they're not. I put them in that locked file, and nobody but you and me has the combination. Should I call the police? I didn't want to do anything until I talked to you."

"We will not call the police about this. It's minor, a couple of temporarily missing packets of photographs of who knows what nuttiness of Beverly's. Probably poultry porno. I'm sure they'll turn up somewhere. Steve Bronstein, your next assistant U.S. attorney, can't afford to look like a flake by calling in the cops over a bunch of misplaced photographs."

Darleen drummed her fingernails on her desk and fumed. "Well, I think you at least ought to tell Beverly the photos are missing."

"No, I'm not telling her. The poor dear is wiggy enough as it is. We needn't fuel the flames of her paranoid fantasies. Like I say, let's just stay calm here. I'm sure they'll turn up."

Bronstein's dismissive attitude infuriated Darleen. If he had so little respect for Beverly and her case, then he should tell her to get another lawyer. And if he had so little respect for the sanctity of his clients' files, then maybe Darleen should find another job. There were plenty of lawyers out there who would appreciate an experienced legal secretary, a person who took her job seriously and who kept impeccable files and records. Bronstein was a jackass.

Ten

One Friday evening a week after Sherlock's visit to Beverly's store and home, Dave worked until nearly ter at the task force office, finishing his weekly reports and poring over the reams of Operation Pillage reports on the surveillance of Beverly, Pancha, and a dozen other small importers in Albuquerque and Santa Fe. By the time he finished, he was tired and thoroughly disgusted. There wasn't an iota of evidence that any of the people Operation Pillage had targeted were involved in anything criminal. Beverly included.

He mounted his bicycle and headed home. Halfway up Coal Avenue, he saw a baby-blue Lincoln Continental parked in front of a rickety old house on Hazeldine Street. He wanted to get home and go to bed, but his curiosity was piqued. He turned onto the street. The car had a whip antenna and a Federal Office Building parking sticker on the windshield—it had to be Zoffke's car. An old white van was parked in the driveway—Elroy's vehicle, if Dave wasn't mistaken.

No lights were on, except one coming from a window at the back of the house. Dave heard a loud groan come from inside the dwelling. Suddenly he heard loud thumping and more moaning. Instinctively, he crouched and reached around his waist for the .38 that wasn't there any more. Then he recognized the sounds and relaxed. He approached the rear of the house and peered into the candle-lit bedroom. A quivering white-whale body was jerking and thrashing on top of a smaller, equally pale body that was twisted up in the bed's rumpled red sheets. A kinky-haired blond head was half buried in a big pillow pushed up against the headboard. Fists gripped the pillow's corners.

¡Coño! he thought. In Dave's sometimes bizarre career, he'd

seen some unusual human behavior. But this was a first. He looked in the window again. The bodies were now collapsed in a twining of sweat, heavy breathing, and bedclothes. The large one turned his florid face toward the window and froze when his eyes met Dave's.

Dave sat on the porch steps and waited. At times like this, he wished he still smoked. Soon, the thud of cowboy boots on the wooden floor of the old house announced Zoffke's approach. Behind Dave, the screen door creaked open and snapped shut.

"I thought it was you," Zoffke said in a high-pitched voice strangled with fury.

Dave neither got up nor looked around as Zoffke stood behind him.

"I want you in my office downtown at zero seven hundred hours, Carney," he hissed. "You got that?"

"Yup," Dave said.

Zoffke got into the Continental, slammed the door shut, and roared away with a squeal of rubber.

Dave got on his bicycle and pedaled homeward. Was this a wonderful stroke of fortune? Did he now have the goods on his fuckhead boss? Goods that would help him secure his promotion? Maybe. But he was also in deep trouble with Zoffke, a dangerous man who would give the thumbs up or thumbs down on the terms of his financial future.

At seven the next morning, Dave, dressed in his gardener's gear, sat in the GSA chair in front of Zoffke's desk, one leg crossed over the other. The boss, wearing his uniform and badge, stood looking out the window.

"Want some coffee?" Zoffke asked.

"No thanks, sir." Dave tried to look casual, but he was nervous. He kept telling himself he had nothing to worry about.

"You know that I was born in Germany," Zoffke said in a small voice without looking directly at Dave.

"Yes, sir."

"I was six years old when the war ended. My mother and I were living in Berlin. My father . . . he disappeared when the Russians advanced on the capital. So it was just my mother and me in a small apartment in the Winterfeldstrasse. We had no food and no fuel. One day, before the Americans had control of the sector, five Russian soldiers followed my mother into our apartment when she was coming back from looking for something for us to eat. They tore her clothes off, they hit her, they toyed with her, they called her a Nazi whore, and they took turns raping her. They made me watch. They told me it would make a man out of me. Now I'd know how it was done. By the time they left, she was nearly dead from the beating and the loss of blood."

Zoffke paused. "I . . . I think this has affected me," he said in a barely audible voice.

"Sir, I . . ."

Zoffke held up his hand and stopped Dave. "I stole food and coal to keep us alive, and with my slingshot, I killed birds in Tiergarten for soup. My mother slowly got well, although she was always nervous and irritable after that, and in the night, she often woke up screaming. In 1947, through her mother's sister in Alabama, we were able to immigrate to Mobile. We lived in my great aunt's motel, and we cleaned the motel rooms for her. It was nig . . . it was work for colored people. But we did it, and we survived, and three years later my father appeared. He had been in Argentina and was able to travel to the states on an Argentine passport and get a job as a policeman. My father, too, was a changed man. He hit me, and he hit my mother and yelled at her and blamed her for all his disappointments in life. They separated for good when I was twelve, and I never saw him again. We went back to living at the motel, where my mother soon met a man, a salesman who often stayed there. He was good to us, he was generous and charming, and he made her happy. What she never knew was . . . I was the one he was really interested in."

"Sir, I . . ."

Zoffke ignored Dave, looked out the window, and continued. "He bought me clothes and football gear and a bicycle. He gave my mother bits of the cheap jewelry he sold, he took her dancing and out to dinner in fine restaurants, and all I had to do was make him happy for a few moments now and then in one of the empty motel rooms."

Zoffke stopped and cleared his throat. "My mother's friend paid my way through the University of Alabama, even though by then our . . . our relationship had come to an end. After college, I spent five years in the Army. Then I joined the agency. It was more money and a better future for my mother and myself. The agency has been good to me. It has been my life. My mother is not well, and she must have nursing care around the clock. It's expensive, but I am able to make her comfortable, and she is very proud of her Reinhardt. I will do anything—*anything*—to see that she is always proud of her little boy. Do you understand me, Carney?" Zoffke turned and stared at Dave.

"Yes sir, I think I do," he replied evenly, hoping Zoffke didn't hear the loud pounding of his heart.

He cleared his throat. "Good. I think we are here to talk about your promotion." He paused and looked hard and long at Dave.

"You can be sure of my discretion, sir."

"Good. I will make the recommendation. You are a fine officer, you are wise, and you will be a man true to his word. Is there anything else you would like to discuss?"

"If it's all the same to you, sir, I would like to conclude my undercover assignment at La Ñapa."

Zoffke lowered his head and shook it from side to side, but said nothing, his lips cemented closed.

"I was wondering if there might be an opening for me at AATA, sir. I only have a year and a half to go before retirement, and I have experience that might be useful to our trainees."

Zoffke sighed. "I'll see what I can do. For now, however, I must ask you to continue your surveillance on this importer. This is a matter of utmost importance to the agency, and you are the most qualified person for the task."

"Thank you, sir." Dave stood and shook Zoffke's hand. He left the office and closed the door carefully behind hi.n. It was all he could do not to dance. His promo was in the bag. A fattened pension. So he didn't get everything he wanted. No big deal. He could handle a few more months of undercover work, and he still had a shot at an AATA job. He desperately wanted a chance to get back into Lita's good graces.

Dave trotted down the stairs to the ground floor of the Federal Building, wondering if Zoffke wanted him to feel sorry for him and his sad tale. Well, he didn't. People were born gay—Dave was pretty sure of that—and he didn't care what people did in the privacy of their homes. So Zoffke had to help his mother clean motel rooms when he was a kid. Big deal. From the time Dave could walk, he'd had to slop pigs and shovel their shit in Iowa's below-zero winters and stinking, sultry summers. And then there was the pedophile preacher he'd had to fend off when he was a ten-year-old at Bible camp. None of it had made him light in his loafers or a Nazi like Zoffke.

Soon enough, whether the AATA job panned out or not, Dave would be a full-time fly fisherman, camping out all over the West. An Airstream or a Winnebago? He'd ask Paulette which one she preferred.

BOOK FIVE

One

March 1989

One morning in early spring, Beverly woke to the buzz of bees in the flowering quince outside her bedroom window. A cool, fragrant breeze slipped in above the lowered sash and spread over her like a swath of featherweight silk. A nightgowned Maja, she lingered in the sheets, contemplating the quince's fluttering pink blossoms and bright green leaves. Suddenly, the telephone's shrill ring intruded into her reverie. She rolled over and answered the phone on her bedside table.

"I have some news for you," Steve said.

Beverly remembered Sherlock's admonition to use a pay phone if she wanted to have a private conversation. "I'll call you right back. Are you home?"

"No, I'm at work."

Beverly threw cold water on her face, dressed, and drove to a convenience store, where she used a public telephone to call Steve's office.

"I found an investigator for you," he said. "His name is Armando Mendoza. He's an Albuquerque lawyer who sometimes works as a private investigator."

"Is he good?"

"He comes highly recommended. I told him a little about

your case, and he thinks he can help you. Here's his number. Call him."

She hung up. Her hands shook as she took another quarter out of her wallet and fed it into the pay phone. Maybe rich people hired private investigators every day of the week, but this was new territory for her. She spoke to Mendoza's assistant, María Chino, and made an appointment to see them the following morning.

When she walked into Mendoza's office in downtown Albuquerque, she thought she'd wandered into a film noir detective story. Dark oak paneling lined the walls and boxy, arts-and-crafts-era furniture sat around the waiting room like scruffy old bachelors. Magazines, their edges ruffled from years of perusal, covered a scratched, glass-topped coffee table, and doors windowed with snowflake-patterned frosted glass let light into interior offices. She picked up a *Saturday Evening Post* and sank down into a sagging sofa with cracked leather upholstery that rode the springs like a thin blanket on a bony nag.

After several minutes, one of the doors opened, and a small, dark-haired, neatly dressed woman, a dead-ringer for Della Street, emerged. "Ms. Parmentier? Mr. Mendoza called to say he and Ms. Chino are going to be half an hour late. Can I get you some coffee?"

"No thank you. Maybe later. I'll use the time to mail some bills."

Beverly walked to the nearby downtown post office, bought stamps, and stood beside a mailbox in front of the building licking the stamps and patting them onto envelopes. A red Cadillac slid to the curb not ten feet away. A man leaned out the passenger-side window and pointed a camera at her.

Setting her pile of envelopes carefully on the mailbox, she took out her point-and-shoot camera, and quickly clicked off several photos of the car and its passengers. Through her lens, she saw the man put down his camera and scowl. He turned toward the driver, a dishy blonde who sometimes followed Beverly around town. In an angry screech of rubber, the Cadillac sped off, hurling a large white poodle leaning over the front seat to the rear of the car like a furry, oversize tennis ball.

This is hilarious! Beverly thought. A poodle? A red Cadillac?

Although her quivering arms and legs reminded her she'd just been assaulted, she was proud of herself for moving quickly, shooting right back, and running the bastards off. With any kind of luck, she'd have clear photos of her assailants and their car. A surge of triumph overcame her frayed nerves and energized her as she watched the car disappear down Gold Street.

She wrote down the license plate number before she forgot it, mailed her bills, and returned to Mendoza's office, where she accepted a cup of coffee from Della Street. Armando Mendoza, his assistant, María Chino, and Beverly adjourned to a conference room behind a frosted glass door.

Mendoza, a small, nattily dressed man, reminded Beverly of a department store men's wear clerk in his tidy but ordinary navy blue suit and red rep-striped tie. His thick black hair, slicked back from a high forehead, matched the well-trimmed mustache that outlined his upper lip. His small, intense eyes, shiny and black as his hair, blinked constantly. She couldn't decide if he was nervous or whether his contact lenses were bothering him. His jitteriness did not inspire confidence.

María Chino, by contrast, was quiet, demure, and elegant. Tall and dark, with striking Indian and Hispanic features, she wore her gray knit turtleneck dress, simple Hopi silver earrings and bracelets, and sleek, shoulder-length raven hair with confidence and grace. Her steel gray eyes, large and intelligent, moved back and forth between her boss and Beverly, as if she were reading from side-by-side texts.

Mendoza toyed nervously with a stack of papers on his desk as he outlined the honey trap he, Steve, and María had devised.

"Our goal is to draw out the people who have been following you and identify them. Once we know who they are, we'll see what legal action we can take against them. We'll have someone pretending to be an important supplier of mysterious goods call you at your store from a pay phone in Los Angeles. He'll suggest you meet him at a hotel near LAX to take a look at something you won't want to pass up. If customs has tapped your phone, this conversation should sucker them into following you. Maria and I will accompany you to L.A. to see who shows up."

"I know just the guy for the role of the sleazy supplier," Beverly said. "A friend's boyfriend in Santa Monica is a bit-part actor always in need of a few bucks."

"Good. You play your role straight, never acknowledging me or María during the setup. We'll be the lookouts, identifying the tails and following them. We'll fly Southwest to LAX."

"My least favorite airline," she groused.

"Well, we're trying to hold down costs here. But more importantly, Southwest's open seating plan will enable Maria and me to see which passengers gravitate toward you."

They finalized plans for the scenario, and Beverly left Mendoza's office. The plan made her nervous. Suckering customs into following her to L.A. seemed like opening the door to the lion's cage. But what could happen? Nobody would be doing anything illegal, and her lawyer would have notes describing the setup in case customs decided to bust Beverly and her phony supplier.

She went looking for a pay phone. Peeling the wrapping down from the roll of quarters she now carried with her, she called her friend Suzanne at her community college office in Santa Monica. They'd been roommates at UNM and had remained friends. Beverly outlined the situation and told her about the proposed set-up.

"I'm sorry to hear about customs' harassment," Suzanne said. "How bizarre. You, of all people. But your scenario sounds like fun. You create your own play and see who shows up to participate in it. I like it. I'm sure Barry will go for it. He loves playing sleazy guys, and he's not busy right now."

After they finished their conversation, Beverly fed another fistful of quarters into the pay phone and called another former UNM classmate, Suzanne's ex-husband, Hal Coughlin, a prominent L.A. trial attorney. "I'm going to be in town next week on business, Hal. Is there any chance you'd be free for breakfast Friday morning?"

"Looks like my calendar's clear until ten. I'd love to see you, Bev," he replied.

She didn't tell him about the setup or the events that had prompted it. They could talk over breakfast. She was hopeful that her old friend, one of the smartest, most cunning people she knew, would have some ideas on what kind of legal action she could take once she knew exactly who was harassing her.

María Chino wrote out the scenario for the setup and faxed a copy to Barry. Several days later, the store's phone rang. When Beverly picked it up, she recognized Barry's voice, although he was calling himself Nestor and talking with a Puerto Rican accent. If Barry knew the Spanish word for tacos, he was doing well. But he did a great job with the scenario. He sounded the way Beverly guessed a smuggler would: oily, whiny, arrogant, and insistent that she meet him in L.A. to see the great treasure he had for her. As called for in the script, Nestor and Beverly agreed to meet in the lobby of the Hyatt Hotel near LAX at 11 a.m. two days later.

Two

Beverly didn't sleep the night before the setup. She was excited, but worried. Something might go terribly wrong, but what? The next morning, she was alert and on time at Albuquerque Sunport. At the Southwest Airlines boarding gate, she immediately picked Mendoza out of the crowd. The investigator had slicked his hair back à la Adolphe Menjou and wore a gray flannel suit. He appeared to be reading a newspaper as he stood off to one side of the crowd gathered around the gate. María Chino was close behind Beverly in line. She was hard to miss, decked out in a bright yellow linen dress with a black-and-white-checked silk scarf wrapped around her neck.

Beverly sipped coffee from a styrofoam cup and made sure she never gave either PI more than a passing glance. Her nerves were jangled, but she did her best to look relaxed and businesslike. Mendoza and María Chino's appearances added to her nervousness, however. Beverly knew little about surveillance techniques, but it seemed to her both PIs stood out like Parisian mannequins in Southwest Airlines' Kmart crowd. Yet she had to trust the pros; she had $2,000 riding on them.

When Southwest announced passengers could board, she surged forward with the shuffling horde that choked the ramp and filed like nervous sheep into the plane's maw. Give me your poor, your tired, your luggage-laden, your crowded masses yearning to reach L.A. Once inside the plane, she looked for an open seat as her fellow passengers struggled with their carry-on baggage, filling every bit of space aboard with strollers, shopping bags, large plush toys, and squirming, bawling toddlers.

She settled into a window seat midway down the aisle. A tubby woman wearing a turquoise-print dress and what looked like a wig of curly gray hair immediately sat down next to her, leaving the aisle seat empty. María took a seat in the row across from Beverly. Mendoza sat up front in a backward-facing seat between an intense young man in horn-rimmed glasses and an elderly lady.

The plane was full, and it lumbered slowly down the runway. Just before it would have plowed into the Manzano Mountains, the metal creaked, the engines roared, and the plane hurtled skyward with all the grace of a pregnant elephant taking flight.

Once they were airborne, Beverly took out a legal pad and started a letter to Doc, but the woman next to her kept trying to read what she was writing. Annoyed, she put away the legal pad and opened up an Edna Buchanan mystery.

During the two-hour flight to Los Angeles, nothing seemed out of the ordinary. Infants wailed, and toddlers ran up and down the aisle. The crew made valiant efforts to be cheery, passing out packets of peanuts, soft drinks, flight information, and jokes. From time to time, Beverly glanced at the PIs. They both seemed engrossed in their reading.

The plan called for Beverly to pretend to make a call from a pay phone immediately after deplaning in L.A. to see who stayed close to her. She filed out of the plane with her carry-on and went to a bank of wall phones, where she dialed a nonsense number and carried on a mumbled conversation with the phone's recorded message: "If you would like to make a call, please hang up and dial again . . . If you would like to make a call, please hang up and dial again . . . If you . . ."

Out of the corner of her eye, she saw Mendoza leaning against a nearby pillar, reading his newspaper. During the several minutes she spent on the phone, no one approached her or used the pay phones on either side of her. She hung up and wandered down the corridor. Mendoza had told Beverly to kill some time in the airport before proceeding to her meeting with Nestor. He and María needed time to change clothes and get to the Hyatt.

Beverly entered a ladies' room, and headed to a stall in a far corner. She saw a turquoise print dress hit the floor in the stall next to hers. Next, black pumps and hose were exchanged for white socks and tennis shoes. A wig of gray curls fell to the floor and was rapidly scooped up. Beverly smiled. She waited until she heard the woman next to her unlatch her door, then emerged from her stall at the same time. The metal doors banged shut behind the two women. As Beverly suspected, the quick-change artist was the tubby woman who'd sat next to her on the plane. She now wore powder-blue sweats, tennis shoes, oversized pearl-rimmed glasses, and a salt-and-pepper straight-haired wig. The turquoise print dress spilled out of her shopping bag. When she looked up into the mirror over the washbasin and saw Beverly standing next to her, grinning like the proverbial canary-eating cat, her jaw dropped.

"I like your new outfit," Beverly said.

Before Beverly could blink, the woman grabbed her shopping bag and fled.

Suzanne was right. This is fun, Beverly thought. Walking with a springy step and trailing her overnight bag behind her, she dawdled in LAX, cruising newsstands and a bookstore while keeping an eye on the clock. Following the script, she left the airport at 10:40, hailed a cab, and directed the driver to the near-by Hyatt Hotel, where she was due to meet Nestor at 11 a.m.

Beverly's taxi came to a halt in front of the hotel just as a tall man hastily left the hotel, gesturing and yelling angrily at somebody inside the lobby. When he saw her in the taxi, he scowled, quickly turned his head away, and got into a black Taurus parked at the curb. Although he had moved quickly, she instantly recognized him as the man who had taken her picture from the red Cadillac in downtown Albuquerque.

Her heart gave a little leap. The plan was working. So far, she counted two fish on the line. Excited to see what would happen next in the movie that Mendoza, María, and Steve had concocted, she pushed open the glass doors.

Walking into the hotel was like walking onto a stage set. All the people in the lobby seemed to freeze in place for several seconds: the clerks at the reception desk answering phones and checking in guests, a bellhop ferrying luggage to a nearby elevator, two men in business suits leaning against the check-in counter conversing.

Beverly blinked, and they all began to move normally again. Her heart beat faster. C'mon, girl, she thought. Stay calm and stick to the script. She stopped in the middle of the lobby and looked around for a familiar face, but there was none. She momentarily panicked. Had Barry forgotten? Had he gotten delayed in traffic? Been arrested?

She sat down on one of the sofas in the center of the lobby and picked up a magazine. Too nervous to read, she flipped through the pages. Just then, her peripheral vision picked up Mendoza stepping out of the elevator. He took a chair along the back wall and began reading a magazine. Although Beverly only glanced at him briefly, she noted he had changed into a navy blazer and khakis, his hair was now stylishly rumpled and moussed, and he wore gold-framed glasses.

As if on cue, a side door opened, and Barry strode into the lobby, carrying a small red box. He wore a brown leather bomber jacket, a day-old beard, a dash of black mustache, and a wise-guy attitude. He surveyed the lobby, saw Beverly, sauntered up to the sofa where she sat, and flopped down next to her. He pecked her on the cheek. "How you doin', baby?" he asked loudly in a Spanish accent. Then he whispered in her ear. "Do you like the look? I call it 'Don Johnson does Nestor.'"

She did her best not to giggle. "Pretty cool, Nestor. But where's your gold chain? Your chest toupee? Your Rolex?" she whispered back.

"Left 'em in Miami, baby," he said. "But I do have this for you."

He handed her the red box. "Don't open it here. It's only a popcorn ball. Don't eat it—it's a little old. Not quite pre-Columbian, but close. Now what am I supposed to do?"

"I think we just sit here and see what happens," Beverly said, holding the box on her lap. "I'm nervous."

"Cool, baby. Gotta be cooooooooooool," Barry crooned.

Coming from Beverly's right, María entered the lobby, wearing skin-tight black jeans, high heels, and an oversized red sweater. Her long black hair was pulled back from her oval face in a swishy ponytail, and large, gold hoop earrings swung from her ear lobes.

Beverly saw Barry's eyes widen as he followed María across the lobby. "That's one of mine," she said.

"Oooooh, weeee! Can you introduce me? If she can act at all, I bet I could get her some parts. Lots of roles for Indians and Latinos now."

"I won't pimp for you, dear. Suzanne wouldn't like it."

Barry laughed. "I'm *scouting talent,* Bev. You have to get the L.A. vocabulary down. I'm only interested in her career."

"Right."

As Barry and Beverly chatted in low tones, the scowling man and the young man in horn-rimmed glasses who had sat next to Mendoza on the plane walked in the front door. Another fish? Or was Horn Rims' presence just a coincidence? She turned the red box around and around in her sweaty hands. Every few minutes, either The Scowler or Horn Rims walked past Barry and Beverly on the sofa. Then they'd take turns leaning against the desk in front of the cashier's window. They watched Beverly and Barry intently, but if either of them glanced their way, the men quickly looked away. Beverly thought they looked awfully obvious, pacing back and forth in front of her and Barry like cops on a beat, but she did her best not to show she'd noticed them.

Are they going to suddenly pull out badges and arrest us? she wondered. Her hands shook, and she gripped the box more tightly.

"Chill, baby." Barry whispered. "You're going to squash that box with your death grip. Think of being waist deep in snow high in the Sierras or under a cool waterfall in a rain forest. Be the snow. Be the waterfall."

Beverly groaned. "I'm not trying for an Oscar, guy. I'm just trying to keep from flying apart."

He patted her hand and grinned. "You're doing great."

As called for in the script, Barry hung around for about ten minutes, and then it was time for him to go. "Got to esplit, baby," he said loudly and tapped the box. "Lemme know what you think of this and if the price is right." He pecked Beverly on the cheek and left the lobby.

She tucked the unopened red box into her tote, stood on rubbery legs, and crossed the lobby to a bank of pay phones, where, as directed by the script, she called Alamo and arranged to rent a car. As she waited outside the hotel for the shuttle bus to the car-rental agency, she saw The Scowler get into his Taurus. When she stepped onto the shuttle bus, he started his engine. Horn Rims came out of the hotel and got into the passenger seat beside him. From her seat in the bus, Beverly looked into the right rearview mirror, watching them tail her to Alamo. They hung around until she got into her rental car, followed her for a few blocks, then sped off.

The plan now called for her to drive to Suzanne's house in Santa Monica. Mendoza and María would spend the rest of the day trying to identify the people who had tailed Beverly to LAX and the Hyatt, and they would periodically cruise Suzanne's street to see whether they could spot any surveillance. She was free until the following morning, when she had her breakfast date with Hal Coughlin.

Beverly carefully negotiated the frenzied maze of L.A. freeways to Santa Monica. Suzanne was at work, but she had left a key underneath a flowerpot by the back door of her little yellow 1940s bungalow. Once Beverly was inside, she collapsed on the living room sofa. Making it to that sofa in Santa Monica had used up every ounce of her mental and physical fuel supply. Her arms and legs quivered, and she felt as if she'd just run a marathon with a piano on her back. Sleep overcame her quickly, and it was a blessing.

She woke a couple of hours later and spent the rest of the afternoon reading an issue of *Vanity Fair* that featured Hal Coughlin and his latest celebrity trial, his successful defense of a best-selling author accused of plagiarism.

Beverly had tutored Hal in English during their freshman and sophomore years at UNM, when he was fresh off his family's feedlot in Clovis. It took some convincing for the short, square-rigged cowboy to trust her that such phrases as "he don't look good" and "she ain't done et yet" weren't acceptable English in much of the world beyond the plains of eastern New Mexico.

She found the article amusing and shook her head in disbelief. The writer gushed over Hal's semantic wizardry and effective courtroom theatrics. Don't that beat all, she thought.

That evening, over dinner in a nearby German restaurant, Suzanne and Beverly discussed the day's events. Beverly was relieved no one was seated close enough to listen to their conversation.

"What are you planning to do if your investigators can prove the people hassling you are customs agents or trainees?" Suzanne asked.

"I'll sue the bastards! If that's possible. I want compensation for my business losses. I also want them to pay me for training their new agents, at a hefty hourly rate, at least as much as I have to pay lawyers to get them to leave me alone."

"You know, if you got the goods on customs, Hal wouldn't be able to resist taking the case."

"Really? It's so penny ante."

"No, it's not, Bev. It could be a big deal—feds picking on a small, law-abiding importer like you. Somebody well known in the business and respected. Using you as an excuse to go on river trips and Caribbean vacations and eat and drink in fancy restaurants at taxpayer expense. Believe me, Hal could make a huge deal out of it, and he'd have a lot of fun doing it. Plus, he owes you."

Beverly smiled. Among other favors, she'd written several term papers for Hal Coughlin when he was in danger of flunking courses at UNM. "I guess he does owe me. But I'm not counting on him."

"I never should have, either," Suzanne said wistfully.

The next morning, Beverly arrived early at a Santa Monica diner for breakfast with Hal. Right on time, the lawyer-to-the-stars strode into the red-and-white tiled diner in his cowboy hat and Lucchese boots and slid into the booth across from her. He leaned over the tabletop to give her a quick kiss.

"So spin me your sad tale of woe," he said.

She was taken aback by his bluntness, but over coffee, she described her plight.

Hal frowned. "What do you want from me?"

"I dunno, Hal. I'm confused by it all. I thought maybe you'd have some ideas about what I can do to get this stopped."

He stroked his bristly Van Dyke beard. "I hope you don't expect me to get involved."

Beverly instantly regretted contacting him. Pompous ass! She came within milliseconds of telling him to go fuck himself. But then her smarter self prevailed. She might need Hal Coughlin on her side in the future. "I am not expecting anything from you, Hal. You can relax," she said coolly. "I have my own spear chuckers."

"Who?"

"I don't think it matters. Like you said, you can't get involved."

She knew his interest was now piqued. Hal didn't want to bother with her picayune problems. But he also didn't want to be left out of anything juicy.

They ordered breakfast. Beverly picked at her fruit plate and yogurt while Hal, eating like a starving cowboy, wolfed down his breakfast of biscuits, fried eggs, bacon, hash browns, and red-eye gravy. Not all the fat was in his head, she thought. He was also getting a little prosperous around his middle.

"Have you got any concrete information on who these guys are?" he asked.

"Some. That's why I'm here in L.A., as a matter of fact. Suzanne and some of her friends are helping me find out who the bastards are."

Hal flinched every so slightly at the mention of his ex-wife. Beverly knew he would now be dying to know who she was working with and what she was up to. But before he could ask, she glanced at a clock on the wall. "Oooops! I've got a plane to catch. Call me if you come up with any ideas for me, OK?" She slid out of the booth and bent over to kiss him good-bye.

Hal smiled. "Sorry if I'm a little gruff this morning. I'm getting ready for a big trial. I'll put on my thinking cap for you, Bev. You've always been a good friend to me, and I haven't forgotten it."

As Beverly wended her way through L.A.'s churning, chaotic traffic to the airport, she chewed her bottom lip and thought about her exchange with Hal. Well, it had been worth a try. He had probably forgotten about her and her quandary the second he got back into his Benz and his important L.A. persona.

Three

In the early afternoon, Armando Mendoza landed in Albuquerque. He made a phone call before leaving the Sunport, then drove to the Airport Marina restaurant, where he sat at the bar and ordered a Coors Lite. Twenty minutes later, a heavy-set man in sunglasses and a floral print shirt sat down on the barstool next to him, slapped a *People* magazine on the counter, and ordered a vodka tonic.

"How'd it go?" the man asked Mendoza.

The investigator shook his head. "Your guys were terrible, obvious as black beans in a bowl of white rice. Why did you bother sending them once you knew it was a setup?"

"They need practice."

"They certainly do. Say, do you have that, uh, . . . article for me? I need to get home to Los Lunas. It's been a long couple of days and I'm bushed."

The man in the hula shirt passed him the magazine. "It's all yours. The, uh, article you're looking for is on page 67. Good luck in the election."

"Thanks, Ray. Be seeing you."

Four

The day after Beverly returned to Albuquerque, she drove to Mendoza and María's office for a debriefing, excited as a sweepstakes winner on her way to collect. She took the steps two at a time up the staircase and burst past Della Street through the open door into Mendoza's office. The PIs greeted her with blank faces.

María, dressed simply in a beige linen dress, her smooth black hair twirled in a bun at the back of her neck, stood beside Mendoza with folded arms, looking at the floor.

The lawyer sat with his hands folded on a few sheets of paper on his desk. "I'm sorry. There were no signs of surveillance," he said.

Beverly was shocked. "What? You've got to be kidding, Armando! What about the kid in the horn rims? He sat next to you on the plane out. He walked back and forth in front of Barry and me at least four times at the Hyatt. He was in the Taurus that followed me to the Alamo office. And he was on the plane back to Albuquerque sitting across the aisle from me."

Mendoza shrugged. María looked out the office window.

"What about The Scowler, that really annoyed-looking guy hanging around the reception desk? And the quick-change artist in the women's bathroom at the airport? I described her in detail to you before we left LAX, and there she was again, sitting in the rear of the plane on our return flight to Albuquerque. You couldn't have missed her. The plane was nearly empty. She was wearing the same thing she'd worn on the plane to L.A.—a turquoise print dress and a wig of gray curls."

Mendoza shrugged. "Maybe we needed more people. But I didn't want it to get too expensive for you."

"Is there something going on here I don't get?" she asked heatedly, looking from María to Mendoza and back to María.

"What do you mean?" Mendoza asked.

"How could you not see those people? Are you guys blind?"

"Ms. Parmentier, I don't appreciate your inference that we didn't do a good job," Mendoza said testily. "Perhaps you should consider the possibility you're imagining things."

For a moment, Beverly was speechless. Then she found her voice. "You're incompetent, or crooked, or both. I'll make sure every attorney in town hears about this, starting with Steve Bronstein," she said heatedly.

Mendoza shrugged again and passed a sheet of paper across the desk to Beverly. "Here's the balance of our bill. It's now due and payable."

She had no recourse but to pay him. On her way out, she left a check with Della Street and hoped it would bounce.

She walked slowly and carefully down the stairs on unsteady legs to Central Avenue, where she'd parked her car. Her head felt as if it were full of day-old oatmeal. She didn't know what to think. She felt like crying, but even that brain function wasn't working. She was out more than $2,000, and it had all been for nothing. In a daze, she drove to La Ñapa.

A pale green, long-bed pickup truck was parked in Beverly's usual spot, and a curly-haired blonde wearing tight blue jeans and a snap-button shirt leaned up against the truck, nervously smoking a cigarette. It was Steve's secretary, Darleen.

"I have to talk to you, Beverly. About Steve."

A lump caught in her throat. "Is he OK?"

"Oh, he's fine. He's just a goddamn jerk. I've been thinking and thinking on this, and I finally made up my mind yesterday. First off, I'm quitting. Today. I found a new job in another law office."

"Oh, my gosh. I'm sorry to hear you're leaving Steve. You've been with him for a long time."

"Six years. But enough is enough. He doesn't appreciate me or how seriously I take my job. That man doesn't care about anybody but himself."

Beverly nodded. "I guess that's true."

"And second of all, he isn't doing what he should for you. You know those photographs you gave us for safekeeping?"

"Yeah," Beverly said, taking a deep breath.

"Well, maybe I shouldn't be telling you this, but I think it's the right thing to do. Last week, somebody broke into the office and took them."

Beverly's blood turned to ice water.

"I spent a whole morning trying to figure out what had been taken. And it was nothing but your two packets of photographs."

"Did you tell Steve?"

"Of course. But he said to keep quiet about it. He wasn't going to report the break-in, and he wasn't going to tell you your photographs were missing, because . . ."

"Because he thinks I'm crazy."

"Well, he didn't quite say that. But . . . well, I believe you about the harassment. I surely do. My whole family's military or police. I have seen enough and heard enough about the weird things that go on in this town that I don't think for one minute that you're making any of it up. You need a better lawyer."

"My aunt told me that, and so did my friends. I should have listened."

"Steve Bronstein is working for one person and one person alone—Steve Bronstein. He thinks he's the next assistant U.S. attorney, and a Supreme Court appointment isn't far behind. He told you to hire Armando Mendoza because he thought it would get him some points with the U.S. attorney, Schwentzle, who told Steve that Armando was looking for PI work. Well, I grew up with Armando in Los Lunas. He's no real PI, and I'm not sure what he was up to, taking a job like that one for you. There's something fishy there, believe you me."

Darleen dug the toe of her boot into the gravel and tucked her hands into her jeans pockets. "Those Mendozas are no good. Nobody in Los Lunas trusts any of them any further than you can throw them. Old Armando Senior, the retired state senator, cheated a lot of people out of their land grants."

"I appreciate your telling me this, Darleen. I know it couldn't have been an easy decision. I'm sorry you're quitting Steve, but I don't blame you. You've been running his business while he's out sailing or 'networking' on the tennis courts. Everybody knows that. He won't be able to find his way to the Xerox machine without you, much less figure out how to run his law practice. If it's any consolation, I have another set of prints and the negatives for both those batches of photos, and they're in a safe place. But please don't tell anyone. Not even Steve."

After Darleen left, Beverly sat down hard on the back stoop. She was stunned. First Mendoza and then Steve. He was one of her oldest, most trusted allies. She'd always wanted to believe that when she really needed him, he'd come through for her. Wrong! Was it asking too much of him to be honest with her? Why couldn't he tell her somebody had stolen her photos? Didn't he understand why they were important? That maybe somehow they could help her get the creeps off her back? That if the wrong people saw them she could be in real danger? Did he simply not give a shit?

Beverly clasped her cold hands tightly together and curled into a ball, chilled to the bone, as if someone had dumped a load of crushed ice over her. If there ever was a time when she needed Magdalena, this was it. Magdalena would wrap her arms around her, feed her a double Scotch, and make her laugh. And then come up with some brilliant ploy to help her regain her privacy.

But would Magdalena have believed there had been at least three people following her to L.A.? That for more than a year, she had been followed nearly everywhere she went, whether it was to the corner store or to St. Barth's? That somebody was opening her mail and packages, listening in on her phone calls, snooping in her store, rummaging through her garbage, her house, her chicken feed, her business, her life? Beverly Anne Parmentier, age 43, storekeeper, poultry raiser, law-abiding American female, was nobody a federal cop should ever have in his sights for any reason whatsoever, goddamn it.

Beverly's head was buzzing as if it were full of killer bees. Her whole body slumped like a puppet whose strings had just been cut. Tears cascaded down her cheeks.

Just then, through the droning in her head, she heard the sound of a car coming up the driveway. Helen Benton's vintage Cadillac rounded the corner of the building. The last person on earth Beverly could face at that moment was her best customer. In a panic she fumbled open the lock to the store and fled inside.

As the door closed, she saw Pancha's faded red Volvo pull into the parking lot. Hallelujah! The first good luck I've had in days, she thought. Pancha can deal with Helen. As she rummaged in her purse for something to sop up the tears, a loud siren erupted, nearly knocking her off her feet. In her haste to hide her tears from Helen, she'd forgotten to turn off the burglar alarm. Just as Pancha trotted up the steps, Beverly turned off the alarm. In the parking lot, Helen Benton slowly emerged from her car.

Pancha grabbed Beverly's shoulder. "What's happened? You look terrible!"

"I'll . . . I'll explain later. I can't see Helen looking like this. Can you take care of her? And call the alarm company before they send the cops. Oh, Jesus!" Beverly ran into the bathroom.

It was twenty minutes before Pancha knocked on the bathroom door. "Bev? Are you OK? Helen's gone. Nobody else is in the store, and I haven't unlocked the front door, so the coast is clear."

Beverly slowly opened the bathroom door, a fistful of Wendy's yellow paper napkins hiding her face. Pancha enveloped Beverly in her arms. "What happened?"

"It's too weird. It's just too fucking weird."

"Ay, mujer." Pancha guided Beverly to the sofa, sat her down, and smoothed her hair back from her teary face. "Do you want to tell me what happened?"

"Oh, it's everything. I can't take it any more. And Steve, I never should have trusted that son of a bitch."

Pancha nodded in agreement. *"Ese.* I know he's one of your oldest friends, but I have never had a good feeling about him. Can I make a suggestion?"

"What?" Beverly asked, her face still hidden in the wad of yellow napkins.

"Even though you don't tell me, I know you're not sleeping, and this stuff is wearing you down. Sure, you make jokes about it, but you're obviously depressed."

"Ayyy, you Santa Fe psychics."

Pancha laughed. "You know John Waldheim? The psychiatrist who buys Guatemalan textiles from us?"

Beverly nodded, dabbing at her eyes. "You think I ought to get my head examined."

"Well, maybe somebody with special training can give you ideas about how to deal with this shit. I mean, I'm here for you, and so are the rest of your friends. But maybe you need somebody who is completely objective, who's trained to listen and help solve problems. Part of the thing is—and I hope you'll forgive me—you're being too goddamn private about all this. I know how spooky and scary it is—better than anybody. Tom and a couple of other people—including you—helped me get through my ordeal. But I finally went to see a psychologist, and she was tremendously helpful."

"I didn't know you'd seen somebody."

"I guess we all feel a little funny about having to admit we need help with our heads. The customs thing still scares me. I still have flashbacks and nightmares. But she helped me develop skills I can use to combat the horror of it all. And you need that, too."

Beverly took Pancha's advice and began to see John Waldheim at his clinic around the corner from the store. His receptionist, Leona, was an old friend of Pancha's. Gradually, Beverly's mood improved, and she began to sleep better. At last, she had found an objective, private ally in whom she could confide her weirdest experiences and fears.

Several weeks later, via Pancha, Beverly learned that the office's outgoing mail had disappeared. Court documents, billings, checks, correspondence, and an important grant proposal that Leona had taken to the Old Town post office never arrived at their destinations. Then the Medicaid fraud office came down like a load of bricks on the practice. When Beverly walked into the Counseling Center one day, a strange woman sat at Leona's desk, going through her file drawers. The entire office was in an uproar. Dr. Waldheim had had to cancel a long-scheduled vacation to Mexico to deal with the investigation, and he had hired an attorney.

In Beverly's session with Waldheim, she mentioned the disappeared mail and the Medicaid investigation. "I'm . . . I'm afraid this might have something to do with me."

Waldheim shook his head. "Don't even consider that. This is going on everywhere. These Medicaid fraud people are ignorant ideologues. Fanatics. It has nothing to do with you."

Beverly wasn't convinced.

Five

One Sunday afternoon in late spring, Hal Coughlin called Beverly from his car phone in Los Angeles. "Give me a call back at home in a few, will you?" he said. "I'm a block from home now."

She went to a pay phone at a Chevron station with her roll of quarters and called Hal's house.

"I think you ought to talk to a PI I've worked with," he said. "He's brilliant, and he comes highly recommended."

Where have I heard this before? Beverly said to herself.

The next morning, on a walk with Pooh along the irrigation ditch, Beverly thought about Hal's suggestion. She needed expert help to document the harassment in hopes of suing the bastards, but her two attempts at hiring professionals—Sherlock and Mendoza—hadn't produced the hoped-for evidence, and she was out $4,000 from the effort. If she hired the investigator Hal was suggesting, was it going to be more hope and money down the drain?

"Should I give it another whirl?" she asked the dog.

Pooh wagged her tail energetically. Beverly decided it was a sign.

A week later, Beverly parked the Dumpster in the airport parking lot and walked into the Sunport. The investigator Hal suggested, Parker Daniels, was due to arrive on an 11 a.m. flight from L.A.

"How will I be able to recognize you?" she'd asked Daniels when she'd called him from a pay phone.

"Well, I look a little like Buffalo Bill," he said.

"Just as long as it's not Kit Carson. He's no hero in New Mexico. People here have long memories, especially Native Americans. You could get an arrow through your forehead even before you get out of the airport."

Beverly arrived at the gate just as the passengers from the L.A. flight were streaming into the airport. There was no missing Parker Daniels. His wavy, russet hair fanned out over the broad shoulders of a fringed suede jacket the same color, and his handlebar mustache topped a trim goatee. Daniels was not going to blend into the scenery. But at least he'd enhance it, Beverly thought.

They drove to a multistory office building in uptown Albuquerque, where Danny Pieri now worked as a real estate agent. He'd made arrangements for Daniels and Beverly to meet in his firm's conference room. Beverly wanted her conversation with the PI to be private.

"You know, people have gotten a lot of zany ideas about PIs from watching TV," Daniels said. "The reality is quite different. A lot of what we do is boring and tiresome. Most of the investigative work my partner and I do is on computers, and frankly, our time is quite expensive."

Beverly already knew that. His twenty-four hours in Albuquerque were going to set her back over $1,000—the $500-a-day fee, plus his plane, hotel, meals, and the rental car waiting at his hotel.

"If you're unsure of me and my story, it's perfectly understandable," Beverly said. "Mental hospitals are full of people who think someone's following them."

He arched his eyebrows and smiled.

"So I think the first thing you should do is look into who I am. Here's a list of people who know me well. I invite you to ask them whether I'm a nutcase. I'm sure you've had some pretty strange clients."

He took the list and nodded. "Lots. I wouldn't have come out here in fact if it hadn't been for Hal Coughlin's telling me that you and he go back twenty-five years. He thinks highly of you and was quite insistent there had to be something to this—you wouldn't have dreamed it up. He did say that you might be a little wacky at times, but you were definitely in command of your marbles."

Beverly was surprised Hal had gone that far out of his way for her.

With Daniels taking notes on his legal pad, Beverly described the strange events that dated from her first letter to Congressman Ovni. She gave him a list of the license plate numbers she'd collected from the cars of people snooping around her or her store and the corresponding Motor Vehicle Department's records Nancy Pieri had gotten for her via the university's computer system. A lot of the cars were registered to people who had rural post office boxes or nonexistent addresses—people whose names or addresses didn't check out in either the phone book or the city directory. Or the vehicles were registered to people who had dozens of vehicles registered to them. For example, a man whose address was an apartment complex on Montgomery Boulevard in Albuquerque had twenty-two sedans under his name.

The most interesting registration, however, belonged to the Cadillac that had stopped alongside Beverly that day at the downtown post office. It was registered through a car rental agency in Chevy Chase, Maryland, to the "junior" of a famous World War II general.

"Are you certain the guys following you are customs?" Daniels asked.

"No, I'm not sure. It seems as if customs is the logical place to start, but I also think it's possible some other agency or agencies are involved. The people pestering me are usually young and military looking. I hear there are a number of hush-hush government training programs going on at the Air Force base in Albuquerque. Maybe I'm target practice."

He brushed his handlebar mustache with his fingers as he considered the notion.

She handed him two envelopes of photographs. "I don't know if these are important. The ones in the pink envelope I took in a restaurant last May. The guy in the Hawaiian shirt is Ray Zoffke, the head customs guy here in Albuquerque. I shouldn't have taken those pictures. We were celebrating my birthday, and José Cuervo had commandeered my brain. I didn't know it at the time, but the Mexican guys are drug dealers. It was probably an undercover operation."

Daniels whistled under his breath. "There's another explanation."

Beverly's eyes widened. "You mean maybe it wasn't an undercover operation?"

He shrugged.

"Oh, my God!"

He looked at the second set of pictures. "Who are these guys?"

She told him about St. Barth's.

He cogitated for a while, then looked at his watch. "As I told you on the phone, I'd like to talk to a few people, read the reports you've written, and then get back with you before I fly out of here tomorrow. I need to get the rental car now and get going. You'd better put those photographs someplace safe."

"I will," she said.

After she dropped Daniels off at his hotel, the Old Town Sheraton, she drove to her gynecologist's office. The bad cramps and heavy bleeding she had been experiencing for months were becoming worse, and an ultrasound had revealed large fibroids on her uterus.

When she told Pancha later, Pancha related the story of a relative who had the same thing, but who in her confused English had described the condition as "fiberboards on her Eucharist."

Beverly knew the condition was serious. Her doctor had recommended a hysterectomy, and she was upset about the prospect of major surgery. She hadn't been in a hospital since the day she was born.

After the appointment, she went home and flopped on the sofa with a Swiss chocolate bar and the latest Tony Hillerman novel. She'd eaten half the chocolate when the phone rang.

"Yo, Bev, what's for dinner?" Steve asked.

"You've got a fucking lot of nerve," she growled.

"Hey, hey! Are we a little touchy today? Why are you biting off my head?"

"Where are my photos?"

"Uh, your photos? What photos?"

"The ones I gave to you as my attorney for safekeeping."

"Ah, *those* photos. Oh, they're around here somewhere. Darleen just misplaced them temporarily. It's just as well she's gone. So, let's have dinner, OK? If you're not up for cooking, I suppose we could go out somewhere, although, to tell you the truth, I'm tired of eating out."

"Tough luck. I'm not your personal chef, and as a matter of fact, you're not my lawyer anymore. Nor are you my friend."

"Oooooooohh. I guess you've had a bad day, huh? Hey, does this have something to do with my going out with Cindi? We're just going to symphony concerts now and then. It's no big deal."

"I don't care if you're dating Mr. Ed, Steve. In fact, you two would be quite compatible. He's a horse and you're a horse's ass. No, this has nothing to do with your love life and everything to do with your being a worthless human being. I'm firing you for incompetence."

"Care to elaborate?"

"You know, I don't. I'm feeling lousy, and talking to you makes me feel worse."

"You're leaving me in the dark here, Beverly. Did Darleen say something negative about me? If she did, I'll put out the word she's disloyal and untrustworthy, and I'll see to it she never gets another job with an attorney in this town."

"It has nothing to do with her. Maybe some day you and I can talk, but not right now." She slammed down the receiver.

Six

Dave walked into the downtown customs office. "You rang?" he asked Melissa.

She nodded. "Zoffke wants you in his office, and he's in a rotten mood, even worse than usual."

"Anybody else in there?"

"That blonde from AATA, Lita," Melissa said with a wry smile.

"Oh, shit," Dave said under his breath, figuring Lita had told Zoffke about finding him and Sherry in the Xerox room *in flagrante delicto.* But why would she go to Zoffke about it now? He thought he'd redeemed himself a little with her the night they took Sherry to the hospital.

With a heart that felt as cold and dead as a bag of wet sand, he opened the door to Zoffke's office.

Ten minutes later, he walked out, followed closely by Lita, who strode briskly out of the office. Melissa motioned him over to her desk with a sparkling blue fingernail. "What's up, Dave? You're grinning and walking with a springy step. Nobody ever looks happy when they leave Zoffke's office."

He shrugged and asked her which cars were available. He chose a Honda Accord with a Hertz registration, and tossing the keys high into the air and catching them behind his back, he left the office whistling a little tune.

Beverly had hired a PI, and Zoffke was livid. Dave also thought he was nervous. He'd never seen the boss so worked up.

Lita and Dave had sat through more than five minutes of Zoffke's rant about women using inherited money to threaten him with fancy L.A. lawyers and hot-shot PIs and fucking up his important operation. In the worst way, Dave wanted to say, "Oh, but Ray, I thought you told us and the agency big shots Beverly

got that money from selling pre-Columbian artifacts and drugs."
Like Lita, however, he just sat there calmly and observed Zoffke's
temper tantrum.

"Get a tap on the guy's hotel phone and a sender on his rental
car—fast," Zoffke ordered Dave and Lita. "I want the tightest
surveillance possible on him while he's in New Mexico. I want
to know everything you can find out about him as well as where
he goes and who he talks to. This is a job that requires first-rate
trackers, you two and whoever else top-notch you can round up
on short notice. But no AATA kids. And whatever you do, don't
get spotted."

Dave laid a little rubber as he sped out of the parking garage
under the Federal Office Building, heading for Old Town. Lita,
driving a blue Corsica, was in his rearview mirror, as was her
large white standard poodle, sitting in the passenger seat.

Dave tuned in to KABQ and sang along with a *conjunto* band.

Seven

Beverly's knees shook as she climbed the steps to the conference room in Danny's office for her debriefing with Daniels. If he told her the whole thing was in her head, she swore she'd drown herself in the teaspoon or two of muddy water flowing in the Rio Grande.

"There's definitely something going on here, but I don't know what," the investigator said. "By the way, everybody speaks highly of you and your business."

"I didn't pad the list, honest."

"I know you didn't. I also talked to folks who weren't on your list. A number of people who have businesses similar to yours told me they, too, have had snoops coming through their stores with regularity for the past couple of years, and they wonder if they're not being followed around at least part of the time. A couple of people reported they'd been tailed while on business overseas, and everyone had a story about being hassled by customs at the border, especially the women. They also say someone's been tampering with their mail and packages. Galo and Pancha's attorney, Lynne Deutsch, thinks the Galería Galo bust was political somehow, but she hasn't yet figured it out."

Daniels crossed his arms behind his head and leaned back in his chair. "Your theory about customs using you as surveillance practice for their trainees may be correct, but I didn't have enough time to get into it. I did find out, however, that the lessee of that red Cadillac registered in Chevy Chase works for Schlachthof International here in Albuquerque. And Schlachthof runs customs' local training program, the All Agency Training Academy."

"Hmmm," Beverly said.

"I talked to my partner last night, and here's what we think." Beverly straightened up in her chair.

"The cheapest and most effective thing for you to do is follow the Freedom of Information/Privacy Act route. Make requests of customs and a number of other agencies as well. It can take a long time, and they'll try a few dodges on you, but if they have records—and they must have them—they're required by law to give them to you. We can then come in and go somewhere with the information you get. We think you ought to work with a top-rate attorney on this who specializes in FOIA/Privacy Act work."

"Can you recommend somebody?"

"Yes. He's in Washington, and he's the best. A lot of lawyers are afraid of tangling with the feds, whether or not they'll admit it. But this guy's fearless." Daniels took out his address book and wrote down a name and phone number for Beverly.

"I'd like to hire you to keep going with this investigation, if you're interested," she said.

"It's not that I'm not interested. But my partner and I are booked for at least another eighteen months with a coffee smuggling scheme out of Brazil. We think you're better off going the FOIA route. We talked about the photos, especially the ones of Zoffke. We think it would be extremely dangerous at this point for you to go to anyone in law enforcement with them. You don't know who's friends with whom. Keep them somewhere safe, and maybe the right time to do something with them will come."

Daniels eyed his watch. "I'd better get going. I hope this hasn't been too disappointing for you."

Of course Beverly was disappointed, but she didn't tell him that. She'd had a fantasy about Daniels and her working together hand in hand to round up the bad guys for a firing squad while soft guitar music played in the background. Alas, it was not to be. The FOIA route could take years and cost thousands in attorneys' fees. But Beverly trusted that Daniels and his partner were giving her the best advice.

"By the way," he said as he put his reading glasses into a leather case, "have you ever been tailed by a thin, gray-haired guy who's about five-ten, late forties to mid fifties, wears granny glasses, and has a kind of a goofy look on his face?"

"Did your guy kind of bounce on the balls of his feet?"

Daniels nodded.

"I think you just described the guy who gardens for me at the store. Oh, my God! I've always wondered about him. He's too smart to be working as a gardener for such measly pay, and he's too serious to be a bum. Also, he doesn't know anything about plants."

"There was a blonde on my tail too, sometimes walking a white standard poodle. Same age as the guy, five-nine or so, straight hair in a pageboy, nicely dressed, pretty, but maybe humorless and brittle."

"I've seen her in Santa Fe, and she's been next to my table in some of the restaurants around town when I meet friends for dinner. I think she was driving the red Cadillac when The Scowler took my picture by the post office. There was a white standard poodle in the backseat."

"They were good, but not that good. I had to make a few quick moves to ditch them, especially when I wanted to talk in private about this with my partner in L.A."

Beverly was dying to hear the whole story, but she knew Daniels had a plane to catch. As they walked out of the office, he put his arm around her shoulders. "Get in touch with the lawyer in Washington. He's good at what he does, and I know he can help you. In the meantime, chin up. Don't let the bastards get to you, OK?"

Daniels headed for a nearby stairwell. "Don't waste any more money on PIs," he said. "They're crooked, lazy, or crazy, and usually they're no good. More often than not, in fact, they're all the above."

"Present company excluded, of course."

"Of course!" he laughed.

Eight

Early one summer evening, Ricky cruised Lomas Boulevard in his wheelchair with Pooh riding on his lap, her ears flapping in the breeze. They were on their way home from a visit to the Baskin-Robbins in Old Town. Ricky and his little dog now shared a large old adobe in the neighborhood between Old Town and downtown Albuquerque with five other handicapped teenagers and a couple of aides.

He rode his chair in the street with his lights on, facing oncoming traffic as he carefully maneuvered around sewer grates, potholes, and trash. The city was beginning to put in curb cuts, but they had a long way to go to make sidewalks negotiable for people in wheelchairs. Pooh jumped down from Ricky's lap and trotted alongside his chair with her tongue hanging out. She had just scored a double dip peach melba cone someone had conveniently dropped in the ice cream store's parking lot, and she was thirsty.

As they approached the block where La Ñapa was located, Ricky saw a Continental park in a handicapped spot on a side street in front of the Waldheim Counseling Center. The driver hung a blue and white handicapped placard from the rearview mirror and got out. A second man, much younger and thinner, emerged from the passenger side carrying a small black tool bag.

Ricky stopped at the corner and turned on his talking computer. The able-bodied men, both dressed in dark pants and shirts, sauntered toward him, laughing and talking. When they got within ten feet of him, Ricky pressed a button on the keyboard of his computer. "That makes me want to barf!" a deep voice boomed out in an odd electronic staccato.

The two men stopped in their tracks. "Did you say something, kid?" the older man asked.

Ricky pressed the button again. "That makes me want to barf!" the disembodied computer voice repeated.

Both men burst out laughing. "Don't I know you from somewhere?" the younger man said approaching Ricky's chair. "Hey, Zoffke, isn't he the kid who lives across the street from Parmentier?"

"Shut up, Elroy, you dummy." The older man turned to Ricky. "That's a pretty nifty gizmo you got there. Lemme see it."

When he stepped closer to the boy, Pooh growled and bared her teeth. The man backed up. "You keep that fucking mutt away from me or I'll kick it into the next county!" he yelled.

Frightened, Ricky put his chair in gear and sped off down the block, Pooh running alongside him. Just past Beverly's store, he turned and watched the men walk down the driveway that led to her parking lot.

He clenched his jaw in anger. Then, with Pooh trying hard to keep up with him, he sped to his house several blocks away. Nobody was home when he got there. He drove the chair into his bedroom, fetched his Batman mask, and struggled it over his head. Breathing hard under the black rubber, he headed for the kitchen, where he opened drawers until he found a large chef's knife. He clasped the knife between his two palsied hands and set it down in his lap. Then he headed out the door, speeding back toward the Counseling Center with Pooh at his side.

It was dark now, and Ricky's eyesight wasn't the best. But it was good enough for him to see that the Continental was still parked in the handicapped spot. He had to be quick. The men might be back at any time. He stopped alongside the car and carefully arranged the big knife between his feet, wedging it between his metal footpads and against the back of the footrest so the knife was aimed forward. He looked up and down the dark street to make sure no cars were coming and no one was watching. Then he backed the chair into the middle of the street, closed his eyes, clenched his feet together, and ran the chair straight at a rear tire.

If he hadn't had his seatbelt on, the impact would have hurled him into the side of the car. As it was, he was momentarily stunned by the impact, but not hurt. A loud whoosh filled the air, and the car tipped toward him. He raised his gnarled fists into the air. Victory!

Pooh began to yip. Ricky turned and saw the men coming around the corner from Lomas Boulevard. He backed up and zoomed away from the scene of his crime, hugging the shadows of the side street, hoping they didn't see him or hear the hum of his power chair. When he got to the corner, he realized Pooh wasn't beside him. He spun the chair around and saw her scrambling out a half-open window on the driver's side of the Continental. She hit the asphalt at a run, speeding toward him.

Seconds later, the men opened the car doors. "Aw, fuck! Dogshit!" one howled.

Ricky was ecstatic. He wanted to stick around and watch the show. But the older guy was as big as Arnold Schwartzenegger, and they were going to be pissed off when they discovered the flat tire. He didn't want to find out the hard way whether they were capable of beating up on a handicapped kid.

Pooh reached Ricky's chair, climbed aboard panting, and collapsed in his lap. Except for Christmas Day, when Beverly had presented him with the motorized chair and the talking computer, this was the most exciting day of his life.

At home, the boy asked an aide to call Beverly. He needed to talk to her urgently. Although it was after nine, she arrived at his house in minutes. Ricky gripped a pencil in his gnarled hands and painstakingly pecked out letters on his talking computer with the eraser end as Beverly knelt at his side.

"2 guys store," he wrote.

She was perplexed. "Two guys were at a store? What store?"

"Yours broke in."

"Oh, my god. Two guys broke into my store?"

"Y," Ricky tapped for yes.

"Tonight?"

"Y 730."

"At 7:30 tonight. What did they look like? Did you see their car? Did you get a license plate number?" Although she had a million questions, she calmed herself down and watched as Ricky slowly tapped his pencil on the computer's letters, then hit the talk button.

"1 big old fat 1 skinny 28ish blue continental forgot license," the Darth Vader voice intoned.

"That's OK."

He began typing again. "Same guys house."

She thought for a while. "Do you mean they were the guys who broke into my house?"

"Y."

She had an idea who the intruders might be. But without a license plate number, there wasn't much she could do. She decided to call the police anyway. It was important to check out the store, make sure everything was OK, and file a report. She drove to La Ñapa and waited in her locked car under a lamppost for the policeman, who arrived twenty minutes later. It was the same officer who had come to her house after the break-in. She could hear him sigh when he recognized her.

She told him what Ricky had told her. He took out his flashlight, walked around the outside of the store, and returned.

"No signs of forced entry, ma'am. Are you sure your handicapped friend wasn't making this up?"

"I'm positive. Would you go inside with me?"

The policeman sighed again. He watched Beverly turn off the burglar alarm and open the store with her key. She followed him in, turned on lights, and together they checked out all four rooms, the bathroom, and her office. Things looked normal, except Beverly could see papers on the sales desk and the desk in her office had been rifled, and a couple of file drawers had not been properly closed. The cash box, which she had forgotten to hide after closing, was still in the sales desk drawer. A quick count of the big bills told her no money was missing.

"Somebody has been in here, but I don't think they took anything," she said.

The policeman scratched his head. "Ma'am, how would they have gotten past the burglar alarm and your lock?"

Beverly shrugged. "I don't know. I'd like to make out a report anyway."

The policeman grumbled and began to fill out a form. "The kid didn't get a license number?"

"He was probably nervous, and he doesn't see all that well."

"Next time, tell him to get a license number."

"There isn't going to be a next time," Beverly said through clenched teeth.

"I hope not," the policeman said.

Níne

Dave climbed the steps to the tire store office and walked in through the open door. Enforcement personnel were scattered around the room, leaning against the walls or sitting in folding chairs, facing Zoffke, who chomped on an unlit cigar and paced as he waited for the Operation Pillage task force to assemble.

Dave grabbed a perch next to Melissa on the edge of the desk and looked around the room. There were a couple of new faces, but somebody was missing—Sherry, of course, and . . . Scarafaggio. It hit Dave like a loaded semi. You have shit for brains, Carney, he admonished himself. Of course! Scarafaggio was the one who had assaulted Sherry. Because he found out she was seeing Dave? Maybe because she wouldn't fuck him? Because he got his rocks off beating up women? Dave seethed with fury— at Scarafaggio, at Sherry, and, most of all, at himself.

Zoffke started the meeting. He spent ten minutes on house-keeping items. It was all Dave could do to sit still and pretend he was paying attention. Scarafaggio. Why hadn't he figured it out before?

Zoffke took a deep breath and plunged into a tirade about what he called "fraternizing." "I'm goddamned if my investigation is going to get fucked up by people who can't get their heads out of their crotches!" he boomed, then stopped abruptly to compose himself. His face was the color and consistency of stewed tomatoes, and the unlit cigar wagged up and down in his mouth like the stump of a Doberman's tail. After a few moments of heavy silence, he cleared his throat and called for reports.

Dave leaned over and whispered in Melissa's ear, "Where's Scarafaggio?"

"I hear he got transferred up to the Idaho border."

They both turned back to the proceedings before Zoffke could call them out of order. The Idaho border, huh. Dave hoped the ape would freeze his ass off or get drilled by some survivalist gun nut. But banishment to the wilds of Idaho for the rest of his career would never be punishment enough for what that bastard had done to Sherry. Dave started to devise a plan. The trout fishing was supposed to be pretty good up in Idaho. Maybe when he retired, he'd head in that direction . . .

He was almost out the door after the meeting ended when Zoffke called him back. "I need to see you in my office, Carney."

Dave's palms began to sweat.

Zoffke shut the door to his office and sat down behind his desk. "Parmentier's allegedly in the hospital, Carney. Did you know that?"

"Yes, sir. It's in my latest report. She had a hysterectomy at eight this morning."

"Well, we need to be certain that's where she is."

"She went in last night, sir. Pancha and her husband drove her to St. Joseph's after they stopped for a drink at Garduño's."

"I want you to make sure that's where she is, Carney."

Dave took a deep breath. "Sir, I think everything indicates she's in the hospital undergoing surgery. She has been visiting her gynecologist a lot recently, and she has been talking on the phone to her doctor and friends about female problems and the hysterectomy. The AATA trainees followed her to the hospital last night. She has a private room with a no-visitors sign on the door. The nurses have a list of people who can visit her, and they're guarding her room like it's Fort Knox."

"But we don't know for sure that's where she is, do we Carney? I need you to make damn sure she's in that hospital room. We need visual confirmation on Parmentier."

"How do you suggest we do that?"

"You go in there as a nurse, Carney."

Dave gulped. "What?"

"You heard me, Carney."

"She'd recognize me right away."

"Right. That's why you go in as a female nurse."

"I hope you're kidding me, sir."

Zoffke's face reddened. "That's an order, Carney."

Dave protested. "Why not send in one of the AATA girls or Lita? I'm sure a number of our women have enough medical knowledge to carry off a nurse's role."

"The trainees and the AATA staff left this morning for Telluride on a training exercise. I need this intel now, Carney. How do we know she hasn't used this surgery business as an excuse to skip town? You're a medic. You're the man for the job. Do I make myself clear? You go to the hospital tonight when it's quiet."

"But sir!"

"Carney, when I tell you to put on a dress and go undercover as a nurse, you don't whine, 'Can't you get somebody else?' You say, 'Yessir! What color dress, sir!' Do I make myself clear?" The SAC was purple with rage.

"Yessir! What color dress, sir!" Dave parroted.

Zoffke waved a hand in the air. "How the fuck do I know. Pink, yellow, white. You figure it out, Carney. That's your job. You'd better do it right, and you'd better hop on it. If she's not in that room, I want to know it. Immediately."

In his long career in law enforcement, Dave had been asked to do some very questionable things. This was one of the most questionable of all, however. He asked to borrow a car, and Melissa handed him the keys to a red Corsica parked behind the tire store. He headed straight for retired customs agent Clive Jackson's house in the South Valley, finding the old man where his wife said he would be, on his hands and knees in the back yard, digging up weeds around the roots of his rosebushes. At Dave's approach, Clive gestured toward a nearby patch of grass.

"Have a seat, Dave. You look like a man packing a bag of troubles."

"You're right on the money." Dave sat down on the grass and told his mentor about Zoffke's bizarre order.

Clive grasped a thorny goathead sticker plant in his gloved hand and yanked it out of the earth. "Zoffke's off his rocker."

"That's been obvious for some time. It's a rotten idea, and it's completely out of bounds. I feel cornered. But I don't think I can go upstairs and make a complaint at this point. It could blow whatever chances I have for a promotion."

"How long you got to go, boy?" the man asked as he stabbed at a weed with his trowel.

"Sixteen months, twelve days, and," Dave looked at his watch, "about five hours."

Clive nodded his wooly gray head, shed his gloves, got up slowly, and brushed off the knees of his jeans. "You ever play any golf?" The sun glinted off the old man's glasses as he looked at Dave.

"No, can't say that I've ever had much interest in the game."

Motioning Dave to follow, Clive walked to the back of his yard. Beneath a huge, spreading cottonwood lay a homemade putting green, its bright, emerald surface smooth and uniform as a newly clipped head of hair. The old man picked up an old-fashioned brass-headed putter leaning against the tree and approached a golf ball resting at the edge of the grass. He hunched over the ball, grasped the putter firmly, and swung his head several times back and forth between the ball and a spot about five feet away, where a little flag stuck out of a lidless tin can buried in the ground. Slowly, he brought the putter back behind the ball and tapped it ever so slightly. The ball rolled straight toward the little flag and dropped with a plunk into the cup.

Clive straightened up, smiled with satisfaction, retrieved the ball, and handed the putter to Dave. "Give it a try," he said, dropping the ball at the green's edge.

Clive showed him how to hold the putter and position himself next to the ball. Dave looked at the hole, drew the putter back behind the ball, and swung it slowly forward, giving the ball what he thought was a light tap. It sped across the grass, missed the cup by at least two feet, and rolled to a stop in a pile of leaves at the far edge.

"Ain't easy as it looks, is it?" Clive said. He ambled across the green and retrieved the ball. He threw it up into the air a number of times as he walked back to where Dave stood holding the putter and dropped the ball at his feet. "You gotta keep your eye on the ball. And that stroke? It's got to be mighty gentle. Just think of it as a love pat on your baby's behind. Give it another try."

Dave set up his shot

"Eye on the ball," Clive coached. "Eeeeeaaasy, easy."

Dave dragged the putter slowly back behind the ball, then swung it forward and connected. The ball rolled a few feet away, off to the right of the cup, missing the mark by a yard. His face flushed with frustration, he strode over to where the ball lay, swept it up, walked back over to the same spot, dropped it, and again lined the putter up behind it. When he hit the ball this time, it rolled to within ten inches of the cup—still a little off to the right, still a little short.

Clive chuckled and shoved his hands into the pockets of his jeans. "Putting's a metaphor for life. You gotta keep your eye on the ball, you've got to stay cool and concentrated, and you just gotta focus on your goal. That's what it's aaaall about." He took the putter out of Dave's hands, leaned it against the cottonwood, and put his arm around the younger man's shoulder. "Let's go see if we can't talk that old gal of mine into a cold drink."

Dave, Clive, and his wife sat at a small table beneath a grape arbor, sipping iced mint tea. The old man cogitated. Then he looked up at Dave and shook his head sadly. "My man, I just don't see how you can get out of this crazy assignment."

Ten

Paulette giggled when Dave told her what Zoffke had ordered him to do. He reddened. "Look, you've got to help me out here, Paulette. I can't go shopping for a fucking dress! If word gets out that I've gone undercover in drag, I'll be dog meat. The guys will never let me forget it."

"OK, honey. What color dress do you want me to buy for you?"

"I don't give a fuck. But you'd better make it long sleeved to hide my hairy arms and that damned jungle rot I got in Peru. Goddamn it, Zoffke's a fucking lunatic."

"Let me get a tape measure. It's going to be hard to find a dress that'll fit you."

While Paulette shopped for the nurse's outfit, Dave called St. Joseph's Hospital, where Beverly was recovering from her surgery. Using a high, croaky voice—"You'll have to excuse me. I think I overworked my voice at choir practice last night"—and calling himself Ellen Davis, he inquired about job openings at the hospital. He knew hospitals were desperate for RNs, especially ones like Nurse Davis. "I speak Spanish, I have an MS in nursing and more than twenty years experience," he told the personnel office.

"Great. We have immediate openings for nurses in surgery, recovery room, OB/GYN, and neonatal. We're especially looking for night nurses."

"Could I go on rounds tonight? I have a daytime job at Kirtland AFB Hospital, and late evening would be the best time for me. I'm especially interested in going on rounds on the women's floor. I just adore newborns," he gushed.

"Oh, me too," the personnel clerk said. "If you can supply us with a résumé and local references, I don't see why you can't do rounds tonight with Betty Valdéz. She's been at the hospital for decades, working in various departments, and I'm sure she can answer any questions you might have. I'll set it up. Show up with your paperwork sometime before midnight, when the office personnel leave for the evening."

Dave called special ops support.

"Happy to help. We'll have someone call from Kirtland Hospital's personnel office right away, and we'll put together a résumé you can pick up on your way to St. Joseph's. Good luck!"

Dave gave himself the closest shave of his life. Then he searched the bathroom cabinets for the makeup he'd need. Damn, he thought, there's enough stuff in here to outfit a battalion of drag queens. He had rounded up an armful of cosmetics when his daughter April came down the hall.

"Dad," she whined when she saw what he was carrying. "What are you doing with my eyeliner? Hey, and that's Junie's new lipstick. She's going to be really pissed off when she gets home and finds out you swiped it."

Dave was in no mood for hassles. "It's part of my job. Don't ask."

Paulette was back in a couple of hours with shopping bags full of Nurse Davis's outfit. In their bedroom, she helped him get dressed. They had an especially hard time with the girdle, which was a little too small, even for his narrow hips.

"Why do I even need this thing?" he asked his wife as they struggled to draw the tight elastic band down over his belly.

"Well, honey," she said, stifling a giggle. "It's this big knot of stuff in your crotch. It'll pooch out of your dress if we don't pack you in. Or, if you want, we could just whack a couple of those funny dangles off." Paulette couldn't hold it back any more. She flopped onto the bed laughing.

"It's not funny, goddamn it," Dave roared.

"OK, OK, honey. I'd miss them as much as you would." She stopped laughing, and finished helping him dress.

They arranged stuffing in his bra, padded his fanny and hips, and pulled a yellow nylon dress over his head. When they finished, Dave stood tall in a shoulder-length brunette wig, nurse's cap, makeup, glasses, white tights, white, thick-soled shoes, a unisex wristwatch, and a stethoscope. Paulette stepped back and gave him the once over.

"OK," he said, smoothing down the sides of his dress. "How do I look? I mean really. I promise I won't yell at you again. This has to be right, OK? How do I look?"

Paulette tipped her head this way and that, and squinted up at him. "The real truth?"

"Yeah," he said.

"I think it'll work. But you look a little like a . . . like a . . ."

"Like a what?" he yelled.

"Like a dyke. But just a little, honey. Honest. I don't think that's a problem. I'm sure they're an equal opportunity employer."

Dave handed in his paperwork to the hospital's administration office and received directions to the women's floor, where, as promised, he found Nurse Valdéz, a diminutive, tightly wound, grumpy old hag. She wasn't too pleased to have Nurse Davis follow her on rounds, but she lightened up when Dave offered to take on some of her less pleasant tasks, like emptying bedpans. For more than an hour, Dave accompanied her as she whisked around the women's floor checking on patients. Worrying he'd give himself away, he spoke as little as possible and asked few questions. Finally, at around 1 a.m., Nurse Valdéz opened the door to a room with a "No Visitors" sign and Dave followed her in.

Except for a nightlight, it was dark. When Nurse Valdéz reached for the light switch, he stopped her, whispering, "She looks asleep, poor dear. Don't you think we should keep the light down?"

The nurse scowled at him but kept the light low.

Even in the semidarkness, Dave recognized Beverly. She was lying motionless beneath the hospital bed's white sheets. Her thick hair was spread out on the pillowcase, and an IV connected one of her hands to a drip bottle beside her bed. She looked pale and drawn. Dave was relieved to see she was asleep. But his heart was pounding. Goddamn, I hope my luck holds, he thought. What if she wakes up and recognizes me? He tried to hang back.

"Nurse Davis," Valdéz whispered, "lift the bedding so I can check this woman's incision."

As the nurse began to peel back the bandage that covered her belly, Beverly opened her eyes and blinked several times.

"We're just checking your dressing, dear," Nurse Valdéz said.

She blinked several more times and appeared to be trying to adjust her eyes to the half-light. Dave averted his face from her line of sight. Jesus, he thought. What if she spotted him, and started to scream? He grasped the edges of the blankets tightly and obliquely watched Nurse Valdez inspect Beverly's wicked-looking vertical slash, which was raw and red, but held together with neat stitches.

As Nurse Valdéz prodded her belly, Beverly moved slightly, and Dave saw she was staring at his hands. Her eyes were wide and woozy, and she was looking at him as if he were a bad dream.

Shit, his hands! Dave realized he'd forgotten that the black hair that covered the back of them like swamp grass, his thick wrists and big, heavy-knuckled fingers were dead giveaways that Nurse Davis was a guy in drag. He hid his hands behind the blanket and waited. Hope to God she's on some good drugs, he prayed. Maybe she'll think she's hallucinating. He closed his eyes, expecting her to start shrieking. When she didn't, he hastily excused himself, saying he had to go to the bathroom urgently.

He waited for the nurse in the hallway outside Beverly's room, finished rounds with her, and with a huge sigh of relief, left the hospital.

It was nearly two in the morning, and heat was coming off the asphalt in the parking lot in waves. Dave's brains were stewing under the wig, and he wanted to fling it into the bushes. But a guy in a crew cut driving through Albuquerque's night streets with his face painted like a whore's was going to get a few odd looks—or get shot. He left the wig on, fired up his pickup, and headed for home.

Dave was in the bathroom taking a leak when a blood-chilling scream nearly knocked him over. Paulette ran to the bathroom door where Junie stood screaming and wrapped her arms protectively around her daughter.

"For chrissakes!" Dave grumbled. "Can't a man even take a leak in his own john?"

"You still have your wig and makeup on, honey. You scared her."

Dave slammed the bathroom door shut, peeled off the wig and the rest of his nurse garb, and stepped into the shower. Five minutes later, he walked into his bedroom, a towel around his waist. He tossed it into a corner and slipped under the sheet alongside his wife.

"Honey?" she said softly. "You're still wearing most of Nurse Davis on your face."

"Mmmmm, he replied, snuggling against her shoulder.

"Honey . . . I . . . I've never been in bed with a person wearing makeup before."

Dave opened a mascara-lidded eye. His wife had a funny look on her face, and he reached for her.

"Honey, in five hours I've got to be at work. Maybe tomorrow?"

Dave drew her closer. "You could call in sick, Paulette," he whispered, nibbling her earlobe. "You never call in sick. I think you need some special care, Mrs. Carney. Nurse Davis will take care of you. Really gooooood care."

Paulette pushed against his chest. "How do I know you're a real nurse? Where's your nurse's dress? Where's your nurse's hat? Where's your stethoscope? And, Nurse Davis, where's that nasty thermometer of yours? The big fat one you're always trying to stick in my mouth or up my butt, you sick thing."

Dave hopped out of bed and put on Nurse Davis's garb. "We'll be right with you, dearie."

Eleven

Rupert Eistopf heard a tap on his office door and lifted his pen from a pile of papers on his desk. "Come in," he commanded.

A petite black woman with straightened bronze hair walked toward him.

"Yes?" he said.

"Sir, I'm Fateema Varnette from the Freedom of Information office," she said in a delicate southern lilt. "I called you a couple of minutes ago, and you said you'd rather discuss the matter in person."

Eistopf put his pen down. "Ah, yes. Miss . . ."

"Mrs. Varnette. Here's the request I thought you should see."

Eistopf gave the paper a cursory glance. "Why are you bothering me with a routine FOIA matter? You get a request from some airport official or importer or little old lady who thinks we're after her because of the strand of pearls she smuggled in from Tokyo forty years ago, you give it the routine. You lose the request and wait for them to write you again. If they write again, you write back and ask for clarification. The next time they bug you, you mistakenly send the paperwork to the passport office in St. Louis. And if they still come back, wanting their goddamn files, you say we're not hiring anybody just now. You know the drill."

"Yes, sir, I do. But this isn't a garden-variety FOIA request. Did you notice the name on the letterhead?"

Eistopf quickly scanned the letter. "Some lawyer in Virginia making a request for some woman in Albuquerque. What's the big deal?"

"Well, sir, I called Albuquerque to find out if they knew anything about the subject. The people there got a little nervous.

They had me talk to a higher-up, and he got very nervous. And nasty, I might add."

"Who was it?"

"Ray Zoffke, sir."

Eistopf moaned. "I still don't understand why you brought this FOIA request to me, Miss . . . uh . . ."

"Mrs. Varnette, sir. Well, Zoffke said he was working under your authority on a high-level matter of critical importance for the agency. I thought you ought to know about this. The other thing is the person making the request, sir. He's not your average Washington lawyer. It's The Doberman, sir."

Eistopf looked up. "Who's he?"

"Bill Donovan. He's about the best FOIA attorney around, sir. Whoever this lady is, she hired the top guy."

The official grunted. "Well, hell, Miss . . ."

"Mrs. Varnette, sir."

"Take it upstairs to the legal department. There's a guy up there they call The Rottweiler."

"Yes, sir, I'll do that."

"Thank you for bringing this to my attention, Miss, uh . . ."

"You're welcome, sir," Mrs. Varnette said. She took the letter back from Eistopf and walked out of his office, carefully closing the door behind her. At the elevators, she pushed the up button. "Fathead," she muttered under her breath.

Twelve

Two days after her surgery, Beverly called Doc from her hospital room. She didn't think customs would bother to tap her hospital phone for her short stay.

"How did the surgery go? How are you feeling?" Doc asked.

"I feel like a tank rolled over me, but other than that, I'm OK. The surgery went fine. I asked the anesthesiologist to give me whatever they give elephants when they knock them out for a couple of weeks. I never knew what hit me."

"Were you able to get a private room?"

"Yes, and as you suggested, I told the surgeon about the hassles from the feds. I also told her I wanted a strict no-visitors policy. But it didn't completely hold the jackals at bay."

Doc groaned. "What happened?"

"As you know, the nurses come around every few hours to harass you for one thing or another. They are terrific, and I bless them each and all. But last night, about one in the morning, Mrs. Valdéz, the night nurse, came in with another nurse. They peeled back my bandages to look at the incision. As they were poking around—me feeling like a trussed turkey—I noticed the new nurse's hands looked funny. I mean very funny. All of a sudden, it hit me. It wasn't a woman in that nurse's dress—it was a guy. I swear to God! Her wrists were too broad for a woman's, she had ape hair on the back of her hands, and her fingers were as thick as railroad ties. The more I looked at her, the more certain I was that she wasn't a woman. She was not quite six feet tall, her hair was a wig, her makeup job was heavy-handed, and she was too stacked and hippy."

"Jesus. What did you do?"

"I wanted to holler, but I didn't think anyone would believe me. They'd think it was the drugs. Maybe I didn't trust myself that I wasn't hallucinating."

"I'm sure you weren't hallucinating. Jesus! A guy in drag, posing as a night nurse, poking around your privates. That's incredible!"

"Well, guess what, I'm a little upset about it myself. This may sound nuts to you, but I think it was Dave, La Ñapa's gardener."

"Your gardener? Oooooooh, that's creepy."

"I've suspected for a while that he's a mole. He's always asking questions and nosing around."

"It's time to do something, Bev."

Thirteen

A week after Beverly's operation, Pancha stopped by her house, carrying a pile of mail, a plastic tub of homemade chicken soup, and a stack of flour tortillas her mother-in-law had made that morning.

"Let's go sit outside, Bev," she said. "Do you feel up to it?"

"Sure. We can go into the backyard where there's some shade."

Pancha took a couple of plastic chairs to a cool spot beneath the black walnut trees and the spreading cottonwoods that shaded the yard. Beverly eased herself down into a chair. Pancha handed her a long white envelope. "I think you better read this first. A young Indian brought it to the store. He showed me a board of nice beaded earrings and slipped me two envelopes, one for me, one for you."

Pancha sat back in her chair and grinned while Beverly read the letter. It was from Doc.

Dear Bev,

How do you like the Indian mail service? One of the kids from the rez was driving to Albuquerque for a powwow, and I asked him to get this to you.

I hope you're continuing to recover nicely. Please believe me. In a couple of months you are going to feel fantastic. Think of it: No more PMS. No more wildly gyrating hormones. And best of all, no more feeling like shit for days on end.

This business with the feds has gone far enough. It's stupid, vicious, and unfair, and the drag queen nurse in the hospital is beyond the pale. I don't doubt it was the feds, playing some stupid paranoid game to see if you were really in that room. What assholes! You need to get away from them, especially now. I am convinced the most important part of a recovery is true peace and quiet. You're not going to get that with people still hassling you or while you are sitting at home thinking about the shop every day.

The River Rats and I had a confab. We think you should disappear for a while. We worked out a wonderful getaway trip for you to a place the cretins will never find: a ranch in Utah that belongs to a friend of Abe's. You'll have a beautiful little cabin all to yourself on a small lake up in the mountains with a nearby hot spring. The place is completely private and remote, with only one road in. A nice family with kids is spending the summer on the other side of the lake, and they will welcome your company when you want to visit or you need something. Ditto the people at the ranch, which is half a mile down the road. Plus the River Rats plan to visit you, if that's OK. The cabin is already stocked with food, vino, Cheetos, a terrific selection of your favorite kind of trashy books, and a laptop.

We've decided these horrible experiences would make a great novel. And an even better movie. We've already decided on the cast. I want Meryl Streep to play me, Andrea wants Demi Moore to play her, and we think Kathy Bates should play you. We suggested Dustin Hoffman could play Flash, but he thinks of himself as more of a Harrison Ford. Abe thought Sylvester Stallone would do for him, although he'd prefer someone taller and better looking. Donnie and Marie Osmond can play the Goodyears.

Here's the plan. By Saturday, pack the clothes and books and things you'd like to have with you for the rest of the summer in a couple of trash bags. DO NOT LIFT THE TRASH BAGS UNDER ANY CIRCUMSTANCES. Call Pancha and ask her to pick up the clothing you're `giving to the women's shelter.' I'll then get the bags from her. She's in on this, of course, and she thinks it's a great idea.

At precisely midnight Friday, without turning on any lights in your house, walk out your back door and go down the ditch to Montaño Street. I'll be parked there in my white Jeep Cherokee. There aren't too

many people out at that hour, but wear a head scarf just in case.
Don't worry about the store or anything. You know Pancha can handle
everything. And don't even think of saying no. We're all excited. The
Great Escape! Take care and we'll see you soon.

   All my love,
   Doc

Beverly put the letter down. "I . . . I dunno, Pancha. I mean, if anyone deserves a break from these idiots, it's you, not me."

"*¡Aaayyyyy, mujer!*" Pancha groaned. "I'm fine. This is something we want to do for you. I have a big, lovely family taking care of me. I have a beautiful son who makes me happy to be alive. And the feds hardly ever bother me anymore. You need a break to recover from this surgery and from the ordeal of being the *federales'* plaything for a year and a half."

"A cool place in the mountains, with a lake and a hot spring, company when I feel like it, time to think, time to write. It does sound awfully nice. And if Doc can pull it off, I'd have privacy, the ultimate luxury. So what do I do?"

"What do you do? *¡Jesucristo, mujer!* You say thank you! And you start packing your garbage bags. Carefully. I'll take good care of the store. Tom's mother offered to take care of Pablito. When you get back in a couple of months, you'll feel like a human being again. Maybe by then, the feds will have the sense to give it up and leave you alone. And maybe the lawyer in D.C. will have gotten the ball rolling on the FOIA request."

The women sat quietly for a few minutes. Then Beverly flashed Pancha a sneaky smile. "Could you do some Xeroxing and mail a few things for me after I leave? And I have something I'd like to get to Ricky. I'll put the stuff in one of the garbage bags. Be careful nobody sees you mailing anything, though."

"You're wearing that smile, Ms. Parmentier. Are you up to something?"

"Me? Up to something? Naaaah. I'm mentally preparing to toddle off into oblivion."

"But you're not going quietly, are you?"

"You know, Pancha, as we stand upon the shit pile of life, every so often there's a whiff of roses. I got a great idea while I was in the hospital. I don't know why I didn't think of it earlier. It's a beautiful way to spend some of Magdalena's money."

Pancha shook her head. *"¡Ayyyy, mujer!"* she laughed.

Fourteen

Dave prided himself on having a sixth sense. It had twice saved him from getting killed, once in a drug bust on the New Jersey wharf and again in a shootout in a Lima whorehouse. One day in late June, when he looked up from weeding the rose bed in front of La Ñapa and saw a white Cherokee with Utah plates drive into the parking lot behind the store, his sixth sense told him the car's stunning driver was no ordinary customer.

He waited a few minutes. When the woman didn't come around to the front of the building to enter the store via the normal customer route, he walked up the driveway to the parking lot, casually carrying a hoe over his shoulder. He rounded the corner of the building and saw Pancha and the blonde loading heavy garbage bags into the Cherokee.

Pancha smiled nervously when she saw Dave and spoke to the blonde. "Beverly's sending some nice things to the women's shelter."

The blonde flashed Dave a winning smile. "We can always use good clothes and household goods. Please thank Beverly for her donation. We'll mail her a receipt."

Dave walked up to the woman. "Have we met before? I'm Dave Carney. I'm the gardener here. And you're . . .?"

"Priscilla. I volunteer at the women's shelter."

Dave's motor revved up. Priscilla was tall, curvy, and gorgeous. "Can I give you a hand with those bags, ladies? They look awfully heavy."

"There's just one more," Pancha said. "I'll get it." She disappeared into the store.

"Where is the women's shelter anyway?" Dave asked Priscilla. "I have some bedding I'd like to donate."

Her eyes brightened and she smiled. "We're not allowed to disclose the location. It's for the safety of our clients, you understand. Just give us a call, and we'll be happy to pick up your donation."

"What's the phone number?" he asked, scratching his chin with a fingernail.

She didn't blink. "I haven't a clue. I'm new in town."

"Oh? Well, hey, I'd be happy to show you around," he said, leaning on his hoe. "It's a great city, and I'm a great tour guide."

"Thanks. My boyfriend's a native Albuquerquean."

Priscilla helped Pancha lift the last garbage bag into the Cherokee, then turned to Dave. "You've got a lovely garden here. You must be quite good with plants." She stepped closer. She was taller than Dave, and he had to look up to see into her cornflower-blue eyes. Her teeth were even and white, her mouth full and naturally red. "Mr . . . Carney, was it?"

"Carney, Dave," he said woodenly, as if he were reciting a name from the phone book. Priscilla was a beauty, but she was intimidating.

"You've done a wonderful gardening job for Beverly," Priscilla said magnanimously and got into her car. With a wristless little wave, she drove off.

Fifteen

The car seat squeaked as the young man turned toward the woman on the passenger side.

"Cut it out, Donny," she said, pushing away his hands, which were steadily moving north under her T-shirt. "We've got to be serious about this. You know, no fooling around on the job."

"Mmmm," the young man replied as he nuzzled her neck, his hands migrating around her back toward her bra clasp.

"Donny." She arched her back away from the car seat so he could unhook her bra. "What if Lita or Orange or one of them comes by and finds you and me necking when we're supposed to be keeping an eye on Parmentier's house? I mean, I don't want us to get fired, honey. With us planning on getting married right after training's over and all."

Donny's bristly hair brushed against her chin as he began to cruise her neck with his mouth. "Nobody's going to come checking up on us, Jennifer," he murmured. With his tongue, he traced the outline of her ear, his hands gently removing her T-shirt. She quivered at his touch, a faint moan escaping her mouth. He pulled her hand toward the front of his cut-off jeans. "It's almost midnight, babe. The badges are all home in bed. Like I wish we were, honey. God, I want you so bad, Jennifer."

She patted the swelling at the front of his pants and sighed. "I know you do, sweetie." Suddenly, she jerked her hand away and sat straight up. "What was that?" she asked, looking out the open windows of the darkened car.

"What was what?" Donny asked with annoyance. "I didn't hear anything."

"I thought I heard something," Jennifer replied in a tiny whisper. "Like footsteps. Oh! What was that? That croaky sound?"

"Those are frogs, you bimbo. The valley's full of 'em. My Dad says in the 1930s, some French guy had the bright idea of growing frogs for frog legs, and when the business went bust, he let 'em loose on the ditch banks."

"I hate frogs! They're so slimy and icky." Jennifer shivered, snuggled into his arms, and tentatively moved her hands across his thick thighs. Suddenly she jumped, let out an ear-piercing scream, and grabbed Donny tightly around his neck.

"Something just jumped on me!" she wailed.

Annoyed, the young man pried her arms loose from the stranglehold she had on him. "You sure are jumpy, babe," he said.

She yelped again, swatting at her bare chest. "Donnyyyyyyy!" she screeched. "There's something jumping on me!" She bounced up and down on the car seat, flailing her arms around and squealing.

Donny groaned. Then he, too, felt something land on him and took a swipe at whatever it was. Suddenly dozens of something live and about the size of a nickel were sailing in the open windows on both sides of the sedan, landing on them. As Jennifer screamed and swatted at the lively creatures, Donny scooped one up in his hand. Holding it in the light that shone into the car from a street lamp, he opened his hand to see what it was. "Shit, baby frogs!" He whipped the little thing out the car window. Just then, a cluster of several dozen tiny wet frogs hit him on the side of the head. "What the fuck?" he yelled.

Jennifer was now screaming loudly, swiping frantically at the multitude of tiny creatures that bounded and hopped all over her naked breasts.

From somewhere close by on the ditch bank, two hearty male voices roared and howled. "Ooooooooh, Donny!" one squealed in a falsetto. "Oooooh, honey, what's that squirmy little thing in your pants? Can I play with it, honey?"

The other voice boomed a big laugh, then chimed in in his deeper falsetto. "Oh, Jennifer, I want you so baaaaaad!"

Donny flung open the car door, sprang out, and whirled toward the voices. In the light afforded by the street lamp and a nearly full moon, he saw two men on the ditch bank, a skinny one with glasses, and a taller, heavy-set man with a black beard. They were laughing and rolling around on the grass.

Donny roared toward the men like an enraged bull. "You're gonna be goddamn sorry, you shitholes!"

The two men leaped to their feet. They grabbed the five-gallon buckets beside them and flung the contents at the man racing toward them, drenching him in stinky, muddy ditch water, tadpoles, and frogs. Dropping the buckets, they took off down different sides of the ditch bank at a dead run.

Donny ran a fast couple of blocks in pursuit of the surprisingly swift and agile big guy, who broad-jumped a five-foot-wide, water-filled ditch and disappeared down a lateral. Slowed considerably by his soggy clothes and shoes, Donny gave up pursuit. He turned around and stomped back to the car. Jennifer stood shivering beside an open car door, her arms clenched tightly across her hastily donned wet T-shirt.

"Clean up this fucking car," he growled, with his hands on the hips of his sodden cut-offs as he surveyed the car that was alive with tiny, bouncing amphibians.

Jennifer looked at him in astonishment. "Me? Clean up the car? Honey, I can't touch those things!"

"The fuck you can't!" He grabbed one of the buckets that lay on its side near the car and tossed it at her. "Get a move on."

Several blocks away, Abe and Flash lay draped across the hood of a white Cherokee with Utah plates. Their chests heaving, they alternately laughed and gasped for breath and slapped each other high fives.

Beverly, a scarf wrapped around her head, slowly walked up to the car. "Did you guys have something to do with all that shrieking and yelling?"

"Abe and Flash were creating a little diversion," Doc laughed. "Let's get a move on, troops."

Abe and Flash, their arms flung around each other's shoulders, stumbled into the car, still laughing and panting.

Fifty yards down the street, Dave stood alongside an adobe wall beneath a large lilac that nearly hid him from view. He raised a pair of night-vision binoculars to his eyes and watched as a woman in a scarf and three other people got into a white Cherokee. He focused on the Utah license plate. Then he put the binoculars down.

A smile slowly lit his face. In the dappled moonlight, he watched the car drive east, then turn north several blocks away. Grinning, he settled the binoculars inside his backpack next to a mobile phone and got into his truck. He drove a couple of blocks south to a ditch bank where two young people stood beside a red Chevrolet Corsica hurling tadpoles and epithets at each other.

Sixteen

A week after Beverly disappeared, Dave was reading the *Albuquerque Sentinel* morning paper over a bowl of Cheerios when a full-page ad caught his eye. He dropped his spoon into his cereal bowl. Milk splattered onto the newspaper and his polo shirt.

In a three-quarter-page photograph labeled "paid advertisement," Zoffke, wearing a Hawaiian shirt and sunglasses, sat at a table littered with food, drinks, and tequila bottles. He was leaning on Ronnie Lechuga's shoulder, while two rough-looking mustachioed men on Zoffke's left hoisted glasses. Beneath the photograph, a caption read: "Pharmaceutical executives enjoy an evening of fine dining and camaraderie at Delgado's, the South Valley's premier restaurant since 1948."

Dave dropped the paper and howled. Then he leaped up and shot his fists into the air. "Yes, yes!"

Paulette came running into the dining room. "Honey? Are you OK?"

"I'm great. Now I get it!"

"Get what?"

"Why Zoffke was after Beverly and her photos." He pointed to the photograph. "Now the shit's gonna hit the fan. Oh, boy, I can't wait. Yes!"

Dave called Herman Naranjo, who had already seen the paper.

"The people at Delgado's Restaurant say they didn't place the ads, and they haven't any idea who might have. And the newspapers can't say who paid for them. Christ, this is awful."

Dave didn't think it was awful. He thought it was wonderful. But he didn't tell Naranjo that.

The office over the tire store was in an uproar that morning.

Various members of the task force gathered around newspapers, talking and chuckling. When Zoffke walked in just before nine, a hush fell over the room. His boots slapping the wood flooring, Zoffke strode up to Melissa's desk.

She handed him a fistful of telephone messages. "Sir, Rupert Eistopf called from Washington and left a message on our answering machine at 6 a.m., 8 Washington time. He says it's extremely urgent, and you should call him immediately. Do you want me to ring him?"

"No!" Zoffke roared. "I'm not here. Hold all my calls. I don't want to be disturbed by anyone or anything."

"Yes, sir," Melissa said.

Zoffke retreated into his office behind closed doors. An hour later, Elroy came into the office with an armload of newspapers and a sheaf of bright pink posters that featured the same photograph and caption as the newspaper ads.

"He says he doesn't want to be disturbed," Melissa said.

Elroy blinked. "I think he needs to see these: the *Los Angeles Times,* the *New York Times,* the *Washington Post,* the *New Mexican,* the *Albuquerque Sentinel.* Plus somebody's putting up these posters all over downtown and Old Town."

Elroy opened the door to Zoffke's office and walked in.

Melissa stopped typing and listened. Nothing. A few minutes later Zoffke stomped out of his office, slammed the door, and left without saying a word. Elroy tiptoed out behind him.

For hours, Zoffke cruised Albuquerque neighborhoods in his baby-blue Continental, scouring telephone poles and bulletin boards for the pink posters. When he spied one, he'd screech to a halt, hop out of the car, and rip it down. Passersby watched in amazement as the husky man, his face the same hot pink as the posters, tore them to shreds, the pieces fluttering away in the breeze like fuchsia butterflies.

In late afternoon, at the Old Town shopping center, Zoffke caught sight of a teenager in a wheelchair tacking up one of the posters on a bulletin board outside a Baskin-Robbins store. The boy was wearing a rubber Batman mask and a Batman costume. Zoffke slammed on his brakes and jumped out of the car. When he tried to snatch the pile of posters from Ricky's lap, his dog attacked, sinking her teeth into his leg. Zoffke screamed in pain and kicked at the dog with his other leg. She hung on. Her snarls and growls, Zoffke's yelling, and Ricky's loud, angry wails quickly drew the attention of ice-cream parlor patrons, including a team of softball players. They jumped out of their truck and pulled Zoffke away from the boy just as a pair of tattooed *vatos* wearing hair nets over their thick black hair trotted up.

"Hey, man," one of the *vatos* said, pushing at Zoffke. "What you doin'? Why you don't pick on somebody big and fat and ugly like you?"

"Yeah, man, you leave the Batman alone," the other said, and he shoved Zoffke's shoulder with the flat of his hand.

"Yeah, leave the kid alone!" The softball players chimed in as they clustered around the *vatos,* Zoffke, Ricky, and his dog.

His face flushed, Zoffke straightened up, whipped a thin black wallet out of his back pocket, and snapped it open. "Official business. Get out of here. All of you, beat it!"

"Eeeee, it's the *federales!*" one of the *vatos* said, staring at the badge. He shrank back in mock terror, his hands across his heart. "Oooooo, I'm so scared."

"That's not such a good picture of you, man," the other *vato* said, looking from Zoffke's badge to his face. Then he picked up one of the pink posters. "Now this, I like this picture more better. You wearin' a nice shirt. You havin' a few drinks, some food, a good time with your homies. Heyyyyyy, you got some interesting friends there, Mr. Federal. Hey, bro," he said, turning to his companion. "Here's some familiar faces. Ain't that Ronnie Lechuga, the guy who sold your brother some very bad shit, and his *mexicano* business partners?"

"I'm warning you," Zoffke growled, shaking a fist in the *vatos'* faces. "You are interfering with a federal officer. I can have you all arrested for obstruction. All of you, vamoose!"

"Official federal business, picking on a handicapped kid?" one of the ballplayers said. "Now I've heard it all."

"Our tax dollars at work," someone in the crowd muttered. "Wonderful way to spend public monies."

"Creep."

"Asshole."

"Thug."

"Say, Mr. Federal," the taller *vato* said, pointing to Zoffke's shiny blue Continental. "Is that your official federal duty ve-hi-cle? Eeeeee, you makin' good money being a *federal,* man. You pickin' up big bucks protectin' the public from kids in wheelchairs. But you know, with you workin' so hard for the citizens and all, your ride ought to look a little more used."

The ballplayers and *vatos* converged on Zoffke, who disappeared in a hail of flying fists and kicks. His yells for help as well as the sounds of shattering glass and the whack of baseball bats against metal were soon joined by the distant wail of sirens. The *vatos* disappeared. The ballplayers quickly loaded Ricky, his chair, and Pooh into their pickup and were long gone by the time the first Albuquerque Police Department squad car pulled up in front of Baskin-Robbins.

The day after Zoffke was released from the hospital he flew to Washington for "urgent consultations."

EPILOGUE

Somewhere deep in the Rocky Mountains, a stand of towering ponderosas swayed gently in the breeze like genteel old ladies listening to the tunes of their youth. On this pleasant summer day, however, the forest's usual serenity was disrupted by a raucous band of naked strangers who sat immersed in a steaming hot springs in a clearing. Their peals and howls of laughter rang out over the treetops, startling jays, woodpeckers, hawks, and other birds into flight, while on the ground, a variety of shy, small and large animals spied on the intruders from the underbrush.

Beverly sat on the edge of the rock-lined spring in a T-shirt and shorts, dangling her legs in the hot water while wistfully watching Doc, Andrea, Abe, and Flash pass around a bottle of wine and a fat joint. "Are you sure I can't jump in?" she whimpered to Doc.

"Maybe next week. How are you feeling?"

"Pretty good. Every day I feel stronger. I'm sleeping better. I walk a little further each day. I nap. I read. And I'm having a ball working on the book, although I had no idea how hard it is to write fiction."

"Is it fiction, Bev?"

"Well, as you can imagine, not entirely. But I think the easiest way to tell a difficult true story is through fiction. That way, I don't have to prove a damn thing."

Doc thought for a while. "I guess you're right," she said. "But is it enjoyable to write this story? Or is it traumatic for you to dredge up all the awful things customs has done to you?"

"It's great fun," Beverly smiled. "I know what the Bible tells us: 'Vengeance is mine, saith the Lord.' But you know, God surely has many more important things to do, and writing this story is my way of giving her a hand."

The River Rats laughed.

Beverly swished her legs back and forth in the hot spring and continued. "I'm not spending all my time writing. I go for my strolls, I sit out under the pines watching the birds and the clouds, I spend hours listening to all those fabulous Motown tapes you left for me. But good as I'm feeling, I'd feel a lot better if I were in that pool with you guys, drinking some of that vino."

"Nope," Doc said. "Not until you've healed some more and you're off the antibiotics. It's only been a week since your surgery. Here, have a toke." She handed the joint to Beverly.

"Really? It's OK?"

"Doctor's orders, Bev."

As dusk and a slight chill descended on the forest, Beverly's friends put their clothes back on, and they all walked downhill to her one-room log cabin. A pot of Abe's elk stew bubbled on an old cookstove, filling the cabin with a savory aroma that woke up everyone's taste buds. A green salad, fresh corn on the cob, iced tea, and crusty French bread completed the menu. The River Rats attacked the dinner.

Beverly wasn't surprised when at dessert time Flash produced two pints of Cherry Garcia ice cream and five spoons. "Oh, it's just like being back on the river," she sighed nostalgically.

"Now all we need is for the Longmont Post Office to show up with that cute little pipe," Flash said cheerfully.

"Noooooo!" everyone yelled in unison.

"OK, OK. It was just a thought," he said.

Beverly became a little teary-eyed. "You guys walk on water."

"You'd do the same for any of us," Andrea said. "Besides, you're a great excuse for us to hang out in this lovely spot now and then. Pass me that joint, would you, Abe?"

After they cleared the dishes from the table, they sat out on the porch to take in the dazzling display of diamond chips in the heavens.

"I have a small request," Beverly said.

"At your orders, ma'am," Flash said enthusiastically, adding slyly, "although I specialize in . . . large requests."

The others groaned.

"Not now," Doc said to Flash. "Beverly will have a headache for several more weeks. So what do you need, Bev?"

"I want you to help me put together a box of presents for our friends in Albuquerque. Something for them to remember me by."

"Uh oh," Andrea said.

"I have a spectacular idea," Abe said, turning to his wife. "Remember that javelina I shot in Arizona a few years ago, babe?"

Andrea groaned. "How could I forget? I've asked you at least fifty times to get that damn thing out of our freezer."

"Here's our chance. We could gift wrap it and send it to that Zoffke creep. A pig for the PIG!"

"Great idea!" Flash said. "Hey, we could send it book rate—collect!"

A week later, on a Monday morning, Melissa walked into the task force office and nearly fell over. The office was filled with a stench that made her turn around immediately and head for the exit where she nearly collided with Dave.

"Christ almighty!" he said when he got a whiff. "What died in here?!"

Melissa held a Kleenex over her nose. "The smell's coming from Zoffke's office. You go look. I can't."

Dave, breathing through his mouth, cautiously opened the door to Zoffke's office. His eyes began stinging, and the overwhelming odor of decay filled his mouth with an awful taste. A large box sat on Zoffke's desk, and a brown liquid was leaking out of it. "Fuck's sake," he said, and closed the door. "When did that box arrive?"

"Friday afternoon," Melissa said. "Priority mail. It smelled a little ripe, but I was in a hurry to get home. I had the mail clerk put it on Zoffke's desk."

Elroy walked in. "Eeeeeuucckkkkkk! What's that stink?"

"I think there's something dead in a box somebody sent to Zoffke," Melissa said. "I'm not going near that thing."

Elroy stood a little taller, strode bravely into Zoffke's office, ripped the brown paper off the box, and tore it open. He took one look at the contents and puked onto Zoffke's carpet. Still retching and vomiting, he stumbled out of the office and ran down the hall to the men's room.

Dave raised his eyebrows and grinned. "Must be good!"

Elroy soon came out of the men's room, a clump of paper towels covering his nose and mouth, his eyes watering. "It's a fucking pig," he said. "And it's crawling with maggots. Who sent him that?"

"I can't imagine," Dave lied.

"Another box came Friday, too," Melissa said, pointing to a parcel on her desk. I haven't opened it. It doesn't smell, though."

Dave put a handkerchief over his nose, went to her desk, and looked at the box, noting it was addressed to La Ñapa Surveillance Team, U.S. Customs Service, 412 Gold Avenue SW, Albuquerque, NM 87103. There was no return address on the package, which was postmarked Boston.

The three gathered around the desk, still protecting their noses.

"You open it, Melissa," Dave said gallantly, and he stepped back.

She smiled up at him. "ATF inspected it already, Dave. You can relax."

He cautiously opened the parcel. Inside was a large box of Snickers bars. Dave and Melissa roared.

Elroy was perplexed. "What's so funny?"

"It's from Beverly, I think," Melissa said.

Dave grinned. "Yeah, it's probably from Beverly. I think she's snickering at us."

Elroy continued to look puzzled. "I don't get what's so funny, you guys," he said. "Besides, I don't like Snickers. I'd rather have a Big Hunk any day."

"I bet you would, kid. I just bet you would," Dave said. He and Melissa burst into laughter.

"Hey," she said. "There's something else in the package." She lifted up the Snickers box. Underneath was a small package addressed to "The Guy in the White Van." She handed the package to Elroy, who ripped the paper off the parcel. Inside were a Big Hunk and a note. Dave looked over the young man's shoulder and read the writing out loud: "Don't litter. Law enforcement people are supposed to set a good example."

Elroy scowled, crumpled the paper, and threw it and the candy wrapper in the direction of a nearby wastebasket, missing the lip by a yard. Then he shoved the candy bar in his mouth and stalked out of the office.

There was one more note in the package, a small folded piece of typing paper with DAVE written on it in large letters. Dave pushed his glasses up his nose and read the note to himself.

"You look pretty good in a dress, Dave. But I think pink would have been a better color for you than yellow. P.S. You're fired."

Dave cocked a big smile at Melissa, wadded the note into a tight little ball, leaped into the air like a ballet dancer, and with an expert hook shot, zinged the paper ball over his head into the wastebasket.

ACKNOWLEDGMENTS

Over the sixteen years I spent writing this book, many wonderful friends, colleagues, book world professionals, and family members helped me in myriad ways.

I'd first like to thank Frank Aon. Frank didn't help with this book, but he was of great assistance to me with *Relicarios: Devotional Miniatures from the Americas* (Museum of New Mexico Press, 1993). When I forgot to thank him in the book's preface, he stopped talking to me. A belated thanks, Frank.

Learning from that mistake, and cognizant of the fact that a decade later, my memory is leakier than ever, I'm not going mention *anyone's* assistance this time around, knowing I'll leave someone out. Suffice it to say, you know who you are, you know how you helped me, and there is no way I could have written and published *Clearing Customs* without you. I am eternally grateful to you for your generosity. Blessings on you and yours.

I dedicate this book to the many fine women and men of the US Customs Service (now the US Bureau of Customs and Border Protection) who unlike some of the characters in this book perform their important duties with courtesy and respect for the public they serve. I remember Inspector Lou Lucetto (deceased) with special admiration. A true gentleman, he only sometimes commented on the abundance of peach pits and hamburger wrappers in my pickup.

Muchas gracias a todos.

Martha J. Egan
Corrales, New Mexico
August, 2004

ABOUT THE AUTHOR

MARTHA EGAN has been an importer and dealer in Latin American folk art and antiques for three decades through her Santa Fe based retail store, Pachamama. She is the author of *Milagros: Votive Offerings from the Americas* (Museum of New Mexico Press, 1991), and *Relicarios: Devotional Miniatures from the Americas* (Museum of New Mexico Press, 1993), and a variety of articles on Latin American decorative art for museum catalogues and magazines. Raised in De Pere, Wisconsin, she has lived in the Southwest most of her adult life. She holds a B.A. in Latin American History from the Universidad de las Américas in Mexico City. She lives in Corrales, N.M. with the ghost of an old cat.

Clearing Customs is her first novel.

Design and composition: Barbara Jellow Design
Text is set in Linotype Bembo with letters in Courier and Linotype Feltpen
Display is set in Linotype Atlantis
Symbols are from *Design Motifs of Ancient Mexico,* Jorge Enciso, Dover Publications, Inc., New York
Jacket/cover images: Retablo by Nicario Jiménez, photograph by Anthony Richardson
Printing and binding: Maple-Vail Book Manufacturing Group, York, Pennsylvania